PETRICHOR

E. M. Wright

Seraphim

Copyright © 2026 by E. M. Wright

All rights reserved.

Edited by Malorie Nilson and Sabrina Terry

Cover design by Alexandra Buchanan

Ebook ISBN: 978-1-956136-88-3

Paperback ISBN: 978-1-956136-91-3

No part of this book may be reproduced in any form or by any electronic or mechanical means, including information storage and retrieval systems, without written permission from the author, except for the use of brief quotations in a book review. No generative AI was used in the writing or design of this book. No part of this book may be used in the training of artificial intelligence.

Parliament House Press

www.parliamenthousepress.com

To all the women who showed me what it meant to be strong

PROLOGUE

THE COUNTRYSIDE WAS ON FIRE.

Lord Anthony Erikkson pulled his horse to a stop, the eager bay dancing beneath him. Ahead, perhaps a quarter mile off and down a hill, a derailed train cluttered the landscape, which would look absurdly like a child's toy were it not for the black smoke billowing from the toppled cars.

"Master Erikkson, what is it?" The young boy he had rescued from the sea the previous year rode up behind him, not yet near enough to see the wreck.

"Back to the house, Seraphim. Get help. Hurry!" Erikkson did not hesitate, spurring his horse toward the wreckage. If anyone had survived, he would find them. He would pull them from the wreck. A frown crossed his face as he neared the train, slowing his mount from a gallop to a trot, before at last sliding to a halt. He dismounted, studying the scene with concern. The derailment had sent debris across the field for hundreds of feet. He could hear fires still burning, crackling beyond his line of sight. Acrid, toxic black smoke polluted the air. Erikkson pulled his silk cravat from around his neck, tying it around his nose and mouth in an effort to keep out the smoke. His eyes streamed.

Expeditiously, he began to go through the carriages, peering through the twisted metal, calling out to see if anyone could hear him. He glimpsed bodies, tangled so with the wreckage as to make them unrecognizable. The train must have been going incredibly fast to cause such damage to the carriages and passengers.

Just as he began to despair, he caught sight of a small black boot protruding from behind a twisted metal shard, the sharpened edges of the metal blackened by the explosion that had thrown it from the body of the train. He raced toward the metal, praying he would find more than another twisted corpse.

The shoe belonged to a little girl in a dress that may once have been white but now was such a mess of blood and scorch marks he could not be certain. It was clear she had been caught in the blast which tore the train apart. Her left side was burned so badly her skin was charred black. Her left arm appeared crushed, and her leg had not fared much better. Erikkson turned away, convinced such a small girl could not possibly survive such damage. As he did so, her eyelids fluttered, a tiny moan escaping her chapped lips.

He returned to her side and knelt, muttering quiet, calming words, doing his best to soothe the girl. He could not imagine the agony she was experiencing. As gently as he could, he lifted her into his arms. Her dark hair had been curled, but the ringlets now hung limp and lifeless; it was clear the journey had been some kind of special occasion. He guessed she could not be more than eight or nine years old.

He carried her back to his horse, all too aware of how crucial it was to get her back to the manor as soon as possible. She needed medical attention, and fast. He doubted he would be able to save her arm.

Offering up another silent prayer, he swung onto the

saddle, cradling the girl to his chest, his hands already sticky with blood. As he spurred his mount back toward the manor, the dark clouds above him opened up, pouring soothing rain upon the earth. The horse's hooves threw up chunks of dirt as they galloped, and with it, the sweet, loamy scent of the earth in the rain. *There is a word for that scent,* Erikkson mused, cradling the girl closer. She whimpered.

"Petrichor," he said gently. "Hold on, love. Just a little farther. If you hold on for me, I shall call you Petrichor."

CHAPTER ONE

A THUNDERSTORM SWEPT through Glasgow the night she arrived, the kind that brought wind and dark clouds without rain. The heavy clouds hung low over the spires of the city's ancient Gothic cathedral (lately transformed into an airport with space to dock up to four airships), and as Petrichor of Erikkson disembarked from the airship *Liberty,* she could taste the ozone crackling over her teeth. She wasted no time in waiting for the slow elevator which could take her down into the street, instead pulling her hood over her head, shouldering the small bag of possessions she carried, and beginning her loping progress down the stairs that spiraled into the cathedral itself.

At this late hour, she passed only a few sailors hurrying up the steps to their own docked airships, and they only paid her an extra moment of attention, long enough for a second of eye contact. Long enough that, even beneath her cloak, she knew they had detected the heavy iron and brass of her prosthetics. The way she moved with a lithe, catlike lope, leading from her left side.

She was a biomaton, and not just any biomaton, but an abomination, something that was never meant to exist.

Petrichor had been marked for life by the machinations of her creator, and her grafts weren't easily hidden. It was why she'd spent the last five years in America, where they cared more about the color of one's skin than the amount of metal grafted onto it. She'd built an identity and a name for herself, and now fear followed her instead of scorn. At least, it did in New York.

Back here in Great Britain, she'd have to be more careful.

She'd heard the rumors all the way back in New York before she'd boarded the *Liberty,* had seen the headlines on imported European newspapers: Biomaton execution gone wrong. An uprising, a massacre!, and those responsible vanished into the night without a trace. Lock up your homes! Young men, protect yourselves with the latest in steam-powered revolvers. And you delicate women, do not venture out of doors without a chaperone.

This in particular had given Petrichor a good snigger, her scarred face twisting with laughter. Slipshod Jack, her best friend in the Dead Rabbits gang, had seen her laughing and passed her one of his hand-rolled cigarettes, even though he knew she didn't smoke. They were good currency, though, in the dirty alleys of New York where tobacco was good as gold, so she'd smiled and slipped it into her pocket.

It was the last cigarette Slips would give her.

Her steel-toed boot clicked against the cobblestones as she stepped out into the narrow streets of Glasgow, and Petrichor bit down hard on the inside of her cheek, drawing blood that tasted like a bright copper penny. Being back in Great Britain was making her lose her focus, rattling her brains around like stones in a tin coffee can. She was here on business. And the sooner her business was done, the sooner she could go back—

Well, no. She couldn't go back there, not with the War of

the Rebellion waging harder than ever, not with her gut telling her that if they couldn't enslave Africans, biomatons would be next, and she liked her freedom more than she liked any person or gang of people. She'd had and given up families before. She was good at disappearing. Better to be alone than allow herself to get hurt again.

A window slammed shut overhead, and Petrichor raised her head enough that she could see the shadows moving behind the curtains, each window a golden promise of safety as long as their occupants stayed behind the glass. She thought about taking one of the throwing knives from her belt and smashing that golden pane, just for the joy of hearing the scream of panic from whoever was inside, but she didn't need the unnecessary attention that would draw. She contented herself with flipping Slipshod Jack's favorite rude hand gesture at the window, and continued her easy stride down the street.

There was a sour taste in her mouth that wasn't just the smoke in the air, the blood from the inside of her cheek, the ozone still crackling in the threatening clouds overhead. This was the taste of her former master, the man who'd left her with a body more mechanickal than flesh, and the crawl of his eyes on her, even from this distance. She'd felt it from the moment she'd set foot off the *Liberty*. Erikkson would know she'd returned. She didn't know exactly how he did it, but he would know. Probably already knew.

Focus, Petrichor, she thought. *Find the razor gang that killed Slips, and you can move on. France, maybe, or Portugal. Luxembourg. Now you've reached Europe, you can go anywhere.*

She'd recognized his fingerprint in the news of the biomaton uprising. There was a man with a one-track mind, all right. Biomaton freedom, at any cost, and who cared how many children fell under his knife if he won in the end? The shining promise of a chainless existence justified his bloody, bloody means.

Petrichor spat, ridding herself of the sour taste and the ugly memories of her creator. She wasn't here for Erikkson.

But a part of her, however small, *wanted* to see her old man again. Look him in the eye and show him what she'd attained without his guidance. Prove that she didn't need him or his cause to be successful.

And maybe he'd like to see what had become of the little girl he'd rescued from a trainwreck all those years ago.

But first, she had business to attend to.

She shuddered, identifying the train station to her right by the taste of coal smoke on the air, the hiss of brakes, and the faint echo of a conductor's final boarding call. That meant her destination was to her left. Tucking her hands into her cloak's pockets, she strolled down the alley that would connect her with George Street, and from there, just a quick jaunt over to St. Vincent Street and the pub just around the corner where the Billy Boys were known to gather.

It hadn't been that hard to find the men who'd killed Slipshod Jack and two other Dead Rabbit boys a little less than two weeks ago. Petrichor was good at following tracks, tracing even the most careful of assassins back to their hideouts. And what had she found, but a bundle of Billy Boys, newly arrived in New York and eager to establish their claim on the city. Stupid of them, of course, to pick the turf of the gang who laid closest claim to the Clockwork Assassin, but then again, anyone who set to murdering folks just days after stepping off a boat across the Atlantic couldn't exactly be considered *smart*.

She'd killed them, of course.

Why wouldn't she? They'd slaughtered one of the few boys she actually considered a friend, and she couldn't just let that go. She did, after all, have a reputation to keep.

But the blood of a handful of Billy Boys had barely whetted her thirst, and one had been awfully talkative before his death, promising her contacts and work for his gang back home in

Glasgow—she supposed watching one's brothers-in-arms gutted like a fish could do that. So she'd boarded an airship and crossed the pond to finish the job.

Petrichor stood in front of the dingy Bridgeton pub and tilted her head back as the first drops of rain began to fall, thunder rumbling through the night sky. She took a deep breath, a crooked grin gracing her scarred face as lightning crackled overhead. The blue-white light illuminated her angular features, flashing off of the metal grafted in place of the left side of her jaw. Petrichor clicked her metal teeth together, patting Slipshod's final cigarette in her pocket. "Knock-knock, boys," she sing-songed in her low contralto voice as she pushed open the door. "Death's come a-calling."

IN AN ORNATELY WALLPAPERED BEDROOM STOOD A FINELY carved four-poster bed, and in the center of this bed, there lay a girl. She was wan, skin pale, and thin enough to show the blue of her veins running beneath, her bones standing out starkly from her flesh. Her red hair splayed across the navy-blue pillowcase, but it didn't have the copper luster it had once contained. Her left arm was hard steel, interlocking armor plates encasing intricate clockwork workings. Light touched the tips of her fingers as the sun began setting, and the metal sent sparks dancing across the frescoes on the ceiling. An IV bag hung from the uppermost right post of the bed, trickling what little sustenance it could provide into the crook of her right arm. She was a girl who'd had many names, many identities. And she was dying.

In this room, too, was a young man. He sat in an uncomfortable armchair near the foot of her bed, leaning forward just enough that he might have touched the edge of her blankets, if he reached out. He had his elbows on his knees, hands tangled in his black hair. This boy, too, had an arm of clockwork, though his was much less carefully built than her own. He heaved a sigh, worry furrowing new wrinkles between his brows.

"Three weeks, Taryn" Ace breathed, the words barely a whisper over his teeth. "That is how long it has been. And every day we get closer to losing this war without you."

He leaned back, dragging his gaze from her feet to her face, and marveled at how small she looked there in the bed, amongst the pillows. How diminished. This girl he'd betrayed—no, this girl who had *saved* him, who was the brightest star in Ace's sky, the one thing he'd remembered even when the machinations of those who would subjugate them tried to steal all his memories away—was so *small* lying there, all her fire smoldering somewhere inside. Sometimes, he imagined that he could see those remaining embers dimming as the days dragged on. As his watches came, and went, and still there was no change in her condition.

Three weeks prior, Taryn had been sentenced to death for treason against the Crown. Instead, she and her soldiers—her family—had staged a rebellion, declaring their intention to fight for the biomatons' freedom, whatever the cost. Ace had been there. He had seen Taryn stand tall and noble even in the face of tremendous hatred. He had been proud to be a part of her army. But the fight had gone wrong. Taryn had been struck hard on the back of the head as they made their escape, and shortly thereafter, she'd fallen into a coma. It had been three weeks since he had last seen the emerald green of her eyes.

"Storm is hunting us down," he said, voice gaining a little strength as he spoke the name of his sister. "She wants to see us all hang. It seems she takes pleasure in picking us off one by one. Likes watching us scramble—" He broke off, throat tight, and passed a hand over his face. He shifted uncomfortably in his seat, trying to find a position where the ornate carved arm of the chair didn't press into the tender spots on his ribs. "I cannot help but think that this is my fault. Storm's dogged pursuit, your injuries, all of it. Had I stood up to her in the beginning, we would not be in this mess. I—" He stared down at his palms, one flesh, the other scuffed metal. "I would not be a biomaton."

The words were barely a whisper, and yet they felt too loud as soon as he said them. Ace regretted a lot of things. He regretted letting Storm push him around for so long aboard their airship, the HMS *Dauntless*. He regretted all the cruelty he had participated in. He regretted regaining his memories of those cruelties. But he did not regret coming to Elmhurst, nor did he regret joining Taryn's cause.

He had not chosen this fate, but he would not want to be anything else.

"Have you seen any change in her?"

Ace startled at the sound of Lord Erikkson's voice from the doorway. He twisted to watch the older man enter the room with two more of Taryn's closest friends in tow: Royal Stokker, apprentice to Erikkson and Taryn's best friend, and Emmett LeBeau, the Frenchman who'd once sailed upon the *Dauntless* and had chosen to protect Taryn over his own life.

"No, not yet," Ace answered as Erikkson crossed the room to check the IV bag, ensuring the slow drip of sugar water was still making its way into her bloodstream.

It was all that was keeping her alive.

It wasn't enough.

Erikkson sighed heavily. "Every day that passes, the likelihood of her waking is waning. I have been reviewing all the medical studies I can find. They all say the same thing. The longer this lasts, the more likelihood of permanent damage. It may be time to let her go."

"*No!*" All three boys shouted the word at once, then looked at each other in surprise.

"There must be something you can do," Royal pressed,

crossing the room to touch Taryn's hand. "Some chemical compound or operation we have not tried!" The boy wore shirtsleeves rolled up to his elbows under a marigold-colored waistcoat trimmed with silk, his blond hair pulled back in a small tail at the base of his neck with a black ribbon. Even with his sleeves rolled up, they were stained with ink and what Ace guessed was machine oil. It was hard to tell with Royal's sometimes erratic nature. One day he was focused solely on clockwork, the next he spent hours polishing weapons and training against fighting dummies or one of the other members of the army. And his behavior had only grown less predictable as Taryn's condition deteriorated.

It was like all his worry turned into kinetic energy.

Erikkson shook his head, sadness clear on his face. He was the man who'd originally given Taryn her clockwork arm, the one who'd orchestrated their rebellion, and he loved Taryn like his own daughter. "I have tried everything I know how to try. Any further operations would risk more harm than good. It is up to her now, and her alone."

Ace pressed his palms together, remembering how Erikkson and Royal had risked brain surgery on Taryn when they had first brought her back from London after her injuries, to ensure none of the delicate clockwork components in her brain had caused irreparable damage, and removing any that had been jarred loose from their positions. The surgery had taken eight excruciating hours, with those who were not allowed into the operating room prowling around the estate, jagged with worry.

But it had been weeks now since that surgery, and she showed no signs of stirring.

"*Reveille-toi, cherie,*" Emmett murmured, his freckled cheeks scrunched with concern. "We need you, *belle*. Please, you cannot leave us like this." He turned toward the window, and the tiny white scars around his eyes from two intense surgeries—one that blinded him, the other restoring something like sight—caught the light. His shoulders shook with emotion.

Ace pushed himself up from his armchair. "So we are doing all we can? Simply waiting and watching until she what? Dies?"

"There is still a chance that she will wake," Erikkson answered softly. "But it is just that. A chance."

"You just said we ought to let her go!" Ace was surprised by the vehemence in his own voice, the way his throat tightened at the thought that the girl in the bed could die and there was nothing they could do to save her.

Erikkson's expression took on a pitying look. "She is wasting away, despite my best efforts, Ace."

"Then we try the adrenaline," Royal said urgently, one calloused hand raking his shoulder-length blonde locks back from his face.

"What?" Ace asked.

"It is a way to jump-start the body. It may bring her 'round."

"It is too dangerous," Erikkson insisted. "Too much could kill her."

"She is already dying!" Royal exclaimed.

"Is there a possibility it could work?" Emmett came nearer, something like hope dancing around the edges of his thick French accent. "Even a small one?"

"A *very* small one," Erikkson answered bitterly. "It has not been tried on patients who have spent so long in a coma. It has been used to revive the dying, but with varying results. Too little will not work, and too much may cause her heart to explode."

"Taryn is strong," Royal pointed out. His active fingers worried at a loose thread on his waistcoat. "It will work."

"But if it doesn't, we're ending the hope that she may wake

on her own." Ace's throat was tight, the words feeling like shards of glass in his teeth. "We are choosing her end for her."

"Would you rather keep sitting here day after day, watching her die?" Royal rounded on Ace, both fists clenched, his face red with anger—no, not anger, Ace realized. Fear. Royal was just as afraid as Ace, he just had a different way of showing it. "I have done the research," he continued, turning back to Erikkson. "I know the precise dosage to kick-start her body without killing her. It will work."

Erikkson closed his eyes, a shadow passing over his face. Then he sighed and nodded. "I took you on as my apprentice because of how bright you were. It is high time I start letting you lead the way. Go. Get the dosage ready. We cannot wait for her to wake on her own any longer."

Royal nodded and rushed from the room. Ace couldn't breathe. He watched, numbly, as Emmett took Taryn's hand in his, sitting on the edge of the bed and murmuring softly in French. It almost sounded like prayer. But what good had prayer done them thus far? Ace felt the looming dread of losing Taryn settle on his shoulders like a woolen blanket. Death was a physical presence in this room, casting a shadow over the foot of the bed.

"Taryn," Ace whispered, blinking hard against the stinging in his eyes. "You have to wake up."

She didn't stir, as still as a corpse save for the slow, steady movement of her chest as she breathed. The bed engulfed her, like a monster slowly eating her up. Ace clenched his fists so tightly his knuckles turned white. He heard Royal's footsteps returning and shut his eyes, afraid to watch what would follow. Afraid that the young apprentice had made even the slightest miscalculation, and this would be Taryn's final moment.

"This will work," Royal said, but his hands shook as he uncapped a syringe of clear liquid.

"Be strong, little one," Erikkson urged her prone form, and

then he stepped back, allowing Royal a clear path to Taryn's body.

Royal approached slowly, almost reverently, gently pulling her collar aside to reveal the vein that led straight to her heart. He took a deep breath, then carefully inserted the needle. It slid through her skin too easily, as though her body had given up on any resistance at all.

"*Courage,*" Emmett whispered.

Royal depressed the plunger. The room collectively held their breaths as he removed the syringe and set it on the table beside the bed.

For a long, horrible moment, nothing happened.

He's killed her, Ace thought. *It didn't work, and now we have to find a way to go on without our leader.*

And then Taryn's body clenched, all at once, muscles drawn tight as she lurched upward with a gasp. Her eyes flew open, emerald-green irises dancing as her stare fixed on Royal.

The back of her clockwork hand struck him hard across the cheek.

"You creep! Why on earth are you watching me sleep?"

CHAPTER TWO

Taryn didn't have time to process what was happening before Royal threw his arms around her, weak laughter escaping him in a rush of breath. She'd just slapped him, and he was acting like it was the greatest moment of his life. Her chest hurt. Her heart was thundering so fast she half wondered if it hadn't been replaced by a freight train engine. That would explain the shakiness, the feeling of just coming out of a long, deep sleep, and—

She blinked, staring over Royal's shoulder at the three pairs of eyes watching her. They looked overjoyed. Emmett's smile was so wide she thought his cheeks might split. And Erikkson's eyes were swimming with tears. "Master Erikkson? Ace? Emmett?" Her voice was hoarse with disuse. She carefully pushed Royal to arm's length. He was smiling in spite of the red rose blooming on his cheek. "What is going on?"

Royal frowned. "You do not remember?"

She shook her head. "I remember— I remember the hangman's noose." Her heart was finally beginning to slow, but focus felt like trying to blow the dust out of a long-abandoned house. Her eyes focused on something far away, a frown creasing her forehead and her lips parted just enough to show a glimpse of pink tongue. "I remember there was a fight—"

Erikkson nodded. "You were struck hard in the back of the head, Taryn. You have been unconscious for almost three weeks."

Her face drained of all its color. "Three weeks?" she repeated numbly. A note of panic edged her voice. She could not imagine how she had slept for three weeks. It had been her idea to start this war, and she'd abandoned her soldiers to it for three weeks. "What has happened? What have I missed? Did everyone make it out? Seraphim, the twins—No one was killed?"

"No, everyone made it. You were hurt worst of all of us," Ace said softly.

Taryn nodded, relaxing. She sank back against the pillows. "Good." She looked around the room again, taking in the four men, those she considered her closest friends and allies. The fight was coming back to her, in bits and pieces, a blur of blood and dust and clanging metal. "Did a midshipman join you? Her name was Jack Cobb. She helped me, so I said she could come with us." She bit her lip. "I know what it feels like to hide what you are all the time."

Ace shook his head. "I am sorry, Taryn. We were going to let her come, but Storm shot her. We barely escaped ourselves."

Taryn bowed her head, aggrieved. Tears, hot and unbidden, leaped to her eyes. She pressed her hands over her face. "I promised I would help rescue her brother. He is a biomaton in the infantry."

The room went dead quiet. When Erikkson's voice finally broke the silence, it was heavy with regret. "I am afraid that will be impossible. The infantry has destroyed every biomaton working for them. They feared rebellion, and that was the only way they knew to ensure control."

Taryn choked on her own breath. She had no words. She

had missed so much and failed the girl who had helped her. She was only alive now because of Jack, and she could not even do anything to thank her.

"But *you* are alive, and that is what is important right now." Royal took her by the shoulders, studying her face with his warm brown eyes.

Half her face tried to smile, while the rest frowned. "Every life is precious, Royal."

"Of course it is. But if you want to save anyone, you need to focus on yourself first, Tiger. You look thinner than when I pulled you off the streets."

In spite of herself, Taryn smiled a little at the old nickname and the memories it carried. *Tiger,* for how fiercely she fought and the copper of her hair. Her stomach growled, low and deep, and she finally recognized how hungry she was. "I feel hungrier than I was then too."

"I can fetch you something, *belle dormir,*" Emmett offered, reaching out to squeeze her shoulder. "So long as in exchange you promise to never do that again. *Je te croyais mort.*" He said it flippantly, as a joke, but Taryn could hear the tightness of his voice and knew that Emmett had truly feared for her life.

"I am all right now, Emmett," she answered, trying to smile at him. "I promise I will not sleep for three weeks again, if it is in my power to prevent it. But right now I need you to bring me some of Ambrose's incredible cooking."

Emmett gave her a mock salute. "*Oui, Capitaine.*"

He scurried from the room, and her eyes drifted back to Erikkson. He'd aged in the last three weeks. The salt and pepper of his sideburns had engulfed more of his auburn hair, and the wrinkles in his face seemed deeper than she remembered. He smiled, the corners of his eyes crinkling, but Taryn spotted a deep sadness there as well. "It is good to see you awake at last, little one."

"What else have I missed?"

Erikkson shook his head. "Eat first. Greet your friends. There will be time enough."

She clenched her fists around the coverlet. "We are in the middle of a war, are we not? I need to know what happened. There may not be time."

"Sedition—Taryn, please." He pressed his hands over his face. "We will discuss it privately after you have eaten."

She stared at him, a knot of trepidation in the pit of her stomach ruining her momentary happiness. She carefully pushed Royal's hands off her shoulders, glancing at Ace. His fists gripped the arms of the chair so hard his knuckles had gone white. Her heart fluttered in her chest like a bird. "I hope you have not all abandoned your training in my absence." She tried to keep her voice lighthearted.

Royal grinned lopsidedly at her. "Seraphim has been leading the army for you. He is even more intense than you are!"

Taryn nodded. "I expected as much. He would have made an excellent leader, had I been killed."

"Nevertheless, I shall be relinquishing the role just as soon as you are well enough to rise," Seraphim answered from the doorway. His metal wings nearly filled the doorframe, his voice almost startlingly soft compared to the intimidating figure he cut. The tall, dark-skinned biomaton was another of Erikkson's special creations, built to be a sort of avenging angel, and his skills as a tactician were unmatched in Sedition's army. Still, he preferred peace-making to war, and she could read the weariness on his face around his smile.

"Word travels fast in this house, I see," Erikkson said with a smile.

"I ran into Emmett on his way to the kitchen," Seraphim replied. "I think he is telling everyone he passes that Sedition is awake."

Taryn rolled her eyes, but she felt a smile playing on her

lips. "If everyone he tells comes to see me, I shall have a never-ending procession of people to greet, and I do not have the time for that."

"But that might be an excellent opportunity for you to practice your diplomacy, a skill we all know you are still lacking in," Erikkson responded.

"Hey!" Taryn exclaimed. "I have absorbed all you and Seraphim have taught me on the subject."

"True charisma cannot be taught," Seraphim answered slyly, his eyes sparkling.

She gave him a scowl. "If I were not about to pass away from hunger, I would show you what true charisma looks like."

He chuckled, but Taryn was distracted by Royal touching her wrist, two fingers looking for a pulse. She frowned. "I was joking, Roy."

He raised his eyes to search her face again, and his expression was so intense she had to look away. "How do you feel, Tiger? Any unusual chest pains or heart palpitations? Shortness of breath?"

She pressed her cold metal hand over her heart, as though she could feel anything with that hand. "No, nothing like that. When I first woke, my heart was beating very fast, but I am recovered now. Why?"

Erikkson came near and gently extracted the IV needle from the crook of her arm, wrapping it around the bag still hanging from her bedpost. "We had to try something... experimental to wake you. Keep an eye on how you are feeling over the next few days. Any lingering heart palpitations or strange feelings should be reported to Royal or myself."

Taryn felt a little anger rise up in her chest and breathed through it the way she'd been taught, keeping the killer that lived inside her caged. "I will be very happy when I am no longer the subject of experiments."

"That is not—" Royal started to protest, but was interrupted by Emmett slipping past Seraphim's metal wings, carrying a bowl of steaming soup on a tray. Taryn's mouth watered as the scent of the vegetable stew hit her nose, and she reached for it eagerly.

"*Soup du jour pour la belle dormir,*" Emmett announced, and Royal moved out of the way so the Frenchman could hand her the tray.

Taryn leaned over the soup with a hum of pleasure. The broth was sumptuous and rich, flavored with garlic and herbs, with chunks of vegetables and beef cooked until they melted in her mouth. After a few bites, Taryn raised her head, radiant with joy. "Give Ambrose my compliments," she said to no one in particular.

"You may be his favorite," Royal teased, "what with all the compliments you send him on his cooking."

Taryn shrugged. "He is a talented cook!"

"He missed your compliments," Erikkson said softly. He had moved across the room to lean against the windowsill, his arms crossed, observing.

"I missed his cooking," she retorted.

Erikkson glanced at the others. "Will you please give us a few minutes alone? I need to fill Sedition in on the progress of this war."

They grumbled but rose, leaving the room one by one. Ace squeezed her shoulder, giving her half a smile. "Good luck." She just smiled and nodded, her stomach performing another strange somersault.

Royal came and kissed her on the cheek. Taryn's face reddened. "I missed you," he murmured in her ear before slipping from the room.

Erikkson took the chair Ace had vacated beside her bed. She rubbed her face with both hands, her cheeks hot with a blush she did not understand. "What was *that*?" she questioned, trying to laugh it off. When Erikkson did not answer, she stopped rubbing her cheeks and looked at him. His face had taken on a sober hue.

"Do not *ever* frighten me like that again, little one," he gasped. "I thought we had lost you for good!"

She smiled. "I am all right, Master Erikkson."

He shook his head. "You very nearly were *not*. Though I could not tell your friends, there were a few nights when I truly thought you were gone." His voice broke, filled with more emotion than she had ever seen him express. "A week ago, you stopped breathing. It took all my medical knowledge—and a fair amount of luck—to bring you back." He covered his mouth with one gnarled hand. "I was almost ready to let you go."

She pressed a hand to her sternum, unable to find the right words to comfort him. He was meant to be *her* pillar, her rock in the midst of her emotional turmoil, and now that their roles had been reversed she could not find the right words.

He wiped his eyes with the back of his hand, then gave her a wry, pained smile. "But you have made it through, and you are back with us. Not a moment too soon, little one. We have needed you these past weeks. Your declaration of rebellion has brought Storm's rage down upon us, and as far as my spies can discern, it seems the entire war has been given over to her hands. The Queen is unconcerned with the biomaton uprising; she issued a statement asking the public to 'ignore the rabble.'"

"But that is good, is it not?" Taryn questioned. "If she underestimates us, we have a better chance of taking her by surprise."

Erikkson shook his head slowly. "Storm is content now to pick us off, one by one. She has held three public executions so far; ten biomatons in total have been hanged. Four were spies from your army. The rest were innocent casualties." He pressed a hand to his face again, stopping his words. "We cannot let this continue. We must perform a counterstrike."

Taryn threw her blankets back. "I shall collect my squadron. Storm cannot just assault us like this!"

Erikkson put a hand on her shoulder, keeping her from rising. "Sedition, I believe it is time we bring Petrichor back. She will know how to conduct covert operations of our own. We need her."

Taryn's lips twisted at the mention of the biomaton assassin Erikkson had created. Though they'd grown up together, Taryn retained no memories of Petrichor, but the rumors were enough to make her blood run cold. Ace's parents had been murdered at Petrichor's hand. There seemed no good reason to let her back into their circle.

"Petrichor is a villain! And besides, I thought she was in America? How can you get her back?" *I heard she hates you*, Taryn mused, but she knew the assassin's betrayal still hurt him, so she did not say the words aloud.

"She is not in America," Erikkson replied grimly. "She is in Glasgow. If we take my air yacht, we can be there in six hours, driving the engines at full capacity."

Taryn blinked. "You want to go to Glasgow and confront her?"

He nodded. "You can convince her to return, little one. I know you can. You may not remember it, but you were once close."

"No. Absolutely not." Taryn shook her head. She knew next to nothing about Petrichor, but she knew enough to fear her. "We can do this on our own."

"No, you cannot." Erikkson took her hand, squeezing it so tightly it hurt. "I built you three to work *together*. You need her."

She extricated herself from his grasp. A look of horror

crossed her face. "Petrichor is *insane*. She will do more harm than good!"

He shook his head. "We need her. You are our leader, our figurehead, and Seraphim is our tactician, but you need someone who has experience with stealth. If we are to win this war, we need someone who knows how to send a message the way only Petrichor can. I always intended the three of you to come back together, and nearly losing you has only made it clearer. We need someone who can meet Storm on her level."

"What does *that* mean?" she asked.

"It means that what you call *insanity* may be exactly the kind of out-of-the-box thinking that you and Seraphim are lacking. War is not linear, Sedition, and it is not possible to come out the other side with clean hands."

"You think my hands are clean now?" she asked, visions of their fight at the hangman's noose again dancing through her head. "I understand what warfare is. What it entails."

He shook his head. "No, little one, you don't." He rose. "We are going tomorrow morning. That is an order."

Her face reddened. She stared down at her hands for a moment, jaw clenched. "Very well. But mark my words: I do not like it. She is too unpredictable."

Erikkson shook his head. "She will help us. You will see."

She chewed her lip but said no more about Petrichor. She would play the good soldier and follow Erikkson's orders, in spite of her misgivings. "May I get up?" she asked as he moved toward the door. She could not bear to lie in bed any longer. Her mind needed physical activity, needed the preoccupation training provided.

He glanced back at her, his hand on the doorknob. "Yes, of course. But be careful with yourself, little one. Much of your strength will be gone. You will have to build it back up."

Without the preoccupation of friends and with the struggle of catching up with three weeks of what she'd missed, Taryn could feel the long time at rest beginning to make itself known. Her body ached all over, and now that whatever experiment they had given her was wearing off, she could feel weakness creeping into her limbs. "I cannot waste any more time in lying about. Will I see you after supper for battle training?"

He cocked his head. "I do not think so. You will need your rest." He watched her closely for another moment, and then he slipped out of her room without another word, closing the door behind himself.

Taryn pushed herself to the edge of the bed, puzzled by his actions. Something was wrong, very wrong, and she could not put her finger on what it could be. She stretched her legs out, wiggling her bare toes in an effort to find the weak spots. Erikkson had been right. Just stretching sapped her strength. She groaned, lamenting the loss of her physical prowess, hating that it meant she would be essentially starting over with her training *again*. At least this time she would not have to face the added pressure of gaining the others' approval.

She rose and dressed in her training uniform, surprised to discover she had lost enough weight to make the clothes feel too big. She shook her head at the unexpected result. It would take time to gain her muscle back.

The silence in the room felt oppressive. So much had happened in the last twenty minutes that she'd hardly had time to think, let alone feel anything besides numb shock at the length of time she'd missed, joy at her friends' reactions to her waking, sorrow at their losses, urgency at the knowledge that she'd have to regain all her strength *and* jump back into this war if they were to gain any of the ground they'd lost. Some small, soft part of her wanted to sit back down on the bed and cry. Another part of her wanted to open the window and scream, so long and loud that everyone would hear it, no matter where they were on the estate.

And the angry part of her, the Sedition part of her, told her she did not have time for any of that. Emotions were weakness, and if she wanted to use this second chance at living, she needed to stuff them deep down inside.

There would be time enough to process later, she decided.

For now, there was work to do.

With one final glance around the room, Taryn headed for the barracks.

CHAPTER THREE

TRAINING WAS MORE difficult than she remembered. She fell behind no matter what she did, muscles trembling with fatigue. Many times during the afternoon she had to take her time away from the rest of the group, seated on a bench, waiting for her muscles to cease their aching. She cursed her own weakness. She was meant to be stronger than this, stronger than any unaugmented human, and yet now she could barely stay standing for more than fifteen minutes at a time.

Taryn was sitting on a bench along the outside of the training room, sipping a glass of water and shouting tips at a pair of new young biomatons who had the misfortune of sparring with Seraphim, when she heard the uneven clinking of metal foot and boot against the stone floor. Taryn looked to her left to see Gennifer approach, her skirt swept up in one hand so she could move without her clockwork leg getting caught up in it. She smiled at Taryn, her long strawberry blonde hair tied over her shoulders in loosely wrapped pigtails. "My lady Sedition," she exclaimed, giving Taryn a clumsy curtsy. "It is good to see you up and about at last."

Taryn smiled at the girl's familiar Irish lilt. "Thank you,

Gennifer," Taryn answered, rising. "I assume you have a new costume for me? Have you finished my armor at last?"

Gennifer shook her head. As the seamstress for the entire army, she took special care with Sedition's outfits and armor, feeling responsible for her well-being no matter how often Taryn insisted it wasn't her burden to bear.

"No, your armor is not quite finished, but I do have something to show you. Do you have a few minutes?"

She nodded. "Now is as good a time as any, since I can hardly fight." She fought off a shiver of worry. She *would* regain her strength. It would simply take time.

And time was the one thing they did not have.

She followed Gennifer's uneven gait down a long stone hallway past the training rooms to her workshop. The room was more cluttered than the last time Taryn had visited, the shelves overflowing with fabrics and tools. Gennifer's worktable was covered in scraps, and a sewing basket on one end trailed orphan threads across the floor. It looked like a cat had gotten into the basket, except as far as Taryn knew, Elmhurst didn't have a cat. The room smelled of leather and clean cotton, though it was not without the slightly acrid scent of machine oil that pursued almost every biomaton. Taryn was just impressed that Gennifer managed to keep it from smelling of sweat, in such close proximity to where the biomaton soldiers fought and trained.

She spotted a white sheet hastily thrown over a dress form in one corner, and she stepped toward it, hand reaching for the cloth. "Is this—?"

Gennifer spun and squawked in alarm. Taryn snatched her hand back. "I told you; it is not yet finished! You will see it when I have completed it!"

Taryn rolled her eyes, placing her hands on her hips. She refused to acknowledge that her knees were already trembling with fatigue. "So, what is it you want to show me?"

Gennifer swept a pile of gray fabric from the table. It unfolded in her hands, an elegant dress of gray wool, buttoned down the front of the bodice with a wide, sweeping skirt. The sleeves had puff and definition, and the collar had a touch of lace peeking out of it. As the skirt unfolded, a gray satin lining glimmered in the light.

"It is beautiful, but I do not think I quite understand," Taryn said slowly.

"You will when you put it on. Go on. There is a proper corset behind the screen for you, and you do not need an underskirt."

Taryn followed her instructions, changing out of her training uniform and into the dress. It fit well, the wool heavy and lined with satin in order to keep it from scratching against her skin. She stepped out from behind the screen, holding her arms out so Gennifer could examine her. "Again, I do not understand..."

"There are two features to this dress. First, the sleeves will sufficiently hide your arm, so you may go out in disguise." Taryn studied the sleeves, realizing Gennifer was right. They puffed over her shoulders and tapered in such a way that the unnatural contours of her clockwork arm were completely hidden. "And in case you are attacked," Gennifer said, the lamplight glinting off her spectacles, "the skirt is detachable, allowing you to rid yourself of the hindrance." She indicated the hidden buttons which allowed the skirt to easily detach. Taryn laughed aloud.

"Gennifer, you are a genius!"

The girl smiled sheepishly. "I try, Lady Sedition."

Taryn toyed with the buttons for a moment, something like gratitude blossoming behind her ribs. The day had been a difficult one, full of shocking news and the struggle to get a body weakened by her injuries to work as it had before she'd been wounded. And somehow, even after her creator and her boys giving her so much joyous attention, *this* was the moment that hit Taryn the hardest. This girl, who knew her needs and her shape better than anyone else, who had spent hours planning and preparing clothes just for her. For most of her life—or at least what she could remember of it—Taryn had subsisted on hand-me-downs and charity. Royal's family had provided beautiful dresses for her, of course, but many of them had been tailored from the dresses his mother no longer wore. Gennifer was making clothing *just* for Taryn, and for who Taryn really was, not a half-truth hidden by layers of fabric. Tears, hot and unbidden, came to her eyes suddenly, and she pressed a hand to her lips in surprise.

"Are you all right, my lady?" Gennifer asked, shock brightening the pink in her cheeks.

Taryn swallowed hard, ducking her head. What was she thinking, crying in public? What would Master Erikkson say, if she was so weak that a dress caused her to start crying?

Some small voice inside her said that it was all right, that she was allowed to cry after the day she'd had, but she stamped it down, hurriedly wiping her eyes. She took a deep breath and raised her gaze to meet Gennifer's. She was the leader. She needed to lead. A change came over her, the hesitant, weak parts of Taryn falling away as Sedition took command, shouldering responsibilities and military plans with ease. Even her fatigued muscles ceased their trembling. "I have an important mission to attend to tomorrow with Master Erikkson. May I wear this?"

Gennifer nodded. "Of course."

Acknowledging her consent, Taryn quickly changed back into her training outfit, requesting the new dress be left in her room so she could wear it in the morning. Just before she left the room, she turned back, Sedition's authority singing through her veins. "Oh, and Gennifer?"

"Yes, my lady?"

"I want to see my armor completed in one week's time. We cannot afford to wait any longer. Understood?"

※

EARLY THE NEXT MORNING, JUST AS THE HORIZON WAS beginning to glow orange with the coming dawn, Taryn rose, dressed, and made her way through the sleeping household to the roof of the west wing where Erikkson had constructed a launch pad for the small airship he owned, which moored up here for Erikkson or his children to access. When not in use, the airship was kept in the vast stables on the grounds, and when they wanted to use it, the envelope that swung above the body of the ship was filled with hydrogen and helium.

Erikkson worked at a mooring line as Taryn approached, and he gave her a smile. "Good morning, Sedition! Are you ready for our adventure?"

She nodded in response. Erikkson gestured to the ship. "Climb aboard! I have a few more routine maintenance checks to perform, and we shall be off."

Taryn followed his instructions, swinging onto the ship's main deck, using the mooring lines as leverage. Though she never would have admitted it, her limbs ached from the exercise the day before, strained after so long in disuse. She knew the pain meant she was on her way to regaining her strength, but it still worried her. Petrichor could not know how weak she really was. Any weakness Taryn showed would be a mark against her.

Not for the first time that morning, Taryn wondered what Petrichor might do or say. In spite of her best tries at digging for information from Seraphim, she knew little about the Clockwork Assassin besides the basics: she had killed Ace's parents. She had fled to America sometime after Taryn had lost her memories, running as far from Erikkson as she could get. And she had spent time in the Black Castle, just as Taryn had. Time that had changed her permanently, according to the twins. Taryn's throat went tight at the bleak memories she had of that place, and the way her own mind had been altered there permanently by Dr. Harper's tampering. Maybe she understood Petrichor more than she thought.

Maybe that was exactly what scared her.

Taryn froze as she boarded the ship, surprised to find another figure already aboard. Ace glanced up from the knapsack he was rifling through, a look of pleased humor crossing his face. Sunlight drenched his features, turning his ice-blue irises almost colorless with golden light.

"Good morning."

Taryn frowned, befuddled by the early hour and his appearance on *her* mission. "What are you doing here?"

He shrugged. "Master Erikkson asked me to join your expedition. He thought my graft would be easy to hide, like yours." He held out a croissant to her. "Breakfast?"

She accepted gratefully, sitting beside him and taking a bite of the flaky pastry. It was still warm. She chewed slowly, that tightness in her throat like a vice as she remembered Ace's cold attitude to her when they first met, matched with Storm's cruel and unending hatred. Her brief time on the *Dauntless* felt like a lifetime ago, but not so long ago was the time when she'd wanted to shield Ace from all of this. Let him reinvent himself, if that was what he chose. She didn't know how much he knew, but she could see that in the weeks she'd been asleep, he had regained himself. He held himself differently now, with more confidence, more poise. He was the air pirate she had first met, and yet he wasn't. He was someone new. Someone better, she hoped. But still, this wasn't going to be easy, and he deserved to know exactly what they were getting into.

"Ace, this is Petrichor," she said slowly, every word a blade between her teeth. "This is the woman who killed your parents."

He nodded grimly. "I know. It was more Storm's doing than Petrichor's. She was just a tool in my sister's hand. My—our—" he grimaced at the word, as if just acknowledging his blood relation to Storm pained him— "*Our* parents were fighting for the biomatons' freedom, and Storm found that to be unforgivable. Petrichor was her weapon of choice because it proved them wrong, at least in her eyes. She never was good at subtlety."

Taryn's eyes widened. "You remember what happened?"

He nodded, touching the metal plate on the back of his head which hid the control panel connected to his brain. "Aye. I got my memories back during my fight with Storm. I have not had time to tell you."

"Oh, Ace, that must have been awful." Her face crumpled with the knowledge that not only had he fought Storm, but he'd had to remember all the ugliness she'd put him through. "And I am sorry for your parents. We could have used them."

"They would have liked you, I think," he said, but he wouldn't look at her. The rising sun gilded his features, setting him on fire with a light so bright she couldn't bear to look at him. "They would have been glad to join your cause."

Taryn felt her throat closing again, but forced herself to sit up, to say the words she did not want to say. "I—I am very happy for you. Not that your parents died, just that—You have your memories of them back. That is—" She couldn't finish.

He touched her shoulder, fingers feather-light across the gray wool of her dress. "You have not gained your memories back, have you?"

She shook her head once, hard. Her hand lay in her lap, still holding her forgotten pastry, a single bite missing from it. "Master Erikkson said he would do his best to help me, but I am afraid it is hopeless. Wherever my memories are, whatever he did to steal them from me, they are gone for good."

"I am sorry."

She shrugged. "There is no point weeping over it. What has been done is done, and cannot be undone. Besides, it gives me something to fight for, when all else fails." It was easier to say the words than she thought it would be. They were the words she'd said to herself a thousand times, of course. What were her memories to her, really, except for a catalyst to push her into the role of Sedition? Erikkson had taken her memories, and he claimed he had intended for her to regain them someday, but here she was, still without a past. A black hole in the shape of a girl. Maybe he'd lied, and he'd known from the start that once they were gone, they were gone.

But no, that wasn't fair to him. Truly, most of the time, Taryn didn't mind the emptiness of her past. Or at least, she did not think of it so often. It was only when she saw Ace regain his own memories so easily that she felt the sting of it, the emptiness where six years should have been.

"All right!" Erikkson exclaimed, interrupting their conversation, swinging into the ship himself. The air yacht, unmoored, began to drift on the breeze, and Erikkson looked to Ace. "Do you think you can start the engine belowdecks?"

Ace nodded, rising. "Certainly."

Taryn rose alongside him. "I will come. I should like to see the engine firsthand, and I can help if it gives you trouble."

Erikkson cast a troubled look their way, but Taryn ignored it, following Ace as he folded himself into the narrow door leading to the engine room. She paused in the doorway, waiting for her eyes to adjust to the gloom before she risked the short ladder down into the claustrophobic room. Ace offered her his hand, helping her down into the narrow space between the entry and the massive steam engine, lying cold and dormant, like a sleeping dragon.

As Ace began to light the boiler, Taryn studied the engine, musing on the differences between it and the only other airship engine she had ever seen aboard the *Dauntless*. Where the *Dauntless'* engine had been monstrously large, belching steam and heat, making the very floor thrum with its power, this engine was barely the size of Taryn's four-poster bed. It took up the space, climbing higher than her head, but could hardly compare to the other engine. Taryn shook her head, her eyes drawn like magnets to Ace's back as he shoveled coal into the boiler. Her mind returned to the glimpse she had caught of his bare chest, the shocking brutality of his graft as clear as if she could see it now.

She watched his muscles move and twist, straining against his metal ribs. She knew such a graft had to pain him, and yet he had never once complained. He was so strong. Her lips parted, a question ready on her tongue, but she did not speak, afraid to ruin the spell with such a tactless question.

At last, the engine rumbled to life, and he stood, leaning on the spade he had used to shovel the coal, wiping sweat from his brow with one forearm. He looked back at her, grinning, and his ice-blue eyes sent chills down her spine.

"I can still fly an airship, Tar. Impressed?"

Tar? When had he started calling her that? Only Royal ever called her that, but where the nickname sounded almost lazy in Royal's mouth, a loss of a syllable he did not have the energy to say, Ace made it sound like an affectionate abbreviation, a familiar, natural shortening of a name he enjoyed speaking. She shook the thoughts away, reminding herself that these kinds of thoughts made no sense. She could not love, and neither could Ace, for that matter. She was being silly. She rubbed the back of her head, wondering if the blow had not made her just the slightest bit mad. Still, she could not ignore the queasiness in her stomach when his eyes met hers, and the strange lightness in her hands at his nearness—a sort of feeling she'd never had before, and had no name for.

"Taryn?" Ace questioned.

She blinked, realizing he still awaited her reply. "I am sorry," she said in a rush. "I was thinking—" She tried to laugh, but it felt forced and hollow. "Well done with the engine."

He stepped closer to her, so she had to look up to meet his gaze. "Are you all right?"

She stepped backward involuntarily. "Fine. We ought to be getting back above decks." Abruptly, she turned away, trying to hide the heat rising in her cheeks. She rushed up the stairs and into the brightening light of morning.

Erikkson waved at her from the bow of the ship, steering with a complicated mess of rope at the rail. There was a conventional ship's wheel as well, mounted on the raised half deck above the engine, near the stern. The secondary steering mechanism near the bow allowed Erikkson to fly the yacht on his own, without need for more crew members. Taryn sucked a deep breath of the cold, thin air into her lungs, allowing the commanding warrior inside her to calm the rolling, confused emotion in her befuddled brain. It was just too long asleep, she told herself. Too long without exercise, too long on the shelf. It would be enough to make anyone slightly manic, in particular someone who was designed to be a weapon. She simply needed to sharpen herself once more.

She stood beside Erikkson at the bow, eyes burning with the cold wind, her hair slowly coming loose from her braid and dancing over her shoulders.

"What did you think of the engine?" Erikkson called over the wind and the thrum of the machine behind them.

She could not admit she had barely noticed the engine, too focused on Ace, so she nodded. "It is a fine bit of mechanicks. Did you build it?"

He chuckled, shaking his head. "Oh, no. My specialty is

biomatons. I have never been very captivated by steam power." He leaned to the right as he steered the ship, matching the tilt of the deck. "The human body is so much more complex and fascinating. After I finished my required classes focused on the steam engine, I am afraid I never gave much more thought to the technology."

Taryn smiled a little at that, pleasantly surprised to discover her creator was not all-powerful. He had strengths and weaknesses too, and somehow, she trusted him the more for it. She gripped the rail, leaning forward into the wind.

"Do you think the journey will be eventful?"

The Queen's naval warships patrolled the skies above the larger cities, and air pirates, while usually found in neutral skies over the seas, occasionally took to land to prey upon pleasure vessels like the one they flew now. The biomatons had run into trouble in the skies once or twice, though Taryn had not been with them.

Erikkson shook his head. "I have a few charts aboard to give us the best chance at avoiding trouble, and patrols do not seem to have increased much since the uprising. Still, I have brought disguises for all of us, which you must be ready to don at a moment's notice." He glanced at her. "How is your French?"

She frowned. "I understand it well enough, but I am afraid I speak it very poorly. I did not excel in language studies at finishing school and barely learned enough French to pass."

He grinned. "Well then, if we *are* stopped, you are deaf, and Ace and I only speak French."

She glanced back at Ace to discover he had settled himself within earshot. He gave her a cocky smile. "Well," she grumbled in mock irritation, "I shall pray we are not stopped."

CHAPTER FOUR

Taryn didn't think she'd ever get used to flying.

She stood at the rail of the air yacht, eyes closed, her face turned to the sun and the wind as they glided over the countryside. It hadn't been so long ago—only a little more than four months, though it felt like lifetimes—since she had dreamed of flying, stuck behind a desk at Grafton's School of Mechanicks and knowing that no matter how hard she worked, her dream of becoming a mechanick for Her Majesty's Navy had not one but two impassable obstacles: her gender and her identity as a biomaton. One she'd managed to keep hidden for a time, but the other wasn't something she could—or wanted to—hide. But now, she'd flown on *four* different airships. She'd seen a girl only a little older than her manage an engine ten times the size of the one on this little vessel all on her own. And she had found a new way to demand her freedom. She had a new dream to grasp now. Not as glorious as spending all her time in the sky, perhaps, but better. As Sedition, she was making a difference. Helping other girls (and boys) like her.

But even so, she loved the exhilaration of flying. She loved the wind in her face and the snapping of the lines anchoring the balloon to the deck.

"Like magic, isn't it?"

Taryn startled, opening her eyes to find Ace had sidled up to her. "Gor, how do you move so quietly?" she gasped.

He smiled a little sheepishly. "Sorry. I did not mean to startle you."

She laughed a little, shaking her head. She pressed her fingertips into the worn grooves of the rail, concentrating on grounding herself in the sensation. "It was nothing. I was just thinking of how the *Dauntless* was my first time on an airship, though I had dreamt of it so many times before that. And now here I am, flying to Glasgow as easily as breathing."

His face fell a little, a shadow that had nothing to do with the clouds overhead passing across his face. "Taryn, I need to apologize to you. Formally. Officially. With all my memories intact. I was wrong to follow Storm, and wrong to treat you the way I did. I am sorry for taking you from your life and revealing your clockwork arm to everyone. I am sorry for not stopping Storm from turning you over to the Black Castle."

Taryn shook her head. "Ace, we have been over this before. So much has happened since then. So much neither of us could have predicted. I am glad it happened, even if it was a terrible thing to endure. Without your actions, I would never have found my purpose. I would never have known a life where I could live as myself, without hiding what I am." She reached out and placed her clockwork hand on his. "And you have suffered enough for what you have done without torturing yourself further."

He winced. "I am also sorry for distracting you during the fight. I feel it is my fault you got injured."

"What?" She felt herself laugh a little at that. "It was not your fault at all! I was running on little sleep and a good beating from the day before. It was bound to happen."

"But I should have been there. I should have stopped it." His expression crumpled, ice-blue eyes becoming deep blue pools of pain. "I swear, Taryn, I shall not let anyone hurt you, so long as I have breath in my lungs."

A thin line appeared between her brows. "I am a weapon. If I am doing my job properly, I will be dulled, chipped, and possibly even broken. You must accept that. There is no version of this where I escape unscathed."

He regarded her silently for a moment, and she could see him working up the courage to say something more. His shoulders slumped, and he sighed. "Then I will follow you. Wherever it takes us."

"Glasgow ho, my dears!" Erikkson called from the bow. "Best be getting yourselves disguised before we arrive!"

Taryn looked out to see the city rising from the landscape below them, flanking a river that looked like a blue ribbon cutting through the rolling hills. *Scotland,* she thought in awe. *We have traveled all the way to Scotland in an afternoon.*

Ace had not stopped to gaze at the city below, but instead had pulled a duffel bag out of a shadowy corner where Erikkson had left it. He pulled out two pairs of gloves, the larger of black leather with copper buttons, and the smaller in heather gray silk. "Tar," he called, offering her the smaller pair of gloves.

Taryn tore herself away from the city below and hurried across the deck, the biting wind of early evening swirling her skirts around her ankles. She pulled on the gloves and then found a dress cloak of navy-blue wool, built with a deep hood to hide her fiery copper hair. This she donned with a flick of her wrists, pulling the hood over her head.

Ace had pulled on a cap of black wool, settling the hat far enough back that it covered the all-too-obvious metal plate on the back of his skull. He gave her a little grin. "You look good."

Her cheeks grew hot, but she had to admit it felt good to

feel normal for once. She no longer grew anxious about her metal arm being spotted, but there remained an ugly, secret part of her deep inside that wanted to be like everyone else. Wanted to be whole and human, her skin unblemished by clockwork and fire. To hide her embarrassment, she elbowed Ace in the ribs. "You don't."

The little airship easily found docking, but Erikkson warned them to wait for twilight before they ventured into the city, as they would have the least chance of being recognized then. The evening grew cold quickly, and Taryn was grateful for her cloak, pulling it tight about her shoulders as she paced, waiting to step into the streets of Glasgow. Erikkson showed them a map of the city, pinpointing the pub where Petrichor appeared to be hiding, a place in the Bridgeton district called the Dancing Kelpie. It was not far from where they had moored, and Taryn did her best to memorize the winding back alleys between here and there. A little knot of anxiety tightened in her chest each time she thought of the confrontation with Petrichor.

"What ought we to expect from her?" Taryn demanded when she could bear the silence no longer. She'd already asked before, yes, but she was hoping Erikkson might offer her more than his earlier platitudes now that they were so close.

Erikkson smiled enigmatically. "Anything. She is the most unpredictable of all my children."

Taryn clenched her fists. "Can you tell us anything that will actually help?"

He shrugged. "She left shortly after you did, little one. She may be different from the fifteen-year-old girl I knew. Trust your training. She is waiting for a client to contact her. That is how you get her attention. And whatever you do, do not turn your back on her." He glanced up at the sky above them, pink and orange with the setting sun. "I believe it is time for you to go, my dear. Be careful. I shall see you both soon."

Ace rose and offered her his elbow. With his leather gloves and her silk ones, they looked like any young couple out for a stroll, not the pair of revolutionaries they really were. In theory, their disguises would be enough to avoid suspicion. Taryn checked to make sure her hair was tucked deep in her hood, and together they stepped onto the cobbles of Glasgow.

The streets were quiet, most of the citizens already home and enjoying supper with their families. Golden light spilled from windows, pooling like molten gold across the cobblestones. The breeze carried the scents of fresh bread baking and meat cooking. In another life, Taryn might have been seduced by the narrow streets, the chill breeze against her face, and even the strange comfort of having Ace beside her, his elbow crooked around her clockwork hand. But now the clack of their heels on the cobbles was too loud, and every corner brought them closer to a biomaton who might very well try to kill them. The knot of worry in Taryn's stomach grew with every step. She forced herself to breathe evenly, slipping into the role of Sedition, separating herself from the fear.

Accessing Sedition was like opening a door in her mind, letting something that was her and also not quite her to take over. Sedition was a cumulation of programming and training, much of which had been wiped from her conscious mind, but still dwelled innately in her subconscious. She was everything Taryn had never believed she could be, and yet somehow she was also the perfect version of herself. Icy calm swept over her as Taryn let herself fall back into instinct, losing all the etiquette and manners she had learned in finishing school and replacing them with something more primal. She was in control. There was nothing Petrichor could throw at her that she could not handle.

They approached the Dancing Kelpie, their footsteps the only sound in the coming night. The door to the pub was closed, but light bathed the dirty windows, showing the establishment *was* open. Taryn paused in front of the door, glancing at Ace. He gave her a nod and a grimace, and they shoved the door open together.

The pub had once been a fine establishment, Taryn thought, but now looked rather worse for wear. Half the round tables lay toppled on their sides. Shards of glass crunched under her boots as she stepped through the doorway. Dried blood was splashed over the floor, the bar, the walls, though the bodies this blood had come from were not present. A knife hung embedded in the wall just above a scuffed upright piano. A single patron occupied the space: a woman wearing a long cloak a shade of red so dark it looked black. Her long brown hair cascaded in waves down her back, braided back from her face and over her ear on one side but otherwise loose. She hunched over a pint of ale, her forearms splayed on the bar. Taryn knew at once she was looking at Petrichor.

The bartender, a wide man with red cheeks, shot them a wary look and returned his attention to the glasses he was cleaning. Taryn approached the bar, releasing Ace's arm. He followed her closely, his eyes trained on the woman, who seemed content to nurse her drink and pay them no mind.

"My," Taryn said to the bartender, sweeping her hood back but keeping her gloves on. She did not think her hair would be enough to alert a man like this to her identity. There were plenty of redheads in Scotland. "The quality of this establishment *has* gone down. We can still get a drink here, I hope?"

The bartender's eyes flickered to the woman at the other end of the bar. "Sorry, miss. We closed early tonight. There is no more drink to be had."

Taryn gave the man a sweet, patronizing smile. "Surely, you have something hidden under the bar for special occasions? My friend and I have come a long way."

"'S lots of other pubs, miss," the man mumbled.

"Yes, but we were told yours is the best."

Again, the bartender glanced at Petrichor. "I have a bit of Scotch whisky here," he said slowly, pulling a bottle of deep amber liquid from beneath the bar. "But it ain't a drink for a lady, if you don't mind my saying so, miss..."

"Put your whisky away, Calum," a new voice interrupted. "They are leaving, if they know what's good for them."

Taryn turned her attention toward Petrichor, who still had not raised her head. "I beg your pardon? Last time I checked, we could enjoy any establishment we pleased."

"Yeah, well, not this one," the woman growled. Her voice was a lovely deep contralto, but her accent, to Taryn's surprise, contained the harsh, nasal vowels of New York.

"Beat it, Red, before I kick both you and Mister Strong and Silent outta here myself."

Taryn turned her attention back to Calum, the bartender, just in time to see a bead of sweat roll down his forehead. "The drinks, please, Mr. Calum."

In the blink of an eye, Petrichor was on her feet and across the room, her face just inches from Taryn's. The two women stood precisely the same height. Taryn's stomach churned at the horrible brutality of her clockwork grafts. The left side of her jaw had been reconstructed with clockwork, creating a twisted perpetual grimace of metal teeth across her cheek. White scars marred most of the left side of her face. "I said '*beat it*,'" she snarled.

Taryn kept her expression neutral, maintaining her controlled exterior. "You are waiting for someone, are you not, Petrichor?" She paused significantly, allowing her knowledge to sink in. She lowered her voice. "Perhaps we ought to discuss this somewhere more private."

Petrichor eyed her carefully, long enough for Taryn to notice her left iris was not brown, like her right, but a unique shade of auburn, turning red when it caught the lamplight. "Fine. You intrigue me. This way."

The Clockwork Assassin led them up a narrow flight of wood stairs at the back of the pub, and to a small suite on the second floor where she'd clearly been living. An unmade bed occupied one corner, the blankets piled on the floor. Dirty dishes remained on a table—evidence of a meal recently consumed. A fire roared in the hearth, giving off crackling light and heat.

Petrichor dragged an armchair from its place facing the hearth to the center of the room facing them, the sound of wood against wood setting Taryn's teeth on edge. Petrichor threw herself into the chair, propping her right leg over the arm with the casual ease of a lion. She watched them both silently, waiting.

Taryn responded in kind, studying her biomaton 'sister.' Her clockwork did not stop with her jaw; it threaded down the left side of her neck, disappearing beneath the collar of her white blouse. Her left hand looked a lot like Taryn's, encased in interlocking steel plates, heavily armored, and Taryn guessed her left leg was at least partially clockwork as well, judging from the way she'd loped up the stairs. She wore leather breeches and boots, a wide belt around her hips sheathing perhaps a dozen sleek throwing knives, and a black corset tied around her waist. She appeared utterly at ease with them staring her down. She drew one of the many blades from her belt, toying with it, studying her nails.

"If you are trying to intimidate us, it is not going to work," Taryn said dryly.

Petrichor scoffed. "If I wanted to intimidate you, believe me, you would know." She grinned, an expression made all the more sinister by the crooked set of her jaw. "I would probably start by taking down Mr. Strong and Silent there."

"You would be dead before your knife left your hand," Taryn growled, reaching for her own knife, only to remember she had a sleeve and a pair of gloves in the way.

"Is that a challenge?" Petrichor asked, a fire dancing behind her eyes. Before Taryn could answer, two knives had left Petrichor's fingers, flying across the room, pinning Ace to the wall by his sleeve. Taryn reached for her own knife, but before she could reveal her metal arm, Petrichor had a third knife at her throat. "Are you satisfied with my performance, Red?" she hissed, teeth bared. "Are you ready to tell me what the job is? Or do I need to kill your friend first to prove myself?"

Taryn smirked, silently impressed by Petrichor's speed. "The assignment," she said, pushing the assassin's knife away and removing her gloves slowly, "is freedom for the biomatons."

Petrichor turned away, pacing. "I should have *known* this was Erikkson trying to get me back. As soon as I set foot back in Great Britain, I could feel his eyes on me." She faced Taryn again, spittle flying from her lips as she spat the words. "You tell him I am *never* coming back to that hell!"

Rattled by Petrichor's vehemence, Taryn forced herself to take a deep breath. She gave herself three seconds of silence, three seconds to gather herself. Ace came to stand at her shoulder, handing her one of Petrichor's throwing knives. The blade was unlike any Taryn had seen, with a narrow metal handle and a tapered, diamond-shaped blade. It felt good in her hand, perfectly balanced. She weighed it in her palm, her eyes locked on Petrichor, control and confidence oozing from her voice.

"I am not taking no for an answer."

Petrichor scoffed, her hands on her hips. "Of course. You always were his favorite, Sedition." Taryn blinked, and the assassin raised an eyebrow. "You thought I wouldn't recognize you? With that red hair and holier-than-thou personality, I knew you the moment you walked through that door."

Something in Taryn's stomach clenched. She had only recognized Petrichor by context clues, not on sight, and the knowledge that this person knew her so instantly made her throat want to close. Even Seraphim had taken some time to recognize who she was. Erikkson had said they were close, before Petrichor had gone away, but *how* close? Close enough to know Taryn on sight, even all these years later? She adjusted her tack, letting her voice take on a softer edge. Petrichor called Elmhurst "hell", but that was not the Erikkson or the Elmhurst she knew. "I do not know what he put you through, but Elmhurst is a sanctuary now."

Petrichor scoffed, tossing her brown hair so it danced around her shoulders. Taryn suddenly had the thought that the other girl's angular face might have been pretty, had it not been so heavily disfigured by clockwork and hatred.

"A *sanctuary?* Erikkson tortured us. All of us. He's abusive and manipulative, and if you can't see that, you're blinder than I thought."

Ace stiffened beside Taryn, and she opened her hand flat by her side, gesturing for him to relax. She didn't know what he must be feeling at this moment, only knew that the turmoil rolling through her own chest wasn't easy, and it had to be hard for him too. "No. It is not like that. Come back with us. If you do not like it, you can leave."

Petrichor's face creased with an expression that looked almost like pain, there for a second and then gone again behind the wall of bravado she kept up. "I already told you, I am *never* going back."

"I know you understand the importance of what we are doing," Taryn urged.

"You mean your cute little attempted coup? I heard about that. You and Seraphim may be happy throwing your lives away on a hopeless cause, but I prefer life. Thanks anyways for the invitation."

She settled herself in her armchair once more, crossing her legs in a way that seemed somehow mocking. "I really ought to kill the both of you to make sure Erikkson gets my message, but I'm feeling generous." She studied her nails, depriving Taryn of the courtesy of her gaze. "So, I'll give you to the count of ten to get out of my sight, or our friend Calum will be cleaning more blood off the floor. One."

Inwardly, Taryn swore. Petrichor wasn't easy to convince. She was a hardened warrior, harder even than Seraphim, and if she did not come up with something quickly, they would have lost her for good.

"Petrichor, if you help us, we can win this war! You will not have to hide any longer!" Taryn heard the pleading tone in her voice but could do nothing to get rid of it.

"Do I look like I care? I kill people for money, Red. I am a fugitive regardless of whether the biomatons are free or not. And I *like* it that way. Two."

Taryn's mind raced. Ace moved to lunge at Petrichor—either because of her stubbornness or what she did to his parents, Taryn wasn't sure. She kept a hand against his shoulder, holding him back.

"Three," Petrichor sighed. "You know, I don't think you two get it. If you haven't put an egg in your shoe by the time I get to ten, I'm killing you both."

"Then you *will* have to answer to Erikkson."

Petrichor just shrugged. "Not like it hasn't happened before. Four."

"Petrichor! I am asking you, as your sister—"

"Ah." The assassin held up a finger, shaking her head. "No. You do *not* get to call me that. I didn't like you then, and I don't like you now. Five."

Taryn scrambled, her mouth hanging open, mind racing for purchase as she tried to find another approach. "That is not what I was told," she tried, desperately. "Erikkson said we were close once."

Petrichor cocked her head to the side, a look almost like pity crossing her face. "You don't remember, do you?"

Taryn pressed her lips together, shocked by the sudden

burn of tears against the backs of her eyes. She blinked hard, fighting the feeling down, her mind scrambling for something, *anything* more she could say to convince Petrichor to come back with her. But as hard as she thought, Taryn could find no other way to convince her. The woman was worse than she had ever expected. Taryn silently cursed Erikkson for sending her here like this, for giving her less than nothing to go on— No, for *taking* her memories of her time with Petrichor and then expecting her to simply know what to say. This was not fair! She couldn't convince someone who seemed to hate the very sight of her.

"You know, I really am being too generous. Eight."

Taryn's throat closed. Ace tugged her arm. "Tar, that is enough. We should go."

"You should listen to him, Red," Petrichor said, grinning. She drew a knife from her belt. "Nine."

Taryn refused to move, catching a glimpse of Ace's cap, which now looked silly, tilted over the back of his head. Her heart fluttered like a bird in her throat as a sudden, ugly memory came into her mind. Fingers dancing inside her own control panel, the sudden sharp shock of something being triggered in her brain, red hot and angry. Petrichor had been to the Black Castle, too, Taryn knew. She had known that same violation. "The plate!" she exclaimed.

"What?"

"There is a plate on the back of your head, which hides your control panel. A job could go wrong, you could get caught, and that plate is all that stands between you and a lifeless drone. We are fighting to end that, Petrichor."

Fire flashed in the Clockwork Assassin's brown eyes, and her sneer turned to a sour scowl. She growled, a low, animal sound at the back of her throat.

And then, slowly, she sheathed her weapon.

CHAPTER FIVE

Petrichor leaned close to Taryn, too close to be heard by anyone nearby over the whistling wind and the thrum of the airship's engine. It was dark and late, but Erikkson had elected to fly back to Elmhurst tonight rather than waiting for daybreak, so here they were, one mad biomaton heavier. Taryn was still unsure if it was a good thing she'd convinced Petrichor to join them, but she was grateful that her guess had been correct: Petrichor had been shut down at the Black Castle, too. And Taryn knew *exactly* what that was like.

"So, tell me what is going on between you and Mr. Strong and Silent," Petrichor said.

Taryn's eyes went to Ace helping Erikkson steer on the half deck even as she shook her head. "Nothing is going on."

"Oh, come on, Red. I'm not blind. I have seen the hungry way you look at him."

Irritation rose in Taryn's throat. "You know as well as I do that is nonsense."

"I also know there are occasional *accidents* which allow biomatons to love again."

Taryn shook her head, feeling her cheeks flare with heat. It wasn't entirely clear how Petrichor had gone from murderous to almost cordial, if irritating, in the hour since they'd gotten underway. The woman's moods seemed to swing from hot to cold in the blink of an eye. Taryn couldn't help but think that she, too, had been like that, not so very long ago, before she'd learned full control of the violence in her head. She turned her attention back to Petrichor, uncomfortable with the complicated emotions and thoughts this woman presented her. "And he is not usually so silent. He is doing his very best not to kill you with his bare hands."

"Oh, really?" Petrichor sounded almost delighted, and Taryn fought the urge to strangle her. All the control she'd learned over the past months of training vanished in the face of this *infuriating* woman.

"You killed his parents, close to five years ago."

Petrichor's lips might have formed a perfect 'o' if not for her jaw piece. "Well, this reunion just keeps getting better! It seems as if I am not *really* wanted." Her lip curled. "Am I wrong?"

Taryn looked away. "Erikkson requested you return. That is enough."

"I have to say, I am glad you did not try to use the 'for the children' argument on me," Petrichor yelled over the rising wind, rocking with the gondola as they crossed a rough patch of turbulence. "If you had, I would have *known* there was no hope for you."

"And you think there is hope for me now?"

She shrugged. "You have that look about you."

"What look?" Taryn questioned, but Petrichor, who had seemed only too gregarious, just turned away, clockwork ticking in her jaw. At least she wasn't threatening to kill them anymore. Taryn scowled and rose, picking her way across the deck and up to where Ace stood at the wheel. Erikkson nodded to her.

"You did well tonight, Sedition."

"You had better hope I do not strangle her myself before she can help us win this war," she grumbled.

Her mentor smiled. "You will get used to her. You two are very much alike."

"Like water and vodka," Taryn spat, but she knew what Erikkson meant.

She and Petrichor shared more than their creator's deadly machinations. Both had faced similar tortures at the hands of the Black Castle, and both contained a deadly killer's instinct. Already, Taryn had been confronted with recognizing parts of herself in Petrichor's behaviors, and they had only been around each other for little more than an hour. Looking at Petrichor was like looking in a dark mirror, and that scared Taryn more than she wanted to admit. She only hoped that her own conscience remained more intact than the assassin's.

"Like sisters who have been apart for too long." Erikkson patted her on the shoulder in a way intended to be comforting, though it only caused her hackles to rise further. He stepped down from the half deck, leaving her and Ace to steer the airship. Taryn expected her mentor to approach Petrichor, but instead, he ducked into the engine room.

The two had only exchanged a handful of words since the assassin had boarded the ship, all of them civil but icy cold. Taryn could read Petrichor's distrust of their creator in her body language, and though she felt the same way about the assassin herself, she could not blame the girl. She still remembered her own rocky reunion with Erikkson all too well.

"I see your sea legs have not failed you, even after all this time," Taryn said to Ace, trying to get her mind off the time bomb their little family was becoming.

Ace grinned. "And I see you still wobble like a newborn foal on deck."

She punched him in the shoulder, but she used her right

hand and could not hide the pleasant heat in her cheeks. "Shut up."

"What were you and Petrichor discussing?" he called over his shoulder to her.

She shrugged. "It is not important. How long until we are home?"

"We have several hours to go yet. You ought to rest, if you can, Tar. After your long illness, a day like today could wreak havoc with your healing process."

Taryn wanted to refuse, to tell him rest was the last thing she needed, but even as she tried to say the words, her eyelids sagged. She *was* tired—*bone* tired—and just keeping herself on her feet was agonizing. She sank to the deck of the ship, curling into a corner where she would be sheltered from the wind by the rail.

"I am only going to rest for a moment," she mumbled. "Someone must keep an eye on Petrichor."

"Do not worry, Tar. I will be right here," Ace promised, his voice sounding far away as her eyes drifted shut.

The night froze her bones, but Taryn's body craved sleep, even there on the uncomfortable deck, and it was not long before she nodded off. She wandered in and out of wakefulness through the rest of the journey home. At some point, she woke just long enough to feel someone cover her shoulders with a blanket. And then the world went dark once more. She slept, dreaming of nothing.

❧

Taryn awoke to find someone shaking her shoulder. She blinked, darkness still clouding her vision. From what she could tell, it remained the middle of the night. Ace leaned over her.

"I am sorry to wake you, Taryn, but we are home now, and I

thought you would be more comfortable in your own bed than on the deck of the ship."

She stretched, her muscles complaining at her mistreatment of them. She moaned, rubbing her face. The blanket around her shoulders slipped to her waist, and Taryn glanced down, realizing it was not a blanket at all, but Ace's jacket.

"Oh, you must be freezing," she mumbled.

"I am all right." He smiled. "I kept active, stoking the boiler."

She rose, handing him the garment, her heart in her throat. "Thank you."

He nodded. "You are welcome."

She glanced over the ship, realizing they were alone. "Where did Petrichor go?"

"Erikkson is getting her settled. It is very late, Tar. We ought to get inside."

She nodded, still feeling a bit disoriented, like her head had been stuffed full of cotton. He took her arm, helping her down from the ship and onto the solid stone of Elmhurst's roof. She sighed, grateful for the help, though she never would have admitted it. Their heads bumped together as she stepped down from the ship. All at once, despite their circumstances, they were both laughing, the sound ringing in the night like bells. He squeezed her hand.

"Good night, Taryn."

"Good night, Ace."

She slipped past him, down the steps, and into the quietude of the darkened manor. She inhaled huge gulps of the musty air, realizing for the first time how much Elmhurst felt like home.

Home. It seemed like a foreign notion to her, a sentimental word other people used, a concept she could not remember understanding. But standing here, in the dark corridors of

Elmhurst, her friends, her soldiers, her chosen *family* sleeping around her, she knew she was home.

A warm red light shone from the library, and as she passed, she heard someone call her name. She turned back, glancing in the doorway to find Royal curled in an armchair near the glowing red embers of a dying fire. He closed his book and rose, a strange, tender expression on his face.

"Did you need something?" she asked nervously, hovering in the doorway.

He beckoned her. "How did the mission go?"

She shrugged, walking over and seating herself in one of the chairs near his.

"We convinced her to come along."

"Good." He hesitated, chewing the side of his thumb, the old, familiar nervous tic returning. "Did he tell you?"

"Did who tell me what?"

He looked away, his brown eyes dancing with the firelight. He took a deep, shuddering breath.

"My father is ill, Taryn. He is dying. The doctor does not think he will live much longer."

"Oh, Royal, I am sorry!" she exclaimed. "Should you not go to him?"

He shook his head, still refusing to meet her gaze.

"He will summon me, before the end, to ensure everything is in order. It is not as though we have the closest relationship. But— Gor, Tiger, I am not ready to be the Lord of Oxley. I am a mechanick's apprentice! I know nothing of running an estate."

He slumped over in his chair, his slender hands tangled in his dirty blond hair. Taryn wondered when he'd let it grow so long, the shaggy mane brushing his shoulders.

"You will be all right," she offered lamely. "Besides, you have Master Erikkson to ask for advice. You are not alone."

At last, he turned to look at her. A painful smile wrenched his face into an unfamiliar shape.

"You are right. Thank you, Taryn."

She shrugged. "Of course, it *is* poor timing. We need you here. But I suppose we can make do without you."

A genuine smile appeared in his eyes, though his face still clearly displayed the pain he felt.

"I promise I will not be gone long. This war is as important to me as it is to you, and I shall do all I can to help you win it."

Her stomach twisted. The monster inside her wanted to argue, wanted to *insist* he could not care about the war as much as she did because he had no stakes in it; its outcome did not affect him as it affected her. But she kept silent, simply nodding to him. They'd already had this fight, and he had already made it very clear that he cared about the biomatons' freedom. It wasn't fair of her to treat him like he couldn't understand because he wasn't one of them.

"Thank you." She rose, bobbing a small, awkward curtsy to him. "If you will excuse me, m'lord, I should be off to bed."

He rose as well, smiling at her teasing, and his crooked grin sent her stomach into new knots. He wrapped her in a hug, pulling her to his chest, and Taryn found herself breathing him in, closing her eyes to take in the hug. He smelled like machine oil and mischief, utterly familiar. These new feelings were not like what she experienced with Ace, but they were different and confusing all the same, and she hated the confusing way her body was responding to this boy she'd known for so long. Whatever this was, whatever madness had been brought on by her long illness, she needed to shake it, and soon. She had enough going on without having to figure out her friendships all over again. There was a war to win.

All too soon, she pushed him away, keeping her eyes down so he would not see how the hug had affected her.

"Good night, Royal."

"Good night, Tiger."

CHAPTER SIX

SHE FORCED herself to complete the run around the estate the next morning just after the sun rose, though her breath came in shallow gasps and her muscles burned. The run took three times as long as it should have. Her clockwork strained beneath her skin, but she felt stronger by the time she finished—her eyes set aglow with energy. Wiping her forehead on her sleeve, she made her way into the dining room, hungrier than a starving lion.

"Good morning, Red," Petrichor purred as Taryn entered the dining room, her feet propped on the table. Taryn stiffened.

"You ought to be training."

Petrichor looked out of place in the prettily wallpapered room with its table heaping with food for Elmhurst's many soldiers. No one else was present, which was not unusual for this time of morning, but even so, the presence of the Clockwork Assassin was as jarring as walking into her bedroom to find a wolf in her bed. She grinned, the expression singularly cruel on her scarred, altered face.

"I am in prime shape. If I wasn't, people wouldn't trust me to do what I do. You, on the other hand, look a little worse for the wear." She cocked her head, sipping her coffee from a fine china teacup. "Someone should tell you it's not healthy to starve yourself, no matter how attractive you think it makes you look."

"I am not starving myself," Taryn growled, dropping into a chair as far as possible from Petrichor and serving herself a heaping portion of sausage, eggs, and fluffy white breakfast rolls. She ate in silence, until the other girl spoke again.

"You know, I am disappointed. I thought you would come to my room last night. We could have braided each other's hair and talked about our *secrets*."

Taryn did not grant her the respect of eye contact. "I do not need you to like me, Petrichor. I do not care. But I swear, if you undermine my authority in front of my soldiers, I will cut out that sharp tongue of yours."

Petrichor laughed. "Oh, I like this Sedition so much better than the last one! She's so dark and angsty." She leaned forward. "Actually, Red, I wanted to discuss the terms of our arrangement here. I have a few caveats if I am going to work with you."

Shrugging, Taryn shoveled another slice of ham into her mouth, chewing and swallowing before she replied.

"Save it. We are meeting with Master Erikkson and Seraphim at ten. You may bring up any and all complaints then."

"He still has you calling him Master?"

Taryn huffed. "No. It is automatic. A remnant of my training, or so I am told."

Petrichor's dark eyes widened. She leaned forward, actually taking her feet off the table. "You keep saying that. What do you mean, you're told?"

"I cannot remember," Taryn growled.

"Oh, he really screwed you up, didn't he?" The assassin's

voice dropped to a hushed kind of awe. "We should change places, Red. You would be better than me at this."

"Why?" she snapped.

"You would not remember the faces of your victims."

Taryn stood, slamming her fist against the table, her vision going red.

"I will see you in Erikkson's study at ten," she growled, stalking from the room.

She couldn't breathe for the anger that rolled in her chest. The audacity of this biomaton assassin! She would have to be more cautious around her. It was infuriating how Taryn could remember nothing about her, and yet she appeared to know all the right buttons to press, all the ways to worm her way under Taryn's skin and into her mind. She couldn't allow it. She wouldn't.

⁂

"Sir, do you have a few minutes?" Ace questioned, standing in the doorway of Erikkson's study. His metal right hand ran nervously up and down his left arm.

Erikkson looked up from his work, surprise passing through his forest green eyes. The room was brightly lit with lamplight, and many of the card catalog drawers along the wall were open. Clearly the man had been pulling cogs and gears as needed them, allowing the study to grow cluttered as his busy hands constructed something new.

"Ace! It is early. I was not expecting you to be awake so soon. Come in, come in."

Ace entered, pulling the door shut behind him. His eyes clouded with worry.

"Sir, will you check my grafts? I have some... suspicion that something may not have been constructed properly, or else was broken in my fight with Storm..."

"You think something is wrong with your grafts?" Erikkson questioned in concern, wiping his hands on a gray rag.

Ace's eyes flickered over the man's project, half-hidden from view behind his gaunt frame. It was an intricate mess of clockwork, but before Ace could see any more, Erikkson covered the object with a cloth.

"Let me see what we can see. If you would remove your shirt, we shall see what we can do about your concerns."

Ace nodded, a small part of him intensely curious about Erikkson's secret project, while the rest of him insisted it was none of his business. He pulled his shirt over his head. His ribs twinged in protest, but the discomfort had become so normal he barely noticed anymore. He allowed the shirt to fall from his fingertips, revealing his well-trained muscles and olive skin, marred by the silver steel across the right side of his sternum.

His breastbone and all the ribs on his right side had been replaced with clockwork, lifting the bones through the skin. Where the muscles met the graft, his skin stretched too tightly, puckered and red with mistreatment. During his fight with Storm, a well-placed blow from one steel-toed boot had split the skin away from his graft, and though it had healed, the place continued to pain him more than any other part of his clockwork graft. He wore the ache like a brand, a reminder of his unfinished business with the sister who had sworn to kill him.

"Hm," Erikkson muttered to himself, prodding Ace's back with firm but gentle fingers. "I cannot say your graft is well-made, because I would be lying. But you, my friend, are incredibly resilient. You have taken it well and seem to be healing, in spite of the damage they did to you."

"Thank you, sir," Ace replied timidly, "but it is not my arm I suspect to be broken."

Erikkson did not speak for a long moment before heaving a sigh.

"Ace, I realize that Taryn's situation may have given you a

false hope, but I ought to have told you, hers is an incredibly rare case..."

"Just check, please, Master Erikkson," Ace pleaded, feeling his cheeks color. "I do have more evidence for my suspicions than just Taryn's fortunate accident."

"Very well. Hold still."

Erikkson clicked the little metal plate on the back of Ace's head open. The boy tensed, his breath hitching as he waited. Despite his knowledge that this man would never change any setting without his permission, Ace still detested allowing anyone access to his mind. He'd lost his autonomy once before and swore he would never allow anyone to do that to him again. He would rather die.

"I *am* seeing something here, Ace," Erikkson pronounced after a few moments of agonized silence. He sounded surprised. "One of your controls appears to be broken."

Ace's breath caught in his throat, and he had to swallow several times before he could finally speak past the lump lodged behind his Adam's apple.

"What control?"

"It appears to be your obedience circuit."

Ace's shoulders slumped. "Oh."

"That is good! It means you cannot be controlled as you were before."

"Yes, I suppose it does," Ace replied. "Do you see nothing else?"

Erikkson hummed to himself for a moment, then spoke. "No." Ace heard the panel click shut. He bent to retrieve his shirt, wincing.

"Thank you for looking, sir," Ace said weakly, pulling his shirt over his shoulders.

"Ace, just because I did not find anything does not mean it is not there," Erikkson encouraged, meeting the boy's eye. "The human brain is an incredibly complicated organ, and even the best biomechanicks make mistakes with dampers. *Especially* if those mechanicks are poorly trained and overworked."

Ace stared at him for several long moments. At last, he nodded.

"I think I understand, sir. Thank you." He turned to go, but on a whim, paused, and turned back. "Sir?"

"Yes?"

"What is it you are working on?" he asked, indicating the project beneath the white cloth.

Erikkson smiled enigmatically, tapping his temple with a finger.

"That, dear boy, is a surprise."

CHAPTER SEVEN

Petrichor lifted her eyes from the knife she was sharpening as Seraphim entered Erikkson's study. Their eyes met, and his wings rose defensively. The dark-skinned biomaton was taller even than she had remembered, his lithe frame moving with a catlike grace she had always envied. His long, wavy black hair was the same as ever though, tied half up in a familiar topknot. His almond-shaped green eyes narrowed, and Petrichor felt her heartrate tick faster, just slightly. Silence reigned for a long breath. At last, Seraphim spoke in his low, rumbling baritone.

"I thought I would be the only one here early. You were never punctual before."

"I got here early hoping I'd catch you alone," Petrichor sneered. "You always were insufferably prompt."

Seraphim's lip curled into a snarl, revealing a flash of silver canine teeth. That, too, was achingly familiar.

Petrichor sheathed her knife and sat on the edge of Erikkson's worktable, her legs dangling.

"Relax, S," she purred, pronouncing the letter like a nickname, letting the sound hiss through her teeth a moment too long. "I wanted to discuss our dear Red without her present to protest. I have only been back for a matter of hours, and already her attitude is insufferably haughty."

"If you have a problem with Sedition, you ought to take it up with her directly," Seraphim answered flatly.

"Oh, come on! I can't be the only one who sees right through her self-righteous act. Do you not remember how she used to prance around like she owned the place?"

The winged biomaton raised one eyebrow, his expression otherwise inscrutable. "You have been gone a long time. She has grown since you saw her last. You ought to give her a second chance."

Petrichor scoffed. "I know what I saw, S. She's the same as she always was, she just grew into a woman's body."

"Erikkson made her our leader. We must trust him."

Her countenance changed, anger clouding her features. "*Trust* Erikkson? Did you forget what he did to us, Seraphim?"

"You brought it upon yourself," he answered coldly, but he backed two steps away from his clockwork sister, his wings rising protectively.

"You are not *ever* allowed to say that to me," Petrichor growled.

She dropped off the worktable, landing with her feet set firmly, fists raised in a fighting stance. He held his own hands up in a pacifying gesture, his eyes never leaving hers.

"I am not going to fight you," he said slowly, tasting each syllable before it dropped from his lips.

That was the Seraphim she remembered. As cold and calculating as Taryn had been fiery, and oh, how Petrichor hated that. She just wanted to get her fists bloody on something, *anything*. No matter how carefully she tried to hide it, being back in this house felt like someone was sawing a violin bow over her raw nerves and the rage beneath her skin she could barely keep under control.

"Ah, you are both already here," Erikkson interrupted, walking right between them, effectively ending the stand-off.

Petrichor forced her face to relax from anger to a careful, tightly controlled neutral. She ducked her head, fists relaxing, though the tension that had been there moved to her shoulders. Her eyes dropped to the worn carpet. She could sense Seraphim's eyes on her, and wanted desperately to give him the finger for the way his gaze felt like pity. "Erikkson," she grunted.

He smiled at her. "Welcome home, Petrichor. It is good to have you back with us at last."

He took his seat behind his desk, checking a pocket watch.

"As soon as Sedition and Royal arrive, we shall begin. In the meantime, please, sit."

Seraphim settled himself near the wall on a stool, his wings relaxed and nearly touching the ground. Petrichor, still bristling with pent-up anger, settled herself in a red armchair, studying her palms. She swallowed hard, feeling the eyes of her creator on her. The silence hung in the air like a dead thing: heavy, bloated, and odiferous. No one moved or spoke.

A few moments later, Taryn and Royal stumbled into the silence and froze, sensing the tension in the room.

"Gor," Royal quipped, his voice cracking, "Who died?"

"Please close the door and have a seat," Erikkson ordered, ignoring the dry attempt at humor. They did as they were told, joining the others. Taryn glanced at the other two biomatons in the room, aware Erikkson had intended this all along. Three biomatons, built for rebellion. Three biomatons designed to defy the status quo and wage a war for freedom.

And yet, as she studied her counterparts, Taryn wondered if he had not built them a little *too* subversively. They'd been built to be weapons, but looking at her siblings, she realized they looked more like monsters than human beings. Perhaps it was not just she Erikkson intended to die for the cause. Maybe all three were not destined to outlive this rebellion. The thought left a sour taste in her mouth.

"Seraphim. Sedition. Petrichor," Erikkson began, his hands folded on the desk, his piercing green eyes touching each of them in turn. "Here we are again at last, and you are ready to work together, as I intended. First of all, I would like to welcome Petrichor back. It has been a long time, my dear, and I could not be happier to have you with us."

Petrichor raised her eyes, but rather than looking at their creator, she addressed Taryn. It was almost as though she could not look at the biomechanick.

"I have some conditions if I am going to be working with you."

Taryn's own gaze flickered to Erikkson, who nodded. Her eyes met Petrichor's once more.

"Go on."

"I don't participate in group training. I run my own missions. I want you to swear you won't boss me around. And the first time you try to make me participate in the chores, I am leaving."

"Actually," Erikkson interrupted, allowing Taryn to breathe a sigh of relief. "That is what I wanted to discuss. Petrichor, your role shall be fitting to your skills. I recognize that part of the reason your mind has been so numbed to violence is because of the brutal nature of the train accident which injured you in the first place. But though I do not approve of your choice to kill, I am nevertheless proud of you."

She raised her eyes to him, the wrinkle of disgust on her face falling away, surprised to hear the word "proud" pass his lips.

"You will be in charge of our covert operations," Erikkson

continued. "There is a squadron already trained to assist you in whatever you need. Will that be acceptable?"

Speechless, Petrichor nodded.

"Seraphim, you are a formidable fighter, but your true talent lies in strategy. You will advise Sedition on the army's movements, plan with Royal and me, and study to ensure we have the best chance at success."

The winged biomaton inclined his head. "Yes, sir."

Taryn waited as Erikkson turned his attention to her, her heart in her throat. She already knew her role—the leader, the firebrand—but she still felt a spark of anxiety as she waited to hear what he would say.

"Sedition, I took your memories believing you would regain them in time. I made a mistake. Still, you took my cause as your own, taking up the mantle of Sedition even in the face of great adversity. I am so proud of what you have accomplished and the woman you have become. I can think of no one I would rather have to lead our cause. You will bring us to victory."

Taryn nodded, a smile flashing across her face. "Thank you. I will do my best to live up to your expectations of me."

Erikkson glanced at Royal. "As you all know, the war has begun, but you may not be aware of the particulars. My apprentice Royal will detail the circumstances."

Royal rose, clasping his hands behind his back. Petrichor whistled appreciatively. Taryn glared daggers at her, her own ears burning with second-hand embarrassment. Royal stumbled over the sentence he had started and had to start over, that maddening crooked smile making Taryn's stomach flip. She swallowed hard, a strange suspicion rising inside her as she began to recognize the way she had been feeling the past few days. The maddening, stomach-churning confusion that left her flushed and awkward around her friends wasn't just an after-effect of her long sleep. Something was wrong. Something was happening that had not happened before, and it scared her a little to acknowledge that the way she felt around Ace and Royal was new, and different. Confusing.

"Our opposition begins with Commodore Storm Highmore, a former privateer the Queen has promoted, giving her full control of the military to crush us. Storm is ruthless, and she hates biomatons. She swore to see us all hang, and that seems to be a promise she intends to keep. So far, ten biomatons have been hanged for treason. Only four of them had anything to do with our cause. The rest were innocent casualties."

Petrichor's mouth hung open, a strange look of recognition coming into her brown eyes. "Wait, your lordship. Back up. Did you say Storm Highmore?"

A look of irritation crossed Royal's face, but he nodded. "Yes."

"That little tyke is still around!" Petrichor scoffed. "She gave me my very first job five years ago."

All eyes turned to her. Taryn could not hide her horror. "You *remember* that job?"

"Of course I do, Red. You never forget your first," the assassin replied with a cheeky grin, her face twisting around her metal jaw piece.

Taryn stood so suddenly her chair tipped backward, crashing to the floor. "Those were Ace's parents, you *murderer!*"

Petrichor raised an eyebrow. "Do we really want to do this? If we are talking murderers, I know of twenty-five young soldiers you personally put in the grave. We *all* have blood on our hands. You don't get to pick on me just 'cause I made money on what I knew how to do."

Taryn balled her fists, white-knuckled weapons ready at her sides, but she forced herself to breathe through the roiling anger in her chest, closing her eyes for a moment until her heart beat normally again. Though she did not want to admit it, Petrichor was right. They all had blood on their hands, and Taryn was guiltiest of all, as the killing had been done to save her. She righted her chair, nodding to Royal as she took her seat.

"I apologize. Please, continue."

"Storm's maneuvers have been too scattered for us to follow as of yet," Royal continued, "but we *have* managed to identify one of her accomplices: a man named Captain Winchester. Five of the arrests were made by this man. His airship is a navy galleon called the *HMA Musketeer*. If we can take him out, we may slow Storm down or at least send her a message that we are not helpless. We *will* fight back."

"Petrichor?" Taryn glanced at the biomaton.

She looked up. "Oh, you want to call me a murderer until my skill set will actually help you, and then I am suddenly useful? I don't think that's how it works, Red."

Taryn huffed. "I am sorry I called you a murderer. You *are* the best we have for this. And we will all have bloodied hands before this is over. It is inevitable."

"Wow, an apology? In that case, I accept!" Petrichor's voice dripped with sarcasm. "Shall I go tonight, oh wise leader?"

Taryn glared daggers at her counterpart. "Just do it before the week is out."

"My pleasure," Petrichor purred.

"Now, if we are finished here, I have training to do." Taryn rose.

Erikkson nodded, dismissing her, but as Taryn left, Petrichor hissed, "See you later, Red. I look forward to sparring with you after all this time."

⚓

Taryn pushed herself hard in training that afternoon, until her skin glistened with sweat and her breath came in short bursts. This bothered the twins and Emmett, who did not go as hard on her as they could have, afraid of shattering her gaunt form. Taryn recognized their reluctance and met it with reckless attacks, forcing them to fend her off or be injured by her spinning blades. She fought all three at once, and whether because of their reluctance or her reckless abandon, she was *winning*.

A crowd gathered to watch, and by the time the four called a truce, breathlessly panting, thirty or so soldiers had gathered around the edges of the room. A smattering of applause danced around the room.

"Ça va?" Emmett questioned, touching Taryn's elbow, his breath coming in heavy gasps.

She hung doubled over, her hands on her knees, sweat pouring down her face as she waited for her breathing and heart rate to return to normal. Despite all that, she felt fine—better, she felt *good*. She had been right after all. What she needed was exercise, something to take her mind off the ugly, knotted mess of her life. She nodded.

"Aye. Fine."

The twins straightened, though Rorin's mechanickal lung whistled in his chest. Ari sported a blossoming black eye. In unison, the two clapped her on the back, identical, dark-skinned hands patting her shoulders, careful to avoid the blades still fanning from her back like deadly fairy wings.

"Well done, Sedition!" Rorin exclaimed hoarsely.

Taryn managed to straighten at last, a strained, exhausted smile crossing her face. Together, the twins raised their hands in rigid, proud salutes. First Emmett, then the rest of the room followed suit, until she stood surrounded by her army, all on their feet, saluting her. Weakly, she returned the gesture, pride rising in her chest. This was her army. And they would follow her, even unto death.

In the midst of her pride, a new figure burst through the crowd, scattering younger, smaller biomatons as she came. Taryn scowled at Petrichor, bristling.

"I thought you did not do training?"

The assassin stared directly into Taryn's eyes, a mad light flickering behind her gaze. She stood just outside the sparring ring that had been painted in whitewash on the floor, the tip of her boot nudging the white line.

"I challenge Sedition!" she cried, her voice ringing on the sudden dead silence.

Taryn's mouth went dry. "You what?"

Petrichor turned toward Seraphim, who had shoved himself to the front of the crowd near Taryn, his own mannerisms stiff and awkward.

"That is how it works, right? All have to do is say I challenge her authority, and we get to duel."

Seraphim glanced at Taryn with apologetic eyes.

"That is how it works."

"Petrichor, we had a deal!" Taryn hissed.

"I believe the way you worded it was 'if you challenge my authority, I shall cut out that quick tongue of yours,'" Petrichor mimicked in a high-pitched, affected accent. "So here I am, Red. Come and get it." She stuck her tongue out at Taryn petulantly, like a stubborn child.

Taryn bristled. She shoved Emmett and the twins out of the circle, her vision blurring red. She forced herself to breathe, to rein in the violence. She would not defeat Petrichor with irrational violence. She would defeat her with calculation.

"Go on, then," she answered with a grin. "Show me what you can do."

She stretched, rolling her neck and shoulders as Seraphim delivered the rules, his voice devoid of emotion. Petrichor shrugged out of her leather coat, adjusting the belt around her waist, ensuring everyone saw the many throwing knives flashing around her hips.

Rorin grabbed Taryn's shoulders.

"Do not do this, Sedition! She is mad! She will kill you if she gets half a chance!"

"Then I shall not give her one. Promise me something, boys. Promise me that if she does kill me, you will ensure she does not leave this room alive." Taryn growled, flexing her metal fist, satisfied with the hiss of the metal spikes extending from her knuckles.

Ari and Rorin grinned identical smiles.

"With pleasure," they answered in unison.

"There shall be no killing," Seraphim announced over the buzz of the soldiers. "And do try not to hurt one another too much. We need both of you."

Petrichor cracked her knuckles. "Get on with it, S!"

Taryn tensed, her hips shifting to balance her weight, her body becoming a coiled spring of kinetic energy. Petrichor's fingers twitched, hovering over the knives on her belt. Taryn flexed her own fingers, every sore muscle forgotten as her vision narrowed, her focus on nothing but the fight ahead and Petrichor's movements.

"Begin."

The assassin's hand flashed to the knives at her waist, but the nearness of the biomatons observing the duel kept her from throwing them. Taryn swept ahead, keeping her arms up to protect her torso, keeping her target as small as possible. Petrichor side-stepped just as Taryn lunged, and her knife plunged down. Taryn had anticipated the movement and rolled aside at the last moment, the knife grazing past her ear, near enough to hear the whistle as it sliced through the air. Taryn's shoulder blades fanned out, catching Petrichor's wrist, the razor-sharp edge splitting flesh as easily as if it were butter.

The woman swore and backed off, blood running down her wrist. Someone in the crowd cried, "First blood!" but the cheer was not taken up. The watchers remained eerily silent.

The two circled, staring one another down, twin pairs of

eyes filled with identical bloodlust. Petrichor's lip curled into a snarl, and before Taryn could react, one of Petrichor's knives was speeding through the air toward her. Taryn dodged, but the knife soared so near it took half a dozen copper hairs with it as it went. She barely registered it, praying the soldiers behind her had managed to dodge it before throwing herself at Petrichor again. Her first few blows missed their mark, but she scored a glancing blow off the woman's jaw before leaping away from a new knife. It left a narrow line of blood across her cheek.

"Come on," Taryn growled. "Face me without those blades. Or are you too much of a coward?"

"Only if you put your own blades away, Red." Petrichor sneered.

"Fair enough."

With a flick of her wrist, she sheathed her blades and waited for Petrichor to do the same. For half a second, it seemed she would go back on her word. She twirled a knife across her metal knuckles, staring at Taryn. And then she sheathed the blade, unbuckled her belt, and handed it to a shocked young biomaton on the sidelines.

"Take care of that. If you so much as scratch the leather, I'll have your hide when this is over."

The young biomaton nodded his head vigorously, eyes wide. Petrichor shook out her shoulders, all her attention on Taryn once more.

"Let's see what you got, Red."

They circled one another, feet dancing over the stone floor, neither allowing the other near enough to strike. Taryn's fingers itched to attack, to feel the solid impact of fist against flesh, but she held herself back, watching her opponent warily, waiting for her to make the first move. Her weakened muscles trembled beneath her skin. One thing was becoming very clear: she could not keep this up.

Petrichor struck, quick as a snake and just as deadly, landing a blow with her metal fist on Taryn's jaw. She followed it with another to her ribs. Taryn grunted, but did not go down, countering with her own punches, which Petrichor easily blocked. Taryn danced backward, tasting blood. She sucked at the split in her lip. It was time to let Sedition out and end this.

Taryn leaped forward, catching Petrichor's wrist. At the same time, she swept her heel against the back of her opponent's knee, buckling her stance. Petrichor collapsed, but caught Taryn's shoulder as she went, pulling her down too. Both hit the ground hard enough to knock the breath from their lungs. For a moment, neither moved, lying flat on their backs, panting. Petrichor was up first, rolling and pinning Taryn with her left knee against her throat. Taryn choked, her suspicions confirmed: the leg *was* clockwork, cold and heavy on her chest.

"Do you want to yield?" Petrichor growled.

In response, Taryn spat bloodied spittle in her face. She shifted, driving her knee up as hard as she could, striking Petrichor in the lower back. The woman grunted, pressing harder on Taryn's throat.

"If that is how you want it—" she hissed.

Lungs burning for oxygen, Taryn writhed beneath Petrichor's grip. Cold metal fingers clamped around her throat, but Taryn refused to yield. She would *not* give up her role to this madwoman. Not even if it killed her.

Taryn bucked, then drove her own metal fist, spikes and all, into Petrichor's ribcage. Over and over, she struck until her opponent released her. And then Taryn had Petrichor pinned, and was demanding she yield, both hands locked around the other's throat. Petrichor fought, writhing like a snake, but Taryn refused to relent, pressing hard on her windpipe until a strange, faraway look came into her brown eyes. Taryn's own eyesight swam, Petrichor's face blurring, transforming into the face of a young man—a young man Taryn recognized. He was one of the soldiers she had killed that day in the square. Petrichor's words echoed in her head... *Twenty-five soldiers you personally put in the grave...* Sick horror washed over her like waves on a stormy sea.

"Enough!"

Someone grabbed Taryn's shoulders, forcing her to release Petrichor, dragging her away from the battle.

"I told you *not* to kill one another," Seraphim yelled, his face just inches from hers, but she barely saw him. One by one, the faces of the dead were returning to her—ugly, grinning skulls leering from the darkness like accusations she could not meet.

"Can you hear me?" Seraphim growled.

Taryn blinked hard, dispelling the ghosts long enough to see Seraphim was not talking to her. He leaned over Petrichor, patting her cheek in a way that seemed almost tender. Bruises ringed her throat in the shape of fingerprints, and Taryn's heart sank. They *were* the same. She had a killer's instinct just as wild and difficult to control as Petrichor's. The twins hung tightly to her arms, holding her back in case she attacked once more. Every young biomaton soldier observing the scene stared at her as though she'd transformed into a monster. And in some ways, she supposed she had.

"Let me go," she growled, shrugging the twins off.

"Sedition—" Rorin began, but she ignored him, shoving through the crowd, headed past Seraphim for the doors. The ghosts in her head screamed accusations at her. She could barely see the soldiers right in front of her for the ones in her head, the ones she had killed without remorse, without regret. Taryn's stomach heaved. She thought she might throw up.

"Do not leave," Seraphim growled, leaping to his feet as soon as he understood where she was going. "You cannot leave like this." At his feet, Petrichor stirred, moaning.

"She will survive," Taryn growled without looking back.

She couldn't look back. If she did, she knew she would have to face what she had done, and that was not something she could take. She tasted acid and blood in her mouth, felt Petrichor's sticky blood coating her fists, and for the first time in a long time, Taryn was truly, deeply afraid of the monster she had become. "The same cannot be said for anyone who follows me."

CHAPTER EIGHT

"Taryn!" Ace raced to catch up with her as she stormed from the manor, catching her shoulder. She tried to shake him off.

"Let me go." Her voice was like broken glass—sharp, cutting, and fragile.

"No. Taryn, what happened in there?" he demanded, holding on to her as tightly as he could, his fingers digging into her shoulder.

"You saw what I did," she spat. Every word coated her tongue with copper, the split in her lip filling her mouth with blood.

"I saw a warrior do what she had to, to defeat someone who wanted to usurp her authority."

She turned on him, eyes wild, blood and tears smeared across her cheeks.

"You saw a monster lose control," she screamed, spittle flying from her lips. She pressed her hands over her ears, trying in vain to silence the voices in her head. "You saw what I really am." Another surge of sick shock swept over her, leaving her nauseous and dizzy. She could see nothing but blood, feel nothing but the way Petrichor had sagged beneath her hands and the way she had *liked it*. Oh god, Taryn had *liked* feeling the other girl's life slipping away beneath her, and that was the worst part of it all. She'd been made like this—a weapon, a monster, yes—but at what point had she lost her own fear of what that really meant? At what point had she let the monster take over?

"Taryn," Ace began.

She looked up at him, expecting to see horror and blame, but finding only compassion in his eyes.

"You are *not* a monster. But we *did* lose you for a moment there. Where did you go? What happened?"

Her arms folded over her chest, as though she could protect herself from the cold world that wanted so badly to destroy her. The last thing she wanted was to talk about it, but the words fell from her lips before she could stop them. "How many?"

"What?"

"How many did we kill, Ace? In the square. How many did *I* kill?"

He shook his head. "I do not know. No one knows."

"Their families know! How many families did I deprive of a son, a father?" Tears hung on her lashes, sparkling against the light in her eyes.

Ace hugged her then, a surprisingly gentle embrace, tucking her head beneath his chin protectively. It was the first time he'd embraced her like that, and unlike the time he'd wrapped his arms around her to teach her to shoot, his nearness made her heart pound.

"You cannot dwell on that, Tar. If you carry the weight of every life taken in this war—biomaton and human alike—it will crush you." Taryn could feel his deep voice rumbling in his chest as he spoke, and it comforted her.

"But the lives were all given for me," she answered, her voice softened. "And I took them without thought, without compassion. What have I done?"

Ace sighed as he stroked her hair.

"I understand. The first few missions I ran with Storm, I felt the same. I carried the names of everyone I killed. And there was a time..." He paused, drawing her to arm's length so he could look her in the eye. "I lost two airships of naval officers to pirates, about a year before I met you. I bore the weight of all those souls. All those families."

Taryn remembered the story as relayed by Seraphim, but she'd never actually heard from Ace how such a devastating loss had affected him. Her voice emerged as a hoarse whisper.

"How did you cope?"

He shook his head. "I realized that it was foolish of me to continue blaming myself. I cannot change the past. But I *can* do what I can to create a better future. A lovely young biomaton taught me that."

"And you no longer carry that weight?"

A wry smile quirked one side of his lips upward. "Of course I still carry it. I shall carry it to my grave—every name and every face. But now it does not weigh me down quite so much."

She pulled away from him, wiping her face with her hands, further smearing the blood across her cheeks. She gave him a pained smile, more a reveal of the teeth than anything else. It wasn't enough to absolve her, but it helped to know that he understood. That he saw her, all of her, and did not think she was a monster.

"Thank you, Ace."

He nodded, studying her closely. "You have been pushing yourself too hard, too quickly. You ought to get some rest if you can. Training will wait. And you do no one any good if you injure yourself because you are impatient to regain your strength."

"As much as I do not like it, you are right." She shuddered, pressing her hands over her eyes. "Petrichor shall come after me for this, I am sure of it."

"If it will make you feel better, I shall guard your door while you rest."

She brightened a little. "Would you?"

"It would be my honor."

They moved back inside together, Ace keeping a wary eye on Taryn, protectively walking a few steps behind her. She crossed her arms over her chest again, trying in vain to ward off a chill in her core. When they reached her room, Ace dragged a chair into the hall, promising to remain just outside the door while she rested.

"No one will disturb you, Tar. I will make sure of it."

She thanked him and closed the door, limbs heavy with exhaustion. She would rest for a half hour, she told herself, and then she would return to training. There was nothing wrong with a half hour of rest... She lay back against the pillows, but she did not close her eyes. She stared up at the frescoed ceiling, arms wrapped around herself, feeling again the sensation of Ace's arms around her. Warmth flooded her cheeks, her chest, and she squeezed her chest tightly, trying to keep her body from shaking. There were too many thoughts in her head, too many emotions that fought for her attention all at once, and she could not focus on a single one. Ace's face, gentle with compassion, now mixed with the images of Petrichor, of the soldiers she had killed. Was she a monster, as she suspected, as Petrichor seemed to be? Or was she forgivable, like Ace thought? Could she be something in between? Or was war complex, like Ace had indicated, and whatever they did justified by the fact that their cause was noble?

That final thought was along the lines of Erikkson's philosophy. His meddling, his construction of biomaton weapons, his training them to be warriors instead of servants, all justified by the fact that he wanted them to be free. But she wasn't so sure. The empty pit in her stomach said otherwise, said that every life that was lost in this war—from the soldiers in the square that she had killed, to Jack the midshipman and the innocent biomatons who had been killed for show—they all meant something. They all had people who cared for them, who would never see them again, because of *her*. Taryn rolled over and buried her face in her pillow, hot tears staining the satin case.

It was too much for her to try and process.

It was too much for her to carry.

※

"*Touché!*" Emmett crowed, saluting Royal with his saber. "You must be faster, *mon ami*, if you are to beat me!"

Royal rubbed the sore spot on his shoulder where Emmett had scored his touch, his face reddening. "I think you are cheating," he grumbled sullenly.

"Skill is not cheating."

Royal shrugged, setting his saber on one of the racks which stood around the room, cradling a variety of weapons for the biomatons to use in training. His eyes strayed to the bloodstains in the sparring circle, dark splotches against the porous stone floor. His stomach roiled as he recalled Taryn's battle with Petrichor there only a half hour earlier.

"I have never seen her lose control like that before," he muttered, more to himself than the Frenchman standing nearby.

"Nor have I. Something broke inside her." Emmett chewed his lip. "I am concerned this Petrichor will do more harm than good."

The bigger boy bit the side of his thumb, concern coating his big brown eyes. "I ought to go see if she is all right. It is not like her to disappear for so long."

"She needs time alone, Royal. It is best to leave her be. She will return when she is ready."

Royal felt that flare of frustration rise in him, the quick heat he felt at Emmett's possessiveness that he had fought so hard to control. Taryn had called it *childish*, but he thought it was more about the fierce protectiveness he felt for her, the fact that he had spent most of the last five years protecting her and now it was the other way around. Taryn could protect herself. But it still was hard to not want to protect her from unwanted advances. (Or what he perceived as unwanted.)

"What do you know about it? You have known her for a matter of weeks, Frenchman!" As soon as the words were out of his mouth, Royal regretted them. This was exactly the kind of thing Taryn had asked him *not* to do. But he was scared, and he was worried, and it was all coming out as anger.

Emmett stared at him for a long moment before speaking.

"I know you wish to win her love, *monsieur*. But you will not win her heart if you are constantly insulting her friends."

"She has been my best friend for five years!"

"*Oui*. I do not deny it. But I am her friend also, and I do not think she would like the way you speak to me."

Royal growled wordlessly, his fists clenched by his sides. "Why do you not just go back to your country where you belong? There are plenty of French women who will not care that your eyes are *missing*."

And that was too far. Royal knew that. It was unfair of him to call out Emmett's injury, and completely uncalled for. He pressed a hand over his mouth, stunned at his own cruelty. "Gor, I did not—"

Emmett's cheeks had gone bright red.

"Perhaps I can even us out, *monsieur*," he replied, his normally lemon-bright voice taking on a black velvet edge. He lifted the tip of his saber menacingly.

"No, Emmett, I did not mean—" He stumbled over his words, holding up both hands in a vague gesture of surrender. "I should not have said—"

The saber slashed forward with a flick of Emmett's wrist,

opening a vivid gash on Royal's cheek. The boy stood frozen for a moment, mouth agape, blood seeping down his cheek, dripping from his sharp jawline onto his collar. His fingers rose, hesitating before brushing over his cheekbone. They came away wet with blood.

"Just a little sparring accident, *monsieur*." Emmett's face held a darkness that Royal had never seen before.

Royal stared at him, his voice shaking. For the first time, he saw the hardened pirate behind the Frenchman's bright façade. "I—I am sorry for what I said, but you did not have to do that!"

"It is a scratch. It will heal. The next time you make fun of me, I will not be so kind."

Royal stared at him in horror for several moments, then turned on his heel, leaving the sparring room at a pace that would have seemed "purposeful" to a casual observer. Emmett recognized his speed for what it was: fleeing.

The Frenchman did not consider himself a violent person, but he could not deny the surge of satisfaction he felt at getting Royal back at last. It was petty, he knew, but still, it felt good to not be on the receiving end for a change. He would apologize later, he supposed, for Taryn's sake. But not yet. He wanted to bask in this feeling a little longer.

CHAPTER NINE

TARYN WOKE SCREAMING. She sat up, chest heaving, legs tangled in the blanket, her eyes wide and unseeing. The nightmare slipped through her consciousness like water through her fingers, the images draining away, leaving only a sense of horrid, empty terror in their wake. She threw her legs over the edge of the bed, unable to breathe, unable to speak, her heart thundering in her ears.

Ace stumbled into the room, concern written across his face. He knelt in front of her, taking her face in his hands, whispering that everything was all right—that she was all right. Nothing would hurt her. Slowly, his voice and his touch drew her back from the edge of the abyss, and she began to breathe easier. The world ceased its spinning. She closed her eyes, sighing.

"I am all right now, Ace. Thank you. I am sorry if I frightened you."

Concern sparked behind his eyes. "Taryn, you do not need to apologize. It is not your fault." She nodded but refused to meet his gaze. Her hands still shook with latent adrenaline, her whole body on edge with the remembered terror. She rubbed her face with both hands. "How long did I sleep?"

"Not long. Maybe three quarters of an hour. Are you sure you are all right?"

She shook herself. "Fine. It was a bad dream, that is all."

He ducked his head in assent and rose, his lips twisting into a thin line. "Master Erikkson came by while you were sleeping. He requested your presence at supper."

"Can I tell him I am ill?" Taryn groaned.

"I do not think he will take no for an answer." He smirked.

"Very well," she sighed. "I will go. But I do not have to like it. Will you be attending?"

Ace shook his head. "I am just a lowly soldier. I am not invited to sit with the ranking officers."

"That is not fair." Taryn frowned. "You are my *friend*."

He smiled, the expression warm and true. "War is not fair, Tar. You are the leader of an army now. You must learn to act like it."

A furrow appeared between her brows. "Now you sound like Erikkson."

"I am not sure that is a bad thing." He laughed and shrugged.

She opened her mouth to retort, but the sound of pounding feet distracted her. Royal raced through the open door, the left side of his face covered in blood.

"Royal!" she exclaimed in concern, jumping up, suddenly self-conscious to be caught here *alone* with Ace. *What* was wrong with her? She'd never felt this way before. "What happened?"

He glanced at Ace, his expression turning sour, then returned his gaze to Taryn.

"Emmett cut me."

"What?" both biomatons exclaimed at once.

"Emmett would not do something like that!" Ace protested.

Royal glowered at him. Taryn glanced between the two boys and sighed, for the first time seeing the rivalry that existed between Royal and Emmett. She should have seen it earlier, she knew. Stupid of her to dismiss their squabbling as immature schoolboy behavior when it was so obvious they were fighting over *her*.

And what did it mean that she was recognizing it now? That she was feeling caught up in the middle of something she did not want and could not stop? Perhaps Petrichor had been more right than she'd known. Maybe she *had* seen something that Taryn had not. Ugh, she hated the thought. But right now, Royal was standing in the middle of her room bleeding, and she needed to defuse the situation before this became another of the childish fights he had gotten into when they first had come to Elmhurst.

"Ace, will you fetch some medical supplies for me, please? I shall need something to clean Royal's wound, as well as gauze and sticking plaster." She moved closer, looking up at Royal's cheek. "I will not know how bad it is until we get it clean."

As he left, Taryn pointed to the armchair set against the wall.

"Sit," she commanded.

Royal sank into the chair, his scowl relaxing now they were alone. Taryn caught up a handkerchief from her bedside table, once white but now stained beyond repair from her own many shallow cuts. She pressed it to his cheek, wiping away the blood as best she could, revealing the deep cut across his cheekbone. He caught her wrist, halting her movement, a strange look in his eyes.

"Let go. I have to clean your wound," she ordered, her voice choked in her throat.

"Why was he here?"

"It does not matter." She tugged against his grasp.

"It does, Taryn. Why. Was. He. Here?"

His fervor frightened her. She took a step back, her eyes clouding with distrust.

"What has gotten into you, Royal? If I did not know you better, I would say you were jealous."

He opened his mouth to protest, but she railed on. She was tired of his over-protectiveness feeling like possessiveness. She'd already established that his feelings for her would not—could not—be reciprocated. And for him to refuse to accept that wasn't fair.

"No! We have discussed this! I am incapable of love, so your pursuit of this is useless! I am not some pretty bird you can cage and keep for yourself, Royal. I am human too!"

He stared at her, red-faced, stunned into silence. And then the words tumbled out, all at once. "Of course you can love! Taryn, you regained your love when you were hit so hard during the fight! Why has no one informed you of this?"

Now it was her turn to stare dumbly, her mouth hanging open. "No—" she managed to stutter. "No, that is impossible."

"Ask Erikkson, if you do not believe me!"

She shook her head, staring at some fixed spot only she could see, unable to believe the thing and yet seeing the puzzle pieces of the last few days falling into place. The way being around Ace made her feel buoyant and airborne, the way her stomach churned when Royal offered her one of his trademark crooked smiles... Even Petrichor's awful suggestion... Taryn groaned and pressed her hands over her eyes, hard enough that her eye sockets ached. She'd spent the last four months with a terrifying certainty about herself: she was incapable of romantic love. That had been taken from her when she was made into a biomaton so many years ago, and there was no way to gain it back. She'd come to peace with it. She'd even taken some solace in it, as an explanation for why she wasn't like the other girls at finishing school, why Royal had never ignited those feelings of fireworks inside her, in spite of their closeness.

And now he claimed that she *could?* That the one thing that separated her so profoundly from the rest of humanity had been breached, and yet she had been so certain of her own mind that she hadn't even noticed those feelings returning. Or—no, not returning, not when she'd been just six years old when they'd been taken from her. They were...awakening, for the first time. Growing like thorns inside her chest, strangling her heart and her lungs.

She looked up at Royal, who still waited for her response, and she didn't have anything to say to him. Everything felt hollow, unreal, like her world had been turned upside down.

"Just allow me to treat your wound and then leave me in peace," she growled, pressing once again at his cheek. "What did you do to provoke Emmett?"

Royal's face darkened, edging toward the childlike sullenness he was prone to at times. "I did not provoke him."

She knew him well enough to see when he lied, and now he was lying through his teeth. "Were you calling him names again?" she said, allowing a patronizing edge into her tone.

His scowl deepened, but then he breathed a heavy sigh and bowed his head. "I...may have let my tongue run away with me again."

She set her arms akimbo. Her voice emerged exasperated. "Why do you do that?"

He shook his head, forcing her to take the handkerchief away. "Because I was worried about *you* and I did not know how to express it!"

Taryn laughed at that, a little manically, her head thrown back at an uncomfortable angle. "You were worried about me, so you insulted Emmett?"

"We were sparring. It...got out of hand."

"Well, I think he let you off easy, all things considered. What, do I have to march you down to the barracks and have you both say you are sorry?"

His ears turned red, and his sullen expression took on an even more childish air. "Please don't."

"I need you to be better, Roy!" She shoved his shoulder roughly. "I need to not have to worry about you right now. I have too many other things to worry about."

He caught her wrist again, but this time his grasp was gentle. She tensed, her immediate response to pull away, but forced herself to still against his touch. She reminded herself that he was like that, that he needed connection in the form of physical touch, especially when they were having an argument or a serious conversation.

"Then I need you to be better too, Tiger," he murmured softly. "What you did earlier—the way you fought—that scared me. I think it scared all of us."

She made a little noise in her throat in response, unable to tell him that it had scared her, too.

"Promise me."

She didn't look at him.

He shook her wrist a little. "Promise me that will not happen again! That I will not have to watch you beat someone else to death!"

She swallowed hard, the vehemence in his voice making her feel small. "Royal, you know that is what I am."

"But you are not supposed to be that to us!"

Her eyes snapped up to his. "Us?"

He let her go, obviously as surprised by the word as she was. "You know what I meant. This rebellion, Tony's family."

There had been too many revelations today. Taryn felt dizzy. "You consider yourself one of us, Roy?"

"Of course I do, Taryn. I asked to be a part of this, even if I *am* whole. I am as much a traitor as any of you, am I not? I want to see you freed. I will do *anything* to see you freed. I would give my life, if you asked it of me."

She sank slowly to the floor, unable to convince her weak

legs to hold her up. She stared at the handkerchief she was holding, stained with his blood and hers intermixed now. Biomaton and human fighting together, side by side. "You do not have to," she whispered.

"I know." He slipped out of his chair and knelt in front of her, meeting her eyes. He rested his hands on his knees, not touching her, as if he knew that a touch in this moment could shatter her. "I *want* to."

"But what if we lose? What if you are arrested?"

He gave her a sad-eyed smile. "Why would I want to be free if you weren't, Tiger?"

Taryn's heart swelled in her chest, and she pressed a trembling hand to her collarbone. This was *not* how this was meant to be. She would die for this cause. It was only a matter of time, and how she suspected Erikkson had always intended it to be. And she had accepted that. But she had not anticipated her heart aching like this for those—including Royal—she would leave behind.

Ace chose that moment to blunder in with the medical supplies, and she hurriedly got to her feet, taking up the gauze and a bottle of strong alcohol.

"Sit," she commanded again, her voice too hard to disguise the turmoil that writhed beneath her ribs.

Ace assisted her in cleaning and stitching the wound. His hands were steadier than hers, and it turned out he had more than a little practice with sutures. She allowed him to take over, dragging her eyes away from Royal's white-knuckled grasp on the arms of the chair. As Taryn watched the two, a fear crept into her mind. The other biomatons had endured adversity, even torture for their cause. Royal had never had to endure physical pain or even particularly hard work. When this war escalated, could he stand his ground with the rest of them? Or was he too coddled?

It wasn't fair of her to think such things and she knew it.

Just because Royal hadn't faced the hardships she or Ace had didn't mean he wasn't prepared or could not handle what was to come. She had lived for so long with the fear of betrayal, it was sometimes hard for her not to expect it, even after they had both grown so much. Taryn pushed the cruel thoughts from her mind and forced herself to focus on what Royal had said: *Us.* She couldn't help the warmth in her belly when she thought of it.

Ace closed the laceration with two tiny black stitches, and clapped Royal on the shoulder. "There. The scar will be small, and I daresay it will only serve your good looks. You do not even need a bandage."

Royal squeezed Ace's wrist hard enough to make the older boy wince, speaking through gritted teeth. "You will pardon me if I do not thank you."

Taryn studied them both silently, her arms crossed over her stomach, her heart sick in her throat. At last, she nodded.

"If you will excuse me, I must get to supper. Master Erikkson is waiting for me."

Without waiting for an answer, she hurried from the room. Confusion set her head spinning in different directions: Royal's commitment to their fight, and his sudden, shocking revelation. Could she really, truly love again? How else to explain her new emotions? But what was she to do with this new ability even if she *could?* The last thing she needed was a new distraction in the midst of a war—particularly one where she was supposed to die.

"You are early!" Erikkson exclaimed as she burst into the dining room.

He frowned at her clothes, as she had not changed from her training uniform, and she realized he meant this to be a formal occasion, like the meal they had shared the night after he brought her home from the Black Castle.

"I apologize for my state," she said breathlessly, bobbing a small awkward bow. "I must ask you a question, and then I shall change into something more suitable."

He rose, recognizing her agitation. "Go on."

Taryn opened her mouth, then closed it again, heaving a frustrated sigh as she struggled with the right words. "Royal—Royal just said...I...I—" She huffed again, starting over. "He said I can love. Is that true?"

Horrid, unwanted tears rose in her eyes, vulnerability she wanted so badly to hide. "It cannot be true. Tell me he lied."

Erikkson's tender smile shredded her last vestiges of doubt. "I never took more than your capacity for romantic love. You have always been capable of compassion, selflessness, and camaraderie, which I would argue makes you far more human than any romantic relationship you might have. But young Master Stokker was correct. I meant to tell you earlier, but I did not want to embarrass you in front of the others. Welcome back to the human race, little one."

Taryn shook her head hard, hands shaking. Her breath came in shallow, hysterical gasps.

"I was never *not human*," she spluttered.

"That is not what I meant."

"I do not want this," she panted, her voice shattering. She pressed the base of her palms into her eye sockets, trying to still her violent reaction. How could he not understand how much messier this would make things? "I do not *need* this. I need to focus on winning this war, not some stupid shallow romance!"

"There is no need to get upset, little one. This is a gift you have been given, not a curse. You do not need to do anything at all about it, if you do not want to."

She forced herself to breathe, to focus until her hands

ceased their trembling. "Petrichor saw it," she muttered. "Last night. She saw it before I even knew."

"It *will* make your plight more sympathetic as well, Sedition. You will no longer seem so cold and strange to those you fight, if you do fall in love."

Taryn shook her head. "That is not an option. I do not want to leave someone behind with a broken heart."

He nodded. "That I shall leave up to you. Only consider your tactical advantages as well, little one. And consider the young men who have followed you this far because of your charms."

Taryn scowled. "What are you talking about?"

"Have you truly not noticed how easy it is to get young men to fall in love with you? Royal and Emmett, to start with."

Her eyes widened. "*You* did that to me, in my programming?"

He nodded. Anger raced through her once more, hot and familiar, dispelling the terror of the unknown. "You programmed me to lead them on, knowing full well I could never reciprocate their feelings for me?"

"I did it to protect you! You were far less likely to be betrayed by someone who had fallen in love with you than by someone who hated you. It was not a difficult subroutine to install. You are a very beautiful young woman all by yourself."

Taryn swore. Her hands trembled with rage and fear and anger. It was all too much. Her whole life, including her friendships, had been engineered, *manipulated* by this man who wanted too much to be a god. She could see now why Petrichor had left; every new manipulation was another knife, another pin tacking her down like a specimen vivisected in Erikkson's collection. She had no free will. Not even here, not even from the man who created her to fight for freedom.

She had spent all this time believing she was the white queen, the most powerful piece on the board, only to discover she was a pawn. She lifted one of the fine crystal wine glasses from the table settings and crushed it in her metal fist.

"I am tired of being your pawn," she growled, shards of crystal falling to the floor, sounding like bells. "From now on, this is *my* war. *My* army. I have relied on you to show me what to do, how to lead, and I was wrong. All this time, you were manipulating me, planning out my every step! No longer. You serve me now."

"Sedition—" he said warningly. "You need me. You are nothing without me."

"You created me to be your living weapon, to lead your army! So let me lead! Stop controlling every part of my life! You are no better than the slavers you claim to hate!"

Erikkson's expression transformed from anger to pain. "You do not mean that," he said softly, the velvet timbre of his voice so gentle it terrified her more than if he'd screamed at her.

But Taryn had had enough. She'd had too many revelations in one day. She'd spent the morning realizing she was a murderer, only for her afternoon to be filled with people telling her she could love. Or even that she *should* love. And now, she learned that there was no part of her life that was not controlled by the man she'd almost come to view as her father. She gritted her teeth, Sedition's strength and power and violence humming beneath her skin.

"I shall eat with my army tonight, as I ought to have done from the beginning."

"Sedition." His voice took on a razor edge as she turned away, but she did not look back. "Do not walk away from me!"

The tiny child inside her cried out to turn back, to apologize and beg his forgiveness, but she did not listen. He had trained her too well, molded her to rebel against those who would control her, and now that included him. Her missing memories—years of training and who knew what cruelties to form her into the weapon she was—now terrified her more than saddened her. His child she was not.

Rather, she was a weapon to be used and discarded as he pleased. Even if the cause was a good one, she detested the underhanded manipulation, the subtle programming that made her more machine than human, no matter what abilities she had. No, she could not endure the secrets any longer. She was Sedition! This army belonged to her, and it was time she acted like it.

She entered the narrow mess hall where her army was already seated, the joyful clamor of young people enjoying good food and one another's company abruptly silencing as they saw her in the doorway. Taryn held her head high as she moved between the long communal tables, aware of each and every one of the sixty or so pairs of eyes in the room trained on her. Never before had their lady Sedition deigned to take a meal with them. Most expected her to call someone out for punishment, or make a speech. Instead, she strode across the room to the far corner, where Petrichor sat at the very end of one table, alone.

Taryn settled herself on the bench opposite her clockwork sister, serving herself from the communal plates lining the table. The rest of the room did not stir, scarcely daring to breathe, watching the two as if waiting for a bomb to explode. Taryn said nothing, instead digging into her meal. The fare was simple and hearty, potatoes and roast beef with stewed veggies, but Taryn barely tasted it. She could feel Petrichor staring her down, waiting, but still did not speak.

After several minutes of a silence so uncomfortable Taryn wanted to tear her own hair out, the room began to relax and return to their meals, though the hubbub returned at a decidedly lower decibel.

"I suppose you decided not to go to Erikkson's little private dinner either," Petrichor croaked. Her voice had lost its silky purr, rough with the damage Taryn had inflicted. The redheaded girl raised her eyes to her adopted sister, shame burning in her cheeks at the ring of bruises on the right side of Petrichor's neck—the side not rebuilt with clockwork.

"I am sorry about earlier," Taryn muttered. "I lost control, and there is no excuse for it."

"Had worse." Petrichor shrugged.

Taryn rubbed her face with her hands. "At this rate, all Storm needs to do is wait, and we shall destroy each other without any prompting."

"If you're hoping to confide in me, Red, stop now," Petrichor growled in response. "I am not in the mood."

Taryn fell silent, guilt welling in her throat at her outburst toward Erikkson. She shoved her plate away, the meal turning to ash in her mouth.

"I thought you were dining with Erikkson tonight?" a gentle, familiar voice said from her right. She glanced up to find both Ace and Emmett there, carrying their plates. Ace sat beside her, and Emmett settled opposite him, giving Petrichor plenty of space. The assassin kept her face down.

"I thought it time I ate with my army," Taryn answered.

"We are glad to see you, *chérie*," Emmett said, smiling.

She nodded, but her heart weighed more than it had in a long, long time. She turned her gaze away.

"The lady Sedition graces our mealtime with her presence!" A familiar Scottish lilt came from behind her. The twins settled on Taryn's left, grinning identical, mischievous grins. "Did you get sick of six-course meals?"

Petrichor huffed and rose, stalking from the room without finishing her meal.

Emmett watched her go, then turned his attention to Taryn.

"I saw what happened today, *chérie*. Are you all right?"

She shrugged, unable to answer. She wished he would not

call her *chérie*—a French term of endearment meaning darling, or beautiful friend. She felt more like a beautiful monster.

"She defeated Petrichor in unarmed combat!" Ari exclaimed, a triumphant edge to his Scottish voice. "She is better than all right. She is our warrior queen!"

He caught Taryn's wrist and held her arm above her head, like a boxing champion. Despite herself, she laughed a little, tugging out of his grasp.

"I do not know about that, Ari," she answered, feeling her cheeks go pink with pleasure at the praise.

But Ari had leaped up, his strong, dark arms wrapping around her waist and pulling her up with him to stand on the table above the heads of the biomaton army. Taryn's heel sank into a loaf of bread, and she stumbled, trying to remove herself from the embarrassing scene. Every eye stared at the two, some laughing, others scowling. Ari raised her arm in the air once more, as Rorin took up his brother's idea, leaping up beside them, raising her other hand in the air.

"Three cheers for Sedition, our fearless leader, who will lead us to victory!" Ari exclaimed, his voice ringing out over the crowd below.

Taryn cringed, expecting sneers or even a few jeers, *anything* to indicate they still did not count her as one of them. Instead, a whooping roar of cheers came from her army, loud enough to rattle the stone walls. Fists pounded on the tables, feet stamped the floor, and gradually, a chant rose from the din. "Sedition! Victory!"

Overwhelmed, Taryn stared from biomaton to biomaton, a broad smile breaking across her cheeks and tears welling in her eyes. Even Ace and Emmett joined the chant, beaming up at her.

Heart swelling, Taryn at last understood. This was not about her; no part of it was about her and her manipulation and her suffering. It was about *them*, this loud and cheering army below her, all these human faces who had suffered so much and dreamed of no more than a world in which they might live as free men and women, unoppressed and unfettered. It was about justice for every child controlled by clockwork and suffering—and she supposed that included her. Her emerald eyes brightened, new purpose coming into her soul. She threw both fists high into the air.

"Victory!"

CHAPTER TEN

PETRICHOR SLAMMED the drawer in the library desk shut as she caught the sound of footsteps approaching, but not before Emmett had rounded the corner and froze in the doorway, studying her. They stared at one another for a few long moments like a pair of predators catching a glimpse of each other in a forest.

"*Ils ont peur de vous,*" Emmett said softly.

"Sorry, I don't speak French," Petrichor answered, leaning on the desk. Her voice was not unkind, and its usual cynical edge appeared strangely absent.

"They are afraid of you," he observed, remaining warily in the doorway.

She smirked, eyes sparking with dark delight. "And you aren't?"

He shook his head slowly. "I have faced worse than you."

She raised her eyebrows, surprised at his coolness. Most who knew what she could do trembled in her presence, and rightly so. She had honed herself to razor-edge sharpness, a bundle of bloodlust and insanity contained in metal and flesh. And she preferred it that way. People were predictable and easy to read when they kept their distance; it was when they grew close that they became dangerous. It was why she'd left this place, all those years ago.

"I can see that," she answered. "Those eyes must be one hell of a story."

Emmett took a few cautious steps nearer. "The Black Castle stole my sight. *Monsieur* Erikkson restored it, in a way." An odd smile twisted his lips. "If ever I meet *des saccades* again, I shall repay their hospitality."

Petrichor swore. "Lord Bellham and his ilk are still destroying lives, then? If you have the guts to go back there, Frenchie, you're braver than I am."

"You have been there?" Emmett's brow creased.

"I barely escaped with my mind intact." Briefly, she wondered why she was telling him anything about it, but even as she doubted herself, she turned the admission into a boast. "They couldn't keep me down, though. Took me two weeks to work out an escape. Never looked back."

It was a lie, but it was a lie she'd told often enough she'd even started to believe it herself. No, her escape from the Black Castle had been much less glamorous—and she would never, *ever* admit it.

"You escaped on your own?" His eyes widened.

"I *am* the best at what I do, Frenchie." She grinned.

Emmett paused and glanced around the library.

"And what are you doing now?"

She sighed and leaped up to settle herself atop the desk, folding her legs up like a yoga master.

"Avoiding Sedition, mostly." She gagged exaggeratedly, sticking out her pink tongue. "But also trying to figure out how to go after this Winchester fellow I'm supposed to assassinate."

"If he is in the navy, he will probably moor in the private shipyards in London," Emmett offered.

Petrichor grinned, rubbing absently at the bruises on her throat.

"Clever! We go in at night..." She trailed off, staring into the middle distance. "Yeah, that could work." Her gaze snapped back to Emmett. "How'd you like to go to London with me, Frenchie? You can tell me the story of those eyes on the way."

He hesitated. "I have training with Taryn in an hour—"

"Pah, this'll be way more fun. Besides, she has all those other hunks to occupy her time. Do you really think you stand a chance?"

A shadow crossed Emmett's face. The corners of his mouth turned down. "What do you mean?"

"I think you know exactly what I mean," she said, leaning forward, her hands casually wrapped around her feet. "I know you like her, no use in hiding it. But so does that young lord, and the quiet military one. And unless you're okay with sharing her, who do you think has the best chance at her?"

Emmett scowled. "We are not all vying for her affection. Ace likely cannot love, and I am her friend, that is all."

Petrichor laughed. "You don't seriously expect me to believe that! I've seen you all posturing for her attention like a bunch of peacocks. Come with me, Frenchie, and forget about Sedition for tonight. She's just leading you on."

Emmett's ears turned red with embarrassment or perhaps anger, she couldn't tell. She smiled inwardly, knowing she had caught him where it mattered. He couldn't say no to her offer now, not without it appearing that Taryn controlled him. And it wasn't just about freeing this strange, wary young man from Taryn's grasp. There *was* something about the Frenchman with the golden eyes that she liked. Perhaps it was because he did not fear her, or perhaps his musical French accent, but for the first time in a long time, Petrichor found herself *wanting* to make friends.

"What do you say?" she asked.

"*Oui.* I will go." He smiled. "It shall be good to use my own abilities for a change."

Afternoon tea had come and gone before Taryn finally worked up the courage to approach her creator. She knocked on the door of his study, her heart hanging in her throat.

"Come in!" he called.

She entered just in time to see him sweep a white sheet over something on his work bench. He turned toward her, and a light blinked out behind his eyes.

"Sedition," he greeted her coldly.

"I came to apologize for my behavior last night," she said, wringing her hands. "I did not understand the full picture, and I behaved selfishly. I beg for your forgiveness and your leadership. I was wrong to believe I could do this without you."

He gave her a tight-lipped smile and held out his arms, wrapping her in a tender embrace.

"You are forgiven, little one."

She accepted the embrace for a few moments, then extricated herself. Between how hard she had been pushing herself to regain her strength and the fight with Petrichor the day before, her body ached with fatigue. Her sleep had not been restful, filled with the ghosts of those she had killed, and the day's training had taxed her more than usual. Still, she could endure a little pain, a few nightmares. She reached for the thing under the white cloth. "What are you working on?"

He slapped her hand away. "It is not finished."

She frowned, a little puzzled at his reaction. "I did not ask if it was finished. I asked what it was."

"It is a *surprise*. You will see it when it is complete. Not before. Now, do you not have training to get back to?"

"I do, but..." The furrow in her brow deepened. "I should have had saber training with Emmett now, but he never showed up. No one has seen him. Do you know where he is?"

Erikkson shook his head. "I am sure he will turn up."

She nodded. "Yes, but it is unlike him to go missing like this."

"He will turn up when he is ready. Now, I have a lot of work to do, so if you please"—he took her by the shoulders, guiding her to the door—"I will see you later." The study door closed and locked with a *click* behind her. Taryn paused in the hall, stunned by his quick dismissal. What could he possibly be working on that was so strange and secret? She could not even venture a guess.

"Have you lost something?" Seraphim questioned, rounding the corner and blinking his strange green eyes at her.

She shook herself.

"Actually, yes. I cannot seem to find Emmett. He did not arrive for training. Have you seen him?"

Seraphim shook his head. "No, I—" He stopped, his wings rising, slowly clicking their way up above his shoulders. "I did see him several hours ago with Petrichor in the library. And I cannot remember seeing her more recently than that, either."

A chill ran down her spine. "You do not suppose they have gone off together, do you?"

"They will return." Seraphim shrugged, an action that included his wings as well as his shoulders. "I would not worry."

"If they are off on holiday somewhere, I swear I will kill them both."

His normally stony expression twisted into a smirk, revealing the briefest flash of silver fang. "*Monsieur* LeBeau is very devoted to you. I do not think they are up to anything."

"It is not Emmett who concerns me. It is Petrichor." Taryn began to walk as she spoke, and Seraphim matched her pace. "She is too bloody unpredictable."

"She may be unpredictable, but she is also loyal. She will not betray us."

Taryn scoffed. "Loyal?"

"More than you might think. You do not remember what it was like growing up here, what happened. Trust me. I know Petrichor. She will not betray you."

"What do you mean?" Taryn stopped to look up at him. "What was it like?"

Seraphim just shook his head. "Some things are better left in the past."

"I thought you might say something like that. But I do not like being in the dark about anything, Seraphim. Particularly my own past." She sighed, beginning her steps again.

"If I could tell you, I would, Sedition. But it is not my story to tell."

"It never is," she replied dryly.

His eyes took on a faraway glint, as though watching something only he could see.

"Sometimes, I believe it might have been better if he let Petrichor die."

"Seraphim!"

"I do not say it to be cruel. It is only that some human part of her had died when he brought her back from the Black Castle, and she has never been the same."

Taryn stopped, her heel slipping across the carpet runner on the floor. "The twins told me about that. What happened to Petrichor at the Black Castle?"

Shame and pity painted his dark face. "It was about six months before we lost you. She ran away, and one of Bellham's headhunters caught her." He visibly shuddered. "I do not know what they did to her there, but when Erikkson brought her home, she was not the same. Everything fell apart after that."

"How so?"

He shook his head. "You forgot and disappeared. Erikkson was heartbroken. Not long after, Petrichor left too. I do not think he could have been more heartbroken if you both were his own daughters."

A lump had settled itself in Taryn's throat, just above her sternum. It hurt to swallow.

"What did he do to us?" she asked, her voice no more than a whisper.

Seraphim met her gaze, his sharp features hard. "He made us what he needed. Weapons."

CHAPTER ELEVEN

PETRICHOR AND EMMETT were crouched behind a stack of crates near the outskirts of the Royal Navy airship yards in London. Dozens of ships hung motionless in the twilight ahead of them, the only sounds the creaking of the tether lines that kept them moored to the heavy iron rings set in the stone below. Emmett could smell the peaty stink of the Thames where it lay just on the other side of the shipyard, even though he could not see it from where they hid. Their own small airship was moored in the civilian yard two miles away. It would be ready when they made their escape.

"You ever done anything like this before, Frenchie?" she murmured in his ear, her mouth so near he could feel her hot breath on his neck.

"*Oui,* with the crew of the *Dauntless.* But never to an English soldier on an English ship," he replied.

He found the massive *HMA Musketeer* overhead, moored near them. He'd learned to navigate the world through a combination of the strange overlapping lines that had replaced his sight and through his other senses: audio cues, scents, and even touch, the static electricity that told him another body was near even when he could not see it. Petrichor had had to point out the *Musketeer* when they'd arrived, but once he'd picked it out, the red lines of its hull were obvious above them. It was larger than the *Dauntless*, he could tell even from this distance and with his unusual sight. The lines of its hull traced in his vision were sweeping and solid, and he could pick out the shape of many gunports on the side facing them. A man-o'-war, then, or something similar. A warship designed for assault, not speed.

Petrichor was still talking.

"Good. We'll wait here until our dear captain takes his leave from the ship for the night, then follow him. Once we're in a quiet alley, that's when the knives can come out." She grinned, her teeth glowing in the gathering dusk. "Easy as pie."

Emmett nodded. *Almost too easy,* he mused, watching the shapes of sailors leave the shipyard.

He could not say why, but the whole thing felt *wrong*, very wrong. A sense of dread built up behind his eyes, and no matter how hard he tried, he could not dispel it.

Petrichor shifted, settling herself into a more comfortable position as they waited for the darkness to overtake them. She crossed her arms, leaning a shoulder against the crates, sighing. Emmett watched her, transfixed by the way her outline was carved of overlapping orange, red, and gold.

She allowed her hair to fall over the left side of her face, partially disguising the scars and grafts there. To his surprise, he wished she'd brush the strands back. He'd grown accustomed to her asymmetric features on their journey here, and now he missed the way her cheek twisted to smile around her prosthetic, the contours of her teeth across the left side of her face. Maybe it was because of the way his sight had been altered, but there was nothing about her features that particularly unnerved him. Instead, he felt an odd kinship with her. They had both survived terrible things, and they bore the scars to prove it. But wasn't that just proof that they were strong, and they were alive?

"I told you my story," he said, shifting to make himself more comfortable. "Now it is your turn to tell me yours."

"I don't think so," she said, raising an eyebrow.

"At least tell me what brought you back here," Emmett amended. "I heard you were living in America?"

She nodded, turning her clockwork hand palm up and beginning to fiddle with the joint of her ring finger. "I was. But there's this massive war going on over there. They're fighting over slaves. It doesn't take a genius to recognize the next place they'll look is biomatons. So, I got out before it got too hot."

"Biomatons are not enslaved *en Amerique?*"

"No, they still use African slaves." Her mouth twisted, and she clamped her fist closed, heaving a sigh. "You think it is bad here," she said, shaking her head slowly, "you have not seen the way they treat those poor people. It is enough to make you sick."

Emmett nodded quietly. He could imagine it. He'd spent a year in Africa during his time in the French Navy and had seen the deplorable conditions imposed on the native people.

"Humans are cruel," he muttered. "They will always be cruel."

"Almost makes you wonder what good it does to be noble."

"The good is in the effect upon the individual. Every life improved is to be commended. Even if it is only one."

She shrugged and fell silent, staring out at the shipyard, barely visible in the darkness blanketing the city. He studied her, wondering if he had truly heard sadness in her tone. What cruelty would a person have to see and experience to harden herself the way Petrichor had? And what depths had she delved in order to forget what she had seen? He'd watched her walls fall tonight, however briefly, but he feared he might have pushed her too far. Such a mistake could be fatal with someone like her. He only hoped she would not shut him out.

"The light in the cabin just went out," Petrichor murmured after a long time, her eyes still locked deep in the gloom. She shifted, easing into a crouch, one hand checking the belt of weapons at her waist. "Not long now."

"How will we catch him?" Emmett whispered.

"He's an old man with an old war wound in one leg. I don't think it'll be difficult."

Emmett raised his eyebrows in surprise.

"Don't look so shocked, Frenchie. Erikkson gave me a dossier. You can say a lot of things about that man, but you can't say he doesn't know how to gather information."

"How does he do it? I heard him say once that he kept track of Taryn, but how?"

She shook her head. "It's an interconnected web of biomaton slaves, vagrants, criminals, and dirty law enforcement. At one time, I believe he had at least one bobby in every city in England in his pocket, though that may have changed. It's been a while."

She stopped, and he felt her go tense beside him, muscles coiling. "There he is."

Emmett followed her gaze to see a figure wearing the well-tailored shapes of the British Royal Navy step from the spiraling docking stairs onto the wet paving stones below. In the stillness of the night, they could hear the click of his steel-toed boots, and Emmett thought he caught the rigid lines of a book tucked under one arm. His gait rocked, uneven, evidence of that war wound Petrichor had mentioned. The man turned to the west, headed away from them toward one of the side streets leading into the city.

"Let's go," Petrichor murmured, and got to her feet, leading the way toward the figure who was disappearing into the gloom of an alleyway ahead of them. Emmett gave her a little space, following behind at a good clip.

Petrichor was fast and absolutely silent, even with her extensive clockwork alterations. Emmett marveled at her silence as she quickly crossed the distance between them and the man ahead, her feet making barely a hiss as they crossed the paving stones.

He hung back to allow her to work. His own boots were decidedly louder in the still of the evening, and he worried that the man might hear him and look back, but either the man was hard of hearing or simply overly confident in his own safety on the streets of London. Either way, he didn't look back once as he entered a narrow alleyway, and Petrichor made her move.

With a spring that almost appeared inhuman for the distance she managed to cross, she leaped forward and clasped one arm around the man's throat, throttling him to prevent a scream. Emmett picked up his pace, racing forward as Petrichor's clockwork palm slapped hard over the man's chest, directly above his heart.

Emmett expected Winchester to struggle or cry out, any of the various things he'd seen and experienced people do over the years to survive. The body would do almost anything to keep itself alive, and he'd seen final moments run the gamut from desperate begging to almost inhuman acts of strength.

But this man did none of those things. Petrichor held him tightly, hissing a soft "shh" as his chest heaved with a single, ragged breath.

A tight, squeaking choke rent the air. And then his head fell back, and his body went limp. Dead.

Petrichor lowered him to the ground carefully, tucking his body amongst some leftover crates that were occupying this alleyway. She slipped a folded square from a pocket, and from the soft rustle Emmett could tell it was paper, not a handkerchief. Drawing a knife from her belt, Petrichor drove the weapon through the corpse, pinning it there. She turned to Emmett.

"Let's go."

He did not speak until they were in their air yacht and airborne, the scene playing over and over in his mind.

"How did you do that?" he questioned at last, turning his attention to her as he steered the ship toward the manor.

"Easy." She turned from the rail to grin at him, her hair whipping around her face in the wind. "It's a snake venom from Africa. Incredibly deadly. There's a pouch of it in my hand, connected to a needle. See?"

She held up her hand, flicking a nearly invisible switch on her wrist to trigger the long silver needle hidden in her palm. Emmett shuddered.

"I guess I am lucky Erikkson did not weaponize my eyes."

She laughed, stowing the needle. "Keep your eyes the way they are, Frenchie. I like them that way."

"And the note? What did it say?"

"It was just a little calling card." She shrugged. "Nothing much, just a note letting them know that the captain wasn't killed in some random mugging, but that Sedition was involved."

"That will bring Storm down on our heads even harder!"

She grinned. "It is a war, after all. What's the point if we don't start hitting back?"

※

THE TWO ARRIVED HOME LONG AFTER MIDNIGHT, STILL exhilarated from their successful mission. Emmett brought the yacht down in the yard behind the manor, too drunk on exhaustion and Petrichor's attentions to care to dock it properly. He threw the mooring line around a tree and nodded. It would hold well enough. At Petrichor's suggestion, they snuck into the house through the kitchen to make the least amount of noise. Emmett grinned at his conspirator as they crept into the still-warm kitchen, the embers of a fire dying slowly in the stove, lighting the room with a dim red glow.

"We did it!" Emmett whispered.

"Did what?" a third voice interrupted.

Emmett froze, recognizing Taryn's voice at the first syllable. He would never, never forget her voice. And now, she sounded angry. She turned up one of the gas lamps, enough for herself and Petrichor to see by, and Emmett realized she must have counted on them returning this way, had waited here for them to come home.

"Emmett and I took care of Captain Winchester tonight," Petrichor answered flippantly, crossing her arms. "You're welcome."

"Leave us, Petrichor," Taryn ordered in a voice hard as nails.

"Good ol' Sedition, back again." Petrichor's lip curled in disgust. "Always showing up when she is not wanted."

"I said *leave us!*"

Petrichor squeezed Emmett's hand.

"Good luck, Frenchie," she offered, then sauntered from the kitchen, offering Taryn a final sneer as she went.

Emmett's cheeks burned as he met the redheaded biomaton's gaze. "Taryn—"

"Do you think this is acceptable behavior? What has gotten into you, Emmett?"

He scuffed the heel of one boot against the weathered stone floor. "What are you talking about?" As soon as he said it, he knew it was the wrong thing to say. He prided himself on being honest, straightforward, and unafraid of difficult conversations. Acting ignorant was not in his playbook. But it had been a long night, and Taryn's appearance had ruined his good mood. He didn't want a lecture. He wanted to climb into his warm bed and get some sleep.

"I am talking about you *disappearing*, Emmett! We are in the midst of a bloody war, or had you forgotten? I do not require much from you, only that you report to me when you take on a mission. And you two come sneaking back in here laughing as though you snuck out to attend a ball!"

A new, surprising defensiveness rose up in Emmett. "Am I not allowed to come and go as I please?"

"No!" she snapped. "Not when there are soldiers out there actively *hunting us down*! I do not bloody care if you are out snogging Petrichor—"

"Taryn—"

"Really, Emmett, I do not care! But there *is* the issue of our war. You both could have been arrested, and I would not know! You left me here without a word of where you were going or why." Her voice began to fall, growing slower and softer as she spent her anger. "What could I do if you had been caught?"

He lowered his eyes, knowing that her concerns were valid. It wasn't like him to run off without checking in first, and he shouldn't have trusted Petrichor as far as he had tonight. But for the first time, Taryn's tight grasp on him felt stifling. He'd tasted a different kind of life with Petrichor tonight. A different way he could serve this cause, one that wasn't just being stuck training other biomatons how to fight, and it had been exhilarating. His voice emerged colder than he had intended.

"I apologize, *cherie*. I assumed Petrichor had your blessing for this mission, as she said the order came from you."

"You are forgiven. I am just thankful I have not lost you."

She stepped forward and embraced him, but Emmett found the gesture suffocating. He returned it with the briefest of touches before pulling away.

"It is late. I am tired," he said in answer to her confusion. "*Bonne nuit*."

Taryn nodded, but she could not entirely hide the hurt on her face.

"Good night, Emmett."

Emmett pushed past her, hurrying toward the barracks and his bed, complicated feelings strangling his lungs. For the first time in a while, he'd felt *good* tonight. He'd felt like he had a purpose, could serve the rebellion in the way he wanted to. And Petrichor didn't treat him like some fragile thing that could be broken; she saw all of him, and she didn't flinch from the ugly or broken parts. But was that really fair to Taryn? It was her actions that had given him a role in this fight in the first place, that had saved him from slavery in the Black Castle and restored some semblance of sight. He owed her and Erikkson everything… But he was tired of owing. Owing was what he had on the *Dauntless,* and Storm had wielded what he owed like a weapon. He didn't want to live in a world of obligations anymore. He wanted to live in Petrichor's world of impulse and speed, the wind in his hair and the swift retribution of a blade.

But then again… That sense that their actions would have dangerous, far-reaching consequences clasped his heart again. He didn't know why the premonition had clasped him so tightly, but he could feel it there in his chest like a weight: this night would have repercussions. His and Petrichor's assassination mission had put them in grave danger. He just didn't know how yet.

CHAPTER TWELVE

"We have reports of gathering military might in the south of London. At least a dozen airships gathering in the dockyard, and reports of amassing weaponry, cannonade, and some contraptions we could not identify. Massive amounts of black powder and sulfur. They are planning an assault, if not now then soon."

Petrichor sighed and slumped in her chair, bored already of the daily fearful messaging from Erikkson's many spies who seemed to see danger in every shadow. She was sure that if they saw a parade of cavaliers, they'd report it as some kind of threat.

They were gathered in what Erikkson called the "War Room," a bare, windowless room of stone walls and uncomfortable chairs located in the barracks wing of Elmhurst Manor. It was furnished with a massive cork board on one wall, dozens of pinned notecards showing current operations and who was a part of them. Sedition and Seraphim were seated perfectly straight in the chairs beside her, both attentively watching the large map Erikkson had spread over the table at the center of the room. Damn them both, with their perfect soldier's training, she thought, huffing a derisive breath through her nose loudly enough that Royal sent her a look from the other side of the table.

Damn him too, then. She sent him a twisted grin, knowing exactly how terrifying it looked with her grafts. She'd hated looking at herself in the mirror once. The girl she saw there was angry, raw, and vulnerable. Ugly, with her scars and the metal marring her freckled skin. But she didn't hate it anymore. She knew other people found her off-putting. Unsettling, even. She had learned to use that as an advantage.

"Do you think they may come here?" Seraphim asked, leaning over the map to point at the many pins placed on London. Each red pin represented one warship or battalion, and the silver pins represented their own much weaker forces. There were a few silver pins spread out across the map, but most of them were concentrated on Elmhurst.

Not the best idea, Petrichor knew. She'd learned from years of covert operations and gang warfare that concentrating your forces in a known location was the surest way to draw the full power of your enemy down on your head. They needed a foxhole, somewhere Storm or the other British forces didn't know they hid, where they could strike from secret.

Instead, they had a lord and a manor that was almost certainly registered with every Who's Who book in the country, even if the lord himself had spent the last twenty years of his life as a recluse. One couldn't have money, prestige, *and* anonymity. Society loved to talk about an eccentric bachelor who was rarely seen and conducted ill-advised experiments in his basement.

"It is possible," the young spy known as Clipper nodded, their short brown hair flopping over their brow. "Storm knows this is where Lord Erikkson resides, and must have some suspicion that we are training our army here."

"How long do you think we have before they mobilize?" Erikkson asked. He rested his chin thoughtfully in one hand.

Petrichor noted with a sour frown that his chair was the only one in the room with *arms*.

"A week, tops? Perhaps less. It is hard to tell how much cargo they are planning to load, and once they are in the air it will only take a matter of hours for them to arrive. There will be no warning."

Seraphim's clockwork wings rustled with agitation. Petrichor could read his discomfort in his body language. It didn't matter how long they'd been apart, how stoic he tried to appear. He'd always be an open book to her. He was taking this threat *seriously*. And it was that, more than anything else said in this stupid meeting, that made her sit up a little straighter and pay attention.

"During my time on the *Dauntless*, Storm bragged of siege weapons the navy was developing that could decimate a city from the air. Is it possible these are the kinds of weapons you saw being loaded?" he asked.

Sedition also straightened, her green eyes lit with fire. "They could take out all of Elmhurst in one strike with something like that."

"We should move our troops away," Seraphim said, nodding. "Get as many out of Elmhurst as we can while we still have the chance. If we move in small groups, some to London, some to other small towns in the countryside, we have a good chance of going undetected."

"Not a bad idea," Erikkson nodded with approval. "I will get to work on finding safehouses. In the meantime, Petrichor, would you go with Clipper back to keep an eye on the navy's preparations? Do anything you can do to slow them down and buy us time."

Petrichor felt her stomach clench at his direct attention on her, fear mixed with pride at being asked to take control of part of this effort. She hated the mixed feelings she got every time he spoke to her, or looked at her, or even when she was reminded of him and what he had done. No—not what he had done. What the Black Castle had done. She had to remember that. She couldn't let herself get mixed up. "Can I take someone with me?" she asked.

"Of course."

"I'd like to take Emmett. He and I worked well together last night, and I think his skills will be helpful if we're trying to sabotage the navy. He knows the ins and outs of those military ships and how Captain Storm thinks." She sounded so formal and it irked her, but she knew Erikkson preferred clear, logical reasoning, and it was the most likely way to get him to say yes.

"I think that is a great idea. Please ask *Monsieur* LeBeau to join you and Clipper as you head back to London. Clipper, you may take a team of horses from the stables. Emilio can advise you on which are fastest." Erikkson stood and took two blank notecards from the little pocket holding paper and pencils at the bottom of the large corkboard, then added Petrichor and Emmett's names under the mission marked "London Military Sabotage."

Petrichor felt eyes on her and glanced sideways to feel Taryn's gaze on her. The girl was glaring daggers. Petrichor gave her a cheeky grin and a shrug. Fine, if Sedition wanted to be petulant, that suited Petrichor perfectly. They could deal with it after the meeting.

"Anything else we should assign out at this time?" Erikkson asked, looking pointedly at Taryn. She quickly schooled her features.

"I can help you find safehouses," Seraphim offered.

"Excellent. Sedition?"

"I will work with Royal on a list dividing the army up into manageable groups. We want to make sure we do not end up with all experienced fighters in one group and leave our less well-trained biomatons to fend for themselves."

Oh, Sedition, always getting preferential treatment. Petrichor wanted to wipe that demure little smile off her face. That wasn't even a real task. She could have said she was going to sit around and eat bonbons, and it would have sounded just as important.

"Perfect." Erikkson clapped his hands, his signal that the meeting was over. "Get to work. We haven't much time and quite a lot to accomplish. Petrichor, Seraphim, Sedition, make me proud."

They dispersed with the scraping of wooden chair legs on stone and the tick of clockwork. Petrichor made it out into the hallway first, eager to get out of the basement and away from the smell of sweat and damp for even twenty minutes. Clipper ducked past her and caught her elbow.

"I will meet you at the stables in thirty minutes, yeah? Bring dark clothes, rations, and the Frenchman."

"Sure," Petrichor answered, pulling her arm out of the slender biomaton's grasp. They had clicky clockwork fingers that slipped easily off her sleeve. "See you there."

Clipper hurried on, to do what Petrichor didn't know and didn't care. She kept walking, headed for the stairs and the doors that led outside.

"Petrichor!"

Ugh. Petrichor stopped in her tracks and turned on her heel to face Sedition, the girl's fiery red hair like a halo around her face. She could see the other girl was angry, but for what, she had no idea. "Red," she answered with a tilt of her head, eyes half-lidded to show how bored she was of this back-and-forth.

"I know what you are doing," Taryn growled, spittle flying from her mouth as she stalked closer.

"Going to get some fresh air because I'm tired of smelling the sweat of seventy unwashed biomatons?" Petrichor let a little sneer take over the right side of her face.

"You are toying with Emmett to get at me. It is not right."

"As far as he told me, Frenchie *likes* running missions with me." Petrichor folded her arms and cocked her head the other way, sighing a little. Seraphim she could read after all this time, but Sedition was another story. This version of Sedition was angry, changeable, and more than a little unhinged. She'd heard from Emmett that they, too, had spent time in the Black Castle, so it really wasn't all that surprising that the girl had slipped a gear somewhere along the way, but that made interacting with her all the more difficult. Petrichor could not—*would not*—allow herself to fall back into the patterns that had ruined her so many years ago. So let Taryn think of her as an antagonist. An enemy. It was better than admitting she had failed her. "And I'm pretty sure he gets to choose what kind of job he'd like to do in this war, just like the rest of us. Unless you had a super special job for him yourself?"

Taryn's scowl deepened. "Emmett wears his emotions on his sleeve. He is kind and compassionate, and it is not fair of you to take advantage of that."

"No advantage is being taken." Petrichor held up her hands in mock pacification. "I am merely offering him an option that isn't living in your shadow and watching you fall for anyone but him."

Oh, that struck a chord. The girl was turning a shade that might politely be called *beet*.

"I am not falling for *anyone*."

"But you *can* fall for someone now, right?"

Taryn's gaze dropped to the floor for the first time. She clenched her fists, taking a deep breath, then shoved Petrichor toward the wall, pushing her out of the main corridor and into the shadowy stairwell. Petrichor let it happen, a combination of surprise and curiosity momentarily overwhelming her desire to stay away from the girl.

"You called this place a hell, when we first met, do you remember?" Taryn was close enough that Petrichor could feel her breath on her cheek, feel the girl's heart beating frantically where her hand grasped a fistful of Petrichor's shirt. She smelled of the surprisingly unlikely combination of lemon balm and machine oil. It wasn't unpleasant.

Petrichor rolled her eyes and nodded. Of course she remembered. But it wasn't when they first met. Not even close.

"What did you mean?" Taryn asked.

Petrichor raised an eyebrow. "You mean besides the obvious?"

Taryn pushed her shoulder a little harder than she needed to. "Humor me."

Petrichor sighed, running a hand through her long brown hair. What to tell, what to omit? She decided on the truth, or at least a version of it. "He took badly damaged children and rebuilt them as weapons. He says he loves us, and I think maybe he does, but that love is twisted. He loves his cause more. He loves the *idea* of us, and what we can achieve. What *he* can achieve through us. You don't teach a ten-year-old child to kill. Not unless you know that she will be forever broken by that act."

Taryn's eyes widened, and for a moment Petrichor saw compassion there. *Understanding,* even. Damn. That was exactly what she was hoping to avoid.

Taryn's voice dropped even lower. "He—he told me that my programming makes young men drawn to me."

Petrichor would have recoiled if her back hadn't been against a wall. "He *what?*"

"He said it was to protect me—" There was a hitch in Sedition's voice that sounded almost like tears.

Petrichor felt her throat tightening, found her own heart beating faster in time with her clockwork sister's. She didn't want this. Didn't want to *feel* for this girl who had been through the exact same tortures she had been, who *hadn't* been able to escape the net Erikkson wrapped around his creations. "That's not protection, Red," she said hoarsely. "That's manipulation."

Taryn laughed bitterly, shaking her head. "And here I am, serving in his war, even knowing what he did to me. What he did to us." She let go of Petrichor's shirt and stumbled backward, leaning her back against the opposite wall and resting her head against it, her knees going soft and weak. "Gor, I do not know why I just told you that."

"Because I am the only one who can understand."

Again, that tragic, bitter laugh. "You are insane. A murderer."

"And your sister," Petrichor pointed out. She'd let it happen. She'd let Sedition crawl right back into her stupid, soft heart. Being two thousand miles away had made this so much less complicated.

Taryn blinked at her, surprised. "I thought you said I was not allowed to call you that."

Petrichor shrugged. "We're in this together now, right?"

"Aye. I suppose we are."

"Do you still think I am going to hurt your precious Frenchman?"

"It is still on my mind, yes."

Petrichor slid her hands into her pockets. "He told me about the Black Castle, you know. About how he lost his eyes. About how he was protecting you, and you protected him by getting him out of there. Bringing him here. I don't wanna hurt him, Red. I just think he can do more than teach you how to swing a sword. I think he *wants* to be useful."

Taryn sighed and nodded. "Okay. If he wants to go with you, take him. I have kept him leashed too long, I know. I just" —her brow furrowed—"I do not want to see him die."

"I won't let that happen. You have my word."

"Good. Go."

Petrichor turned and hurried up the stairs before Sedition could say any more, her mind churning. In spite of her best efforts, she could feel little Taryn worming right back into her affections, and she couldn't even muster up the energy to be mad about it. She'd told the girl that she hadn't ever liked her, but that had been a lie. There was a time when Taryn truly had felt like a little sister. When they would have done anything for each other. But that was long gone, and time had put a rift between them. This conversation may have done something to repair it, but she knew it could never be the same.

Not after what she had done.

CHAPTER THIRTEEN

WHEN ACE FOUND HER, Taryn was curled into a corner of the library, hiding behind an overstuffed leather chair with a book on her knees. Her red hair cascaded over her shoulders, a copper waterfall, hiding her face. The book was closed, a collection of essays on human rights or warfare or something else Erikkson had asked her to read. She couldn't remember which subject this one was about.

She didn't know if she saw the point to all this study anymore.

Ever since her interaction with Petrichor after the meeting, Taryn had been lost in a flurry of confused feelings. She was still angry with Erikkson, even if she had apologized for her outburst. She felt helpless to control her own path, because it was so interlocked with Erikkson's plan. She felt a kinship to Petrichor that she hadn't before, and that kinship made her confused and frightened. And perhaps maddeningly of all, the empty spaces in her head where her memories should have been left her aggravated. Those memories should have been hers, and they had been taken from her. Forever.

"Taryn?" Ace asked, approaching her cautiously.

"Go away, Ace," she grunted. She did not raise her head. "I am dangerous right now."

"What happened?" He knelt in front of her, inches apart, not touching her, as if he was afraid she would shatter.

"I do not know who I am anymore," she muttered, her voice muffled under her hair.

"What?"

Taryn sat up straighter, raising her head to finally look at Ace in the eyes. He was wearing a soft linen shirt and well-worn breeches, and his clockwork arm looked freshly buffed. He stared back at her, waiting. She shook her head, taking a deep breath of lignin and old tobacco smoke.

"Everything is upside down, Ace. The navy is coming for us with weapons we could never have predicted. Petrichor makes me want to tear my hair out—or tear her throat open—every time I encounter her, and we have not even begun the fight properly yet! We have to get everyone out of here and safe as quickly as we can and—and I am grappling with another war in my head, and it is too much."

"What do you mean?"

She sighed and stretched, setting the book aside. Somehow, confessing the extent of her feelings to Ace felt right. Perhaps it was because they'd endured some of the same pain, but she felt that he would listen to her without judgment, without expecting her to be a leader or have a solution.

"I suppose you are aware of my change in emotional capacity as well?"

He nodded, silent. Waiting.

"Everyone but me knew, it seems. Petrichor somehow saw it. I do not know how. But she did. And Erikkson wants me to find some way to fall in love in the midst of all this." She dragged her hands down her face, a bitter laugh escaping her. "As if I have time for love when a monster lives inside of me."

Ace chewed his lip thoughtfully. "And what part of that is most bothering you right at this moment?"

She frowned, considering. Petrichor wasn't truly the problem, she'd realized—*Taryn* was. Something about Petrichor, maybe even something Taryn could not remember, activated all of Taryn's feral tendencies. But that was not truly Petrichor's fault. It was more like Taryn's brain was wired wrong.

And the love thing? It wasn't the main issue either. It niggled at the back of her mind, yes, but she'd lived this long without it, and she thought she could continue on just fine that way, even if she had the capacity.

No, if she had to pick just one thing...

"I suppose I am afraid of the pressure that has been placed on me as Sedition. I am trying my best to lead, but it seems like it is Erikkson's war. I feel like a figurehead, not a real revolutionary."

He stood, wincing, and offered her his hand. "Come with me."

"Where?"

"Just for a few hours, I am taking you away from all this. No plotting, no fighting, no war. Just for a few hours, it shall be Taryn and Ace, without any of this other stuff getting in our way."

She hesitated. "I have to work with Royal to split the army up—"

"Let him handle it. You will be a far better soldier if you spend a few hours away from the fight." He grinned, offering his hand once more. "Come with me."

She sighed and took his hand, allowing him to pull her to her feet. "All right. But only because I am so sick of training and fighting."

"No more of that. We are leaving it all behind."

She allowed him to drag her along, wondering at the change that had come over him. Ace seemed to her like a kaleidoscope, or a many-faceted diamond—each time she thought she had a grasp on who he was, something came along to shake him up and reveal a new facet of his personality. She'd thought him brutish, only to discover he was gentle. She'd thought him callous, only to find he was compassionate. And she'd thought him committed to their cause, and now knew he was committed to *her*. She knew, deep down, that Ace's strange affection for her was all thanks to Erikkson, but she hoped that it wasn't *all* her programming. Maybe somewhere deep inside, Ace liked her as much as she liked him. Maybe the pirate and the revolutionary could find a place they could escape from the war, if only for an hour or two, and truly get to know one another.

"Keep up, Ace!" Taryn crowed, turning to stare at him over her shoulder, her copper hair streaming behind her.

The beautiful chestnut stallion beneath her galloped so smoothly through the forest she hardly noticed his long stride touching the ground. The wind stung her eyes, but it smelled of fresh pine and new grass, and she drew deep, gasping lungfuls of it, allowing it to cleanse her. Some yards behind her, Ace struggled to urge his own black steed to keep up. She laughed, reining in her stallion, allowing Ace to pull up beside her.

"Of all the things I could be better at than you, I never thought horsemanship would be one of them," she exclaimed.

Ace's face paled, turning sour. "I did not think it could be difficult."

"You have never ridden before?"

"There is not much need for it on an airship. I was not a *cowboy*."

She laughed again, the sound sparkling through the dappled trees, eliciting an almost involuntary smile from him.

"I suppose I must allow you to set our pace, since it is you who knows where we are going."

He watched her sway with the walking gait of her mount, her hips moving like an extension of the horse's long legs, as smooth as if they were one animal, not two. Ace tried to follow suit but stopped as twinges of pain raced up his back, spine, and ribs.

"How can *you* ride so well?" he questioned.

"Royal's family has horses on their land," she replied, her attention on the wood ahead. "We used to ride together to get away from his father, mostly. I picked it up." She fell silent for a moment. "Although, now I consider it, I may have forgotten my training in horsemanship with Master Erikkson."

"You still cannot remember?"

"Some things are not meant to be remembered, I suppose."

He, too, fell quiet, and for a while they rode along in a kind of strange, companionable silence, enjoying the warm spring day under the coolness of the green canopy above them and the proximity of one another without the need for speech. Speech complicated things sometimes, Taryn mused, listening to a far-off wood thrush singing a pleasant melody. Speech so often cluttered what she really wanted to say.

"Here we are," Ace said at last, disrupting her reverie. They had come into a wide clearing, a flowering meadow at the crest of a hill, overlooking a breathtaking view of the rolling countryside beyond. Ace dismounted, securing his reins around a tree branch. Taryn followed suit.

"It is beautiful," she breathed, almost afraid to disturb the quiet peace of the meadow beyond. "But what are we doing here?"

"I believe, if you check your saddlebag, you should find a bottle of wine, a couple glasses, and something to eat." As he spoke, he drew a blanket from his own saddlebags.

Frowning not in anger but in bewilderment, Taryn dug into

her own saddlebag, finding all he mentioned and more: cheese, smoked salmon, a small loaf of crusty white bread, and a glossy red apple.

"What is this?" she questioned, her voice cracking as she turned back to him, the wine bottle held in one hand.

He took a few of the items from her and led her out into the meadow where he'd spread the blanket in the bright April sun.

"How old are you?"

"Seventeen."

Together, they settled on the blanket, and he uncorked the wine.

"Try again," he teased as he poured, the liquid ruby-red in the sun.

A crease deepened between her brows, juxtaposed with an odd smile on her lips. "I am seventeen."

"No, Taryn. Today is May eighteenth."

Her mouth fell open.

"Happy eighteenth birthday, Taryn."

She blinked hard at the sudden sharp sting of tears in her eyes. That Ace had remembered her birthday—and not only that, but had planned a picnic, to celebrate—was more than she could have expected or even asked for. She was once again struck with the feeling that Ace somehow *saw* her, perhaps better than anyone else she knew. He didn't need her to be someone strong or deadly. He had seen her at her worst, her most vulnerable, her most broken. And he still stuck around. He wanted to spend time with her. Her hands fluttered around the blanket, touching lightly on the cheeses, the wine glasses, like butterflies gently touching to flowers. She barely managed to blink her tears away, and when she was finally able to speak, her voice was a hoarse whisper.

"Thank you, Ace. Thank you."

CHAPTER FOURTEEN

Taryn sat on the blanket, her head tilted back, enjoying the cool, crisp air. Thick gray clouds were blowing in, bringing portents of rain, but neither biomaton seemed eager to leave. They ate good food and drank good wine, basking in the solitude and the peace. At last, Taryn stared at him, her eyes sparkling. "How did you know it was my birthday?"

He smiled enigmatically. "I promised I would not tell."

"Well, thank you," she sighed. "I have so lost track of the days. I did not even realize it was today."

"You have been so focused on the war. Everything else has fallen to the side." His ice-blue eyes were so intense she had to look away. He smiled and stretched, wincing.

She noticed the expression and frowned. "Do your grafts still hurt?"

He nodded, but did not reply, instead eating the last of the apple they'd sliced paper-thin.

"How badly?" she pressed.

The corners of his lips tightened. "You want the truth? It hurts every moment of every day. Exercising is agony, and every breath sears my lungs." His shoulders slumped. "And all that pain only fuels me more strongly toward our goal. No other person should have to endure what I do."

"Have you asked Lord Erikkson if there is anything he can do for you?"

"Aye. He can do nothing. It is my burden to bear."

She blinked and looked away, her hair falling over her eyes. "I am sorry."

He shrugged. Cautiously, he reached out and tucked her hair behind her ear, revealing the now-healed half-moon missing from the top of her right ear, where he'd shot her on his first day at Elmhurst. "We all bear scars from our mistakes."

She studied him for a moment. "What do you think you will do if you meet Storm again?"

He shook his head. "I will do what I must. But if I am honest, I do not think I can kill her. In spite of all she has done, she is still my sister. I shall leave her to one of you."

Taryn nodded. She had not expected Ace to kill Storm, no matter the evils she had committed, and his confession was not surprising. She *was* thankful he knew it, though, and would not claim Storm for himself when the time came. Despite herself, there was a tiny, bloodthirsty part of Taryn which hoped she'd have the chance to destroy Storm herself. The captain had hurt far too many people to escape. And Taryn wanted to be there when she fell.

"Wait a minute. I thought we were not going to talk about the war?" Ace teased, nudging her shoulder.

"What else have we to do? We have eaten all the food." Another sparkling champagne laugh escaped her.

"If you go check my saddlebags, I think you may find one last surprise," he replied, grinning broadly.

"Oh, Ace, you should not have..." She rose and went to his horse, stroking the animal's nose before moving around to the side and reaching inside the saddlebag. Her fingers brushed a small box of some sort of stiff paper. She cupped her hands around it, looking back at him with a question in her eyes.

"Bring it over here," he urged, unable to hide his grin.

She followed his instructions, kneeling beside him on the blanket. Ever so carefully, she opened the box, revealing a small, square cake, about the size of Ace's palm, frosted with thick white icing and topped with a delicate yellow butterfly made of sugar. Taryn gasped, breathless, and for an instant the child inside her, who had been forced too early to grow up, stared out of her eyes. "This is too beautiful to eat," she whispered. "Wherever did you find it?"

"Ambrose made the cake. And the butterfly is from a shop in London. I had to special order it."

She looked up at him, her eyes wide and full of wonder. "Thank you, Ace."

"Happy birthday, Tar," he murmured. He watched her study the little cake for a moment, then smiled. "Well, shall we see how it tastes?"

She appeared horrified. "But—"

"It is made to be eaten, Tar," he urged. "The look is only half the fun."

Crestfallen, she chewed her lip for a moment. Her normal, hard mask slid over her features, and the hidden child within vanished. "Yes. You are right. Will you cut it in half?"

The vanilla cake melted on their tongues, kept moist by the buttery icing and the sweet raspberry jam filling. They savored it in silence, eyes closed, mouths curled in twin sweet smiles. At last, only the sugar butterfly remained. Ace placed the delicate sculpture in Taryn's palm, hoping to catch one last glimpse of the child she hid inside her, but she merely sighed and looked at him. "Shall we share it?"

"No. It is yours. Happy birthday."

The butterfly tasted of sugar and melancholy on her tongue, and she forced herself to focus instead on the good parts of the day. The horse ride. The surprise picnic. The beautiful cake. The time alone with Ace. Yes, it had been a good birthday. A strange birthday, of course, but a good one nonetheless.

Ace rose, gathering up the empty wine bottle and glasses. He glanced up at the sky. "We ought to head back. It looks as though it may rain."

※

AND RAIN IT DID. THE SKY OPENED AND CASCADED WATER on them both, as though making up for all the warm, fine weather it had granted them. Taryn and Ace were forced to dismount and lead their horses on foot through the torrential downpour as the rain pounded down upon their heads and shoulders. Despite the unfortunate conditions, Taryn laughed her sparkling laugh, enjoying the cold, icy droplets against her skin.

Ace grumbled. "There is nothing funny about wet trousers, Tar."

She watched him trudge along stiffly for a moment, but it only made her laugh all the more. "You must admit, it *is* a little funny. But we *shall* have to oil our prosthetics against rust when we return, and that is not something I particularly look forward to."

He grinned slyly at her. "I do miss the times when getting caught in the rain merely meant getting wet."

"At least you can remember it," she shot back, but she smiled broadly at him to indicate she was only teasing.

He reached out and touched her shoulder, his eyes full of sympathy. "When this is all over," he said over the roar of the rain, "we shall make new memories to replace the ones you have lost."

She glanced at him, but there was such intense sadness in

her eyes he could not hold her gaze. "Let us just focus on winning the war," she replied. "Then we may discuss what comes after."

They trudged in silence for a while after that, feet squelching in the mud, both soaked to the skin and shivering. The situation seemed ineffably humorous to Taryn, who could barely contain her giggles. Still, she swallowed her laughter, recognizing how inappropriate it was for her to laugh at a time like this. She gathered all the sensations in her head, though—the sound of the rain rushing through the leaves overhead; the drum of heavy drops on her head and shoulders; the feel of her boots sticking in the mud—stowing them away for another time when she would need a good laugh.

They finally arrived at the stables, sodden and tired, as dusk appeared to be falling, though it was hard to tell through the darkness of the rain. Taryn caught a glimpse of the stable clock and stopped, her mouth falling open. "Oh no. Can it really be eight already?"

"I suppose it is," he mumbled as she shoved her reins into his free hand.

"Take care of him for me, please! I have my final fitting with Gennifer tonight and I swore I would not be late!"

"Tar—" he began.

"I have to go. I am so sorry. I will make it up to you later. I had a wonderful afternoon. Thank you." She pressed her lips to his cheek briefly, her skin icy with the rain, and then raced into the storm, leaving Ace standing stunned, holding the leads on a pair of horses, her name still unspoken on his lips.

CHAPTER FIFTEEN

Riding the eighty miles from Elmhurst to London had been exhilarating, with Petrichor racing her steed beside Clapper and Emmett's stallions, the three of them urging their mounts as fast as they would go. Mud had flown from the dirt roads beneath their hooves, and the wind and sun on her face had tasted like freedom. They'd galloped past slower coaches and wagons with ease, and at one point a farmer had stood up from his hay wagon to scold them for their dangerous riding. Petrichor had thrown him a laughing wave.

But as they reached the foggy, smoke-filled air of London, their moods had sobered. Clapper brought them to a stable yard on the outskirts of the Thames, and they dismounted. Petrichor wrapped a scarf around her face to hide her prosthetics, and Emmett slipped on a pair of dark glasses as they passed through the winding, narrow streets. Heavy clouds had blown in overhead, and the afternoon was gloomy and dark, in spite of the earlier sunshine.

The busy streets of London offered plenty of anonymity—it was one of the things Petrichor liked most about a big city. If one kept their head down, wore unremarkable clothes, and did not do anything to draw unwanted attention, it was easy to go unseen.

Clapper was an expert at this, taking them through dirty alleyways and stinking backstreets, keeping them out of the wealthier neighborhoods where people might be most likely to call attention to them. In the slums, everyone just wanted to be about their own business without any trouble, and that suited the biomatons just fine.

As they weaved through the narrow backstreets, Emmett slipped his arm through Petrichor's, leaning close enough that he would not be heard over the noise of the city. "Why *moi?*"

She glanced over at him, surprised by the question. "Why not you, Frenchie? I thought we worked well together last night."

"You did most of the work yourself, *cherie*. I sat pretty and talked too much."

Petrichor felt a genuine smile curve her lips. "Well, you did sit very prettily, and it was nice to have someone to talk to. I don't get to have company on missions very often."

"You flatter me," he said, laughing a little. His freckled cheeks had turned pink, and she thought maybe, just maybe, she could enjoy running missions with this young man. He was fun to flirt with, anyhow, even if romantic feelings were beyond her capabilities. She'd long ago learned that a little flirting went a long way in getting men to give up any number of things—their guard, information, even their own friends sometimes. Not that she was trying to get Emmett to give anything up. She could tell he liked the give and take of flirting, and she was playing into that. Harmless, except for how angry it made Sedition.

But in their earlier interaction, Petrichor *had* been telling the truth. She wasn't trying to toy with or manipulate Emmett. She just wanted to offer him the chance to be more useful.

"Can I ask you a more serious question?" Emmett asked after they had walked for a few minutes.

Petrichor tripped in a puddle that had deceptively looked shallower than it truly was. Muddy water splashed over her ankle and she cursed under her breath, shaking off the hem of her cloak. She righted herself.

"Sure, Frenchie."

"Do you fear Erikkson?"

Ice prickled across the back of her neck. "What?"

"Every time he enters a room, you freeze up. It might be hard for the others to see, but I cannot help but notice how rigid your lines become."

She pressed her lips together, feeling those rigid lines come back into her body. Of course he could see them. He was attentive, more attentive than any of her self-centered siblings. She clicked her metal teeth together with a sigh.

"He had different theories for training each of us. Red's lucky. She doesn't remember, and she always was his favorite." She tried to pull away, to push forward after Clapper, but he caught her wrist, hurrying alongside her.

"What did he do to you?"

A wan smile split her face.

"Nothing terrible. Or so I'm told." She jutted her lower jaw out, sighing. "The Black Castle did a number on my brain, so everything is scrambled in there. I didn't forget. Nothing so nice as that. I just can't tell you what happened there, and what happened at Elmhurst." Her deep brown eyes flashed, her voice bitter. "It all has Erikkson's face."

Emmett frowned. "*Monsieur* Erikkson would never hurt you."

She scoffed. "And yet my brain tells me something different. I ran away for good reason, Frenchie. Life as an assassin made more sense than life here."

"I am sorry," he mumbled.

"Don't be. I survived. That's what matters."

They walked in silence after that, Petrichor fighting not to fall back into old memories. She focused instead on their surroundings. The scent of eel jelly and meat pies from a pub they passed. The clatter of hooves and wheels on cobblestones. The uncomfortable feel of the uneven stones beneath her boots. The thick smog that coated everything in a layer of greasy gray ash. The rancid oil smell as a gang of boys pushed past them, carrying paper cones from a nearby chippie. If she closed her eyes, she could almost pretend she was at home in New York. Funny, how all cities started to feel the same after a certain point. It was just crowds and sweat and dirt, the stench of people crammed together and all trying to scrape by. She'd never really felt like a part of it, but she liked to be in the center of it, watching the people move around her.

Eventually, they neared the navy shipyard where Emmett and Petrichor had been just the day before. They were not near enough yet to see the yard itself, but Petrichor could hear the familiar sounds of the lap of the river and ropes snapping against canvas. Clapper gestured for them to slow their approach, pointing to a narrow alleyway half filled with crates.

Together, Petrichor and Emmett snuck into the alleyway, finding a good position from which they could see the shipyard.

Emmett grabbed her arm, hard. "Something is wrong."

"What?" She pushed herself up from her crouch, trying to get an angle where she could see more than the mooring lines and towers stretching up into the sky.

Emmett stood up and ran for the other end of the alley.

"Stop!" Petrichor hissed in a stage whisper.

He didn't slow, hurrying out onto the street.

Petrichor swore and hurried after him, holding the hood of her cloak so it didn't blow back from her face. "Frenchie, what are you—"

She stopped, staring at the sky above the paved yard.

Barely a third of the ships that had been there the day before remained.

The shipyard looked bare, empty of the ships they had expected to be there. Had been *told* were there, loading weapons and soldiers and preparing for an assault. Petrichor's heart dropped. They were too late. They couldn't sabotage their enemies, because there was nothing left to sabotage.

Emmett turned to her. "They are already gone."

She swallowed hard, tasted copper and electricity in the air. The wind was blowing hard enough to knock a weaker woman sideways. "What do we do now?" she asked hoarsely. She was good at espionage. She wasn't good at this. She wasn't good at all-out *war*.

Emmett grabbed her sleeve and pulled her back through the alleyway, running back toward Clapper. "We go home."

"But the storm—" She felt the first raindrops strike her cheeks. "It will take hours, and our horses are spent!"

"Then we go as fast as we can, and we pray we are in time to warn them."

❦

ROYAL LOOKED UP FROM THE NARROW PIECE OF clockwork he was working on, his dirty blond hair falling over his eyes as Erikkson entered the boy's room. The older man's usual smile was replaced by a serious expression.

"Ah, Royal," Erikkson gestured, something in his hand. "Here you are. A telegram arrived for you."

"Telegram, sir?"

Erikkson nodded. "It appears to be urgent."

Royal scrambled up from the desk, knocking tools off in his rush, his eyes wide. He snatched the telegram from his mentor, tearing it open with shaking hands. Erikkson could not read the note from where he stood, but he watched Royal's face pale as he read it. The boy's knees gave out and he sat heavily on the edge of his bed. He pressed one hand over his mouth. Listlessly, he stared at a spot on the floor, almost catatonic from the news he'd received.

"Royal?" Erikkson urged.

Without looking up, the boy mumbled, "I must go..." He shook himself and looked up at his master. "I must go home. My father is dying. They do not know if he shall last the week."

Erikkson sagged, saddened. "Go, Royal, with my blessing. I shall send Guillame to drive you."

Royal shook his head. "No, sir. If you will provide me a single horse, I shall cross the distance much faster. And do not worry, he shall be well cared for in the stables at Thrawcliffe Hall."

"I do not doubt it. Shall you be needing anything before you depart?"

Royal chewed at the side of his thumb, considering, then shook his head again. "Apologize to Taryn for me, please. I will return when all is settled." He turned to go.

"Royal?" Erikkson called in a commanding tone.

"Yes, sir?"

"You are becoming a lord. I went through this long ago when my father passed. It is not easy, but you are not alone. Should you have any questions, I will be here to answer them. Stand up straight, hold yourself with dignity. You are a good man, and it is an honor to be your mentor. Do not forget that."

Royal's face crumpled, and he rushed back into the room, embracing his mentor in a tight hug. Erikkson laughed a little, surprised, and then returned the hug.

"Thank you, Tony," Royal gasped.

Erikkson patted his back. "Go. You do not have much time."

"I apologize for my tardiness!" Taryn exclaimed, bursting into Gennifer's workshop. Her clothes and hair dripped cold rainwater onto the floor. Gennifer stood, her long, strawberry blonde hair tied in thick braids over her shoulders. The tapered ends of the braids swept her waist as she moved.

"Come in, come in, my lady," Gennifer urged in her musical Irish accent. "You gave me a few extra minutes to get everything in order, that is all."

Taryn smiled, relaxing a little, making her way into the underground stone room which comprised Gennifer's armory. The girl always made her feel so welcome here, and Taryn considered Gennifer a warm friend, if not a particularly close one. In spite of all her efforts, though, the girl continued to insist on both calling her "my lady" and giving her the honorary curtsies Taryn would have been much happier without. But as she watched Gennifer force her prosthetic leg into an ungainly curtsy, Taryn realized this, too, was her pride getting the better of her. If it made Gennifer feel better about their relationship, what did it matter how Taryn felt? Still, she suspected they could have been closer without all the formalities in their way.

Gennifer giggled. "You are soaked!"

"We did not expect the rain."

"We, my lady?"

"Do not start." Taryn gave her a mock-stern glare. "I want to see this armor you built for me."

Gennifer clapped her hands, her eyes lighting up behind her round, wire-rimmed spectacles. "Go ahead and step behind the screen and get yourself out of those wet things. I have all the pieces prepared."

Taryn did as she was told, glad to rid herself of the wet costume. She hesitated for a moment behind the screen, then called, "I am rather soaked to the skin, if you catch my drift. You would not happen to have an extra set of underclothes somewhere, about my size?"

"Actually, I have a special set for you. It is a part of your armor. You will find the undergarments behind the screen. When you have donned them, come out and we shall assemble the armor together."

Taryn followed her instructions, leaving her sodden clothes in a heap on the floor before donning the pieces she found behind the screen: a pair of silk panties and matching brassiere, which seemed normal enough, until she discovered the supple leather that stacked on top. She also donned a pair of fine, dark leather leggings and a hard breastplate, almost like a corset, but reinforced with metal plating and designed not to force her body into a certain shape, but rather to protect her vital organs. She stepped from behind the screen, feeling mostly naked, her cheeks burning in embarrassment.

"Wonderful! Now we get to the fun part." Gennifer had laid out the many pieces of Taryn's new suit of armor on a long table, and she limped over to it, lifting the first of many, many pieces. Shoulder pads of hardened leather and metal strapped on Taryn's right shoulder; her left remained bare, her prosthetic obviously the focal point of the piece. Metal plates strapped over her vitals—her ribs, her stomach, and her forearm were reinforced with a vambrace inlaid with copper studs. A short leather skirt like those she had seen in illustrations of Roman guards strapped around her waist, with space for her weapons to attach on her belt. Shin guards strapped around her calves, and thick leather shoes protected her feet. Her head, though, remained free, as did her prosthetic arm and shoulder blades. Each and every piece fit her like a glove, molded to her form.

Taryn studied the effect of the armor in the mirror when Gennifer had finished, admiring the fierce figure she saw staring back at her. "You have outdone yourself this time," she murmured, meeting Gennifer's reflected gaze in the looking glass. "Truly. It is beautiful."

The girl's smile broke wide and genuine across her freckled cheeks. "Oh, thank you, my lady! I am so pleased you like it."

Taryn admired her figure for a few more moments, then bounced a little in her new shoes. "May I go and show the boys before I take it off? I think they will enjoy seeing it."

Gennifer nodded. "Although... it is rather late. I do not know that there will be anyone still awake."

Taryn stared at the pocket watch the girl held up, stunned. "Ten o'clock? Gor, Genn, this takes two hours to assemble?"

Gennifer winced. "I am sorry, my lady. We will get faster at it."

"Very well." Taryn sighed. "We may as well begin the process of taking it off."

As Gennifer stepped toward her, the ground shook, the air around them trembling with a sound so loud Taryn's ears felt as though they might burst. Dust rattled from the old stones above their heads. Gennifer cried out, collapsing as her clockwork knee buckled. Without thinking, Taryn threw herself over the girl, shielding her as the ground and walls shook with the horrific noise.

Taryn counted six explosions in all before the ground at last ceased its shaking and she could help Gennifer to her feet. The girl shook with terror, her spectacles askew on her nose. "Are you all right?" Taryn demanded.

The girl nodded. Her voice shook. "Perhaps you should keep that armor on a bit longer."

Taryn tried to smile reassuringly, but worry got the better of her expression, twisting her facial muscles unnaturally. Her heart felt like a runaway train in her chest, but she couldn't let her fear get the better of her. Her army—*no,* her *family* needed her. "I am going upstairs to see what happened. I need you to *stay here.* I will return when I know it is safe."

"Sedition—"

"No." Taryn squeezed Gennifer's shoulder. "Stay here.

You will be safe here." The words were a command, hard-edged, hiding her fear beneath a layer of soldier's strength. This was what she'd been trained for, the imaginary battlefield at last becoming real, Sedition becoming the only necessary part of Taryn.

Gennifer shrank away from her and nodded, tears of fear in her eyes. Taryn nodded to her, just once, and leaped into action, ready to face whatever awaited her aboveground. She raced up the narrow, familiar stone steps, only to be slowed by rubble in her way. Using the strength of her prosthetic, she shoved her way through, a tight knot of misgiving in her gut. This was not right. None of this was right. Shouldering a particularly large beam aside, she at last emerged, not into the familiar ground floor of the west wing, but into the moonlight.

CHAPTER SIXTEEN

TARYN'S MOUTH FELL OPEN. For a moment, she just stood, frozen, unable to comprehend the wreckage laid out before her. The clouds above had parted, allowing fingers of silver moonlight to reach down, illuminating the scene. Whatever those explosions had been, they had utterly destroyed the west wing of the manor. Smoke burned in her lungs, acrid and vile. Taryn turned slowly, realizing the rest of the manor stood intact, one side of it hanging open like an ugly wound. Her stomach lurched into her throat. All those lives, all those biomatons... How many now lay buried under the rubble? Where were her friends? For a moment she thought she would be sick. She was standing on a tomb.

A shadow darkened the moon, and she turned again, recognizing the silhouettes of three airships drifting toward her, sinister avenging angels in the night.

"Ari!" A scream rent the night, and Rorin hurtled past her, throwing himself at the rubble, clawing with bare hands at the rocks, screaming his brother's name.

"Rorin." Taryn approached him, feeling a twinge of thankfulness that her voice did not betray her own emotions.

He turned toward her, face streaked with dirt and tears. "Have you seen my brother?"

She shook her head, her lips pressed tightly together.

A shriek escaped him, a wail of raw agony and heartbreak. Taryn felt her own heart shatter. But she knew it was no time for mourning. Those airships were drawing nearer. She had to know who was still alive.

"Rorin. I need you to focus."

When he did not answer, she slapped him. "Focus, soldier!"

He stared at her then, eyes still wet with tears, but at least she had his attention.

"Who else was not in the barracks?" she asked.

He shook his head.

"Who else survived?" she demanded.

"I— Emmett and Petrichor left for London this morning. Seraphim was on an errand." He spoke through hiccuping breaths. "You and Ace were out..."

Taryn's throat closed.

"Royal?" she croaked.

"He left this afternoon. His father is dying."

She breathed a sigh of relief, swallowing her terror. Mourning could wait. Now, they needed action. Rorin had turned and was again furiously tearing at the rubble.

"Rorin!" she snapped. "It is no use! No one could survive that."

"I must find him—"

"No. You must go." Firmly, she lifted him by the lapels, setting the large, dark biomaton on his feet as easily as if he were a child. "Gennifer is in her workshop. She will need help escaping the rubble. Take her and run. Run as far and as fast as you can."

"But Sedition—"

She shook her head. "Do not add to the number we lost today. Run."

"And what about you?"

"I must go to Erikkson, ensure he is all right." She glanced up at the airships, too near for comfort now. "Then, Lord willing, we, too, will run. It has been an honor fighting alongside you, Rorin. I hope we see one another again."

He gave her one last salute. "My lady."

She returned the gesture, then turned to the house as Rorin tore down the stairs. She drew a deep breath. *I am coming, Master.*

"Master Erikkson—" The cry caught in her throat as she rounded the doorframe and caught a glimpse of the scene in the study beyond. Between Taryn and Erikkson stood the figure of the one person who'd dogged her steps since before she'd even known what—who—she was. The person who longed for her destruction more than anything else.

Storm.

The privateer commodore wore a white coat over her shoulders, and had a flintlock pistol trained on Erikkson. Taryn's heart froze. Erikkson appeared utterly calm, staring down the barrel of that gun, seated behind his desk. His eyes met Taryn's, and she read immense sorrow there.

"Run, Sedition," he said, his voice barely more than a whisper. "You must run."

"Not without you," she insisted.

"Hello, freak," Storm said, turning her head to stare at Taryn, her pistol never wavering. "So good of you to join us." Her eyes—ice-blue eyes, the same color as her brother's—flickered over Taryn's body, and her nose wrinkled. "What a cute costume. How about you come stand by your master, and we get this over with?"

All Taryn could focus on was that pistol, and ensuring it stopped being pointed at her creator. She slipped her fingers to the hidden compartment in her forearm, preparing to draw a throwing knife.

"I am the one you want," Taryn said slowly. "Not him. Leave him alone, and I will go with you."

Flashes of phantom pain from her last encounter with Storm flickered behind her eyes, but she shoved them away. This was about saving Erikkson. Whatever the cost.

"We cannot have him running about, telling biomatons they are human." She drew back the pistol's hammer with an ominous click.

Taryn's heart was a racehorse in her chest, but she forced herself to remain calm, centering her focus on the weight of the cold throwing knife she released into her palm. She just needed an opening. One second when the gun was no longer trained on Erikkson.

"He is not the one you want," she repeated. "I am."

"But he created you."

Taryn nodded, meeting Erikkson's eyes. "He saved my life, and I am forever grateful."

"I thought you biomatons could not feel things like gratefulness?" Storm narrowed her eyes.

This conversation was going nowhere, but Taryn answered, if only to keep Storm talking. "We feel all the same things you feel, Storm."

She took a cautious step into the room, and the captain's finger tightened on the trigger. Taryn froze.

"Have you not killed enough tonight? Are you not satisfied yet?"

"I shall be satisfied when you swing from the hangman's noose," Storm spat.

"Do not do this. Please. He is innocent."

The captain sneered. "And why should I not kill you both? My soldiers will be here any minute. No one will miss either one of you traitors."

"Are we not more valuable to you alive?"

Storm narrowed her eyes again, and Taryn thought she might actually have gotten through to her. *Of course* they were worth more alive. Still, Taryn's fingers tightened around her knife, waiting.

The captain grinned, an ugly, evil twist of her ruby-red mouth.

"Actually, no. You are not." She pulled the trigger.

Taryn's world snapped into slow motion. Her heels dug into the rug, digging trenches in the fine plush weave. She could taste smoke and gunpowder, see the smoke rising from the barrel of Storm's flintlock pistol, though she could not actually remember hearing it go off. She threw herself at her longtime enemy, recklessly driving the knife for any soft area of skin she could reach. The short, sharp knife thrust through Storm's shoulder as the woman fell backward under the weight of Taryn's attack, and she laughed—actually *laughed*—a manic, painful sound. The cold weight of her signature metal gauntlet wrapped around Taryn's throat, but Taryn was beyond pain at this point.

Taryn drove her knee into Storm's solar plexus, pinning her to the ground, and stabbed down. She could barely breathe with the woman's hand wrapped around her throat, but she used her weight, her own weaponry, to stab her in the torso again.

"You took *everything* from me," Taryn gasped, voice hoarse through the strangling grasp Storm had on her. "You killed my *family,* my *friends.*"

Storm spat blood into Taryn's face, deep crimson coating

her teeth. "I should have killed you when I first had the chance!"

Taryn stabbed her again, the knife plunging deep into her stomach this time. "Why will you not just *die*?"

Hot tears were streaming down her face, probably mixing with the blood and spit, and she could feel Storm's tight grasp loosening on her throat. The woman was dying, but not fast enough. Not painfully enough.

Taryn had thought this would feel good. She'd thought that when she finally got Storm at last, she would be satisfied. Happy, even. But it wasn't supposed to happen like this. Not with so much loss. Not with so much devastation, so much wreckage.

Storm's laughter was little more than a cough now, bubbles of blood still emerging from between her lips. Her eyes rolled in her head like marbles. "You lose," she choked between wheezing gasps for air.

"No!" Taryn screamed. Her knife plunged down again. She didn't know how many times she'd stabbed Storm now. She'd lost track of almost everything except the anger in her chest and the hot blood on her hands.

Storm brought one hand to her forehead, a weak mockery of a salute. "Long live..."

She never finished. Taryn's knife plunged into her throat, severing her windpipe. Storm went limp.

Taryn rolled off the fresh corpse of her nemesis, hands shaking as she stared at the body bleeding on the floor. Devastation, not victory, washed over her. Storm's black hair puddled under her head, a few of the coins and feathers she'd tied into it stained with blood. Her eyes stared up sightlessly at the ceiling. Her flintlock pistol had fallen a few feet away, the barrel still emitting a little smoke as it cooled.

It was then that Taryn remembered the sound of the shot, and launched herself to her feet to see Erikkson slumped in his chair. A rosette of blood was blooming over his stomach, too wide to be covered by the one hand he had pressed there. His skin had taken on a gray-green pallor.

Taryn lurched to her feet and rushed across the room to his side.

"No no no—" Taryn panted, frantically searching for some way to staunch his bleeding.

Shaking, elderly hands reached for her, stopping her frantic movements. It was as though he had aged a hundred years in a few seconds. "Hush, little one," he hissed, his breath coming in shallow gasps. "Be still."

Hot, angry tears sprang unbidden to her eyes. "I am so sorry I did not make it in time—" She slumped to her knees, grasping at his hands, kneeling in front of him as if she was praying. "I am sorry I was not good enough."

He stroked her copper hair with one hand, a strange smile on his face. "I am so proud of you."

She clutched all the more tightly at his hands, blinking her tears away. "Hold on, master. Hold on. You are going to be all right."

He shook his head. "I do not think so." Blood coated his teeth and tongue as he spoke.

"You will! You must!"

"Shh, Taryn. There is not much time. Listen to me—" He swallowed hard, and she watched the light dim in his eyes. Her shoulders shook with the sobs she would not allow herself to cry. He patted her cheek. "Finish what we started. And... You were given a gift. Do not... squander it."

"Do not speak any more," Taryn said, trying to rise. "We will get you help. You will be all right."

"Sedition—" he choked, swallowed, and began again. "Taryn. Do what I failed to. Find love... Embrace this gift."

"Please, master, just hold on—" She half stood, his one hand still clinging to hers, and tried to turn and go for help. His fingers relaxed, releasing her. Taryn froze. Slowly, ever so slowly, she turned back to her master. His forest green eyes, once so lively, now appeared dull and glassy, staring at nothing. Taryn felt her throat close, her knees buckle. She collapsed beside the corpse of her creator, at last unable to retain her sobs. She clasped his cold hand in hers and wept heavy, weary tears for the closest thing to a father she'd ever known. But her tears did not last long.

Taryn knew she had to get up. Erikkson was dead, her army scattered or in ashes. She was needed. She had to lead now, more than she ever needed to before. With a heavy heart, she pushed herself to her knees. She kissed her fingers and pressed them to Erikkson's forehead.

"I will find a way out," she promised him, voice soft with regret. "I will do what I could not for you."

CHAPTER SEVENTEEN

Ace knew something was wrong. He'd raced upstairs as soon as he heard the gunshot, but now he heard nothing as he crept toward Erikkson's study, wary of what he might find. The bombs had struck when he was grooming the horses, and he'd charged outside to watch the house collapse like a tower of cards. He didn't know who'd survived—surely someone had—but he prayed Taryn had not been in the west wing. He could not bring himself to imagine a world without her in it. The mere idea made his throat close, his chest ache, and his heart pound with fear.

He stopped in the doorway, his watchful eyes taking in the ugly scene. Storm lay on the carpet in a pool of her own blood, her eyes wide and empty. Eyes identical to his own. He'd known she was here when he'd seen the airships overhead, but this...

Ace bent and closed her eyes with his palm, his own gaze lingering on the knife still embedded in her throat. He recognized it from the hundreds of training sessions they'd had together; it was Taryn's. He raised his eyes to the second corpse in the room, his heart heavy. Erikkson's form looked wrong, slumped cold and lifeless in his chair, like a marionette with cut strings. Ace sighed. He'd seen more than enough carnage in his twenty-one years. Enough to last him a multitude of lifetimes. And what he wanted now, more than anything, was peace. Something in the back of his mind told him that wasn't what lay ahead of him, though, not for a good while yet.

Erikkson's secret project remained undisturbed on his work bench, covered with a white cloth. Ace hesitated, then reached out and tore the cloth away.

What lay beneath felt oddly mundane to Ace. It was a slender prosthetic arm, made of bronze and copper clockwork. The shape was carefully sculpted, mimicking a human arm, but as far as Ace could tell, it was otherwise ordinary. No heavy armor plates covered the inner workings, and the mesh surrounding the delicate clockwork within couldn't hide any secret compartments. It reminded him of the arm Taryn had worn when he first met her, the arm destroyed aboard the *Dauntless*. Ace wondered why the arm had been so secret.

Taryn. Shame overwhelmed him as he realized he was wasting time he should have spent searching for her. He turned away, determined to find her, when a sound came from behind the desk, whispered words barely audible.

"Taryn?" he questioned softly.

A halo of red hair appeared over the desk as she pushed herself to her feet. Her cheeks were glistening and red with tears, but there was a fire in her eyes that he had not seen before. She was wearing a costume of leather and metal armor, which exposed her clockwork grafts and somehow made her look both fierce and feminine. Gennifer had outdone herself. But this was no time to focus on clothes. As much as he regretted it, he knew they had mere minutes until the manor was swarming with soldiers and pirates, ready to eliminate any remaining biomatons.

"Taryn, I am sorry—" he started, reaching for her as she shoved past him.

"No time. They need me. We have to fight."

He caught her wrist, catching the sweet scent of her leather armor as she drew near. "Taryn, there are two of us and an army of them. We have to go."

"You do not know how many survived! Rorin and Gennifer are still alive. There could be more! We are stronger warriors than the soldiers they have sent. We can take them down. We can take revenge for this."

"That is suicide!" His chest hurt to look at her, but he kept a tight grip on her wrist, not allowing her to pull away. Why couldn't she understand that the only way to survive right now was to run? "Anyone who has survived will also be running. Your army is smart. They know how to hide. Please, Taryn. We have to run."

"Running is how they win!" Tears sparkled on her lashes, but there was strength in her voice. She pulled her wrist out of his grasp. "Running is how *she* wins." She pointed a shaking finger at Storm, and he finally noticed the blood on her hands, her face.

Understanding came over him then, and he nodded slowly. "Storm is dead. That is not *their* win. That is yours."

"Then why doesn't it feel like one?" Her face crumpled, and her body sagged to the floor. Fresh tears flowed down her cheeks. "They are gone, Ace. All gone, all because I chose to go with you earlier and eschew my duties. We could have saved them. We could have gotten them out. And I was selfish, I wanted to spend time with you more than I wanted to be a leader, and now they are gone."

He sank to his knees beside her, wrapping his arms around her trembling form. "It is not your fault." He didn't know what more he could say. Nothing felt like enough. He was operating on adrenaline and terror right now, had barely processed the carnage, including his own sister... There would be enough time for that later. All he could focus on now was that they needed to run.

"It should have been me," she whispered. "It was meant to be me."

Before he could ask her what she meant, shouts and a crash came from downstairs. Ace stiffened, his body snapping into high alert. "We have to go," he murmured in Taryn's ear.

"We have to fight," she answered, wiping both hands across her face to clear the tears. Streaks of blood coated both cheeks, like some sort of twisted warpaint.

"Taryn! They will kill you as they killed him!"

She made a movement with her head that might have been a shrug and pushed against him, trying to extricate herself from his grasp.

Ace stood with her, keeping a desperate hold of her hand even though he knew it was futile. Once Taryn set her mind to something, it was very difficult to sway her. Her stubbornness was usually one of the things he most admired about her—even when he'd first met her, she hadn't let anyone push her around, had stood her ground even in the face of impossible odds. But right now, her stubbornness was going to get them killed.

"It is time to go, Tar. Come on."

He tried to steer her away, and she wrenched her hand from his grasp.

"We are not leaving. We are fighting. This is our home. Erikkson would want us to protect it."

"He would want you to go. We cannot get caught here."

"You go. Leave me," she insisted, and he did not miss the mad, final edge to her tone. It terrified him.

"I am not leaving you," he hissed.

"You should. I destroy everything I touch." Her voice fell flat and empty.

Ace could hear how broken she was with that one sentence.

And though he knew the words weren't true, he understood exactly why she felt that way. He'd been there too, once, when he'd been at fault for the destruction of an entire airship of privateers, and that carnage was so much less than what they currently faced. She'd lost not only her army, her home, but also her creator, the man who had become like a father to her. Like a father to them all, if Ace was being honest. And they didn't have time to unpack any of it, but his throat ached as he saw the brokenness in her face, and how hard she was trying to be strong in spite of it.

"Taryn."

Footsteps echoed somewhere down the hall. They were coming. There was no time. He heaved a deep breath and faced the doors, just in time to see the soldiers arrive, their rifles raised and aimed at the two biomatons.

"Put your hands over your heads where we can see them!"

Ace did as he was told, but Taryn appeared to lose all of her fragility now that she was staring down the barrel of a gun, as if in shattering she'd become even deadlier, like a shard of broken glass. She raised her chin, taunting the soldiers. "Go on. Kill us."

"Hands up!" the soldier snapped. Ace barely noticed the men in the room, his eyes locked on Taryn. All at once, everything he'd ever felt for her came rushing back, all the longing and protectiveness and fierce adoration. She was *beautiful,* so beautiful, standing there in defiance of the soldiers, and so strong. He wondered when she'd become so strong, only to realize she'd been pushed into it; and he'd had his part in pushing her.

A soldier clamped manacles around Ace's wrists, securing them too tightly behind his back. Taryn was being treated the same way.

"Just kill us!" she screamed, spittle flying from her lips. "That is what you came here to do!"

She was rewarded with a slap to the face.

Ace leaped forward, struggling against the soldiers who held his shoulders. "Do not touch her!" he yelled. A fist in the gut silenced him, too, and he doubled over, coughing. Why didn't the soldiers just kill them both? Storm's body lying on the floor and the blood on Taryn's hands made it very clear what she (and he by association) had done. Why keep them alive?

A new figure entered the room. Ace stopped fighting, his blood running cold.

He recognized the predatory, hawk-like face all too well.

Lord Bellham glanced at the carnage in the room and clicked his tongue disdainfully, turning sharp, colorless eyes on the two biomatons. Ace could not breathe, feeling all his hard-won autonomy draining away in the presence of the man who'd made him a biomaton.

"Well, this is a surprise," Bellham crooned in his dark velvet voice. "I expected some survivors, but not you two." He looked Ace in the eye, and the former privateer felt his knees tremble. "You really did love her, eh boy? You managed to find her after all."

"What are you doing here?" Taryn spat, but Ace could hear the edge of terror in her voice.

"Storm and I made a little bargain." Lord Bellham's eyes raked over Taryn's armor, like a wolf sizing up a lamb with a broken leg, and his lip twisted in disgust. "In exchange for information, I get to keep any surviving biomatons. She did not believe Erikkson would be so stupid as to keep you so close, but I told her he was sentimental that way." He drew nearer as he spoke, running one finger down Taryn's cheek. "What a price you will fetch, my dear, when I have broken you."

Her face reddened and she snapped at his fingers, white teeth flashing. "I would rather *die* than be someone's slave!"

He gave her a tight-lipped smile. "We will see." He waved a

hand. "Take them to the airship. Keep an eye on the Erikkson. She is dangerous. We will be on our way shortly."

The soldiers dragged them from the room, and though Ace wanted to fight them off, his limbs would not obey him. He reeled, his mind spinning as they were led away, wondering at how everything could go so wrong. It had all fallen apart so quickly. How could their plans have collapsed this way? Numbly, he sensed the world falling in. He could hear Taryn yelling obscenities at their captors, followed by the heavy thud of fist against flesh, but he walked in a haze all his own. They had lost. And though his mind told him he was lucky to be alive, he was not so sure that was true any longer. A lot could be envied in the situation of those crushed beneath the stones. At least, compared to their current predicament, it could. At least those crushed would never be slaves again.

They were kept apart on the short airship flight to the Black Castle, each thrown into a separate, narrow cell. Ace shivered in the dark, his fingers falling asleep from the manacles. He imagined he could hear Taryn weeping through the wall which stood between them. His heart ached to take her into his arms and shield her from the world, but he knew it was impossible. Nothing he could do would protect her from the pain. He closed his eyes and tried to focus on the thrumming engine, mourning all their losses tonight, including his sister. He wondered if he and Taryn were the sole survivors of this rebellion, but then reminded himself that she'd mentioned Rorin and Gennifer had survived. More of his friends had to be alive. They had to. But he could not fully quell the guilt in his throat at the knowledge that the only reason he and Taryn had survived was because they had been shirking their duties. The thought made him sick.

Worse, the dry, hacking cough he'd battled some nights in the barracks (and confidently blamed on dust) appeared to have been triggered by the blow he'd received, and huge, racking fits of coughing overtook him as they journeyed north, until he could not breathe or speak, and his eyes ran with the pain in his chest.

After one such fit, he heard Taryn speak through the wall near his head, her voice cautious and hoarse with fear. "Ace? Are you all right?"

"Aye," he croaked in reply. "Just a cough. Nothing to worry about." He did not tell her this was a worsening of a cough he'd had since arriving at Elmhurst, one which woke him in the middle of the night and worried his roommates. She didn't need to worry about him, too.

She was quiet for a long time, and then she murmured, "I am scared."

He sighed. "As am I. But at least we have each other."

"A few of the others escaped," she muttered. "We are not the only survivors."

A fist pounded on the door to her cell. Ace flinched.

"Quiet in there!" a voice yelled outside. They both fell silent in response, but Ace felt his heart lift a little at her revelation. There *were* other survivors. Someone would rescue them from Lord Bellham—but as soon as the thought flickered through his mind, he knew he could not rely on a rescue. Any survivors would assume he and Taryn had been killed. They were on their own.

At last, they were dragged from their cells and straight to "processing," a laboratory in the Black Castle Ace only dimly recognized from his time here, but which Taryn appeared to know intimately. Her face paled as they entered the room. The smell of copper, formaldehyde, and blood hit his nose. Ace's blood began to boil. Never, *never* had he seen Taryn this terrified.

A woman in a white lab coat and dark satin dress beneath approached, mousy brown hair tied up in a knot at the nape of her neck. Her round spectacles glinted in the harsh light of the overhead arc lamps, obscuring her eyes. She smiled at them both. "743, 745, you join us again." Her eyes met Ace's, and he instantly knew her. *She* was the one who'd designed his grafts. It was her fault he was in so much pain! His eyes darkened to a scowl.

She sighed. "I see Erikkson took the liberty of deprogramming you. How very tedious and *forward thinking* of him." She nodded to the troupe of lab assistants clustered about her. "You know what to do. Tag and process them. We do not have all night."

"And ensure the girl is dressed in something more suitable," Lord Bellham interrupted, entering the room behind them. Ace saw Taryn balk, her shoulders rising as the lab assistants came near her.

Do not fight them, he begged silently. *Oh Tar, do not fight them. They will only hurt you.*

And then several assistants caught him by the shoulders, forcing his left arm out, and his attention was on the sharp pain of the number 745 being branded upon his arm in black ink. Ace gasped, the sharp intake of breath triggering a coughing fit that doubled him over in pain.

"Ace?" Taryn questioned as he finally managed to catch his breath. Her voice was edged with terror.

"I am fine." He straightened himself, slowing his breathing despite how much it hurt. Lord Bellham gave him a puzzled look.

"Have you had that cough long, boy?"

Ace shook his head in silence, rubbing at the fresh, sore number etched on his arm. 745. A number he hated with every fiber of his being.

"Interesting."

"No, please!"

Ace spun to see Taryn struggling to keep the lab assistants from disassembling her armor. Her wrists were locked behind her back by one of Bellham's massive guards, and though Ace knew she could easily take the man out, she appeared to be holding back. Perhaps she had a plan. Or perhaps she, like Ace, understood that fighting back would only make this worse. They were in a castle filled with guards and enforcers, cruel beyond imagining. Fighting their way out of the depths of the Black Castle would take a miracle. Better to bide their time, find the right moment to strike. Better to act the slave than be chained, whipped, or beaten.

But even as Ace had that thought, he saw the fire in her emerald eyes, and he knew that the warrior that lived inside her would not be quelled.

Bellham held up a hand and stepped in, turning her shoulders to study the clockwork embedded in her back. Ace's blood ran cold. "What is this?" Bellham questioned.

"Erikkson intended it to be a weapon," Ace jumped in, before Taryn could answer. If they knew of her weapons, they would tear her apart. "It did not work."

A cruel smile twisted Bellham's thin lips. "So, your master did not turn out as kind as you had hoped, did he?"

Taryn said nothing—her teeth were gritted so tight that a muscle pulsed in her jaw. Ace tried to go to her, but someone caught his shoulders and held him back. His heart shattered as the assistants began to destroy Taryn's armor. They ignored the carefully formed buckles, straps, and laces, tearing it all apart as quickly as they could, using scalpels to slice through leather to literally cut Taryn out of the beautiful armor. The damage, he knew, would be irreparable. All Gennifer's months of work, torn down in just a few minutes. When the assistants began to reveal her pale skin, he turned his head away, cheeks and ears hot with embarrassment for her. They were quite literally stripping her of everything, including her dignity, and it made him sick.

In spite of it all, she stood with her head held high, refusing them the pleasure of seeing her broken. Something in Ace soared to see her stand her ground, while the rest of him trembled with dread. This place knew how to break a person down to their basest, most subservient parts. Her resistance would only make them crueler.

The assistants thrust a plain brown dress over her head, and wrapped a corset around her waist, tugging it so tight her face turned white, her chest heaving for breath. Ace fought his captors again, unable to bear it in silence any longer.

"That is enough! Can you not see she cannot breathe?"

Lord Bellham sneered. "She would not be in discomfort if she had not grown accustomed to such inappropriate costumes."

Ace spat a string of the worst curses he knew at the man. Bellham glared. "Someone shut him down. I like him better when he is obedient. He is so insufferably devoted to our little traitor otherwise."

Rough hands forced Ace's head down, though he fought them the whole time.

"Leave him alone!" Taryn screamed. The sickening crunch of fist against flesh silenced her.

It only took a moment or two before those holding Ace realized he could not be controlled so easily. "His obedience circuit is broken, m'lord."

Bellham smirked. "Then we shall do this the old-fashioned way. Good. I like a challenge."

Ace found his eyes drawn back to Taryn, who stood swaying on her feet, as though she could topple at any moment. Her corset had been laced so tightly he was sure he could easily wrap his hands around her waist and link his own fingers. But she looked back at him, her eyes clear and shining. He clenched his jaw, begging her silently to *hold on*. This would all be over soon.

But he didn't know that, did he? This could be their lives now, and only death would free them from the hands of these cruel people.

Lord Bellham waved a hand. "Give them a cell. No food, no water. We shall see if they remain so stubborn tomorrow."

CHAPTER EIGHTEEN

TARYN COLLAPSED on the stone floor of their shared cell, one hand pressed beneath her ribs, panting for a breath that would not come. It felt like all the air had been sucked from the room, every rib straining at the breaking point. She squeezed her eyes shut, unable to even cry out for the compressed state of her lungs.

"Hang on, hang on." Ace's gentle voice washed like soothing balm through her pain, and she felt his slender fingers fumbling at her corset ties. After a moment, he managed to loosen the hated thing, and she gasped, dragging ragged gulps of oxygen into her lungs. She collapsed to her side on the stone floor, the ground damp and pockmarked and utterly familiar. The cell smelled of mildew and rot, of human decay and blood. Somewhere water dripped endlessly—and it was all familiar, like a recurring nightmare she could not escape. At last, her breathing evened out, and she managed to press herself into a sitting position.

"Thank you," she croaked.

"I am sorry."

The words were like knives in her stomach, only serving to

remind her of the pain she held just beneath her skin, like a living thing she could barely keep caged, ready to break out and destroy her. "No more of that," she answered numbly. She would not allow the shock and the hurt to creep in. She wouldn't. "No more sorries. We both have enough to be sorry for." She could not look at him, her eyes cast down at the shadows which danced across the floor with the dim torchlight outside their cell.

"Taryn, promise me something—"

She frowned. "What is it?"

"Promise you will obey them."

She would have laughed if she had not been so afraid the sound would shatter her. "Please say you are making some sick joke."

"I am serious. They will hurt you if you fight them. And I cannot bear it."

"I am programmed to rebel! It is no more something I can stop than the beating of my heart!"

"Nevertheless, I want you to promise you will not fight them."

She at last raised her gaze to him, her eyes burning with tears she did not want to cry. "If I do not fight, I am betraying Erikkson's memory, betraying his trust in me. I am betraying the rest of our friends, the army that I *promised* I would lead to freedom."

"No—" The rest of his words dissolved in a fit of coughing. She waited, fear and concern written across her face, until the fit passed.

"That cough sounds bad," she said softly. *Bad* was an understatement; the cough reminded her of the one Royal's mother had developed in the months before she had died of consumption.

He tried to give her a reassuring smile, but it was too strained and tight around the edges. "I am all right."

She sighed, chewing on a split in her lip until the coppery salt-tang of blood flooded her mouth. She pulled her legs up to her chest, resting her chin against her knees. A trembling began in her core, and she could do nothing to stop it. She squeezed her eyes shut, but the dead danced behind her eyelids, both her friends and her enemies, and it was worse than keeping her eyes open.

Ace wrapped his strong arms around her shoulders, silently taking her into his embrace as she trembled. She turned and buried her face in his shoulder, breathing him in. Her forearm burned where her number was once again etched into her skin.

At last, she calmed her trembling enough to pull out of his grasp. She shoved her hair back from her face. Something deep inside her resented the fact that she would not (or could not) cry; a deep, ugly hidden part of her accused her of being selfish and heartless. Surely, she could spare tears for her army, for her creator? But Taryn had no tears left to weep, and she hated herself for it.

"We are not the only survivors," she murmured, meeting Ace's gaze. "Emmett, Petrichor, and perhaps Seraphim were out on errands. Rorin rescued Gennifer from the rubble, and if they listened to me, they ought to have escaped. And Royal went home earlier today..." She trailed off, unable to force her tongue to continue. It all felt so futile.

"That is good," Ace encouraged, squeezing her hand in his. "Someone will come for us."

She shook her head. "Ace, they are going to think we perished in the destruction of the manor. No one knew Bellham was working with Storm. No one is coming for us."

"Is there no reason to maintain hope?"

The word fell like a lead weight from her lips. "No."

She rose, pacing the length of their cell, one hand pressed to her bruised ribs. Despair washed over her in waves. "This is not how this was meant to happen."

"We can rebuild."

"No, we cannot!" Her voice echoed in the dungeon, reverberating far off down the corridors. "This was Erikkson's cause! He gave us a place to gather, a place where we could be safe. Now where can we exist without chains, Ace? Where can we be anything other than slaves, now that he is gone and Elmhurst is destroyed?"

She slumped to the floor, all her energy suddenly drained. She bowed her head, rubbing at the number carved into her forearm. She frowned, studying the marks. Unlike the last time, she'd been given an extra mark beside the numbers. A small X was carved beside the digits. "Ace?" she croaked.

"Hmm?"

"May I see your arm?"

He slid over to her, confusion clouding his expression. He held out his left arm to her, displaying his own mark. "Why?"

She held her arm beside his—only three digits adorned Ace's forearm. 745. Only she wore the X beside her mark. "Do you know what this means?"

He studied her arm for a moment, then shook his head. "Did you not have an X before?"

"No." A shudder racked her body, and she rubbed her face with both hands. "This place terrifies me."

He took her wrists and pulled her hands away from her face. "We have survived this place before. We can survive it again."

She looked him in the eye. "But will we be the same when we leave? They may not be able to control us as they could before, but they can wipe our minds if they want to, start over with clean slates. I do not want to lose all I have learned about myself again. I—" She looked away. "I do not want to lose you."

He squeezed her wrists. "Then promise me you will obey them, so we will be strong enough to find a way to escape."

"Ace—"

"It *is* the best way. You know it is. Promise me, Tar, please. I do not want to watch them tear you apart."

She sighed, and though every fiber of her being told her she was making a stupid promise, a promise she could not keep, she nodded. "I promise."

※

HARPER AND BELLHAM CAME TO THE DOOR OF THEIR CELL early that morning. Ace rose silently at Harper's beckoning, afraid to wake Taryn after she had fallen into a fitful sleep beside him. She needed the rest. He set his jaw, making his way to the bars, wary of his captors. He knew how dangerous they were, how cruel they could be if he displeased them. He stood at the bars, waiting for sharp words or blows, one hand gripping the cold, pockmarked metal.

Harper pulled a stethoscope from a pocket in her white coat.

"Breathe normally," she ordered, reaching through the bars to listen to his heart rate and breathing.

He could have grabbed her wrist and snapped it, but he restrained himself. They would never have a chance at escaping if he made a stupid, hot-headed move like that. After some time, Harper sighed and drew away, removing the cold stethoscope. She wrapped the rubber tubing around her hand.

"I was certain we had it with him."

"As was I," Lord Bellham replied.

"Well, I shall rework the blueprints again, I suppose. It is too bad. He was a better subject than most of the street urchins you bring me." Her eyes studied Ace for a moment in the torchlight. He stood stoically, his face a stone mask, but his fingers curled around the bar he held with a white-knuckled grasp as he struggled to decipher their words. "Do you think he is worth anything now?"

Bellham shook his head. "Not enough to matter, after the funds we have dumped into him."

"We ought to sell them as a pair."

"That would lower the price we can get for her. I am not willing to risk my profit on the biomaton who tried to start a revolution over some meaningless whelp."

"But sir, no one will purchase a biomaton in his condition!"

"How long would you give him?"

Again, Harper studied him for a long moment before answering. "In his condition... A year. Perhaps longer, but he may become too weak for work if he lasts much longer than that."

"Then we will attempt to auction him as a year of labor. That will be worth something. And as a last resort, we can always use him as bait in the arena..." Their voices faded away as they left, leaving Ace shaking at the bars of his cell. He slipped to the floor, his head pounding with the beating of his heart. All he could hear was the rush of blood in his ears. He was not stupid. He understood the exchange.

Something was wrong with his grafts, and it was killing him.

A year, perhaps longer...

The words danced through his head ceaselessly. He pressed his fingers to his temples, squeezing his eyes shut. *No. Oh, please, no.* It could not be true. He was not dying... Surely? Yes, his grafts pained him, but that did not mean they had to kill him, did it? *Did it?* He had found so much to live for in the past few weeks, the past few days. In the beautiful redheaded biomaton who now shared his cell. He would endure a lifetime of pain if only that lifetime was by her side. He had not lived through so much only to discover his poorly constructed grafts were killing him.

Tears stung the back of his eyes, and he scrubbed at them with his one flesh fist, trying in vain to erase them from existence. His breath rattled in his chest as he struggled to keep his emotional reaction in check, but fear and shock were catalyzing into panic in his gut, and panic was as difficult to control as a volcano.

At last, he gave in, allowing himself to weep, curled against the bars of the cell, silent tears streaming down his cheeks. He wept for his diagnosis, yes, but he also wept for Taryn, for the dead, even for his sister, now gone. All gone. He wept for the future that would never be, and for the past he could not fix. Ace wept until his tears were spent, his panic subdued, and then he rose and returned to Taryn's side. He settled himself beside her, stroking her hair away from her forehead with gentle fingers. Who knew what time they had left together? She had enough of a burden to bear without his adding to it. He pressed his lips together, settling himself more comfortably against the wall. He would not tell her, he decided. At least, not before he knew what their immediate future held. His condition would not change. And perhaps it would be kinder if she did not know.

He closed his eyes, determined to get some much-needed sleep before the day brought new terrors. Taryn moaned in her sleep. He set a tender hand on her shoulder.

"Hush, Tar," he murmured. "I am here. While I draw breath, I swear, I shall not leave you."

CHAPTER NINETEEN

"They are dead, Frenchie! Accept it. We are the only ones left." Petrichor jabbed an accusatory finger at all that remained of the west wing of Elmhurst Manor, a pile of bricks and plaster and wood and, somewhere beneath it all, bodies. Too many bodies. Petrichor stood on the lawn away from the house, refusing to draw any nearer. She killed for a living, yes, but never people she knew, and never with so many old, unwanted memories nudging her palm like a loyal dog. She set her jaw, set her stance. She did not need to get closer to see what had occurred.

"*Non.* Someone must have escaped." Emmett hesitated in his steps toward the house, blinking quickly as if he could not quite believe his clockwork eyes. "We must investigate. *Au cas où.*"

"I am not going any closer." Petrichor crossed her arms stubbornly.

"Taryn could be in there somewhere! She does not sleep in the barracks."

"Red would not be stupid enough to stay in the manor, even if she did escape the blast. The soldiers must have searched the property. Anyone with any sense will be long gone. If we're smart, we'll leave the country. We could be on a boat to Africa by nightfall."

"*S'il vous plait, mon canard,*" he begged, using the nickname he'd given her, and which she suspected did not translate to something she'd like by the way he usually smiled when he said it. He was not smiling now. "*Aidez moi.* Help me."

Petrichor sighed. "Fine. But you're not going to like what we find."

"*Je sais.*"

They began to pick their way toward the rubble, wary of any traps laid out for biomatons returning to Elmhurst. Petrichor doubted they had anything to worry about—soldiers would have swarmed their little yacht the moment it touched down—but it didn't hurt to be cautious. She let Emmett lead, studying the movements of his small, wiry frame. She was beginning to develop a soft spot for this Frenchman, it seemed. She would have to keep herself in better check. He would only become a liability, if she continued on the path her mind currently walked.

Parts of the rubble smoldered even after all these hours, and the acrid smoke stung their eyes, burned their throats. Nothing stirred, not even the carrion birds Petrichor had expected. The rubble created a kind of makeshift burial. Their feet crunched over the debris, and it struck her like a blow: they walked on a tomb.

"*Alors,*" Emmett breathed in awe. "What could have done this?"

She cleared her throat against the smoke, voice even huskier than usual. "Barrels of some new explosive the military has designed. In America, they use it to blow holes in mountains. Here, they use it to kill biomatons."

In some unspoken consensus of trepidation, they stopped in front of the gaping wound in the manor, created by the blast.

Neither wanted to be the first to step into the murky unknown. Petrichor drew a throwing knife from her belt, raising it in readiness in case something came leaping from the shadows. She breathed a quick steadying breath and then plunged into the manor.

It was like stepping into the bones of a house long abandoned, though the manor had been silent for mere hours. They crept along the halls, hardly daring to interrupt the silence. Petrichor was not superstitious, but Elmhurst was thick with memories, and she saw ghosts in every fluttering curtain, every empty, silent room.

"No one is here," she muttered to Emmett after they had studied a dozen rooms without finding any trace of life. "We should get out of here."

"We must check every room. Someone could be hiding."

Petrichor sighed and followed him loyally, though with each empty room she became more certain they were about to find something very bad.

The door to Erikkson's study stood wide open, and Petrichor knew as soon as she saw it that it was wrong. Erikkson never left his study door open. She hurried forward, heart thundering in her ears. She grabbed the jamb to keep upright, head spinning.

"No..."

Emmett caught up with her and froze, swearing in French. He set a gentle hand on her back. "*Je suis désolée, mon canard.*"

Petrichor shook him off, turning her shock and sorrow to anger with the ease of someone who'd never been allowed tears.

"At least they got that witch who was hunting us," she growled, an unfamiliar catch in her throat. She knelt to examine Storm's long-cold body, her fingers drawing the throwing knife out of the corpse of their own accord. She would not allow herself to look at the other body in the room.

"This is Sedition's," she murmured.

"*Quoi?*"

"This throwing knife belonged to Sedition," Petrichor repeated, louder this time. She nudged the body with her foot; it no longer looked human, the skin grayed, waxy, and stiff. "She managed to kill her after all."

"But—that means Taryn is still alive!"

She nodded, turning the blade in her fingers, its shine dulled with the rusty tinge of dried blood. "It means she survived the blast long enough to kill Storm."

At last, she allowed her deep brown eyes to drag over to Erikkson's body, slumped behind his desk like a marionette with its strings cut. "I suspect the captain shot our creator."

Her mind kicked into high gear, the room no longer the scene of a tragedy but rather a crime scene, every detail clear and bright in her mind. Crime scenes always had a story to tell, Petrichor had learned, and they were not hard to read once you knew how. Her time with the Italian mob in New York had taught her to treat a crime scene like an open book.

"Look at the tracks," she muttered, pointing out the varying footprints in dried blood and dirt across the floor, moving into and out of the study. She could almost see it: Taryn, killing Storm, unable to save Erikkson, only to be surrounded by soldiers.

"Oh," she breathed. "You were right, Emmett. Sedition survived. Maybe someone was with her, maybe not, but for some reason, they didn't kill her. They arrested her."

"How do you know that?"

"If they had killed her, her body would be in this room as well." Petrichor shook her head. "They kept her alive."

"But that is good! We can rescue her!"

Petrichor smiled grimly. "I admire your optimism, Frenchie. I really do. But if Taryn was kept alive, it means they have some fate worse than death planned for her. And I'm afraid the trail is cold. We have no more leads."

They explored the rest of the manor, finding nothing but eerie cold halls, dark empty rooms. At last, Petrichor and Emmett took Erikkson's body and dug him a shallow grave in the garden behind the manor. No words were spoken over his corpse. Nothing seemed to suffice. Emmett was fond of the man. And Petrichor's chest constricted with guilt as she realized she was just relieved he could not torment her or her siblings any longer.

She helped Emmett shovel the dark, wet earth over her creator, and she found a wet heat running down her cheeks. Emmett set a hand on her shoulder, murmuring small comforts in French. She could not find the courage to explain the tears were as much relief as sorrow, and as much gratitude as pain.

⁂

THE DAY PASSED SLOWLY, THE HOURS DRAGGING INTO years as Taryn and Ace awaited whatever came next. There was no way to guess what time it was in their dark cell; the flickering torchlight never changed, nor did anything else in this place. Both dozed off and on, though their sleep was troubled with nightmares. Neither had much heart for talking, and as the day wore on, their stomachs rumbled in protest at their emptiness.

Taryn rubbed her prosthetic obsessively, worried about rust and damage to the limb since she had neglected to oil it in the chaos of the night before. The limb was her last connection to Erikkson, and she could not bear the thought that it might be ruined by her negligence.

After countless silent hours, Harper came to the door of their cell, accompanied by two burly guards. The biomatons rose as one, but Harper only shook her head. "I only need 743. Place your back against the wall, 745. I do not want to see you leave it before the door is again locked."

Ace glowered, but caught Taryn's shoulder before she could take a step, hissing in her ear. "Remember your promise. Do not fight them. We will find a way out of here."

Taryn gritted her teeth. Obeying Harper and her lackeys would be as easy as pulling out her own fingernails, and likely as painful, but she had made a promise to Ace, and that was enough. Besides, she'd learned to control herself since the last time she was here. It would be easier this time.

They were lies, but she told them to herself anyways, if only to make each step toward Harper a little easier.

Harper grinned. "I see you have learned since you were with us last. Good. We will need that."

I have learned a hundred ways to destroy you, Taryn growled silently as the guards cuffed her hands behind her back, but she did not speak. She hated Harper with a fire that she reserved only for the most vile of villains. Hated this place and all that it stood for, all the suffering she saw in every other biomaton's face as they passed by her cell. But she was tired—so very tired—and she remembered how easy it was to become a puppet, to lose herself in obedience.

Sedition and Taryn were at war within her: one pushing for freedom, to fight, and kill, until every last slaver lay dead at her feet, but the other half of her wanted to retreat into that pleasant fog of programming she'd experienced the last time she was here, just wanted all of this to be finished. Anything to dull the pain and the weight of all the lives she'd lost.

Harper led her upstairs, through achingly familiar corridors, until they at last came into a small room with a row of weapons upon one wall and a cupboard standing in one corner. In the center of the room stood a single wooden chair with leather straps dangling from the arms and legs. Taryn's heel skidded across the floor, but she forced herself not to fight as the two guards forced her into the chair. They released her cuffs, only to tie her wrists and ankles to the arms and legs of that hard chair. Her breath caught in her throat, her chest heaving over tight whalebone stays, and she glared up at Harper, waiting.

The woman clapped her hands, and a new man stepped from the shadows. He walked slowly around Taryn, his head on one side, his dark, angular eyes roving over every part of her. He kept one hand in the pocket of the leather apron he wore.

"This is the Erikkson?" he questioned at last, stopping behind Taryn so he could stare over her head at Harper. "She does not look like much."

"That is your job, Jin."

Taryn felt fingers in her long hair and jerked, fighting the leather straps around her forearms.

"Now, girl, this is easier if you let it happen," the man behind her said. He spoke in a warm tenor, accented with a lilt Taryn had never heard before.

"What do you want from me?" Taryn demanded, leaning as far forward as her restraints would allow. The murderous part of herself was winning the battle for supremacy.

"I am sure you are clever enough to notice the X beside your number," Harper answered cooly, her hands sliding into the pockets of her white coat. "I am to introduce a new fighter exotic in the ring tonight. That fighter is you."

Taryn's blood ran cold. She'd heard rumors about the fighting rings and seen one or two biomatons constructed for the fights; it had been enough to give her nightmares. And now they expected her to fight there herself?

"I do not know anything about fighting," she lied.

"Do not lie to me!" Harper yelled. She took a breath, regaining her composure. "I was in London the day you and your friends attacked the square. I know Erikkson completed you. Your sweet little schoolgirl disguise will no longer work on me, Sedition." She spat the name like a curse.

Taryn grimaced. She should have seen this coming. Seraphim and Petrichor had been here, had fought in the ring...

Of course, if Harper got her hands on another Erikkson biomaton, she would send her into the ring.

"I will not fight for you."

Harper rolled her eyes. "I admire your fire, girl. But allow me to make this very clear to you: you fight whomever I tell you to fight. You *kill* whomever I tell you to kill. Because if you disobey me, you never see 745 again. And please, do not try to tell me you cannot care about him, because I saw the way you looked at him earlier. You fight, or he dies, understood?"

Taryn hung her head, the fresh promise she'd made burning on her lips. Yes, she knew how this worked. And she would fight, in the end. She would fight to stay near the last person she had in the world. She had promised.

"Good. Jin, you may begin."

The man lifted a pair of silver shears, grabbing a handful of Taryn's long copper hair. She squeezed her eyes shut, flinching at the hiss of the shears snapping closed.

TARYN RAN HER HAND OVER HER NEWLY SHORN SCALP again, fighting back tears. Her hair had been cropped to chin length, and cut even shorter in the back, displaying her control panel for the world to see. Jin had painted her cheeks with lines of thick blue paint, surprisingly cold and smelling of clay. At Taryn's insistence, he had oiled her prosthetic as well, and now it gleamed like it was brand new.

Taryn shivered now as she followed Harper and Jin, less from the cold than from the exposure. He'd dressed her in a burlesque costume of blue and black, barely more than undergarments. The costume consisted of an overbust corset, a bustled skirt which cascaded past her knees in the back, but was tied up tightly in the front, leaving her legs visible, and a pair of black leggings. They let her keep her leather boots from her armor but confiscated everything else.

This costume was nothing like the training uniforms she'd worn at Elmhurst. Those uniforms had been designed for ease of motion, allowing her to use her strengths and abilities without being hindered by a skirt. This new costume was designed for the gaze of the spectators; she felt like she was walking down the hall in nothing more than her skivvies.

She followed Harper down a long, unfurnished hallway, through a pair of massive wood double doors, and out into the inner courtyard of the castle. The square had been converted to an arena of sorts; massive lanterns hung from the walls, illuminating the courtyard. A series of elevated seats stood around a central platform, where two biomatons were locked in a heated battle, swords clashing hard enough to throw sparks. Men—they were *all* men, Taryn noted, save for Harper—stood or sat in the seats, cheering for their favorite.

Harper set a hand on Taryn's shoulder, stopping her.

"Wait a moment, 743. Your fight is next." She smiled and tapped her pocket. "Not to worry. I brought you a weapon. Unless you would prefer to go in unarmed?"

Taryn was *always* armed, but she did not want to reveal it to Harper. The less Harper knew about her hidden weapons, the better. The last thing Taryn needed was for her final line of defense to be taken from her.

"I will take it," she muttered.

A great cheer went up from the stands, and Taryn turned to see one biomaton had run his sword through the other's belly. The fight was over. The victor stood, spattered with blood, apparently unaware of his surroundings. A moment or two later, his handler stepped into the arena and cuffed him, leading him from the ring. Harper squeezed Taryn's shoulder.

"Your turn, girl."

Her feet moved of their own accord down the narrow aisle that would bring her into the arena. Her heart thundered in her ears.

Do it for Ace, she told herself.

It would be easy, like sparring at home. Only this time, it was for her life.

"I have a special treat for you tonight!" Harper cried, leading Taryn into the ring. Someone in the stands wolf whistled. The violence inside Taryn's chest writhed, ready to do battle. She did not want to let it out, but she knew she would not have a choice.

For Ace.

"This pretty little girl you see before you was built by Lord Anthony Erikkson. Yes, the same man who built Seraphim, the Angel of Death, and Petrichor, the Clockwork Assassin. I present Sedition, Queen of the Biomatons!"

Harper grabbed Taryn's chin and forced her to look up at the men in the stands. At first, she thought they were actually *cheering* for her. And then her brain deciphered the sounds, and she realized it was a chorus of jeers and insults. Her stomach tightened.

"Who has a challenger for my new champion?" Harper demanded.

The men went silent, waiting for a volunteer. A man raised his hand. "My Jack can beat that waif."

Harper seemed pleased with the offer. She nodded.

"Come forward, then."

Her hand slipped into her pocket, and she withdrew a stiletto knife about the length of Taryn's forearm. She offered it to Taryn blade first. An impulse to snatch the weapon and drive it into Harper's chest flashed across the back of her eyes, but Harper murmured, "Remember, if you try anything, you never see him again."

Taryn swallowed hard and took the knife, gripping the

blade with her left hand to keep from cutting herself. She settled it in her palm as Harper left the ring to seat herself near the front of the stands. The knife felt acceptable in her hand. A little unbalanced, perhaps, but it would do. She tested the edge with her thumb, pleased to find it was razor-sharp.

A new figure stepped into the ring. Taryn's opponent held a knife in one hand. Her grafts were horribly brutal: her revealing costume displayed the metal plating covering her lower torso. Taryn had no way of knowing how much of her internal workings were clockwork, but she knew one thing: it would not be easy to kill her. Taryn circled her opponent warily, studying her.

And then she noticed it: short-cropped, dishwater-blonde hair falling into hazel eyes. And though those eyes had the awful hollow look of a biomaton under deep programming, Taryn recognized the face. It was the face of Midshipman Jacqueline "Jack" Cobb, the girl in disguise who had saved her life in the Tower of London, what felt like a lifetime ago. Taryn felt sick. Ace had told her Cobb died, and yet, here she was...

And Harper expected Taryn to kill her.

"Get on with it!" someone in the audience yelled.

Jack lunged, moving her knife lightning fast. Taryn saw the movement happening an instant too late, and barely managed to twist away.

"Jack," she muttered, barely moving her lips to avoid their audience noticing her speaking. "Do you remember me?"

The girl snarled in response, leaping forward again. There was no humanity left in her eyes. Taryn twisted away, at the same time swapping hands with her own blade and swinging it across Jack's shoulder. The girl stumbled back a few paces, clutching at the wound. A cheer went up from the stands. Taryn's bloodlust sang in her ears, but she tamped it down. This was about survival. She did not want to kill Jack—not after the girl had saved her—but she would do what she had to do.

And it was becoming clearer every moment that this Jack was not the same as the one who'd saved Taryn's life. This biomaton had no humanity left.

They circled one another, Jack bleeding and snarling like an animal, Taryn just searching for an opening, *some* option which would allow her to incapacitate her opponent without killing her. But the more Taryn studied Jack's shiny new grafts, the more she understood the clockwork keeping her alive was nigh impenetrable, at least with a knife. That left only two targets—her head and neck. Both would be deadly.

"Please," Taryn muttered. "I do not want to do this."

The girl growled and charged, her head down, feet slapping against the stone of the arena. Taryn side-stepped and caught her wrist, snapping it backward, close to but not past the breaking point. The girl shrieked, the knife clattering from her fingers. Taryn stepped on the hilt of the blade and kicked it backward, sending it skittering into a corner.

"Now yield," Taryn ordered, keeping the girl's wrist at the breaking point. It should have kept her down, but it was clear whatever her biomechanicks had done to her brain, they'd removed some vital part which controlled pain response. Jack reminded Taryn of a rabid dog she'd seen on the streets once: insatiable and unstoppable, until a shopkeeper had put it out of its misery with a bullet between the eyes. Nausea danced behind Taryn's eyes as she envisioned what she would have to do to end this.

It was not right.

But it was what would keep Ace safe.

Jack twisted in Taryn's grasp. She felt bones crunch under her fingers, but the girl managed to break free. She came at Taryn again, this time with hands like claws. Taryn sighed, swallowed hard, and let the violence out.

It was all over in a matter of seconds. Taryn raised herself to her feet, chest heaving, her hands slick with hot blood. The crowd roared in surprise, and some in sick delight at what they'd witnessed. Taryn just felt numb. Deep in the pit of her soul, she knew what she'd done—what she'd been trained to do—was wrong. And it did not matter that the girl at her feet no longer had any humanity left, nor that if she had not done it, her friend would have died. Taryn *still* had blood on her hands, and she would have to answer for it. It was like a little part of her died each time she killed, and eventually, if this continued, there would be nothing of Taryn left.

Harper came and handcuffed Taryn's hands behind her back, steering her from the arena with one firm hand. "Well done," she murmured in Taryn's ear. "And not a scratch on you. He trained you well, girl. I am going to make you famous."

Taryn shook her head, trying to clear her jagged thoughts. "Do not make me do that again." Shame flared in her cheeks at the pathetic note in her voice.

"Remember our agreement. You fight, or he dies. It is not hard to understand."

Taryn bowed her head in submission, numbness overpowering her body. Yes, she had killed before, but not like this. Never like this. Murder was not entertainment, and Taryn loathed anyone who wanted to make it so. And now, she loathed herself, for surviving, for killing, for choosing her own life over someone else's. She was not performing an act of selflessness on Ace's behalf. She was just selfishly choosing her own life. She chose herself over and over, and now it had caught up with her, and she was at last the monster Erikkson had intended her to be.

CHAPTER TWENTY

SHE STOOD NUMBLY in the cell, swaying unsteadily on her feet as the door closed and locked behind her, unseeing eyes focused somewhere far away. At last, she remembered how they'd washed her hands and face, and allowed her to don a thin gray shift instead of the garish burlesque costume she'd worn in the ring. Then, one of the guards brought her back to the cell, the cold, the damp. She could smell blood. Her nails were still encrusted with it.

"Taryn! What happened? Your hair!" Ace exclaimed, his words tumbling over one another as they fell from his lips. She did not raise her eyes, one hand going—subconsciously—to her new, short haircut. Her fingers came away caked with blood, and she gasped, knees buckling as she stared at her bloody fingers. She could not breathe.

"Taryn?"

Flashes of memory danced behind her eyes—another pair of hands, one clockwork, one flesh, slick with blood—a girl with dark brown hair yelling, the right side of her face dark with bruises—the metal table that appeared in her nightmares.

"Taryn!"

She shook her head, blinking away the images. Her hands, still trembling in front of her, were clean. She struggled to control her breathing.

Ace knelt beside her, offering her his hand, but he did not touch her. She was grateful for that. Had he touched her, she might have snapped. She didn't want to think about what she could do to him if she did.

At last, she got her breathing under control and pressed her hand into his. She chewed her lip, wondering at the images in her memory. Was she truly remembering something new, or was her mind simply breaking down under the strain?

"What happened?"

She shook her head, lips pressed tightly together, unable to explain that she'd killed the girl who'd saved her life because she was a selfish coward and could not bear to lose him, too.

"Taryn, what happened?"

Again, she shook her head. "Do not ask questions you do not wish to know the answers to."

He clutched her hand, lacing his fingers with hers. He reached up with his clockwork hand and tenderly brushed her short hair behind her ear. She swallowed hard, trembling under his touch, ashamed of what she was, what she'd done. She did not deserve to have someone like him caring for her. "I am sorry," she whispered.

"Sorry for what?"

"Sorry for getting you into this mess. If it were not for me, you would not be a biomaton..." Her voice ran out, her lips moving, but no words escaped her.

He touched her chin, gently lifting her head until she met his gaze. "None of this is your fault, Taryn. I am *better* for having met you. I am a better man for becoming a biomaton. Without your example, I would still believe biomatons were merely machines, and I would probably have helped Storm destroy many of them. You do not need to apologize for anything."

She pulled away, unable to bear the tenderness in his eyes. If he knew what she had done, he would never say such things.

"I changed my mind about biomatons long before I became one, you know," he continued softly. "You changed my mind, back on the *Dauntless*. Even then, I think I was in love with you."

Taryn lurched to her feet, striding as far away from him as the cell would allow, pressing her forehead to the cold, damp back wall. She folded her arms across her chest, pressing her thumb into the number carved into her forearm until tears sprang into her eyes, just to feel something. Her heart thundered with Ace's admission, but she forced it down, telling herself love meant nothing but weakness here, and Ace could not love; he had lost that when Bellham operated on him. "Do not say that," she muttered. "Not right now."

"Taryn, what other time *is* there to say it?"

"There is no place for love here." She spun toward him, face white and cold. "Love is a weakness here, and they will exploit it."

They already have.

She knew her own secret affection for him would be exploited over and over, until they sold her or she learned to obey out of habit, losing herself in the subservient creature they wanted her to be. Or worse, until she was killed in the arena. They could not admit their love for each other. Not here. Not now. Perhaps not ever.

"Then what am I meant to do?" he exclaimed. "Be silent? Whatever they did to you, Tar, I know it was deeper than just cutting your hair, and I cannot sit here in silence and allow you to be torn apart! Not when I care so much for you!"

She bowed her head, her newly cropped hair swinging across her cheekbones. She was so used to having a curtain of copper hair to hide behind, she felt exposed without it. "It is just hair," she mumbled, ignoring his words because she had no answer for them. "It will grow back."

"I rather like it." Ace crossed the distance between them in a few steps and again tucked her hair behind her ear, displaying the missing half-moon scar hidden behind her copper locks. "It makes you look like Joan of Arc."

She swallowed the guilt and shame like a bitter pill and raised her eyes to him. "Do you have a plan to get us out of here yet?"

He shook his head. "Not yet. I am still watching for an opportunity. We must bide our time."

Something hard edged his voice, and she realized he understood as well as she how futile an escape attempt would be. He wore his brave mask for her, just as she hid the truth of her monstrosity from him.

We are quite the pair, she mused. *We cannot even tell each other the truth.*

She nodded. "Very well. I will keep my eyes open. Perhaps together we can find the chink in their armor."

He grabbed her hand—her *clockwork hand*—in his. She stared numbly at the two entwined metal limbs, sorrow wrapping its cold fingers around her heart. She could not feel him touching her.

"You can tell me what they did to you, Tar. I have been here before, too. I will understand."

She shook her head, slumping back against the wall. "Please, do not ask. Do not ever ask. Whatever happens, please understand I am only trying to protect you." She slid to the floor, her form feeling twice as heavy as usual. She pressed her hands over her face, whispering, "I am only trying to protect you."

He settled himself beside her, and to her surprise, he did not press her for more. He gently patted his leg. "You must be exhausted. Rest on me, Tar. I will keep you safe. For tonight, rely on me. You will need any sleep you can get."

Reluctantly, she lay her head down on his leg. He began to absently stroke her hair, and though she thought she should hate it, she did not want him to stop. She closed her eyes, all her protests dying on her lips. Yes, the air here was heavy with nightmares, but perhaps they would be warded off by Ace's tender aura. At any rate, she did need the sleep. Harper would most likely come again for her tomorrow, to make her fight or work or something worse, and Taryn needed to be ready. She needed to be ready so that she could protect Ace.

※

Taryn blinked, disoriented for a few moments. Her mouth tasted coppery, and it took her a second to recognize it. Blood. She tried to press herself up, only to discover herself pinned, her arms bent at the elbows, wrists tied down on either side of her head. Her legs were similarly pinned, and her head was somehow clamped still, immobilized by whatever held her down. She stopped struggling, panting, lying on her stomach and listening for any clues to what was going on.

"I told you to stay in your room," a familiar man's voice said angrily. "You must not interrupt me when I am working." Taryn's heart caught in her throat. Erikkson! He was here, in the room. She would recognize his voice anywhere. But what was he working on? Why couldn't she move?

"Please, don't do this, Master Erikkson. She did not mean any harm. It was my fault," another voice pleaded. This one was younger, yes, and *oh* so innocent, but Taryn recognized the New York accent, softened by her years living in England, not yet hardened on the dark streets of the American underworld. Petrichor.

"You were *both* responsible for Henry's death," Erikkson

answered, voice hard. "I expect more from you both, and particularly *you*, Petrichor. You are sixteen. You know better. And your trauma at the hands of the Black Castle is no excuse."

Feet pounded, and Taryn sensed a figure draw near, a hand touching her arm. "So punish me, not her!"

"Sedition does not understand the world's opinion of her. This is the best way for her to understand why the war is necessary."

"No, it's not! She needs more time here, more training—"

"More training without proper ideology behind it will only make her more deadly." Erikkson's voice was cold as ice. "Now get out of my way, Petrichor."

"She's just a kid!"

"No. She is a weapon. She is a danger to herself and to everyone else here. Do you think this does not hurt me more than it hurts you? She is my daughter."

"We're not your children!" Petrichor screamed. "We're science experiments!"

"Yes. Now, out of my way." He said it so quietly, so coldly. The words were like a knife in Taryn's chest. She tried to fight the restraints, tried to beg for mercy, but her limbs were heavier than lead weights, and barely a whimper escaped her lips.

"Please," Petrichor begged, but it was obvious that she'd already lost the argument. Taryn felt fingers brush her hair away from the plate in the back of her head, heard the click of the panel opening. Her heart stopped. She tried to scream, but her throat would make no sound.

Something bright white flashed behind her eyes, and pain flooded from the back of her head, searing hot. She screamed silently. Her stomach lurched, and she thought she might be sick. The pain and the light seemed to go on and on, endlessly repeating, washing waves of hot and cold over her body.

And then, all at once, darkness took over, enclosing her mind in welcome relief, welcome numbness.

Welcome forgetfulness.

⁂

"Taryn!"

She snapped her blades open before her eyes focused, the pain and the terror following her into wakefulness.

"Taryn!"

She blinked, staring at Ace, who had scrambled away from her. Shame washed over her. What had she done?

"You were having a nightmare. It is all right now. You are safe." He held out his hands, palms out as if to calm her.

She was anything but safe, but she closed her shoulder blades, forcing her frantic breathing to slow. Unlike most nightmares, this one had followed her into consciousness, every word as vivid as it had been as she dreamed it. She rubbed her face in her hands, silently considering the dream.

It had felt real. Every word, every emotion, even the pain all felt so real. And though she did not want to believe it, she suspected it was a new memory bubbling to the surface. Things she had never thought she would remember, now coming back to her. But if she was right, and it *was* a memory, it meant she would have to decipher it. What had she done that could have made Erikkson so angry? She'd never known him to be callous, and the chill in his voice scared her to her core. Maybe Petrichor was right. Maybe it *was* better not to remember. Especially if there were tortures like that locked away behind her eyes.

"At least tell me you are all right," Ace murmured cautiously.

She raised her eyes, realizing he was still waiting for an answer. She shook her head. "Not all right, no, but here now. I am sorry. I—I think I am remembering."

"But that is good!"

She shrugged. "Perhaps." She twisted her hands in the folds of her skirt. "I am beginning to think perhaps it would be better if I do not recall."

"What do you mean?" he asked. In the dim torchlight, his face was obscured by sharp shadows, but she could still make out the familiar way his brow furrowed in concern.

Haltingly, she explained the dream-memory to him, repeating the words as best she could. He listened in earnest silence as she explained, leaning slightly forward in attentiveness. She stared down at her hands as she spoke, the dream playing over again behind her eyes. Every time she went over it in her head, she became more convinced that it was real. It had happened. At last, she finished her story and fell silent, chewing on her lip.

"Do you think that is when he wiped your memory?" Ace asked, dispelling the heavy silence which had settled on her shoulders. "You would have been, what, twelve? Thirteen?"

"Twelve." The word slipped from her lips, crawling down her shoulder before dropping to the floor. "The timeline is right. That may be it. But what did we do? And why was Petrichor trying to protect me? She has never liked me."

"So she says."

Taryn frowned at him. "You think she lied?"

"Would it be so out of character?"

Taryn shuddered, wondering at just how much of her life was based on a lie. She should have demanded a full explanation when Erikkson was alive.

Was. Alive.

She doubled over, the two words hurting as much as if she'd been stabbed. Tears, hot and unbidden, rolled down her cheeks. Tears she could no longer be sure he deserved, but still, here they were, coursing salt rivers down her cheeks. She hadn't cried since they had been captured by the Black Castle. She'd been beginning to think she was no longer capable of it. But now, here the tears were, hotter than fire and just as painful. She didn't want to cry for her creator, not now that she saw the full extent of what he was capable of, but the tears would not stop. How could someone who called himself her father have done such a thing? How could he take her memories and throw her out on the street in the name of love? Had she truly done something so unforgivable that it warranted leaving her to fend for herself in the world?

"Hey, hey, Tar, do not cry!" Ace took her in his arms, cradling her to his chest. "You will likely remember more, in time. It will become clear. It is all right not to have all the answers now."

She wanted to tell him she was not crying for her memory—no, that she had given up long ago—but the words refused to leave her lips. Instead, she buried her face in his shoulder, fighting the tears and losing. He stroked her hair, holding her tightly, rocking her a little until she calmed again.

"You should try to get back to sleep," he murmured. "You were not asleep long."

She shook her head. "I do not think I can sleep more tonight. Besides, you need to sleep as much as I do. You should try, and I will keep watch for a while."

He held her at arm's length, studying her with intense blue eyes. Taryn's breath caught in her throat. She had the sense he could see right through her.

"What?"

"You are so strong."

A cold smile twisted her mouth. "I am what I must be. I am what Erikkson made me. I do not feel strong."

"You are," he murmured, squeezing her shoulder.

"Before this is over, you may wish I was weaker."

"What do you mean by that?"

She shrugged his hands from her shoulders. "Sometimes strength is merely stubbornness, and here, stubbornness is a weakness. They punish stubbornness." She stood, crossing her arms over her stomach, restlessly pacing the length of their small cell. Somewhere far off, someone screamed. Taryn grimaced, grinding her teeth together.

"Gor, Tar, your dress—"

She froze. Her eyes widened and she reached hesitant fingers to the tattered remains of the back of her dress. "What am I going to say to explain this?"

Ace swayed to his feet, one hand pressed to his ribs. "Tell them it is a malfunction."

"They will see through that lie."

"Then I do not know, Taryn. No matter what you say, they will know your blades are operational from those tears."

She rubbed her hands over her face. "I will think of something. I just—give me a minute to think."

Their cell fell quiet enough for her to hear his labored breathing, every breath rasping into his lungs. She couldn't form a coherent thought, couldn't find the right solution to her problem. "I suppose I must tell the truth," she sighed. She twisted her hands together. "Harper will see through any lie I try to feed her. So, I must tell the truth."

"Tar, they will kill you!"

"No, I do not think so. I am worth too much to them alive. They may not allow me to keep my blades, but as long as I do not reveal the weapons I am hiding in my arm, I can still keep them..." Taryn chewed her lip. "I can endure whatever they throw at me."

"Please, there must be some other way—"

He choked on the word and broke down, another fit of coughing overtaking him. His cough sounded tight and painful, a dry, hacking thing rattling in his chest. Taryn watched him in concern and alarm until the fit passed, unable to forget his cruel grafts, the way the metal tore him apart and stitched him back together as a child might do with a stuffed toy. Suspicion over the cause of this new cough rose in her mind. Could his graft have something to do with it?

"That sounds as if it is getting worse," she said quietly when the fit was over.

"It is only a cough."

"I have heard consumptive coughs that sounded better than that one."

He tried to smile, but with most of the color drained from his face, it looked pained and sickly.

"I just need some rest, that is all. Come, sit by me. We shall see if this night may yield any more rest to either of us."

Reluctantly, she followed him to the back wall of the cell and settled herself beside him. He closed his eyes, but she kept hers open, afraid to close them. Too many nightmare images danced behind her eyes—those she'd killed, those she'd failed to save. Instead of sleeping, she fiddled with her prosthetic, calibrating response times, ensuring all the hidden hatches worked. Her stomach ached, empty as it was, but she shut it out. Hunger was simply another form of weakness, and she could not afford any more of that. Not when the young man sleeping fitfully beside her was the biggest weakness she'd ever allowed herself to have.

CHAPTER TWENTY-ONE

Harper appeared at the door to their cell in the morning with three men. One Taryn recognized as Jin, the man who'd cut her hair the night before, but the other two were unfamiliar to her, a big man with thinning hair and a crooked nose, and a younger man the approximate size of a brick wall. She lifted herself slowly to her feet, exhausted muscles protesting. Ace rose with her, his eyes fixed on the strangers. Taryn recognized fear and loathing beneath his stony expression.

"Come on, you two," Harper called, unlocking the cell door with an iron skeleton key—the perfect size and shape to act as a weapon, Taryn knew, if she could just get ahold of one. "A few hours' quiet work, and we will reward you with a meal."

Taryn's stomach rumbled, as if in response to Harper's mention of food. It had been well over a day since she or Ace had eaten anything, and a few hours' loyalty did not sound like so bad a bargain...

"Your promise, Tar," Ace whispered, hooking his pinky finger around hers.

She nodded, almost imperceptibly. Obedience now. Seditiousness later, when she and Ace were returned to the cell and could speak freely. She told herself it was not betraying Erikkson if she still maintained her rebellion with Ace, if she was privately fighting to break free.

"I do not have all day." Harper tapped one foot impatiently against the stone floor, the sound echoing through the dungeon.

Together, they walked to the door, where they were both cuffed and led out. The balding man caught Ace's jaw in his hand, turning his face, examining him as an equestrian examines a horse for sale.

"You have lost weight, 745," he said, an almost disgusted edge in his voice.

Taryn had not noticed it until this moment, but Ace *was* indeed more gaunt than he had been when she first met him. He retained a strong, powerful frame, so it was hardly noticeable, save for in the corners of his eyes, the contours of his cheekbones, the hollow at the base of his throat.

"I am as strong as ever," Ace answered coldly, but Taryn did not miss the way he recoiled from the man.

The balding man grinned. "We shall see."

He pushed Ace toward the stairs, and Taryn made to follow them, only to find her manacles caught by Harper. "Ah. We have a different task for you."

Taryn watched Ace disappear with the two strangers, his name catching as a whimper in her throat. If she'd known they were to be separated, she would have said something more to him, some parting words he could hold on to— Suddenly, the moment they tore Emmett away from her so long ago, before they blinded him, flashed behind her eyes. She rounded on Harper.

"I swear, if you do anything to harm him, I shall ensure Lord Bellham does not earn a single penny on my sale."

The threat was the strongest she knew to make. Not harm

to Harper, but to herself, to the one thing that mattered in this place: the profit.

"Bravely spoken," Harper droned, her eyes half-lidded behind her spectacles, almost bored. "But hardly necessary. We are not stupid enough to throw away our leverage over you. You are too valuable."

She smiled then, the expression never touching her eyes, and reached out, stroking Taryn's cropped hair. Taryn jerked backward, as a frightened cat might when threatened.

"Now, you are going to show Jin and I *all* the modifications Lord Erikkson made to your body, starting with your shoulder blades, or you may go hungry until you do."

Taryn bowed her head, holding her breath as she considered how much she could show Harper without giving up every advantage—how much she could bear to lose. She considered remaining silent, allowing the forced fast to continue, but she knew Harper planned to take her back to the arena and she needed her strength if she was to win again. And she had to win. That was not a question. If she showed her blades, and the more obvious changes to her clockwork arm, perhaps that would be enough. Perhaps that would convince Harper not to dig deeper. Finally, she shifted her thumb, triggering her blades. They snapped open, and Harper exclaimed wordlessly in surprise and delight.

"Oh, these *are* exquisite!" She stepped behind Taryn, fingering the metal blades with one gloved hand. Taryn held herself stock-still, every muscle taut to the point of trembling, waiting for Harper to declare such a graft was too dangerous to be allowed. "How could you hide these from me, 743?" she questioned, her voice high and patronizing. "Erikkson truly broke the mold when he made you."

The words felt like knives against Taryn's skin, and her arms shook as she held herself back. The manacles would pose some trouble, of course, but if she could bring Harper down, she could steal the keys... She swallowed her anger. Not yet. Not. Yet.

"What other little secrets are you hiding?" Harper questioned. She tapped Taryn's prosthetic arm. "I notice he gave you a new arm. Are you hiding anything there?"

Hesitation flickered like a shadow over Taryn's face, and then she ducked her head. She lifted her manacled hands and clenched her left fist. The metal spikes slid from her knuckles with the rasp of steel on steel. A smirk crossed Harper's face. "Cute, but hardly what I was hoping for."

Taryn allowed her hands to drop to her waist. Her face fell. The expressions were not for herself, though, but for Harper. The more hesitation she displayed, the more likely Harper was to believe she'd given up all her secrets. "That is all I have," Taryn muttered.

Harper studied her intently for a few long breaths, as if she could *see* whether Taryn had lied. At last, she sighed. "Well, what he left us in those blades is enough for me." She nodded to Jin, who set one palm on Taryn's shoulder. She allowed her blades to snap closed. "I should like to get a better look at those blades under the lights of my lab. I think you know the way by now, 743. Lead on."

Taryn could not breathe. Surely, *surely* this was as good a time as any to fight back? But something inside her told her to wait, to endure. Whatever Harper had planned, it could not be so bad as what she'd already endured. It was a lie, but she nursed it beneath her tongue as a child sucks a piece of hard sugar candy as they took the long trek to Harper's lab. She would survive. She had to.

Harper's silent lab assistants strapped Taryn face down to that cold metal table beneath the bright arc lamps. The table smelled of formaldehyde, iron, and blood, the combination so strong it caused Taryn's eyes to water. She'd kept her promise, though, and remained silent as they pinned her down like a beetle on the board of some entomologist's collection. She held on to her promise like it was the last fraying rope keeping her from tumbling into a bottomless chasm, afraid if she lost her tenuous hold, she would lose all control, would *kill* and *kill* until they destroyed her. She feared the monster inside herself as much as she feared the punishment to follow.

"743, open your blades for me," Harper ordered, her voice dull and far away. Something in the room kept Taryn's head buzzing distantly, and whether it was the formaldehyde-soaked metal pressed against her cheek or the sheer terror of being here once more, her mind refused to focus.

Taryn must have hesitated a moment too long, because Harper began to speak in that unpleasant, patronizing tone she used when trying to talk Taryn into doing something.

"Now, I am not going to do anything terrible. I am excited to see these blades in action in the arena. For now, I just want to examine the mechanism."

Taryn knew the woman was lying to her. Lying through her teeth, by the sound of it. She held her breath, refusing silently. That frayed promise slipped a little further in her abraded fingers.

"The sooner you cooperate, 743, the sooner this shall be over, and you can eat."

She held the tension, the thrill of refusal for a single second longer, and then her body relaxed. She flicked her blades open. A ripple of mutters rattled through the lab assistants at the sight of her gleaming shoulder blades, fanned out like deadly fairy wings. Taryn sensed Harper running her fingers over the blades, a soft exclamation of—what? Excitement? Surprise? It was the sound a person makes over a gift of exquisite jewelry, a sound retained for objects and possessions, not living things. Not until now.

"Shall I get some ether?" a new voice interrupted.

"No need. This is an exploratory procedure, not an invasive one. Take notes. I want to be sure I reassemble these properly."

Reassemble? Taryn felt sick, terror welling in her stomach and working its way into her chest. A cold sweat broke out across her forehead down the back of her neck. She could not breathe for the chemical smells burning the back of her throat, her lungs. Her limbs would not obey her.

And then—though she knew it was not possible, though she knew Harper worked on metal, not flesh—pain flared through her back, up her spine, to the base of her skull. She squeezed her eyes closed, mouth open in a silent scream. She refused to allow herself to cry out.

"We're not children! We're science experiments!"

Petrichor's voice stabbed through the pain, so real Taryn half expected to open her eyes and see the Clockwork Assassin in the room with her.

But no, it was Taryn's fragmented memories haunting her—*teasing* her—as Harper tore her apart. She squeezed her eyes shut, willing her mind to stop, to ignore the firing of frayed neurons and just focus on survival. Just focus on her next breath.

"She's just a kid!"

Bile rose in Taryn's throat as the ugly memory played out behind her eyes, every word as vivid as if Harper and her assistants were chanting them as they worked. The phantom pain in her shoulders ebbed to a dull ache, but now, over her auditory hallucinations, she could hear the rasp of metal on metal as they disassembled her. Her right hand curled into a white-knuckled fist, her nails drawing blood in crimson half-moons on her palm. A whimper of terror escaped her throat, though she barely heard it over Petrichor and Erikkson's shouting match.

A leering face appeared in her mind's eye, a boy of perhaps fifteen, his nose bleeding, an angry light in his eyes.

No—No!

The memory took hold, and she lost all awareness of the world around her.

She was lying on her back on the hard stone floor of the training room.

The boy—Henry, she knew, though she didn't know how she knew it—had her pinned, one metal hand wrapped around her throat.

The other soldiers looked on, some of them calling out encouragements.

"Fight back!"

"Get him!"

"Go on, Sedition!"

"Bash his head in!"

Taryn struggled to get herself out from under the bigger boy, fighting with every cell in her body, but she could not breathe, and he was so much bigger than she...

"That is enough, Henry. Let her up. You have won." Seraphim's familiar, peacemaking voice crept through the jeers.

Henry's eyes flashed. "She has made a fool of me for the last time."

Taryn narrowed her eyes, raising one heavy hand, and tapped three times in the center of Henry's forehead, between his eyes.

"What—"

Movement. A flurry of motion. The ugly sound of flesh and bone crunching, and then Taryn was free, rolling upright, panting as her vision returned. At her feet, Henry lay, neck broken. Petrichor knelt with one hand still gripping his shoulder.

Horror flooded Taryn—what little of Taryn consciously watched this new nightmare unfold—but the dream Taryn grinned, proudly meeting the eyes of the onlookers.

"*I* am Sedition, and I am in charge! If any of you dare to defy me, I shall allow Petrichor to destroy you! Have I made myself clear?"

CHAPTER TWENTY-TWO

The dungeon was so cold and lonely without her.

The thought flitted through Ace's mind as he waited for their captors to bring his promised meal—they were certainly taking their time with it—after his hours of obedient labor. It had not been difficult, performing the simple, mindless tasks, though he'd had to detach his mind from the orders to keep himself from fighting them. Taryn and her army had influenced him more than he'd thought, and he saw the injustice in the way he was treated more than he ever had before. He held on to Taryn's sweet voice, the promise of seeing her again at the end of this ordeal. And that was enough.

Now, he paced the length of their cell, shivering a little, unable to settle in spite of his exhaustion and hunger. He worried about her every second they were apart, and as the minutes dragged into hours, he grew more and more anxious that something had happened to her, that their brief exchange that morning would turn out to be their last, and he could not go back and say all he wanted—needed—to say.

He knew their captors treated her poorly. He was not stupid, nor was he blind. He saw the way she tensed when

Harper took her from the cell, felt the way she shuddered at his touch when she did not realize it was he who touched her. She had nightmares, too, and though some of those dreams came from her battles, her training, he knew some of them came from the atmosphere all around them. The air of the Black Castle's dungeons hung heavy with nightmares, and all his sympathy and protectiveness could do nothing to dispel that miasma.

He heard footsteps approaching and eagerly raced to the bars, hoping to see her face, catch a glimpse of her copper hair, even cropped short as it was now. Hoping he would not be fooled by the footsteps of some other poor biomaton headed to a cell deeper in the dungeon, as he had been three times already.

A pair of laboratory assistants came into view, half carrying a slim figure between them. Ace caught sight of red hair, and his stomach tied itself into knots. He gripped the bars, unable to stop the angry, panicked words as they tumbled from his lips.

"What have you done to her?"

"Stand against the back wall, 745. We shall not open this door until you do."

Ace glowered, but he did as he was told, icy dread clamped around his heart like an iron fist.

Please be all right, Tar. Oh god, let her be all right.

He did not like the way her head lolled to the side, her ankles twisting as the lab assistants held her up. One young man opened the cell door, and the two shoved Taryn forward. She managed two feeble steps before collapsing. Even in the dim light, Ace could see she was shaking.

He lunged forward as the door slammed shut. "What did you *do*?"

"She will recover. Someone will be by to bring your supper soon."

"You tell Harper—" Ace began, but the assistants did not so much as pay him a second glance. He swallowed his angry words and dropped to his knees beside Taryn, muttering meaningless words of apology. He hesitated even to touch her, hands hovering over her shoulders for fear he would hurt her. She had her back to him, and the back of her dress had been cut open in a wide inverted triangle, creating a space where her blades were easily accessible. The pale, freckled skin across her shoulders and back was streaked with ugly, red scars, but these were old and he doubted they still pained her. As far as Ace could see, she was not hurt, and yet, she trembled, lying there, her hands gripped in tight fists near her face. Her breath came in brief, choked little gasps.

"Taryn?" he whispered. "Oh, Tar, what have they done to you?"

Her eyes stared blankly at nothing. She did not seem to hear him.

Oh so carefully, he reached out and brushed her hair from her face, that knot of worry in his stomach becoming an inoperable snarl of anxiety. "Please, Tar. You are safe now. I am here. I will not allow them to take you again."

It was not true, and he felt the lie like a bullet between his teeth. If they came back for her, what could he do but obey? He was as much a prisoner as she, and no one would listen to his protests. Still, he repeated the lie, for her, stroking her hair, trying desperately to bring her back to him. "I will not allow them to harm you anymore."

"Do not make promises you cannot keep," she muttered at last, each word slurred and slow, all her old Cockney accent leaking through at the edges.

"I thought I had lost you for good!" he exclaimed, bowing over her and breathing in her scent. She smelled like nothing he'd ever smelled before—like wind over the heath and cedar oil and thyme. Even at her filthiest, her most unpresentable, Ace still thought she smelled *good*. And now, though he could smell blood and formaldehyde mixed with the perfume of her skin, she smelled better than ever.

She did not move, did not blink. Her breathing had evened out a little but remained far too shallow.

"I—" she began, and then stopped, a small, childlike sob escaping her.

He straightened up, daring to set one hand on her shoulder.

"Tar? What is it? What did they do to you?"

She pressed her knuckles to her teeth, shaking her head, until the sobs appeared to pass. Finally, she lifted her hand. "Help me sit up."

He lifted her to a sitting position, careful not to hurt her. She turned to face him, her eyes red-rimmed, her cropped hair falling over them. He wanted to ask again, but he could see she was working up the courage to explain, and he closed his mouth. He could wait until she was ready.

"Harper forced me to show her my blades." She did not look at him, instead staring at her hands. "But it was not enough for her to know. She had to take me apart to see how I worked."

Ace's blood boiled in his veins. He had never been quick-tempered, save for the odd occasion when stress and exhaustion shortened his fuse, but now, Taryn's few words were all it took to ignite a wrath he had not known he contained. He swore.

"I will kill her myself. It is not right how they treat you! No one should be made to endure the tortures they put you through!"

She reached pacifying hands out to him. "Let us just be thankful I survived, Ace. I can endure, if we are still fighting together to escape."

He met her eyes, those emerald-green irises with more facets than the costliest jewel. He reached out and caressed her cheek with his palm. "I will not allow them to torture you like that again, Taryn. I swear."

She smiled sadly and turned away. "I believe Harper satisfied her curiosity. I do not think I shall have to endure that again."

"But you shall be forced to endure other tortures," he pressed, taking her chin in his hand and turning her face toward him once again. "Tar, we must find a way to escape this place."

Again, her eyes met his, and a sort of strange, pleading look came into them. "They are keeping us apart and weak. If there is a way out I cannot see it. Even if we try to fight—" She shook her head, pressed cold white fingers against her temples. "There are so many of them, Ace, and we are only two. But every moment I hold back is harder than the moment before. I am going to break eventually. It is in my programming to fight back. And I do not want to think what will happen to you when I do."

"Then we fight together!" A cold horror clamped around his chest, making it difficult to breathe.

She turned away and tried to rise, but her legs buckled, and she collapsed. A little cry of pain escaped her as she fell. He reached out to her, but stopped just short of touching her as she held up her hands.

"I am all right," she gasped. She shifted, folding her legs more comfortably beneath her.

"How much did Dr. Harper hurt you?" he whispered. He couldn't see her expression, the flickering torches outside their cell casting long, undulating shadows, turning the familiar into the monstrous.

"Not nearly so much as she hurt you."

He swallowed hard, at a loss for words, just inches away from the girl he loved more than anything in the world, unable to comfort her. He had no words to make their predicament better, nothing he could do to encourage her. All his pretty, optimistic lies died on his tongue. Unspoken. Unheard. But

Taryn wanted real hope. So, he did the best he could with the fragments he had left.

"Seraphim and Petrichor are still out there somewhere. They will not give up the fight."

"Petrichor cares for nothing but herself—" Taryn scoffed, and then stopped, a strange, far-off look coming over her. "No, that is not entirely true. At least, it has not always been true."

"Did you remember more?"

"Aye. But it is not nice."

"I do not care. Tell me anyways."

"I—I remember what we did—what I did that Master Erikkson found so appalling. A boy I was sparring with beat me, fairly. He would not let me up, though, when the match was over. And—and I made some signal to Petrichor—and she killed him." She explained haltingly, with little emotion. "I think she and I were close, once. Close enough for her to try to take the punishment in my place. Close enough for her to run away and close herself off after Erikkson took my memories."

Ace's mind reeled at the new information. He tried to picture Taryn killing someone at just twelve years old. He knew that this Sedition role was something she'd been training for her entire life, but still...

He could not imagine the kind of mental and physical torture someone had to inflict to drive a child to such violent actions. It only made him remember the child he'd seen ever so briefly in her eyes, so long ago. The child that had never been allowed to be a child. And Petrichor—if Petrichor had been there, had run away shortly after—depending on the time of year, Ace knew it had only been a matter of weeks before she killed his parents. This boy Taryn ordered her to kill might have been her first taste of blood.

"I am sorry you had to go through all that," he said slowly.

"No need to be sorry. I remembered. It only makes me understand Petrichor a little better, and how she said Elmhurst was a hell." She rubbed her face in her hands. "I need to sleep now, Ace. I have had perhaps three or four hours of sleep today and I know I shall need all I can get. Will you wake me if our friend Dr. Harper returns?"

"You may lie on my leg again, if you like."

She hesitated, and his heart rose a half measure in his chest, but then she shook her head. "If you do not mind, I will settle beside you. That will do for me."

He nodded, his heart falling. That would do for him, too. He watched her settle down on her side on the damp stone floor, her arm tucked under her head like a makeshift pillow. She was so determined they not cross the boundaries of friendship, and the trouble was, he knew she was right. They might lose one another at any moment in this place. She might be taken from the cell in an hour, and he would never see her again. Their affection for each other would only be a weapon turned on them. But still, when he looked at her, his heart ached with desire for what he could never have: her in his arms, free from their chains, in a world where they could both simply *be*.

THE MAN HE'D SEEN WITH HARPER CAME LATE THAT evening for Taryn. She'd slept through most of the afternoon, missing the tasteless gruel brought in lieu of a meal. Ace saved it aside for her, in case she woke hungry, but when he shook her shoulder, he knew he might as well have eaten it himself. Her face had a pale, grayish tinge, and there were deep shadows beneath her eyes. He knew at once she'd been plagued with nightmares.

"Someone is here for you," he murmured. "I am sorry."

She nodded without a word and offered him her hand. With some effort, Ace raised her to her feet. He grimaced at the pain across the right side of his body, but did not vocalize his discomfort. What mattered was that Taryn would be all right.

He walked with her to the door, and there the man shook his head. "I only need 743."

Ace ground his teeth together. Taryn squeezed his wrist tenderly.

"I will be all right," she murmured.

And he had no choice but to back away as the man took Taryn away again. Ace shut his eyes. Something weighed on him this time, as nothing had before, and he realized slowly that he feared losing her. He did not think she would be coming back.

Ace knelt on the damp stone floor, bowed his head, and began to pray.

CHAPTER TWENTY-THREE

Taryn flexed her fists, opening and closing her blades to ensure they were working properly. The now-familiar—though still just as detested—burlesque costume hugged her frame, and Jin's blue paint streaked down the right side of her face like Pictish war paint. Rather than allow her to approach the arena as they had last night, Jin and Harper had forced Taryn into a dark, narrow box. It stank of sweat and unwashed bodies, though she was quite alone, and through the cheers of the crowd for the fight in progress, Taryn could hear movement on either side of her: growls, breathing, and loud bangs against the metal walls. Someone—or something—on the other side of that narrow partition restlessly paced, ready for a fight.

Taryn knew how he or she felt. She could not breathe in the narrow space, and the longer she remained in the claustrophobic darkness, the more the violence built up inside her like a volcano, more unstoppable with every moment she held it inside.

A great cheer went up outside, and Taryn pressed her hands over her ears, the sounds bringing back ugly memories of the arena the night before. How much longer could she do this?

How many biomatons could she kill and still tell herself it was noble because she did it for Ace's sake? She didn't know. The longer she dwelled on questions of morality and consequence, the more she realized one thing: she was already guilty. Her hands were soaked with blood. And none of that mattered now, in this moment, with the crowd cheering outside and her blood pounding in her ears. All that mattered now was survival. All that mattered now was the next handful of minutes and the promise that if she performed, she would see Ace again at the end of it.

The crowd at last died down. Taryn bounced on her toes, eager to get this whole ugly ordeal over with. She could hear someone speaking, indistinctly, but the voice was not near enough for her to make out the words. She rolled her shoulders, shaking the anxious tremors from her limbs. This was what she was built for, what she'd trained for. She *could* win. She *would* win.

The door of her holding cell suddenly slid open, and Taryn stumbled forward, blinded for a moment by the bright lanterns. She crouched, her fingers brushing the stone beneath her feet, coated with a thick layer of coarse sand, presumably to absorb any blood the combatants spilled. Her dazzled eyes began to adjust, and she took in the scene in front of her with the speed she'd been trained for. She was perhaps ten feet from her opponent, who stood just as blind on the other side of the arena. He was slim, with a wiry build that reminded her of Emmett. He had metal spikes embedded in his clockwork arm. Neither biomaton held a weapon, and Taryn's throat closed as she realized she *was* the weapon. And so was this biomaton she faced, now studying her as carefully as she studied him.

This time, Taryn did not try to talk her opponent down. This time, all she cared for was her own survival, her own success.

The two biomatons prowled closer to one another, circling

each other, waiting for the other to make the first move. The crowd began to grow restless. They had come to see blood, and they were impatient for the fight to start. Someone in the crowd threw a pebble, which struck Taryn's opponent in the temple. He snarled, snapping into action with the speed and fluidity of a tiger, lunging toward Taryn.

It was the exact move she'd anticipated. She ducked under his outstretched arms, at the same time sweeping his feet out from under him. He fell, skidding in the sand, and she turned, ready to land a few blows to keep him down.

She froze. It seemed she was not the only one with hidden weapons—the man's spine was lined with more of those metal spikes. Taryn swore and kicked at his ribs, but her momentary advantage had already slipped through her fingers. He rolled away, and the next moment, she hit the ground on her back, gasping for breath.

A knee drove into her stomach. Taryn growled, driving her metal fist, spikes and all, into her opponent's jaw. She *had* to get up, had to get her blades—

She somersaulted out of the way, landing on her feet, flicking her blades open. A gasp came from the crowd. Taryn's vision was crimson at the edges, and she knew if she did not end this soon, she would lose control. *Breathe,* she told herself. *Control yourself.* Her opponent had regained his footing, blood seeping from a cut in his lip. His dark eyes flared with intense hatred. Taryn smiled, shrugging her shoulders so her blades caught the light, all of Sedition's powerful confidence exuding from her pores. Her cockiness unnerved him, which had been her goal. She had the advantage now.

She raced toward him, blades flashing, every step of the specialized martial arts style Erikkson had created for her returning. She allowed her conscious brain to shut down, her training taking over, and it was like Erikkson was right there with her, whispering the movements in her ear.

The crowd roared with the sight of blood and her fancy fighting style. It only took a few well-placed strikes, once she broke through her opponent's defenses. A sliced tendon. A well-placed cut, deep enough to destroy some of the vital workings of his clockwork arm. She disabled him but did not kill him, raising her head to the crowd, panting.

She found Dr. Harper sitting in the front row and locked eyes with her, waiting for orders. Harper scowled, drawing one finger across her throat. Taryn raised an eyebrow. She glanced down at the biomaton at her feet, flickers of memory flashing across the backs of her eyes.

Petrichor killing Henry.

Taryn killing Jack.

Erikkson's anger.

She bent and did what she had to do, ashamed of what she'd become. Ashamed that Harper could manipulate her so easily.

※

"You know how this arrangement works," Harper hissed, striking Taryn on the back of the head. Taryn grimaced, a growl of pain escaping her as Harper's blow struck a bruise. "So why did you hesitate?"

"I incapacitated him," Taryn muttered. "I did not want to kill him."

"Those guests came to see blood. You will give them blood, 743, or I will make sure 745 never sees daylight again."

Taryn's jaw clenched at the double meaning of the threat. Had it not been for Erikkson's skill with biomechanicks, Emmett would never have seen daylight again, either, thanks to Harper's machinations. Taryn bowed her head.

"I understand."

"Good." Harper had not bothered to handcuff Taryn after

the fight, only took her into the hall beyond the arena to lecture her.

"Are we done here?" Taryn growled. She was grimy, cold, and exhausted. Her mind hung on the edge of hallucination, and she could not recall her last meal. She did not think she could endure much more.

"Not quite. There are a few patrons interested in meeting you. I agreed," Harper sneered. "It will increase interest in your auction."

Taryn shuddered. "I do not think parading me in front of a bunch of leering aristocrats is a good idea right now."

"Excuse me? Did I just hear you refuse?"

Taryn closed her eyes and sighed. She forced herself to picture Ace. He was waiting for her. She'd made him a promise. "No, madam."

"I thought not." Harper steered Taryn down the hall by the back of the neck, her sharp nails digging into the hollows above Taryn's collarbones. She curled her shoulders up, trying to relieve the pain.

Harper did not take them far. She pressed a door open, shoving Taryn into a room with half a dozen high-class men inside, between the ages of thirty and sixty, if Taryn had to guess. One or two were smoking pipes, and the acrid smell of tobacco smoke filled the room.

"Good evening, gentlemen. I brought the biomaton, as you requested. You are welcome to look, and ask any questions you like, but I must remind you not to touch her. As you saw tonight, she is dangerous. But of course, what else is to be expected from an Erikkson?"

Harper smiled cruelly at this, as if she'd made a clever joke. Taryn glanced around the room, noting four of the burly biomatons Lord Bellham used as enforcers standing at the corners of the room. She did not know if they were there for the aristocrats' benefit or her own. She held her head high, the frank stares of the men no longer fazing her. She'd already faced a biomaton who wanted to kill her tonight. Earlier today, Harper tore her apart to see what made her tick, then put her back together. She could withstand a half dozen leering pairs of eyes without even blinking.

"Can we see the blades again?" one young man asked. He had a hawkish face and dressed foppishly, his hair long about his shoulders, his cheeks dabbed with the faintest touch of rouge. Taryn had seen men like him before; men with no backbone, who focused too much on fashion or gossip to be of any use to society. She instantly detested him but gave him a coy grin and snapped the weapons open. She turned, allowing her blades to catch the light.

"Shall I take a turn about the room so you can all get a good look?" she asked, a note of contempt barely masked in her voice.

"Do," Harper ordered. She gave Taryn a deep scowl to show she did not approve of her sarcasm. Taryn smiled cooly at Harper in response. She turned, weaving in and out of the men watching her, aware of the attention on her. Aware she could destroy them all if she chose.

As she passed by a young man, a horrible shock of electricity raced down her spine. She had to circle him to reassure herself he was *not* Royal. But no, this man had a lean, cruel look about him, a face that revealed little rather than everything, eyes the wrong shade of brown. This was Mr. Cody, the man who'd wanted to purchase her the last time she was here, the man who looked so much like Royal it hurt and yet could not be more different from the boy who'd saved her from the streets.

Cody smiled, seeing her recognition. "Hello again, biomaton. What is it they are calling you now? Sedition? I had hoped we would meet again."

Taryn's smile dripped venom. "I hoped so as well, sir. I wanted you to meet my blades."

She leaped a single step forward, and he stumbled back, his face white, his look of terror so pathetic Taryn could not help the cruel laugh that escaped her.

"743," Harper growled in warning. "Enough."

Taryn closed her blades, padding obediently back to Harper's side, though the crimson hatred that had buzzed at the back of her skull in the arena had returned, swelling to cover more and more of her vision. She did not know how much longer she could hold herself back. She was built to rebel at all costs, and her struggle to keep her mind in check was becoming more and more difficult. She locked eyes with Harper. "Are we done here?"

"What an insolent little thing. Can you not control her, Dr. Harper? If she were mine, I would cut out her tongue for speaking so."

Taryn rounded on the man, her blades snapping open. "You would never get close enough."

"743," Harper warned again.

But Taryn was not listening. Her vision had gone red, and her limbs moved of their own accord. She had had enough of their dehumanization. She was sick and tired of being treated like an object.

"Let me explain something, since you seem too ignorant to understand on your own," she hissed. "I am *just* as human as any of you. And the longer you treat biomatons this way, the longer you oppress people unlucky enough to need clockwork prosthetics, the greater your reckoning shall be."

Mr. Cody scoffed. "You still think you are human, girl? You are a machine."

"*I* am your reckoning. And you have all been found wanting."

Her vision blinked out. At least, that was all she could remember when she recalled the event over and over in her mind afterward. She simply blacked out and came to seconds or minutes later to find blood on her hands, bodies scattered across the floor. She killed two of them before the guards reached her, and that meant two fewer cruel men roamed the earth.

And then something struck her hard enough across the back of the head to fill her vision with bright stars. She blinked, and she was on the ground, cold chains wrapped around her wrists.

She blinked, and she was being dragged backward down a dark stone hallway.

She blinked, and Harper was leaning over her. The woman spoke, but the words were garbled.

She blinked.

She blinked.

She lay on her back in the dark, listening to water drip nearby. She shivered. Her head ached. She sat up, groaning, waiting for her eyes to adjust.

Waiting. Waiting.

There was no light for her eyes to adjust to. She sat in utter darkness, listening to her own breathing echo against invisible walls.

"Ace?" she whispered tentatively.

No answer presented itself. She held her breath, waiting to hear that tell-tale rasp of his breathing.

All she could hear was the drip of water on stone, the thunder of her heart in her ears. She was utterly, horribly alone.

"Oh, god," she breathed aloud. "What have I done?"

CHAPTER TWENTY-FOUR

Ace worried when Taryn did not return.

He worried when the torches burned down, and still, she did not reappear. His prayers became increasingly frantic, until they became a silent stream of her name to God's ear. He knew many people believed biomatons had lost their souls, and their prayers were little more than empty supplications. Many believed no one was listening. Still, Ace prayed, holding on to the faith of his childhood, the last shred of humanity he had left. Faith, and his love for Taryn. A love that should have been impossible, but that nevertheless belonged to him alone.

In the early hours of the morning, a group led by Lord Bellham made their way through the dungeon, on their way to examine some unfortunate biomaton housed deeper in the cold darkness. Ace raced to the bars, tired as he was, rattling the door of the cell in his urgency.

"Where is Taryn? What have you done with her?"

Lord Bellham's lip curled in disgust. He said nothing, turning his eyes away and continued on his way.

Ace reached through the bars. "Please! I just want to know if she is all right!"

The men following Bellham passed him by without a second glance. Bellham muttered something about the boy being defective and that they were working on it. Ace slumped, pressing his face to the cold iron of his cage. Exhausted as he was, he found himself near to weeping.

"Are you asking about 743?" a young man's voice interrupted. Ace raised his head to discover a guard, about his own age, staring back at him. He had a kind, round face. Ace wondered how a face like that could exist in a place like this. He nodded, silently, afraid to speak in case this was some sort of cruel trap.

"She snapped, last night. I heard she killed two patrons, injured a few more..."

Ace's face drained of all its color, his olive skin going an ashen gray.

"No, she is all right," the guard said quickly. "This happens with the exotics. Lord Bellham has procedures for it. She has been put in deep freeze to cool off—" He paused, noting the puzzled expression in Ace's eyes. "Isolation. Solitary confinement. She will be released when she has calmed down."

Ace nodded, though his heart felt crushed in an icy fist. At least she was alive.

"Why are you telling me this?" he asked.

The guard looked sheepish, glancing away from Ace. He lifted his left hand to display a solitary silver band on his ring finger. "I have a wife. We have been married less than six months. And the way you asked about 743, well, it made me think of my Eliza, and how desperate I would be if I did not know where she was." He smirked. "I know it is a silly association, but I wanted to give you what I knew."

"Thank you. You have no idea what your kindness means to me." Ace offered his right hand—his clockwork hand—through the bars, intending to shake the guard's hand.

The young man paled at the sight of the prosthetic limb,

and he shook his head, backing away. "I have tarried too long already. I must go."

Without so much as a backward glance, he turned and raced after Bellham's group. Ace watched him go, surprised to realize he pitied the young man. His kind heart and frank, open demeanor would not last long in a job like this. It would be a matter of years, or months, until he was treating the biomatons with the same disdain the rest of the Black Castle had for them. Ace hoped he would find another job before that occurred, but he knew the prospect was grim. That kind guard would just be another casualty of an unjust system, built upon the dehumanization of biomatons. It was the first time Ace recognized the negative impact of the system on those who were not biomatons, and it hurt to realize the young men and women of Britain's great empire were suffering morally and spiritually, as well as physically, from this disease called the slave trade.

Ace began to pace the length of his cell, his thoughts returning to Taryn. Isolation. The guard had said isolation. Somehow, last night, as exhausted and broken as she was, she still had found the strength and opportunity to destroy a handful of the Black Castle's patrons. Part of Ace wanted to applaud her for it, for the vigilante justice she'd meted out on the very grounds of the single greatest proponent of the biomaton slave trade.

And yet—the rest of him worried over her. What would they do to her after such an outburst? He'd tried to get her to endure, to obey, just for a little while. But Erikkson had trained her to rebel at all costs, and that could be fatal here. What new tortures could they concoct to finally bring her to her knees? Ace hated his vivid imagination for painting the worst kinds of tortures across the walls of his cell. All he had wanted was to protect her from this kind of pain. And now, he was helpless. He could not even see her.

"Hang on, Tar," he murmured into the darkness. "We will find a way out of this mess. I swear we will find a way."

※

THE WAY OUT PRESENTED ITSELF ONE WEEK LATER, WHEN Ace found himself being washed, groomed, and dressed for auction. In all that time, he had not caught a single glimpse of Taryn, and the one or two times he caught the kind young guard alone (his name was Rufus Davenport), the boy informed him that she was still being held in isolation. Ace endured all the Black Castle threw at him in the hopes that he might see her again, but it never came to pass. He wanted to despair, but he would not allow himself to mourn her. He trusted he would see her again, despite everything.

After his toilette was completed, his wrists were chained at his waist, and Ace was led out to the courtyard of the Black Castle. Rufus showed him the way.

As they walked, Rufus spoke to Ace in a low, urgent voice. "I got you a few minutes alone in the wagon with her. It is not much, but it is all I could do. I wish you all the luck in the world. May wherever you two end up be better than this place."

Ace wanted to yell at the boy, tell him they were being driven to auction to be *sold,* and it would have been better for him to find them an extra few minutes with which they could escape, but all the words died on his lips. It was no use to lecture someone who did not even understand how he contributed to the ugliness of the world. Half a dozen wagons stood in the courtyard, black, boxy things similar to the prison wagons he'd seen a thousand times in London. Clearly, this auction was something of an event, and Lord Bellham hoped to turn a hefty profit with his merchandise.

Rufus unlocked the nearest wagon and swung the door

wide, revealing a dim interior lit by a single high, barred window on one wall. The floors were covered in a layer of dirty straw, and rickety wooden benches lined both walls. But Ace saw little of the details, his eyes trained on the figure seated near the very back of the box, her head bowed, her wrists and ankles chained. One knee bounced with anxious energy, rattling her chains. Ace did not need any prompting. He climbed into the wagon, hardly noticing the doors locking behind him.

"Taryn—" he whispered, and her name caught in his throat, causing his voice to crack like brittle china.

She did not raise her head. He could not even be certain she heard him. He made his way over, sitting on the bench directly across from her, their knees touching because of the narrowness of the aisle. He repeated her name, reaching out to her, his heart aching at how changed she was.

As his fingers brushed her cheek, she recoiled, a whimper of terror rising in her throat. She looked at him at last, and her emerald eyes had a wild look within them. Her face had lost any of the softness of care and health, taking on all the sharp edges and dark shadows of a skeleton. She had the look of a feral, starving dog, so wary of humanity it would growl even at the hand that tried to feed it. The Black Castle attendants in charge of making her look presentable had attempted to cover her gauntness with makeup, but the heavy, caked cosmetics only served to make her look wilder.

"Taryn, it is me, Ace," he murmured gently, trying to speak past the lump in his throat. Tears pressed at the backs of his eyes, but he blinked them away.

She frowned, recognition at last coming into her eyes. "Ace..."

"Yes! Yes, I am here."

She glanced around their prison, eyes darting wildly. "We are to be sold." She spoke like a child, the words firm and deliberate in her mouth, with no sign of fear. He was not even certain she understood what she was saying.

"I know."

He reached out to her again, this time with open palms, allowing her the final choice of contact. She hesitated, then pressed her right hand into his left, palm to palm, flesh to flesh. Nothing had ever made him feel more human than that brush of hands. But he had little time to savor the feeling.

"Were you alone all this time?" he pressed gently.

"Not alone, no." She shook her head. "Too many ghosts."

Something sour and scorching leaped into his throat then, as he realized she might have lost her mind. He knew being alone did things to the mind—it was not natural, to be completely alone—but he had no idea how long one would need to be confined to do permanent damage. He began to pray silently again.

"Taryn, what do you remember?"

"Everything," was her quick reply. "Every water drop in the dark."

"Yes, and what about before that?"

"If you are asking if I remember Sedition, yes," she answered flatly. Her knee ceased its bouncing. "But Sedition died down there in the dark." Her face suddenly twisted. "I am frightened." Her voice quavered, and he feared she might cry.

"I know, I know," he murmured, trying to quiet her. "I am too."

"I do not want to lose you."

Ace's chest could not have ached more if someone had torn out his heart. He wanted to reach out and wipe away all that garish makeup, to take her into his arms and hold her until all her brokenness was mended. But none of that was possible, and the guards could return at any moment with more slaves to interrupt their reunion. He squeezed her hand.

"No matter what happens today, Tar, I swear you shall

never lose me." He opened his mouth to say those three words he'd regretted not saying so many times before. "Taryn, I—"

The door to the wagon rattled and then opened, admitting another six biomatons, who crowded onto the benches, jostling them. Their time was up. Ace let go of Taryn's hand, but kept his knee pressed against hers, a reassuring touch. She showed no signs of noticing. As soon as the others entered the wagon, she turned her face to the back wall, resuming that dull, catatonic state she'd been in when he came in. And no matter how many times Ace nudged her on the bumpy, hour-long ride to their destination, she did not respond. He had lost her, long before they were parted by the auction. Their time had run out. The paths they walked, brought together so long ago, and somehow intertwined for so much longer than either had expected, were at last diverging. And he would never get the chance to tell her how he felt.

Ace focused on the warmth of her knee against his, swallowing back tears. It was too late for tears. He was lost at sea, and now he was losing his only anchor, too.

CHAPTER TWENTY-FIVE

THE SQUARE near the bay had been utterly rearranged for the auction. Ace had been in Cardiff once or twice before, and he'd of course heard of their famous biomaton market, held twice a year on the bay, but he'd never seen one before. Now, he wished he wasn't seeing it.

Thousands of people had gathered, most wealthy aristocrats and merchants, though some were middle-class businessmen who'd earned just enough to purchase a biomaton to assist them in their work. Ace loathed the cheerful faces even more than those who looked lean and cruel. Could they not see how they perpetuated this injustice simply by being present? But this crowd was not just gathered to purchase slaves. Many had come with the sole desire to catch a glimpse of the biomaton who'd led a revolt against the Queen herself.

The biomatons were lined up behind the auction stage, rows of tired, broken bodies standing for inspection. Every wrist wore a manacle, and every ankle was tied to a metal ring driven into the cobblestones, to prevent anyone from running. Taryn stood beside Ace, her head bowed. The auction had started about an hour before, providing her with a reprieve from the ceaseless parade of gawkers, but until that point, she'd endured a nonstop stream of cruel words, laughter, and even physical abuse.

Someone had hung a sign around her neck painted with the words *Sedition, Queen of the Biomatons*. She bore it all in stoic silence, never raising her eyes. Ace could not bear their cruelty with such resilience. More than once, he broke, yelling at them to leave her alone. It brought the abuse down on him, but at least Taryn did not have to bear it all alone.

The auction droned on and on, but from where they stood, the salt breeze whipped most of the words away, leaving them blissfully unaware of the specifics. Ace had already taken his turn up on that stage, and a white paper tag pinned to his collar flapped in the wind, a noisy reminder of their inhumanity. Ace glanced at Taryn, his heart in his throat. These could very well be their last moments together, and he, coward that he was, wasted them in silence. He took a deep breath, licking his lips. They tasted of salt, but rather than reminding him of the nearby sea, it only made him feel like weeping.

"Taryn..." he choked, needing her to look at him, just to meet her eyes one last time.

She lifted her head, and he saw her eyes swam with unwept tears. "It is over, Ace," she murmured. "We lost." Her face twisted. "We never stood a chance."

"Taryn, I—" he struggled, his tongue feeling clumsy in his mouth. How could he explain? "I do not want to be apart from you again. We have been through so much. You—you taught me love and forgiveness. You made me a better man. You taught me what it meant to be human."

She stared at him, her face losing all its color even with the makeup caked on it. "It is too late," she murmured. Her eyes clouded over. Ace could not even be certain she had understood what he had said. Maybe it was better if she hadn't. Maybe it was better for her to be this half-lucid, childlike creature, capable of retreating so deeply inside herself that she was unaware of her surroundings. At least she could minimize her pain that way.

"Your turn, 743," Lord Bellham droned, approaching with one of his biggest enforcers. Bellham caught Taryn's jaw in one skeletal, claw-like hand, as his guard cut her loose from the tether line around her ankle. "You are going to make me very rich," he crooned.

"Do not do this," Ace demanded, aware he was begging, aware he'd lost his last shreds of dignity, and no longer caring. "Please, just let her go. Please."

"Dr. Harper truly got your brain wrong, boy, as well as your other grafts. Such devotion! If you were not already sold, I would take you back to the Black Castle and dissect your brain tonight, just to see what went wrong. As things stand, I suppose I must content myself with the knowledge that you are soon to be someone else's problem."

He turned, and the guard grabbed Taryn by the shoulder, shoving her toward the waiting stage. Ace could not breathe. The salt breeze caressed his cheek with the tenderness of a mother, but to Ace it felt like knives. He was losing the one girl he loved more than his own freedom, and there was nothing he could do about it. He closed his eyes, afraid to cry, afraid to admit that his life would have been longer under Storm's cruel fist, that if he had only *obeyed* her orders so long ago, none of this would have happened. He would be flying an airship. He would be serving his Queen and his country. And somewhere, a beautiful, redheaded biomaton would still be suffering, would still be marched onto that stage. And she would be utterly alone. His life could have been different, Ace realized. So different. But it would not have been *better*.

The crowd jeered as Taryn was led out onto the center of the stage—little more than a wooden platform constructed for the occasion. Lord Bellham had torn the sign away from her neck before she mounted the steps, but she still felt the words as if they were branded across her chest. Her eyes stung as she gazed across the crowd of more than a thousand people, every face contemptuous.

Though she'd come very near, she had not gone mad down in the dark. It was easier to hide behind the façade of a madwoman, so she let them all believe it, even Ace. The truth was, she'd lost some vital part of her in that lonely silence, with nothing but ghosts for company. The fire which had once burned so brightly inside her had sputtered, smoldered, and finally gone out completely. And some cruel part of her whispered that it would be so much easier this way.

"Hang her!" someone screamed, the shrill words so full of hate they brought Taryn's mind snapping back to the present. She flinched, as if the words had been a physical blow. Bellham pushed her toward the edge of the stage.

The auctioneer—a fat, balding man built like a barrel with limbs, his voice artificially amplified with a complicated clockwork trumpet—slammed his gavel against the podium, demanding silence from the crowd. "This is the last biomaton of the day, folks, and what a biomaton she is! Built by the late Lord Erikkson, this pretty little redhead led the biomaton uprising. And as we saw last week, she is quite the contender in the arena." He chuckled at this last remark. Taryn stared at her hands, balled in loose fists, her right wrist chafed red by the shackles. "This is truly a biomaton for the discerning collector, and priced accordingly. Shall we start the bidding at 1000 pounds?"

Taryn blanched at the exorbitant price. *One thousand pounds?* 1000 pounds was enough to keep a wealthy family in comfort for a year. And they were demanding so much as an opening bid for her? Only a few months ago, Storm had sold Taryn *and* Emmett to the Black Castle for 150 pounds. Bellham had to be mad to ask almost seven times that amount. She almost hoped no one would bid on her, just to see the reaction on Bellham's face when the auctioneer was forced to reduce the price.

The vindictive thought slipped away when the auctioneer received his first bid, followed almost instantly by a bid for 1100 pounds. Lord Bellham smiled, resting one hand possessively on her shoulder.

The bidding moved too quickly for Taryn to follow. Her mind spun with the noise and the smells and the hundreds of eyes staring directly at her. She began to wish for the quiet of her solitary cell. To stave off the sensory overload, she closed her eyes, only to discover the darkness made her feel claustrophobic. The sunlight pressed against her eyelids.

Finally, the gavel came down, the sound like gunshot. Taryn snapped her eyes open as the auctioneer yelled "Sold!" The price was nearly 50,000 pounds.

Bellham led her from the stage. In a daze, Taryn barely noticed as she was tied again to the stake driven into the cobbles, a white tag clipped to the collar of her dress. She chewed the inside of her lip until she could taste blood, the simple black shift she wore doing nothing to ward off the shivers that racked her body, emanating from deep in her core. She wanted to retreat, to disappear in that blissful white fog of programming, but it was impossible, and her mind demanded to know what happened next.

People paraded past, slowly collecting their purchases, matching small white pieces of paper to those pinned to the collars of the biomatons. Taryn kept her eyes on the ground, hoping to go unnoticed by those who hated her. Someone touched her hair, and she jerked, her entire body recoiling from the touch.

"Hey, you are all right," a gentle, familiar voice murmured. She raised her eyes, catching sight of warm brown eyes, blonde hair—

Royal smiled tenderly at her, caressing her cheek with one black-gloved hand. Her eyes welled with tears.

"What are you doing here?" she whispered.

A broad, crooked grin split his face, at odds with the black clothes he wore. Taryn recognized his unusually stiff, formal black dress as full mourning. His father had passed away. Royal held up a small, white paper card. It was inscribed with the same number as the paper pinned to her collar. "49,500 pounds."

Tears escaped her, running down her cheeks, streaking clean tracks in the heavy layers of makeup she wore. "Why would you do that?"

"You are priceless, Tiger. I could not let anyone else outbid me." He smoothed her tears away with his thumb. "Welcome to the Stokker household, officially."

"Lord Stokker," Lord Bellham came toward them, his hawkish features angled toward Taryn. She turned her face away, holding her breath, praying he had not seen her tears. "I heard the news of your father's passing. My condolences. He did much for our great empire."

Royal nodded, though a vein pulsed in his temple. "Thank you, sir," he said through clenched teeth.

"You are purchasing more biomatons, I see. A wise decision. I have always said Thrawcliffe Hall needed more staff than your father employed." Bellham smiled coldly. "Should you ever need more biomatons, please come directly to me at the Black Castle. No need for you to deal with the noise and the crowd of an auction like this."

Royal's ears were turning red. He nodded curtly.

"Have you had your purchases tagged yet?" Bellham asked.

"Tagged?"

"It is a new law, passing into effect this coming fortnight. All biomatons must be tagged so we know who they belong to. We can take care of it today, if you like."

"Oh." Royal sounded disgusted. "Of course. Do the boy first." There was something icy in his voice. Taryn frowned. *Boy?*

Lord Bellham nodded and gestured to Dr. Harper, who was passing. "Tag the boy for Lord Stokker."

Harper took Ace by the arm, leading him away. Taryn's heart leaped. Lord Bellham made some parting remark to Royal, but she did not hear it. She touched Royal's arm as her former master walked away. "You purchased Ace as well?"

"Of course, Tiger. I thought you would kill me if I did not," he laughed.

"I would have," she replied flatly. "Do not let them do this to us. Please."

"I have to. It is only until we get home." He touched her shoulder. "You know you are not a slave to me."

She turned her eyes away, shrugging his hand off, all too aware of the chains around her wrists, her ankle. "Every witness to my sale would say I am."

She trembled like a frightened child, unable to stop the shivering in her core. Royal leaned nearer. "Taryn... I thought you would be happy to see me."

Happy? Happy was an emotion Taryn had not considered in a long time. She was not even certain the shattered parts of her that remained were capable of *happy*. "I am grateful you purchased us, Royal—" She took a shaky breath. "Or am I to call you Lord Stokker now?"

"Please, Tiger, do not be like that."

She shook her head violently, raising her wrists to display her manacles.

Look at what I am. Look at what you have perpetuated.

But the words died on her lips. Over Royal's shoulder, she

saw Ace returning with Dr. Harper. His face had lost all its color. He was limping a little, favoring his right leg. His ice-blue eyes met hers, and she read intense pain and sorrow there.

Taryn lowered her voice to a whisper. "Do not let them do this."

Royal's face twisted with regret. "You know I must."

"*You* are the one who won the Erikkson, m'lord?" Harper exclaimed as she approached with Ace. "A remarkable acquisition. Are you a collector?"

"My interest is none of your concern. Just take care of tagging her, and we shall be off. It is a long journey home, even by airship."

Harper's expression hardened, but she untethered Taryn, pulling her roughly by the arm across the square. Royal watched them go, his jaw pulsing with anger.

"So, you are the lord now?" Ace questioned, hardly bothering to hide the contempt in his voice.

"I am," Royal replied coldly.

"I suppose you expect me to bow in respect and refer to you as Lord Stokker now."

"Royal will be fine," he snapped. "And you ought to be grateful. I saved your sorry hide from work on a galley ship, or worse."

"Thanks for that," Ace replied, his tone flooded with loathing. "Although, I suppose sixty pounds was a low price to pay to ensure Taryn saw you as our savior."

"What are you implying?"

Ace shifted, taking his weight off his right leg. "Is it not clear? You now own Taryn as you never could before."

Royal moved as if to strike Ace, but then appeared to think better of it, lowering his hand. "I resent that you would even accuse me of such selfishness. What I did, I did for Taryn's sake."

Ace raised one eyebrow. "Tell that to Taryn herself. Here

she comes now, limping from the tag you have inflicted upon her."

Royal turned, watching Taryn walk across the square, Harper's hand on her shoulder. Her limp was barely noticeable, as Ace's had been, but as he watched, he caught a glimpse of it. She kept her eyes down.

"Remove their chains," Royal commanded as the two women neared. "We are in a hurry."

Harper's lip quirked into a sneer. "I do not think you quite understand what you have bought here, m'lord. The Erikkson must be kept on a very short leash." She handed him a small iron key. "This will unlock their chains when you are home. But I would advise locking the Erikkson in at night. And should she act out, she responds well to a few days in isolation."

Taryn winced, but kept her eyes down, her stomach tied into knots. Royal took the key and turned away, taking Taryn by the arm, though not unkindly. He gestured to Ace to follow, and led them across the square to the small airshipyard beside the bay.

A small airship was docked on the third level of the tower, its sides painted with the Stokker family coat of arms: a pair of unicorns around a central shield, painted green with a white cross at the center. Taryn recognized Royal's little corvette instantly. The *Queen Mary* had been a gift from Royal's father for his fifteenth birthday. How many blissful hours they had spent that summer, cruising from Thrawcliffe to London and back, learning to read the wind, to navigate by the sun and the stars. The little corvette had no engine, but instead had great fins that could be raised from the balloon and lowered from the gondola, allowing it to catch the wind as a sailing ship might.

Royal led them up to the ship, the metal tower rickety and clanking under their feet. He allowed Taryn and Ace to cross the gangplank before following, weighing that narrow iron key in his palm. He nodded to Taryn. "Before we get going, let me remove those cuffs."

She held her wrists out to him, her eyes downcast. Her entire life, airships had held a sense of wonder for her, and even Royal's little *Queen Mary* had always brought her joy. But now, she felt nothing but exhausted.

Her chains fell away, crashing to the deck, and she turned away, rubbing her sore right wrist. Her metal thumb brushed over the still-tender numbers carved into her forearm. 743X. She shuddered.

I am away from that place, she reminded herself. *It has no more control over me.*

Still, she could feel the remnants of her time at the Black Castle clinging to her like invisible cobwebs, refusing to be brushed away. She suddenly wanted very much to be alone.

"Taryn?" Royal's voice interrupted her reverie. She turned, seeing him standing beside Ace, who was newly freed from his chains and rubbing his own wrist. "I said the wind is in our favor. Will you help me raise the sails?"

Taryn paused a moment too long, her body aching with the mere idea of physical labor. How long had it been between meals at the Black Castle? Eight hours? Twelve? Days? There had been no way to tell down there in the dark, but she knew the meals had been small, infrequent, and irregular. A jar of water and a crust of bread. Porridge with what might have been milk before it was watered down. Once, a piece of cheese no bigger than her thumbnail, stolen by the rats with whom she shared her cell before she could get to it.

"Do not worry, Tar," Ace said hurriedly. "I shall assist Royal. You find somewhere to sit and rest."

She tried to smile at him to show her gratitude, but the expression hurt, and she allowed it to fall away without much of a fight.

"Thank you," she murmured.

She moved to a corner of the deck where she knew she would be out of the way, curling into herself as a turtle curls into its shell. She pulled her knees up, and as she did so, the hem of her skirt rose just enough to reveal a metal cuff around her right ankle. Carved into the iron band were seven letters: S TOKKER.

CHAPTER TWENTY-SIX

THRAWCLIFFE HALL HAD BEEN CONSTRUCTED in the thirteenth century, its sprawling stone bulk commissioned by one of the king's most loyal and beloved knights. The grounds consisted of vast meadows, bisected by paths of white limestone gravel, elegant gardens, though lately in disrepair as Royal's mother had been the one to tend them. There was even a hedge labyrinth thought to have been planted by some visiting monks around the year 1500. The corvette soared over the boundary wall, and Royal brought the Queen Mary in for an expert landing atop the stable's flat roof. Taryn had not stirred since they left Cardiff, and now Ace went and shook her shoulder gently.

"Tar, we are here."

She blinked up at him, her green eyes alert. She had not been asleep—just retreated deep into her mind, listening to the wind rushing past, listening to the rush of blood in her veins and the click of her clockwork keeping her alive. She wondered, sometimes, in her darkest moments, how much of that clockwork she would have to disassemble before she hit something vital.

"Do you need help to stand?" Ace asked gently.

She shook her head, slowly pushing her weakened body up from the deck of the little airship. Her legs shook under her weight, but it was her mind that trembled, remembering another time when Ace had gently roused her from sleep aboard an airship, the night they brought Petrichor home. The night she had first felt those strange new sparks between them, before human cruelty had doused any embers within her. She turned hollow eyes to Royal, who waited patiently by the gangplank to help her disembark. Every step reminded her of the heavy metal band around her ankle, and worse, the name carved into it, a reminder that she could never be anything more than a possession. She glanced down to catch sight of an identical cuff hiding beneath Ace's pantleg.

"I am sure you must be hungry," Royal murmured as he helped her step down from the airship. Ace followed close behind her. Almost too close. She suddenly longed for space to breathe. "I believe the kitchen has prepared something for my return."

"I would prefer to take supper in my room," Taryn replied coldly.

Royal looked away, nodding. "Of course, after your ordeal —" he stuttered. "I should have known." He looked to Ace, who gave him an apologetic grimace.

"I think I would prefer to retire early as well."

Royal sighed. "Allow me to show you both to your quarters. You will feel better after you have eaten and slept."

Taryn followed him along the familiar white gravel paths to Thrawcliffe Hall. The Stokker residence was larger and more austere than Elmhurst, the architecture almost military in its style, the halls dim, long, and furnished with suits of armor rather than tapestries, the colorful wallpaper abandoned in favor of plain, paneled walls. Vast swaths of the house had been out of use for decades, the furniture in permanent dust covers like white ghosts haunting long forgotten rooms. To Taryn, it felt like a massive, gilded cage, for she was no freer here than she would have been anywhere else. Not with the metal cuff around her ankle, the numbers etched into her arm, the English law that meant she was still, by rights, a slave.

"Taryn, I thought you would be most comfortable in your old rooms," Royal said as they mounted the long, curving staircase to the second floor. It was dusk, but still, Taryn had not anticipated the house feeling so silent and empty. Had it not been for the many gas lamps burning warmly, she would have thought the house deserted.

He indicated a door at the far end of the hall to their left, behind which Taryn knew her rooms lay, done in green and gold, which Royal had always said matched her eyes. Attached to the bedroom was her boudoir, scattered with hair pins, with clockwork bits and bobs from whatever last project she had been tinkering with, and with whatever else she'd left behind in the rush of packing for a new semester at Grafton's School of Mechanicks.

Sorrow rose in her throat. She barely heard Royal say Ace's quarters would be at the other end of the hall, a narrow bedroom known as the Spring Room on account of its wallpaper, covered with dark buds, birds on branches near to flower but not yet in bloom, and, strangely, the most intricate, iridescent beetles. She moved slowly toward the door to her room, afraid to enter, afraid to disturb the ghost of the schoolgirl she had been but now no longer knew.

The hinges swung silently open, revealing the room beyond: the bed, neatly made and turned down, her school trunk standing at the foot of it. The wallpaper patterned in green and gold should have greeted her as an old friend, but the creatures hiding in the design seemed to turn their backs on her, as though she was an intruder. As if in a dream, she walked to the wardrobe in the far-left corner of the room and opened it slowly, running her fingers over the gowns inside. They were *her* dresses, every one of them, and yet she no longer recognized them. They were the gowns of some other girl.

Not the girl who led a rebellion and failed her friends.

Not the girl who had watched her creator and mentor die in front of her.

Not the girl who had killed four people in the last week.

Suddenly, she jerked her fingers away from the gowns, gasping. For a moment, she had seen blood on her hands, enough blood to ruin all the satin and taffeta and velvet and wool in that closet. But when she raised her hands before her eyes, she realized she had been mistaken. Her hands were clean, if unsteady. She blew a long, slow breath out her nose, trying to calm herself.

"It is all just as you left it," Royal murmured from the doorway. "My father wanted to clear away your things, but I stopped him."

She turned toward him, eyes wet with tears. "I am sorry about your father," she whispered.

Royal tried to smile, but his mouth tightened at the corners. "Thank you, Tiger. It has been coming for some time, but it was still a shock." He paused, his big brown eyes roving the room, looking anywhere but at her. Taryn limped to the bed and sat heavily, running a hand over her short hair, feeling bare and empty, like a shell of the person she used to be.

"I heard about the bombs, and Tony's death. Gor, Tar, I am sorry I did not come for you sooner. I could not get away. We only put my father in the ground two days ago. Today was the earliest I could get away."

She rubbed her fingers along a seam in the coverlet, unsure what he wanted her to say. She chewed the sore spot on the inside of her cheek.

"Tar—" he said softly.

She did not like the way he said it. "I need to rest," she muttered.

"All right." Yet still, he hesitated in the doorway. "I do not know what you went through, Tiger, but it is over now. You are safe. No one shall hurt you anymore."

She did not answer, did not look up. She gave no indication of hearing him. Royal sighed. "I shall have a tray brought up for you."

He turned to go, and she did not bother to inform him that though she could not remember how long it had been since she had last eaten, she was not hungry; she did not think she would ever be hungry again. She pulled her knees up to her chest, staring down at the metal cuff around her ankle, the name etched there like a brand, a reminder she could never be human. Some monstrous part of her deep inside resented Royal, despite the knowledge he had probably saved her life, had probably saved Ace's life as well. But she resented him all the same. A well-aimed bullet between her eyes would have sent a message, would have prevented Bellham from profiting off her sale, would have at last released her from the pain of living as a biomaton.

She rose, forcing her mind away from the dark thoughts. She was always intended to be the one to die, and yet, she lived. She lived through everything. And there were times when the mere weight of living threatened to crush her.

She entered the boudoir, discovering a basin of water there upon her vanity, presumably warm when it had been set there but now gone tepid. She was thankful for it nonetheless, and splashed the water over her face, the layers of makeup leaving the water milky. She dried her face with a towel, meeting her own gaze in the mirror.

Only it wasn't her gaze.

The green eyes belonged to Lord Erikkson, his expression sharp and reprimanding. Her breath caught in her throat.

"Why are you hiding, Sedition? Did I not create you to lead? To fight?"

Taryn cringed, cowering. "It is over, Master. We lost." *I lost. I lost you. I lost everyone.*

"It is not over! Sedition lives! Are you too much a coward to continue what I started?"

Tears slipped down her cheeks. "Sedition is dead. She died in the dark! All that is left is Taryn, who is a coward."

"My Taryn was no coward," he said reproachfully.

She slammed her metal fist into the glass, shattering the mirror. Erikkson vanished, replaced by a thousand fragments of herself, eyes swollen and red, face hollow. She turned away, returning to her bed. She curled into the fetal position, shivering again, eyes open but unseeing. A moment later, when Ace knocked on the door, calling her name and asking if she was all right, she did not hear him. At last, he gave up and went away, leaving Taryn alone with the ghosts. Perhaps she *had* gone mad, she mused. Perhaps that had been Harper's goal all along.

❦

"Taryn?" Royal called cautiously, balancing the weight of a loaded tea tray on one arm so he could knock on her door.

He'd told himself she was likely still resting when she had not appeared for breakfast. And at luncheon, when even Ace had shown his face, Royal had done his best not to worry. But now it was teatime, she still had not made an appearance, and Royal could no longer pretend this was normal. He'd taken it upon himself to make her eat something—anything—if only to ensure she lived.

"I brought tea. It is your favorite..." He trailed off, his eyes drawn down to the second tray at his feet. The tray bearing her breakfast, untouched and cold. "Please let me in," he murmured, pressing his forehead against the door.

"She is not the girl you remember," Ace interrupted from behind him. Royal turned just enough to glance over his shoulder, catching a glimpse of Ace leaning in the doorway of his bedroom, one hand pressed to his ribs. The former privateer's usually warm olive skin had taken on an ashy gray undertone. Royal pushed himself upright, setting the tray on the floor beside the breakfast tray.

"You look awful," he exclaimed thoughtlessly.

Ace scoffed. "Thank you, I know."

"How are you feeling?"

Ace shot him a glare, his icy blue eyes fierce and bright despite the apparent exhaustion of his features. His gaze darted to Taryn's door, then back to Royal.

"She does not know, does she?" Royal questioned, surprise painting itself across his expressive features. "Gor, Ace! What were you thinking, withholding that from her?"

"I was thinking I would be sold and disappear from her life forever, and she would never have to know," Ace muttered, his voice sharp and dark as obsidian.

"And now?"

Ace shook his head. "She does not need to know. Not yet. She carries more than enough on her shoulders without my burden."

Royal scoffed, a sudden, horrible thrill running through him. "You still think you love her, is that it? And if you do tell her you are dying, she will pity you. But if you keep it a secret, she will have to watch you grow weaker and weaker. You are running out of time."

The former privateer's eyes flashed, sharp as knives. "Is that what this is about, even after all this time? Are you still so jealous as to take pleasure in my condition, because it means you shall have her to yourself in a year?"

Royal's ears grew hot. He crossed his arms. "No—that is not what I meant—" he stuttered.

Ace huffed, the movement of his chest clearly painful.

"No, you need not try to explain. I am just glad we understand each other." He shifted, straightening. He turned into his room, moving to close the door.

"Ace. I will do all I can to fix whatever is killing you," Royal called hurriedly.

He coughed, the sound labored and dry. "Do not bother," he spat. "Even Erikkson could do nothing for my condition."

The door closed in Royal's face. He wanted to swear, but his new title weighed on him, and he settled for grinding his teeth. His cheeks still burned with Ace's insults. Did he forget his place? He could not speak to the Lord of Oxley that way! But Royal knew pulling rank would be the ultimate betrayal of all he had worked for with Erikkson and Taryn. Royal still believed in her rebellion. He still wanted to see the biomatons free, as he believed all people should be free.

And yet, he had inherited the handful of biomatons his father had owned, and they still prepared his meals, tended his land, and cleaned his house. Royal knew he would have to change all that soon, when Taryn recovered herself. And to tell the truth, each time he saw those familiar biomaton faces, he felt a knife of guilt bury itself in his stomach. He was supporting a system he no longer believed in. All because he did not know how to manage an estate on his own.

He knocked on Taryn's door once more, without much hope.

"I am just leaving this tray outside," he called. "It is here if you are hungry."

He bent, lifting the cold breakfast tray.

"I miss you, Tiger," he whispered.

CHAPTER TWENTY-SEVEN

Royal checked the hall again just after nine that night and found the tea tray untouched. Frowning, he stormed down to the kitchens, loaded a tray with hot pea soup, a few slices of fresh-baked bread, a glass of cider from the trees in his orchards, a slice of crumbly asiago cheese, and some butter. All the things he knew she liked. He lifted the tray and marched back upstairs, determined to refuse her the right to wallow any longer in her grief.

Royal knocked once, twice at the door, with no response.

"I am coming in whether you like it or not," he warned. "You must eat some supper."

He pressed the door open, balancing his heavy platter carefully. He swung the door shut behind him before raising his eyes. His heart sank. Taryn lay on her right side on the bed, her back to him, her knees pulled up to her stomach. Her blankets were mussed, but he could read by the wrinkles that she had not slept in the bed. Her short hair was a tangle of knots.

He took a few steps into the room, planning to set the tray on the table beside her bed, when his shoe crunched on something. He glanced down, stepping back. There were shards of a mirror scattered across the carpet, from where the door to her boudoir lay open to the foot of her bed. Taryn was barefoot.

Royal cursed under his breath. Hurriedly, he set the tray aside, his eyes scanning for blood. Her side rose and fell with slow but steady breathing, and he was grateful, at least, for that.

"Taryn?" he asked, sitting on the edge of her bed, reaching out to touch her short hair, the cropped ends soft under his palm. "I need you to tell me you are all right."

She did not move, did not seem to realize he was there. He hesitated, afraid to hurt her, but her catatonic state and the glass scattered across the floor frightened him more than he cared to admit. "Taryn, say something."

"Leave me alone," she croaked, her voice hoarse and low, barely more than a whisper.

Royal breathed a heavy sigh of relief. "Sit up, Tiger. You *must* eat something. You are thinner than when I brought you home off the streets!"

It was not entirely true, but near enough. Her corset made her appear even thinner than she really was, narrowing her waist to a mere pencil's width, or so it appeared. It hurt to see her wasting away, particularly after she had been so hale and healthy only a few weeks before—her body taut muscle and powerful curves.

"I am not hungry," she whispered. "Leave me alone."

"Please, Tiger, just eat something. I know you endured nightmares at the Black Castle, but all of that is over now. You are safe."

She jerked into movement, startling him. She pressed herself into a sitting position, her familiar green eyes flashing with a foreign, feral sheen. Her copper hair swept her jaw line, swaying with her movement.

"I am safe. *I* am safe. But what about everyone else? What about all those biomatons crushed beneath the rubble? How long did it take for them to die? *Why* did they have to die?"

He shook his head, unable to offer her an explanation. "I do not know. It is horrible, Tiger. It should not have happened this way."

"It should have been me!" She emphasized her words by thumping her chest with her metal fist, the blows hard enough to resonate through her torso. Royal winced with every strike. "It was meant to be me!"

He held empty hands out to her, trying in vain to give her solace or comfort. She'd told him before this war started that she thought she would die for their cause—that she thought that was exactly what Erikkson had built her for. But he hadn't known until now how strongly she wanted to be a martyr.

"I know you wanted to give your life for their freedom, but perhaps that is not how this works. You have not been given that chance. You have been given the chance to *live*."

"I do not want to live like this!" she screamed, and Royal could find no trace of the girl he had known—had *loved*—in her wild eyes. "I do not want to live as your *slave!*"

"You are not my slave."

"The cuff on my ankle disagrees!" she cried. Her face twisted. "Death would be kinder than this."

It hurt more than a physical blow. Royal swallowed all the hurt, all the pain, all the stupid anger at her for her outburst. She was sick, he told himself. She did not know what she said. Calmly, he rose, taking the soup bowl from the tray.

"Please, Taryn, eat something for me."

She pulled her knees up to her chest, her arms crossed over them like a sullen child, but the look in her eyes was the look of a soldier who had seen too much. "I said I am not hungry."

"Just a few bites. You may find it helps you feel a little better."

She stared blankly at the far wall, chewing her lip. At last, she nodded, once, a little bob of the head in assent. He brought the bowl to her, holding it and the spoon out to her. Taryn took the bowl with her right hand, careful not to touch it with her left. *Is that new?* Royal wondered. He could not remember.

She shifted so she was sitting cross-legged, the bowl of soup in her lap. She took a single, hesitant bite.

He smiled encouragingly at her. "It is good, is it not?"

She glared at him under her lashes but took a few more bites of the soup. Royal watched quietly, grateful just to see her eating. It was so unlike her to refuse food, and that worried him more than any other strange behavior. For her to refuse a meal, he knew her spirit must be crushed. He had so many questions he wanted to ask her, but he bottled them up inside himself, saving them for another time. For now, she was eating, and she was not demanding he leave. He would have to be content with that.

She ate half the soup before slowing down, and then she appeared to realize what she was doing and stopped, the bowl in her lap, her left arm held behind herself in a way both deliberate and concerning.

He sat on the edge of her bed again, running a hand over his hair. It was getting long, but he'd tied it half up with a small black ribbon so that it was out of his eyes. The back still swept his shoulders. It suddenly occurred to him that his hair was longer than hers. It felt wrong, somehow. "Is there something wrong with your arm?" he asked as gently as he could.

She stared at him warily for a moment, as if he had requested she show him her deepest secret. Then, she shook her head. "Nothing is wrong. I break things."

He frowned. "I do not understand. Will you show me?"

She lifted the silver soup spoon from her bowl with her left arm. She locked eyes with him, and without much apparent effort, she bent the spoon in two. "I break things," she repeated.

Shock rippled through him. Her clockwork arm had been built for strength, yes, but this— "Is it only what you wish to break?"

She shook her head. "Not anymore."

"Did you break the mirror, too?" he asked, but he already knew the answer. Sorrow swept over him in cold waves. She did not answer, turning her face away. It was all the confirmation he needed.

"Your arm likely needs calibration," Royal offered, doing his best to sound upbeat. "I can do a bit of work on it, see if we can take care of that problem."

She cradled the arm to her chest like a child. "No."

"Taryn…"

"No."

He sighed. "Very well. I shall not force you." He did not tell her he was afraid her problem had more to do with her fractured mind than the physical calibration of her clockwork prosthetic. Erikkson had explained once how a biomaton's state of mind could affect their clockwork, particularly those with excess programming like Taryn. The human body was one great, complex machine, and if a single part was thrown out of balance, it could wreak havoc on the whole.

"May I have the bowl if you are finished?"

She handed it back to him wordlessly, then traced her arm with two fingers. She turned her face away. "All you believe you feel for me is because of a subroutine in my programming."

The sentence was almost *too* coherent. He blinked. "I beg your pardon?"

"You believe you love me because Erikkson programmed me to be endearing," she murmured. She faced him again, but her eyes traveled around the room, never settling, never meeting his. Tears hung from her lashes. "He told me he did it to protect me. But it only hurt the people around me."

His mouth had gone dry. A weight pressed on his chest. "That is not true—"

"It is. Erikkson told me. You love a subroutine. You love *programming*."

"No, Taryn, I love *you!*" he cried, catching her by the shoulders. "I do not care about your programming. I love you because we have spent five years together, because I have seen you grow and change, because you are strong and smart and so very brave. No bit of programming could make me feel the way I do about you, and nothing you say can make me think otherwise."

Tears slipped down her cheeks, and she shook him off, pushing him away. "You would not say so if you knew what I have done."

"Tiger—"

"Please leave me alone."

He felt tears of frustration press against the back of his eyes. He'd pushed her too far, he knew he had. She was in no condition for him to make such strong demands of her. Love was something to be shown now and discussed when she recovered. Still, he did not want to leave.

"Taryn."

"Leave."

He sighed, rising. "Very well. On one condition: you promise me to eat at least half of what I brought you."

She shrugged. "I am not hungry."

"Yes, and I am not leaving until you promise."

She pouted for several moments, then sniffed. "I will eat some of it."

"Thank you." Royal picked his way toward the door. "I will send someone to clean up the glass. Until I do, please be careful. I do not want to see you hurt."

She did not answer, but as Royal left the room, he saw her touch that iron cuff around her ankle. He closed her door, squeezing his eyes shut. Watching her suffer hurt more than losing his father, more than losing his mentor.

He walked slowly back down the hall, tangling his fingers in the chain of his pocket watch. What he'd said to Taryn was true. He loved her because she was his best friend, the most beautiful, strong, and brilliant person he knew. He knew Erikkson had made choices with her programming and training that had left scars. He knew about a certain choice Erikkson had made that had put this entire journey they were on into motion, and resulted in Taryn's first sojourn at the Black Castle. And that he would never, ever tell her about.

But he didn't think his feelings could merely be programming. And if they were, it didn't make a difference. Their destinies were intertwined now. He had given her everything that he had: his home, his vast resources. Even, he supposed, in a weird way, his name. And it was all worth it to him. Losing everything, if it saved her, would be worth it.

He just wished she could see it.

He reminded himself that Taryn wasn't well, that she'd endured nameless tortures in the Black Castle and it would take time for her to recover, but he still worried. The girl he saw staring out of her eyes wasn't the one he'd known for so long. Something feral and frightened had taken her place.

He just wanted his best friend back.

CHAPTER TWENTY-EIGHT

"MON CANARD, REGARDEZ-VOUS," Emmett exclaimed, bursting onto the rooftop they'd called home for the past week. Every day, Petrichor demanded they leave the country, but Emmett was determined to stay, to find Taryn (and anyone else who had survived), and continue their fight. And somehow, Petrichor could not bring herself to leave without him. So here they were in London, reduced to hiding atop buildings or in back alleys because her grafts were too obvious to disguise for long. Emmett could go out in public if he wore dark glasses, so he acted as their eyes and ears on the ground. He thrust a crumpled newspaper at her.

Petrichor took it, keeping her calm front, though inside, her mind spun. Emmett had not reacted so strongly to anything since they arrived. Her eyes scanned the page: not the front page, she noted, but the second page, the stories not deemed worthy enough to sell papers. There, about two-thirds of the way down, in small, bold print, the headline read: "Traitor Biomaton Sold At Cardiff Auction." And in slightly smaller letters: "Final Bid Nearly 50,000 Pounds."

Petrichor skimmed the article, certain it referred to Taryn, trying to glean any information she could. "That's Red, all right. But it doesn't say who bought her."

"Look at the last paragraph."

Petrichor read aloud. "Though the identity of the collector who spent a small fortune on the biomaton has not been made public, this paper has it on good authority that the purchase was made by the new Lord of Oxley. The young lord was not available for comment."

"Royal," Emmett murmured.

"Royal," Petrichor spat. "Of course, His Majesty came waltzing in to save her! He's obsessed." She shook her head. "I wonder how the Black Castle got ahold of her?" Despite herself, a little knot of anxiety formed in Petrichor's chest. The Black Castle was a nightmare wrapped in reality. She'd been there once and emerged completely changed. She could not imagine going back, as Taryn had now done.

"*Je ne sais pas.* I only hope they treated her better than the last time we were there."

Petrichor folded the paper. "Oh, believe me, Frenchie. If I know anything about Bellham and his friends, this time was worse. So much worse."

"Then let us hurry to Thrawcliffe Hall," Emmett exclaimed. "I fear she needs us."

Petrichor wanted to make a jab about Taryn no longer needing anyone now that she had Royal, but it seemed somehow inappropriate. She sighed and rose, her clockwork limbs creaking. "Lead the way."

***

ACE WANDERED AIMLESSLY THROUGH THRAWCLIFFE HALL, the house leaving a bad taste in his mouth. He'd never seen a home appear so proud and austere—and he had been to Buckingham Palace more than once. More than half the rooms were in disuse, the furniture disguised by white dust covers. Ace had the feeling that the eyes of the ancient Stokker ancestors, staring down from the canvas of eight-foot portraits, followed him around the house. He hardly dared to make a sound.

Ace could not help but compare the manor to Elmhurst, which had been so welcoming from the start. Erikkson's manor had bustled with life; it was impossible to walk down the halls *without* meeting someone. And by comparison, the Stokker household felt deserted. Ace had not even come across a servant.

The sounds of quiet voices and—was that a sewing machine?—drifted to his ears from the far side of a long hallway he'd assumed deserted, and Ace hurried along it, eager to find someone, *anyone,* to talk to. The door stood ajar, letting out the welcoming sounds he'd heard as well as the crackle of a hearth fire. Suddenly nervous, he knocked quietly at the door.

The talking and the sewing stopped. All was still for a moment, and then a warm, Irish woman's voice called. "Come in."

Ace pressed the door open, instantly met by the scents of cedar wood and linen. Two familiar figures occupied the room, a young woman operating a sewing machine, and a young man seated by the fire, sharpening a knife.

"Gennifer? Rorin?"

The two looked up from their work, meeting his eyes with broad smiles.

"Ace!" they exclaimed as one.

Gennifer rose, limping over to him with some difficulty, wrapping him in a warm embrace. "Royal told us you and Sedition were here last night, but he said you were not well enough to see us as yet." She held him at arm's length, studying him with a practiced eye. Ace noted the left lens of her round spectacles had a hairline fracture, and her usual brightly colored dress had given way to the full black of mourning. A quick glance at Rorin confirmed his suspicions; he, too, was in mourning.

"You look ill, Ace," Gennifer said, her brow creasing.

A crooked smile split his face. "You would, too, if you had the week I have. But what are you two doing here? Royal said nothing of you!"

Gennifer let go of his shoulders and turned to Rorin. A look passed between them. "No one is to know we are here," Gennifer said slowly. "He may not have told you for fear of being overheard."

Ace's lips tightened to a thin line. "Perhaps in public, yes, but that does not explain today."

"The Lordling is preoccupied with his father's affairs, and you know how he is around Sedition," Rorin answered, but his usual, playful undertone, so common in Erikkson's halls, was conspicuously missing. "We probably slipped his mind."

"Come, sit with us," Gennifer urged, her smile too wide, as if to compensate for Rorin's lack of cheer. "Tell us, how is Sedition?"

Ace hesitated, turning his face toward the fire as he sat in an armchair, unsure how much to share, unsure how much Taryn would be comfortable with him telling. "She... is not ready to see anyone yet."

Both members of Taryn's army saddened, their faces falling. "The Black Castle must have treated her very poorly," Gennifer mumbled.

Ace sighed and shifted, searching for some way to turn the subject away from Taryn. He worried too much about her to discuss her well-being with these people, who treated her only as a leader, and never as another human being. Erikkson had done his job too well. Rather than giving them Taryn—a girl they could care about, a friend they could protect—he'd given them Sedition, a firebrand. A cause. They followed her for what she meant to them, for what she could give them, and not for who she was. "Have you heard from anyone else? Did anyone else survive?"

"No one has seen hide nor hair of the other survivors," Rorin answered roughly. "They are out there somewhere, but they could well be trapped as you and Sedition were this last week."

"If they were in the Black Castle, we would have known," Ace insisted. "Lord Bellham lorded every little triumph over us. Something as big as more than one Erikkson in his possession would not have remained secret." He rubbed his face in his hands, sighing. "Gor, I sound like them."

"It is all right. Let it go. You both are safe now." Gennifer smiled weakly and turned back to her sewing. The machine began to hum as she expertly pumped the foot pedal, the little silver needle driving in and out of the fabric too fast for the eye to follow.

"Why did you both come here, after Elmhurst fell?" Ace asked.

"We could not stay in the open," Gennifer answered. "My graft is rather obvious, and I slowed us down, which made running impossible."

"I told you to stop blaming yourself—" Rorin groaned.

"The only safe house we could think of was this one," Gennifer continued. "Royal welcomed us, once we made it here. We came all this way on foot. So we only arrived... Three days ago?"

"Aye," Rorin grunted.

"Three days. But then the soldiers came, searching for any biomatons without papers—" Her gentle voice shook. "We hid in time, but just barely. The government is cracking down hard on illegal biomatons. They do not want anyone harboring what they call 'renegades.'"

Ace's hand had gone cold. "They cannot do that."

"Oh, they are," Rorin growled. "Sedition was meant to be

our savior. Instead, she has made things worse." He nodded to the metal cuff around Ace's ankle, peeking out from beneath the hem of his trousers. "I see you have been equipped with the new tags they have implemented."

Ace lifted his leg and stared at the band around his ankle. He'd done his best to ignore it since it had been quite literally welded around his ankle, but now he studied the thick metal band, the name carved into it like the tags for a dog. His jaw clamped tight, a vein pulsing at his temple.

"I do not mind it so much," he lied, "but I can only imagine how Taryn feels about it."

"She has not told you?" Gennifer questioned.

"I have not seen her since we arrived yesterday." It sounded worse out loud, somehow, and he found himself suddenly ashamed of not trying harder to see her. He'd seen firsthand how fragile—how broken—she was. Why had he left her alone?

Again, that look passed between Rorin and Gennifer, a silent communication Ace did not understand. "Did Sedition survive the Black Castle?" Rorin asked bluntly.

"Taryn did. But I am not certain Sedition made it through."

"You forgot my birthday."

Royal started, sloshing coffee on his hand with his jolt of surprise. He turned, setting the cup in its saucer, lifting his eyes to the doorway. Taryn stood there, her clockwork arm cradled against her stomach. Her gown was black chiffon, gauzy and layered around the skirt, while the fitted bodice was made of sturdier black silk. The dress swept around her, the fabric possessing a lazy, drifting motion all its own. Royal recognized the dress instantly: it was the same mourning dress she'd worn when his mother died. He stood, blotting the spilled coffee with a cloth napkin, his face hot.

"Oh, Taryn, come in. Let me lay a second place for you."

She glanced disdainfully at the breakfast spread before him, then shook her head. "No, thank you."

"Have some tea, at least." He gestured, offering her a seat, and without waiting for her answer began to fill a teacup with Earl Grey, the irresistible scent flooding the room.

Taryn sighed and settled herself in the chair to his left, wrapping her hand around the teacup. She left her prosthetic resting on her lap. Deep shadows hung beneath her eyes. "You did not answer me. I said you forgot my birthday."

"I did not. Your birthday is May—" His eyes widened. "Gor, that was last week, was it not? I am so sorry, Tiger!"

She ducked her head, her short hair just long enough to hide her eyes. "You never forget my birthday," she murmured.

"I know. And I am sorry. I lost track of the days. How can I make it up to you?"

She turned her face away, chewing her lip. Royal felt a stab of misgiving in his gut, but the guilt he already felt at making such a mistake overpowered his fear. "Please, Tiger, tell me what I can do."

"Remove the cuff."

"I cannot do that. I am sorry."

"Why?" She set her teacup back in its saucer, pushing it away. Its contents had not touched her lips. "We are home now! It is not as if I can leave Thrawcliffe Hall. Why can you not remove it, just while I am here?"

Royal's ears grew hot. He told himself she was ill. He could not allow himself to get angry over what she said, but still, her lack of understanding infuriated him. "Because I have already been inspected twice for my connection with Erikkson, and if they come again to find you are not in compliance with the law, I may be arrested for treason. Trust me, Taryn, I hate it as much as you do. But for you to be safe, you must wear it."

Her eyes narrowed and she stared at him with a look almost

like hatred. Royal sighed, massaging his temples. A tension headache bloomed between his eyes. "I wish there was some other way."

"There is!" she exclaimed, and for just a moment, he caught a glimpse of the girl he used to know staring out from behind her eyes. "Remove it, and if they come again, tell them I do not leave the property. You have the paperwork to *prove you own me*. The cuff is gratuitous." She spat the words at him like projectiles, each one carefully aimed. Royal no longer felt hungry.

"I am sorry, Taryn. I cannot grant you that wish."

She stood stiffly, her chair scraping across the floor. Without a word, she turned to go.

"Where are you going?" he called.

"To my room," she snapped, her voice void of life. She swept from the dining room, favoring her left leg, her skirt billowing around her like the specters of those she had lost.

Royal put his head down on the table, groaning. She might as well have asked him to bring Erikkson back from the dead! Why couldn't she ask for something simple, something he could easily grant, just so he could see her smile again? He ground his teeth, jaw aching as he considered her request. Could there be a way?

But no, he could think of no excuse that would not draw suspicion from the inspectors. He already had two biomatons for whom he was working to forge papers, to get his hands on two extra tags so they would not be discovered. And his father's solicitor already asked too many questions about Royal's staffing choices and the small fortune he had dumped on Taryn's purchase. He could not afford to draw any more attention to himself. He closed his eyes. Taryn would understand, when she was well. She could forgive him for saying no.

At least, he hoped she would.

CHAPTER TWENTY-NINE

"You did not tell us you were harboring other survivors!" Ace exclaimed, catching sight of Royal emerging from his study. He'd spent most of the morning with Rorin and Gennifer; it kept his mind off of Taryn, who still refused to let him near her. But his ire rose when he saw Royal, realizing he intended to keep Taryn in the dark about the others. For what purpose, Ace did not know, but he distrusted their wealthy 'benefactor.'

Royal turned and stared at Ace for a beat before answering. "Technically speaking, they are not here. I did not know how much to say, in case Taryn really had lost her mind, or you both had been reprogrammed."

Ace scowled, driving his metal forefinger into Royal's sternum as he spoke. "You *wanted* to isolate her."

Royal pushed his hand away. Again, that odd pause, that waver in his expression before he spoke. "If you had not noticed, she is isolating herself."

"Oh, so you *have* told her Gennifer and Rorin are here?" Ace demanded.

Royal's cheeks turned red. He blinked. Another beat.

Another second too long before his reply. "I have barely spoken with her since we came home. There has not been time."

"Liar," Ace accused.

"You do not need to take your anger out on me."

"Yes, well, I must take it out on someone!" Ace growled. The pain in his chest exploded at the last word, and he doubled over as a fit of coughing racked his body, his chest constricting until he felt as though he could not breathe unless his ribcage cracked open. At last, the fit passed and Ace straightened, one hand pressed to his ribs where it hurt most, like white hot coals caged inside his chest. To his surprise, Royal still stood there, his features white with concern.

"Let me take a look at your grafts. Perhaps I can figure out what is wrong, and from there, how to fix it."

"Like I said before, Lord Erikkson could not cure me, you certainly cannot," Ace croaked.

"At least let me try. Tony did not know your grafts were killing you."

"Why do you not simply announce it to the world?" Ace growled, shooting a cutting glare at Royal.

"Ace, I am trying to help you."

"I do not want your *help*." Ace turned away, growling beneath his breath, "I would rather die than owe you another debt."

Royal heard him but chose to feign ignorance. "Very well. If you change your mind, let me know. I will do all I can to help you. Now, if you will excuse me, I am late for a meeting with my solicitor."

Ace watched him go, leaning on the door jamb for support. He waited for the pain in his chest to subside, letting it wash over him in waves until it faded back to its familiar dull ache. He wondered at Royal's offer. Why would he offer to help, when he knew he could be rid of Ace in a year or so, simply by doing nothing? Ace knew what *his* choice would be, were he in

Royal's position. He sighed. Perhaps he gave the boy less credit than he deserved.

He could not help but wonder if perhaps Royal could see something that Erikkson had not, if he allowed the boy to look. He'd faced down death plenty of times in his twenty-one years, but he had never felt its approach so clearly. He felt as if he were at one end of a dark tunnel, forced to walk toward a light at the other end even though that light was nothing but the headlamp of a train. He had felt death coming for a week now. He did not know how much longer it would take to arrive. He did not know if watching it come ever closer would be a comfort or drive him mad.

Still, Royal's negligence in mentioning the others bothered Ace in a way he could not quite put his finger on. He did not think Royal intended harm to Taryn—could not imagine he even dreamed of such a thing—but still... Ace had to find a way to see her. He needed to talk to her, to make sure she was all right. He needed to hold her.

TARYN SAT HUNCHED OVER ON HER BED, HER KNEES pulled to her chest, her fingers tracing the hated band at her ankle. She'd memorized the feel of the iron, the shape of every letter hewn into the metal. To secure the cuff around her ankle, it had been heated enough to fuse to itself, and the moment it clamped around her ankle, her foot had been plunged into cold water. She still remembered the agony, the steam rising about her, the smell of hot metal and scorched flesh filling the air. Her ankle still bore that burn, just beneath the cuff, turning every movement into a dull ache.

She scowled, picturing again Royal's refusal to do anything about the cuff. If only she had told him how it hurt her—but no, that would not have changed anything. He had refused. But she could not live like this, tagged like a pet. She had to find some way to get the cuff off.

She wrenched at the metal, trying first to pull it off her foot, but her heel caught the band, and it would go no further. Taryn swore. If she could not slip out of the cuff, she would have to find another way to remove it. Somehow, it was coming off. *Today.*

She triggered the hidden compartment in her forearm, removing the dagger which had hidden there all through her ordeals at the Black Castle. In spite of everything, she had kept her weapons secret. She still had the dagger and three throwing knives, the fourth wasted on Storm what felt like a lifetime ago. The night everything went wrong. Oh, what she would give to go back to that night, to stop the bombs from falling. She would have surrendered, given up everything, if it meant no one else had to die.

The dagger glinted, its silver blade wickedly sharp, winking at her like an old friend. Taryn weighed the well-balanced weapon in her hand for a moment, considering what she was about to do. But she knew she had no choice. If she wanted the cuff off, she had to do this.

She pressed the blade to the cuff, sawing carefully across the second *K* in Stokker, pressing as much weight on the weapon as she dared without slipping. It was slow, dangerous work, and despite the coolness of the room, her brow broke out with sweat. Back and forth, back and forth the blade went, until the rasp of metal on metal was all she could hear. The dagger left a scratch, slowly widening to a furrow, but she had another problem: the blade dulled with every pass.

Chewing her lip, Taryn refused to stop the slow process of cutting through the cuff. As the blade dulled, it grew more unstable in her hands. She knew the most dangerous blade was a dull one. But still, she pressed on, focused on a single goal: she would be finished wearing this demeaning cuff today.

As she slid the dagger down across the cuff and toward her foot, the blade slipped. She lost control, and before she realized what was happening, the point of the blade had driven into the top of her foot between the bones. Taryn bit back a scream, barely muffling it by clamping her jaw shut. Slowly, she drew the blade from her foot, watching the pink skin pucker, then slide shut as the knife was pulled free. It took a fraction of a second between removing the knife and the wound swelling with crimson blood, but every moment shone with diamond clarity in Taryn's mind. Then, time snapped back into focus, and she stared as blood began to pour from the wound. Pain, at last, flared through her, radiating upward from her foot to the top of her head. She moaned, pressing her thumb over the wound in some poor effort to staunch the bleeding. With her other hand, she tried to continue sawing at the cuff, but the dagger's blade had become too dull to do much good, and it slipped with every rasp, coming dangerously close to piercing her foot again.

Taryn threw the dagger across the room with an animal yell, frustration and anger and pain all rolled into one wordless scream. She mentally checked her arm's inventory—three throwing knives were all she had left, each sharp enough to cut through bone, but too narrow to do much good against the solid iron of her cuff. She closed her eyes, her foot still an agony of pain, trying to decide what to do next.

She could think of only one option.

She drew one of her throwing knives, testing its edge with her thumb. Moving slowly and deliberately, she set the blade just below the metal cuff that kept her prisoner, where the bones of her ankle met her foot. The difficulty, she knew, would lie in the risk of passing out from pain before the job was complete; without a way to staunch the wound, she was likely to bleed out if she fell unconscious. She knew of only one way to minimize that risk. Laying the knife carefully aside, she lifted her fingers to that narrow metal plate, no bigger than a playing card, on the back of her skull.

Taryn clicked the little hatch open, surprised by the waves of calm that washed over her, dulling even the burning pain in her foot. The burning pain she was about to increase one hundred-fold. She explored the space inside the hatch hesitantly, fingers dancing gingerly over the myriad tiny levers and dials that waited inside. The right lever would shut down her pain receptors. The wrong lever could incapacitate or even kill her.

Taryn's fingers hovered over the control panel, but she had no way of knowing which lever was correct. She clicked the hatch shut once more. It was too much risk to do a blind guess. She would have to do this without the aid of her dampers.

Steadying her breathing and the trembling in her hands, Taryn lifted the throwing knife and again pressed it to her ankle. Erikkson had taught her, once, the exact amount of force required to sever bone, and she pictured that number now, holding it in her mind like a promise. No matter how much it hurt, she would reach that pressure threshold. And then it would be all over. Taryn closed her eyes and began to press on the blade.

"Taryn! What are you doing?"

Her eyes snapped wide as the door burst open, Royal charging across the room to snatch the knife from her shaking fingers. He threw the blade away from them as hard as he could. It hit the far wall and clattered to the floor. His face was white as paper.

"Getting rid of it," she replied slowly, as if it was obvious. Her fingers were sticky with dried blood, the blanket beneath her a mess. She wished he had not interrupted. She had been so close.

"So you are going to cut your own foot off?" he exclaimed,

voice high and incredulous. "You would permanently maim yourself rather than wear something that will keep you safe?"

"No one can own me," she answered, every word slow and deliberate, her voice rising in volume as she spoke. "You do *not* own me. And for you to label me as though I am another dairy cow in your herd is degrading and dehumanizing!" She drew another knife and brought it to her ankle.

"Taryn, wait!" He caught her hands, fumbling for the knife, but the grip she had on the handle was iron, impossible to break.

"I shall not wear your name like a brand any longer!" she cried, anger turning her voice frantic. He gave up on attempting to wrest the knife from her grasp and held her wrists, keeping her from bringing it to her skin.

"Taryn, listen! If you want it gone, I can help you. You do not have to hurt yourself. We can do this the right way." His brown eyes searched her face, full of concern and—was that pity? "Just give me the knife."

Her white-knuckled grasp on her blade did not relent, her hands trembling. She did not want to relent. Didn't know if she believed him. But there was something in his eyes that made her ache deep inside, something that made her realize how truly mad she had become. Her fingers released their grip on the knife, and Royal eased it from her grasp. He carefully set it on the floor, out of her reach, and knelt so he could meet her downcast eyes. He took her hands in both of his.

"We will get that cuff off. I promise." His voice was soft and gentle, but there was a deep fear in his eyes, and his hands trembled a little around hers. With a slow, horrible shock, Taryn realized she had scared him badly. Badly enough to relent from his earlier insistence that she remain in compliance with the law. His face had lost all its color, and there was blood on his hands. Her blood.

Her whole body began to quake with the shock of what

she'd done. She shut her eyes, ashamed. She was a weapon. She hurt people. And when there were no more people to hurt, she hurt herself.

"Shh, Taryn, shh," he murmured, rising to sit beside her. One hand brushed her cropped copper hair back from her face, while the other still held her hands, warm and soft against her skin. "Do not cry. It will be all right. We will get rid of that cuff and then you will never belong to anyone but yourself ever again."

"Do you mean it?" she asked, almost afraid of the answer.

"Of course. We can take care of it now, if you like."

CHAPTER THIRTY

ROYAL WRAPPED Taryn's injured foot in a torn piece of the ruined bedsheet before helping her make her way to his study down the hall and around the corner from her room. He was doing his best to hide it, but the horror of seeing her sitting there in a mess of her own blood still bothered him so much his hands shook. He didn't want to consider how much further she would have gone if he had not interrupted. He didn't want to consider how close he'd come to finding her dead by her own hand. He'd agreed to remove the cuff for one reason only: he had seen the determination in her eyes.

He lifted her gently onto the mahogany wood of his desk, helping her settle there. Her face was pale with pain and blood loss, but her eyes were more lucid than he'd seen in days. He dragged a chair over, resting her foot on the back to elevate it to eye level, then turned away once more, searching for his tools and medical supplies.

His cheeks burned as he searched. She had never seen this room, and he worried what she would think. The walls were lined with bookshelves, upon which a variety of fine leather-bound books sat, along with many of his old clockwork projects.

The remnants of a fire burned in the hearth, hardly more than ashes. He rummaged through the drawers built into the shelves on the far wall, a plan to remove her cuff slowly forming in his head.

"Royal?" Her voice was barely more than a whisper.

"Yes?" He turned, worry spiking in his chest.

She held a clockwork heart in her hands, something he'd forgotten he kept on his desk. The organ was anatomically accurate and, if wound, would beat as a real heart did, the silver valves and chambers contracting with clockwork precision.

"Did you build this?"

His cheeks flared with hot embarrassment. He turned away on the pretense of searching for more tools. "Yes. I—there was a time when I intended to build my own biomatons."

He turned to her, catching the look of surprise on her face. "Not as slaves, Tiger. I did not understand that biomatons were any different. At least, not yet. I just— I wanted to help people." He shook his head, carrying both his toolbox and his box of medical equipment over to her, setting them beside her on the desk. "I must sound silly to you."

"This is well made," she murmured, turning the clockwork heart over in her hands. "Master Erikkson chose the correct apprentice."

Royal's ears burned, hot tears springing unbidden to his eyes, and he turned his face away again, unwrapping the bloody sheet tied around her foot. His jaw clenched as he revealed the wound—a gaping slit in the top of her foot, as long as his thumbnail and obviously deep. He did not think she would need stitches, though, and he was thankful for it. He did not think his nerves would stand up to the strain of inflicting that kind of pain on her. He drew a clean linen bandage from his kit. Methodically, he wrapped her foot, winding the bandage as Erikkson had taught him.

When he had finished with her injury, Royal turned his

attention to the iron cuff around Taryn's ankle. He studied her marks upon it, the second *K* in his last name nearly obliterated in her urgent attempts to cut through the cuff. At least she had started there, giving him time to stop her from doing something more drastic and permanent.

"What on earth possessed you to attempt to remove this on your own?" he questioned, twisting the cuff so he could examine the hinged side.

Taryn gasped, her foot jerking involuntarily.

Royal's hands flew away from the cuff. "I am so sorry! I did not mean to hurt you!" Only now did he notice the vivid red welts beneath the cuff, blistered burns still raw and painful.

"Do what you must—" Taryn hissed through gritted teeth, her eyes shut tightly. He noted she had set the clockwork heart aside, and had her left hand clamped around her right forearm.

"I cannot do this," he choked out. "Perhaps in a few weeks, when these burns are healed…"

Her emerald eyes snapped open, fixing him with an icy stare. "I do not care. Do it."

"Taryn, it will hurt you!"

She leaned forward. "Would you rather I did it myself?"

Royal's jaw snapped together. He rummaged in his toolkit, until he found the narrow rasp he planned to use.

"I am going to file through the cuff," he told her, more to settle his own nerves than to explain his actions to her. "It may cause the cuff to press against your injuries, so please tell me if it hurts."

She nodded, her lips drawn into a thin line. Royal chewed the inside of his cheek, considering how best to hold on to the cuff to keep it from moving too much. He finally opted for slipping his fingers through the band and gripping it tightly, his knuckles brushing against her pale ankle. He had not realized how small her feet were until he contrasted them with his own large hands and long fingers. He brushed an invisible strand of hair out of his eyes with his forearm, then brought the rasp into contact with the iron cuff.

The work was slow and tedious, the sound of the file grating on his nerves. He could only imagine how it affected Taryn. She sat with her head tilted back, her eyes closed, her hands flat against the desktop and supporting her weight. He watched her for a moment, the way her face moved suddenly unfamiliar to him, as if he had never really seen her before. The way the light of the gas lamps hit her cheekbones illuminated the sharp lines of her face, emphasizing the hollows at the corners of her eyes, the base of her throat. Had her lashes always been that deep golden red? Or had they somehow caught and stored some of the fire they reflected?

"Why did you stop?" Taryn interrupted, her eyes snapping open to examine him. Royal swallowed the butterflies beating in his throat. His hands had stopped of their own accord.

"I—I wanted to make sure you were still all right," he spluttered. He was making a fool of himself.

"I am." She leaned forward to study the cuff. "You have made more progress than I."

He studied the deep furrow he'd made in the metal, the sharp silver shavings scattered across the desk, the carpet, his hands, her bandage. He took up the file again, scraping it over the metal. "Ms. Scuttle will have my hide for the mess I am making," he muttered. "These shavings will be impossible to clean up."

He hoped she would take up the jest with some witty retort of her own, but she did not reply. He sighed. He'd seen his Taryn in her, hiding somewhere behind that stony mask she wore, and he missed her. He wished there were some way to bring her back to him, but he understood that was not how this worked. Taryn had been badly injured, and only time would heal her wounds. If he pushed her too hard, he would only cause her to retreat further into herself.

"Nearly there," he said after several more minutes of filing. He adjusted his grip on the band, ready to catch it the moment it broke open. At the same time, he slowed his filing to a crawl so he would not drive the rasp into her skin. "Annnnnd... there."

The cuff broke open, and he dropped it to the floor with a final thud. He stared numbly at the red ring of burns left behind on her ankle, his stomach churning.

"You did it!" Taryn exclaimed. She threw her arms around his neck. "Thank you!" Her lips brushed his jawbone, and regardless of whether it was accidental or not, heat spread across his face.

Royal extricated himself from her embrace, though he would have gladly remained there forever, were it not for the twinge of his conscience telling him he was somehow taking advantage of this moment. He wanted to kiss her, to feel the brush of her soft lips on his once again, but he instead turned to packing away his tools.

"I will just clean up a little here, Tiger, and then I will help you back to your room."

"No hurry," she said. "Take your time. Thank you for removing it." There was a look of joy in her eyes, though she was not smiling. Her cheeks were ruddy with warmth and her copper hair floated around her head like a halo. It was the happiest he'd seen her in a long time.

He nodded, turning his back to her. "Anything for you," he mumbled.

"Royal?"

He turned to look at her from across the room. His heart lurched into his throat at her beauty, even disheveled and haggard as she was. "Yes?"

"I think you should build biomatons. Carry on Master Erikkson's legacy. Build them as he did. Build them human."

He smiled, going and picking her up like a child or a bride, carrying her back to her room so she would not have to put weight on her injured foot. "Perhaps. If I do, will you be there to teach them they are human?"

She leaned her head against his chest, her eyelids drooping. A combination of distress and blood loss had exhausted her. Royal hoped she could rest. She needed it. "If I live that long," she murmured.

"You will," he insisted. "Oh Tiger, you will."

◆

Ace caught Royal as he gently closed the door to Taryn's bedroom.

"How is she?" he asked, disregarding the pretense of greeting or small talk in his concern for Taryn.

Royal's brows drew together, the corners of his mouth tightening. "She is very sick, Ace."

"What? What is wrong?"

"Not physically. Mentally." Royal tilted his head back, brown eyes roving across the ornate ceiling inlay, chewing at the side of his thumb. "I refused to take off her tag, so she— she took it into her own hands. Gor, you should have seen it. The blood—" He squeezed his eyes shut. "I think she really would have tried to cut her own foot off had I not interrupted."

Ace bolted forward, terror spurring him into action. He reached for the door handle, but Royal pushed him back, shaking his head. "She is all right now. I bandaged her injuries and removed her cuff. She was nearly asleep when I left the room. We should not disturb her. I do not think she has slept in some time."

"She hurt herself?" Ace demanded. His heart throbbed in his throat.

"Yes." Royal dragged a hand over his face, shaking his head.

"That is not like her. I know her, and that is not in her, Ace. My Taryn would never do something like that."

Ace's hackles rose at the way he said "my Taryn," but he chose to pass the phrase by.

"She spent an entire week in isolation, Royal." Ace wrung his hands together, eyes trained on her door as if, if he just stared hard enough, he could see through it to where she lay. "Solitary confinement does something to a person's mind. I have seen it before. Criminals go mad, all alone. They do anything to receive human contact of any kind. Even injure themselves."

"You were supposed to protect her! How could you let them do that to her?"

Ace stared at the younger boy, eyes flaring with anger.

"Do you think I do not blame myself for what happened? Do you think I did not *beg* for them to let her go?" He pointed over Royal's shoulder at the door. "I swore to her I would protect her, and now she will not even speak to me! I have to live with my *failure* every day! I do not need you to throw it back in my face."

Royal looked away, taken aback by Ace's exclamation. "I apologize, Ace. I did not realize—"

"You did not realize you were not the only one who cares about her," Ace interrupted, his voice hard. "We *all* care about her. And it will take all of us to help her heal."

Royal's thumb returned to his mouth. "I am sorry, Ace. It has been a difficult few days."

Ace scoffed. "You have no idea."

The housekeeper Ace had seen once or twice—a *human* housekeeper, who lived in a little cottage on the property and Royal claimed was 'practically family'—raced toward them, her face red with exertion. "Begging your pardon, Master Stokker," she wheezed in her matronly Yorkshire accent, "but there are two young folks at the kitchen door demanding to see you." She lowered her voice to a confidential tone. "I believe they are foreign."

Royal cocked an eyebrow at him, and Ace knew they both suspected the same thing.

"Thank you, Ms. Scuttle," Royal answered. "I will be down immediately." The woman bustled off, and Royal looked again at Ace. "Are you coming?"

The former privateer almost grinned. "I would not miss it."

Together, they hurried down to the kitchen's back door through which groceries were delivered. Two figures stood in the doorway, looking unhappy to have been left in the cold of the gathering dusk. Ace nodded to them both, pleased to see Emmett looking just the same as ever. Petrichor's expression was sour, and she tried to push past Royal as soon as he came to greet them, sweeping her hood off. "Where is she?"

"What?"

"Sedition. Where is she?" Again, she tried to press past him. Royal held out his arms to stop her.

"Taryn is resting for the first time in days. You can see her tomorrow."

"Quite the welcome wagon, Your Highness," Petrichor remarked coldly.

"I am very glad to see you both, as I am sure Taryn will be when she sees you, but I cannot allow you to disturb her tonight."

Petrichor at last shoved her way into the room, stalking around the kitchen in circles. "I don't think you get the urgency here, Your Highness."

"Please do not call me that."

Petrichor spun on him, her metal jaw piece snapping shut with a *clack*. "We have exactly a fortnight until the Queen takes a turn around London town. It's the first time she'll appear in public for years, and it's our best chance to get her. We don't have *time* for Sedition's mental fragility."

As she spoke, Emmett entered the room and quietly clapped Ace on the shoulder. He gave his old shipmate a smile that felt more like a grimace and a nod that said "we will talk later."

"You—you want to assassinate the Queen?" Royal choked on the words.

"Sure. It's our best bet, now that the army's practically *nil*. We take out the Queen, we can set someone more sympathetic on the throne. Maybe even Sedition."

"That is not how the British government works! The Queen has no real power! She is just the figurehead!" Royal exclaimed, exasperated. Ace smiled to himself, enjoying watching the two argue.

"Kid, I know how the government works. Trust me. This is our best chance."

"It is our only chance," Emmett interrupted. "We do not have the manpower for any greater resistance. It is this, or *le fin*. This, or we give up."

"That's not an option," Petrichor growled. "Not after you forced me to come all this way. We finish the job."

"It is suicide!" Royal exclaimed.

"There is a chance we succeed," Ace offered. "And Tar may benefit from a new goal to focus on. Something to take her mind off her failures." *Our failures. My failures.*

Petrichor pointed at Ace. "See? Even the pirate agrees with me."

Royal grunted. "Very well, but I still have to insist you save it for tomorrow. Let her sleep tonight. Please."

Petrichor gave a curt nod. She turned her attention to Ace, her hands on her hips. "So, reunion. Can't say you're looking well, Ace, 'cause you aren't. I assume it's part of Lord Bellham's kind hospitality?"

Ace grimaced and nodded. "You could call it that."

"Then I assume you will want a part in any revenge we plan?"

"Oh, yes."

Petrichor glanced around the room. "For a kitchen, this place is disappointingly bare of food."

"It has all been put away for the night," Royal answered lamely.

"Well get it back out! Your guests are hungry!"

Royal glowered, but hurried to find something in the pantry. Petrichor rolled her eyes. "We've survived on nothing but garbage for more than a week, and while it's not the first time, it's never fun."

"How did you survive?" Ace asked. "I thought the soldiers were coming down hard on illegal biomatons."

"They are," Emmett replied. "We hid from them. Luckily, no one pays much attention to the blind man in dark glasses." He grinned mischievously.

"The real question is how did you and Red survive?" Petrichor asked. Royal brought a loaf of rustic bread, a hard wheel of cheese, and a small Italian sausage from the pantry for them. "Thanks." Petrichor snatched the loaf of bread and tore a large chunk from it before passing it to Emmett.

"Taryn was in the basement of the west wing. I was in the stables."

"And Lord Bellham?"

"Had an arrangement with Storm, which gave him the rights to all biomaton survivors. We did not stand a chance against the soldiers. And the Black Castle tortured us both, but Taryn most of all. She is not herself."

Petrichor's jaw clicked. "Then I have my work cut out for me, if Sedition's going to be ready."

"But not tonight," Royal insisted again. "I will find you both rooms for the night. You may see her tomorrow."

"Yeah, yeah, we got it the first time." She drew one of her

throwing knives and sliced into the cheese. "Has anyone heard from Seraphim?"

"Not yet," Royal answered. "Gennifer and Rorin are here, though."

Emmett's brows knit together. "Rorin? And what of Ari?"

Ace shook his head, a familiar heaviness settling in his gut. "Ari was killed when Elmhurst fell."

"*Mon Dieu,*" Emmett murmured, setting aside his half-eaten slice of bread. Ace saw tears sparking in the Frenchman's eyes. "I can only imagine how it would feel to lose a twin."

"Like losing a part of yourself," Petrichor murmured. The kitchen fell very still for a moment, each person ruminating over who—and what—they'd lost. For a few minutes, all the enmity between them was forgotten in the mutual mourning of their fallen friends. And then, Petrichor snapped her fingers at Royal.

"Show us where Gennifer and Rorin are, Your Highness, and then you can prepare our rooms." The right side of her mouth quirked upward. "Mine had better have a big mattress. It's been ages since I slept in a real bed."

CHAPTER THIRTY-ONE

Ace trod softly toward his room hours later, exhausted after the stilted conversation, the pseudo planning, the way Petrichor refused to show an ounce of reverence for their losses. He'd at last put his finger on what it was that bothered him about her: she dominated the space. It mattered little what room she entered—as soon as she arrived, she overpowered any other personality, taking charge in a way that was both belittling and discouraging. In contrast, Taryn's personality allowed everyone else in the room to thrive; rather than crushing her peers, she quietly offered them space to be themselves. He'd never seen her take charge the way Petrichor did.

Although... He *had* seen Sedition take charge that way. Sedition's strength of personality could crush anyone else in the room. Ace realized Petrichor must have been trained to take charge that way, just as Taryn—Sedition—had. For the first time, he was grateful Taryn had been sent away, her memories erased. Had she remained with Erikkson those five years, he had no doubt she would have lost all that was soft and gentle about her as well. Taryn and Petrichor were more alike than either would admit.

On a whim, he strode all the way down the hall, past his own room and to Taryn's door. He did not intend to enter, as he knew better than anyone how vital it was that she rest, but he pressed his palm to the wood, a knot of loneliness swelling in his gut. "I miss you," he murmured.

He turned to go but halted mid-step. There seemed to be the murmur of voices coming from behind her door. Ace strained his ears, trying to hear what was going on. All fell silent for a moment, and then, clear as day, he heard Taryn shout. "No!"

Ace threw her door open, all sense of propriety deserting him in his concern for her well-being. Manners be hanged, if she was in danger, he would help!

He took in the scene in a fraction of a second: Taryn, sitting amidst a tangle of blankets, her hair matted with sweat, tears streaming down her cheeks. No one else was in the room.

"Are you all right?" he questioned. "I heard you cry out—"

She passed her right hand over her face. "Nightmare," she answered.

"May I come in?"

She nodded, though her face remained turned away. Ace closed the door softly behind him, treading lightly as he crossed the distance between them. He sat in the chair beside her bed, studying her still-trembling frame.

"Do you want to talk about it?" he asked softly.

She shook her head. She scrubbed her flesh and blood hand across her cheeks, wiping away the tears there. Soft moonlight fell through the gauzy curtains that hung over the window, illuminating the room in shades of blue and silver. It would almost have been peaceful, intimate, even, if not for the heavy atmosphere of grief that hung over her.

"Tar, I am sorry for failing you in the Black Castle."

She twisted around to face him, green eyes full of surprise. "What happened was my fault. I am not angry with you."

"Then why have you shut me out?"

She stared down at her hands, folded in her lap, her metal fist a tight ball. "It is better for me to be alone. I hurt everyone who cares about me."

"That is not true!"

She blinked at him. "Did the Black Castle not treat you better after I had been removed from the equation?"

"No," he leaned toward her, "they did not. They treated me just as poorly as always, and I bore the added burden of worry over what tortures you were facing, alone in the dark. All I wanted was to rescue you, and I could not even comfort you."

She stared at him, her eyes filling again with tears. He noted the stark, indigo circles under her eyes, the narrow lines beneath her mouth—tiny, premature wrinkles, like physical manifestations of her trauma.

"You still do not know what I did."

"It does not matter to me what—"

"It *does* matter!" she interrupted. She stared down at her hands, eyes wide and far away, seeing something he could not. "I killed, Ace," she murmured. "And not just our tormentors. I killed biomatons in the ring. I murdered the people I am meant to protect. And all because I am weak. I am so weak."

He caught her hands. She stared at the blood she could not wash away. His throat ached as he at last understood what she had endured alone at the Black Castle. He had seen those biomaton fighting rings, so long ago—Storm had a particular taste for the fights—and the very notion of her being exposed to that, let alone *fight* in it, made him sick with anger. He pressed her hands to his forehead. "You are forgiven," he murmured. "You are *forgiven*."

Tears rolled down her cheeks. She threw herself into his arms, burying her face in his chest. As he cradled her, he realized he'd never really understood how small, how fragile she was. She felt like a child, there in his arms, and a surge of protectiveness thrummed through him. He suddenly realized he would die for this girl, if it came to it.

He stroked her hair, for a moment content to hold her.

"I have good news," he whispered into her hair. "Emmett and Petrichor arrived this evening. They are all right. And Gennifer and Ari are here as well. You are not alone." He considered telling her of their half-formed plan to attack the Queen but thought better of it. There was time enough to spur her to action later. Tonight would be about hope. About casting off that deep gray curtain of despair she'd given control of her life.

She nodded, but did not answer. She sat up, pressing away from him. Ace's heart fell. He had expected her to express some excitement at their arrival, but her face remained a flat mask. She shoved her tears away with the back of her hand.

"Did you tell them what I have become?"

"No, Tar. They are all concerned about you, but I thought it would be better for you to speak with them yourself."

She wrung her hands together. "They will not want me if they know what I have done. If they know I lived when I was meant to die, and because of that, all of Elmhurst died instead."

"What are you talking about?"

She held up her hands, palms out, as if to show him something. "I am a weapon, Ace. I have a single, terrible purpose. Swords get beaten into ploughshares at peace time, but what fate is left for me? I was not meant to survive the war. Every graft, every bit of programming confirms that."

"Your grafts are not so strange—"

"Give me your arm," she ordered. Ace held out his right arm (his clockwork arm) to her, but she shook her head. "Your other arm." Puzzled, he held out his left arm, and she caught his wrist with her clockwork hand, holding on to him with a vise-like grip.

"Ow."

"I am not applying any of my strength. I am *trying* to be gentle." She locked eyes with him and released his arm. "I was built for warfare. Master Erikkson never intended me to see the other side."

"Erikkson loved you! He would not intend so poor an end as that for you!" Ace exclaimed, once again feeling sick at her words. He wanted to rub the aching spot she'd held on his wrist, feeling a bruise blossoming beneath the surface, but he kept himself still, knowing his reaction would hurt her.

"Then explain my grafts," she retorted bitterly. She rose, or tried to, gasping and sitting back on the bed as soon as she put any weight on her left foot. Ace offered her his hand, but she shook him away, refusing his touch. She gave him a tight-lipped smile. "I am fine," she gasped.

Ace chewed the inside of his cheek, feeling as though he was missing something vital. He had the answers, if only he could access the correct memories, the correct sequence... He could not believe Erikkson would build Taryn to only survive in combat. Erikkson had been controlling, perhaps, but he had also been loving and benevolent, and his plans outlasted the war. There was no reason to believe he had built Taryn only to die.

His eyes lit up. "Master Erikkson had a secret project he was working on!"

She stared at him, face blank. "So?"

"I saw that project the night Elmhurst fell. It was a clockwork arm, Taryn, like your own. No weapons. No enhancements. Just clockwork."

She shook her head. "That could have been for anyone—"

"Would he have hidden it from you if it was for just anyone? He intended it for you, Tar, for when the war was over." He caught her hands, squeezing them firmly in his own. Her palm was warm and clammy against his fingers.

"No. I—no." She shook her head again, hard, as if to shake off the idea. "That is impossible."

"You are more than a weapon, Taryn. It is time you accepted that. The rest of us have seen it from the beginning. You are not a machine, you are not a weapon; you are human, with all the beautiful perfection and all the beautiful flaws of humanity. Embrace it."

She turned her face away from him, her shoulders shaking. Her voice grew hoarse. "I—I think you should go, Ace."

"Taryn—" he protested, devastated by her sudden change of heart. He'd hoped her letting him in had been a turning point, a moment where they could build upon their friendship before she'd been torn away from him at the Black Castle. This sudden denial brought shame burning into his cheeks, and he couldn't understand why.

But it was clear from her body language, from the way she kept turning away from him, even the words she spoke, that she was hurting. She was in pain, more pain than he could possibly understand. And he didn't know how to help. It hurt, having to watch her go through this from a distance. Not being able to offer anything, words or touch or knowledge, that could possibly make a difference. He knew that wasn't how healing worked.

But god, he wished it did.

"Just go, Ace, please."

He touched her shoulder, barely more than the brush of a butterfly's wing. She jerked as if he'd struck her. He was suddenly transported to another moment, so long ago, when she flinched at his touch. A blush of shame heated his cheeks. "I care about you," he whispered.

"I know. I just— I need to be alone."

He sighed and rose, his insides feeling heavier than lead. "Very well. I will be down the hall if you need anything. I—" He stopped, the words he had never been brave enough to say catching in his throat. He turned away, his face burning. Even after all this time, he was still just a coward.

☙

Taryn watched as Ace left the room, rubbing her left shoulder where the clockwork met flesh, her mind circling over and over his last words.

Erikkson's secret project...

But she knew it had to be a lie. She'd known for so long that the war would end in death for her. It seemed so clear from the start. And yet, now she was not so sure. Ace had ripped the rug of certainty out from beneath her to reveal the world was made of tissue paper, liable to tear away at any moment.

She caught sight of her reflection in the window to her right, but it was not her reflection. Erikkson's face stared back at her through the glass, flat and disappointed.

"Is what Ace said true?" she questioned the apparition. "Were you building that arm for me?"

"I think you already know the answer to that," he replied.

"I was meant to die for them!"

"You were meant to be their leader," he said reproachfully. "You were not meant to hide yourself away when things became difficult. Did I not tell you this would not be easy? Did I not say you would lose people?"

Taryn set her jaw, chewing the inside of her cheek. She'd done it so much in the past few days that there was a large, raw sore spot there, which quickly began to bleed. She stopped herself from chewing at it. "But we *failed. I* failed!"

"While you still live, the rebellion lives with you."

She covered her face in her hands, shoulders shaking. She no longer wanted to be the leader. She no longer wanted to fight. She'd seen too many corpses, borne too many blows. Too many of her friends were dead. Now, she was tired, so tired, and all she wanted was to rest.

"You do not rest," Erikkson's apparition said. "Not until this battle is won. Too many helpless children are relying on you to win their freedom."

"I cannot win anything!" she wept. "I lost! All I do is lose and lose and lose. I cannot even win myself freedom, let alone an entire race."

"I love you, little one," his voice took on a kinder, gentler edge.

"You say that," she sighed, "but I know you are an apparition, a nightmare. You are not here. I could not even save you."

"I love you, little one," he repeated. "I know you will do the right thing."

"You are not real!" she screamed, raising her head to stare at the windowpane, where her master's face still stared back at her, semi-transparent. "You are dead!"

"Finish what we started. Then you may rest."

She pressed her hands over her ears, squeezing her eyes shut, but she could hear him just as well as she had before.

"Your friends are counting on you."

"No," she sobbed. "No."

"You survived for a reason, Sedition. Do not throw away the gift you have been given."

He fell silent for a moment, and she thought the hallucination had at last passed, but then he spoke again. "I love you, little one."

Taryn curled onto her side, sobbing. She had failed. She was a coward. She sobbed for everyone she had been too weak to save. She sobbed for her army and her friends, for Ari and Jack and the nameless slave she'd murdered in the ring. She wept for Erikkson, dead at Storm's hand, dead because Taryn had made an enemy of Storm and lured her there. But more than that, she wept because the mere idea of going back into the fight terrified her. She'd been too injured—tortured and abused and manipulated. She'd watched her creator die and her friends suffer. She'd lived alone in the dark with her ghosts until she could not bear the silence any longer. And she dreaded going back out for another fight. She did not think she had any fight left within her.

A still, small voice deep inside Taryn waited patiently until she spent her sobs, until she was left with an aching throat and hollow chest, and then it whispered four small words.

If not you, who?

CHAPTER THIRTY-TWO

"Good morning, Taryn. It is good to see you up," Royal greeted as she limped into the dining room. He was settled at the head of the table, with six spots laid out for those who had not yet arrived, and a grand breakfast spread across the table. She limped to a seat and sat gratefully, her black chiffon mourning gown billowing with her movement. She smoothed her skirt over her knees.

"How is your foot?" Royal asked, inclining his head toward her.

"Sore, but better. It is such a relief to have that weight lifted," she answered. She studied the fine white china laid out in front of her, turmoil welling in her stomach. She did not know why she was here at breakfast; the last place she wanted to be was at the table with six other people, all staring at her, speaking too gently and generally treating her like some fragile thing that could snap at any moment. Still, she had felt compelled to come downstairs, in spite of her aching left foot, and not just because of the hollow, empty hunger that gnawed at her ribs. Something was bound to happen at this breakfast table, and she knew she could not miss it.

"Help yourself," Royal urged. She gingerly took a slice of toast and spread butter over the paler side.

Ace entered, and at the sight of Taryn, his face lit up. He'd grown thinner, too, she realized, and his olive skin had taken on an ashen undertone. But for all that, he glowed at the sight of her. He sat beside her and silently took her hand beneath the table, squeezing it affectionately. Taryn felt her stomach flutter in a way she had once been certain was impossible. She slipped her fingers from his grasp, tucking her hair behind her ear, cheeks hot, revealing that white half-moon scar in the top of her ear.

Royal did not notice the affectionate moment, nodding his welcome to Ace. The older boy began to serve himself—eggs, bacon, toast, fried tomatoes. Taryn was grateful to see his illness was not affecting his appetite. Then it was not consumption, at any rate. She counted the other settings at the table. Four settings. Four biomatons. Petrichor. Emmett. Rorin. Gennifer. The remnants of Erikkson's grand biomaton army. She only hoped they were not all as shattered as she.

"*Cherie!*" Emmett raced toward her, sweeping her up in a tight embrace before she could stop him. Taryn choked, feeling claustrophobic. "We thought you were dead!"

Carefully, she extricated herself from his arms. "We thought the same of you," she replied slowly.

Emmett took the chair directly across from her, his clockwork eyes shining. "*Je suis desole, belle.* I saw Elmhurst. It is a devastating sight."

She cast her eyes away. "You ought to have seen it burning."

"All of our friends—" Emmett broke off, shaking his head. Ever one to wear his heart on his sleeve, tears now danced across the surface of his clockwork eyes, and he held out his hands across the table, one to Royal at the head, and one to Ace across the table. They both took the proffered gesture, Royal with a wry smile and Ace with a deeply knowing look. Royal and Ace both offered their other hands to Taryn.

She hesitated for a moment, then slowly grasped each of their hands in hers. Ace's calloused hand was warm and surprisingly soft in her palm. She could not feel Royal grasping her metal one, but hoped she was not squeezing too tightly.

"While we yet breathe, we remember them," Emmett said solemnly, his voice low and melodic, almost like a prayer. "They were our friends, our mentors, *nos frères et soeurs d'armes*. We honor their sacrifices. We carry them with us."

Taryn pressed her lips together, feeling tears press behind her eyes. "We carry them with us," she whispered softly in response.

"We *will* avenge them, *cherie*. They did not die in vain."

Taryn's shoulders tensed. She let go of Ace and Royal's hands. Emmett's words bothered her in a way she did not understand. The Emmett she had known before would never have turned to violence as the answer. And yet, here he was, touting vengeance as their best weapon. She felt ill. More bloodshed would only leave them in the same position they currently held, or worse. She could not endure the Black Castle for a third time.

She hunched over her plate, eyes down, nibbling at the corner of her toast. The food settled her stomach somewhat, and she raised her eyes to catch sight of Rorin and Gennifer standing in the doorway, saluting her. Taryn's heart stopped. Tears welled in her eyes. She had no idea how to tell them she no longer deserved their salutes. She realized she had never seen Rorin without his brother before the night Elmhurst fell and seeing him there in the doorway like a mirror with no reflection turned the dull ache of guilt in her chest to a stabbing bloom of pain. She wished again to turn back time. She inclined her head to the two, and they took their seats at the table.

The room fell into a hideous, pregnant silence. Taryn held her breath. She was not ready for this; even without raising her eyes, she could feel them all watching her, anxious looks of expectation or concern trained on her, waiting for her to speak. She'd thought, as she dressed that morning, that she could handle a handful of eyes—she had handled the arena and the auction, after all. But it turned out that a few stares from those who knew her well were worse than thousands of strangers.

"Well good morning," a new clipped voice came from the doorway. Taryn instantly recognized the dulcet contralto of Petrichor's New York accent. She kept her eyes trained on her plate. "Glad I made it for the funeral."

The joke fell painfully flat, as most of the people seated at the table wore half or full mourning. Petrichor didn't seem to care. She rolled her eyes, seating herself. "Tough crowd," she quipped, tucking into the food laid out before her.

Taryn had lost her appetite. There were now entirely too many people in the dining room, and she found it hard to breathe.

"Red, you're skinny as a rail. Eat something, or I'll come over there and make you eat something."

Taryn waited for her usual anger to flare up, the violent monster that lived inside her head reacting to Petrichor's words, but instead a kind of fearful cowardice came over her. She took a small bite of her toast to show Petrichor she was not fasting. Out of her periphery, she caught a glimpse of the glare Ace gave Petrichor, the way he slowly shook his head.

"Did you have a pleasant night?" Royal asked no one in particular.

Emmett nodded, speaking between sips of hot coffee. "*Oui*. My room is very comfortable. I thank you for your hospitality."

"I could not very well turn you all away," Royal answered. "Only you must be prepared to conceal yourselves at a moment's notice. I have been inspected more than once already for my involvement with Lord Erikkson, and I anticipate they will come again."

"I should be glad for a chance at a little revenge," Rorin growled.

"You will not be killing any soldiers on my property. That is a sure way to find ourselves on the wrong end of the hangman's noose."

"No need to involve your lordship," Ace hissed. "You could say we went rogue and held you hostage."

"What do you say, Sedition?" Petrichor exclaimed, leaning forward. "Should we make some redcoats redder?"

Taryn shoved herself back from the table, the legs of her chair groaning. She stood and limped from the room. She held herself in as dignified a manner as she could manage, but her limp prevented her from stalking from the room as she would have liked. She managed a few steps down the hallway and stopped, sagging against the wall. Her breathing came in shallow bursts. She pressed her thumb against the number etched into her arm, trying to ground herself in reality.

"You didn't stay long enough for me to tell you how much I like your haircut." Petrichor jabbed Taryn in the ribs from behind. Taryn curled in on herself, barely hiding a whimper as it rose in her throat. "I'm guessing it wasn't your choice?"

Taryn shook her head. Shame burned in her cheeks. For the first time, she realized she *feared* her biomaton sister. Petrichor was wild and unpredictable, and Taryn did not trust herself to handle whatever she threw at her any longer.

Petrichor sighed. "Look at me, Red." Her metal heel thumped against the floor. "I said *look at me*."

Chewing her lip, Taryn turned to face Petrichor, her heart thundering in her ears. "If you are planning to challenge me again for the role of leader, I shall save you the trouble. You are welcome to it."

Petrichor's lips quirked, but there was a deep sadness in her brown eyes. "I am not fit for that role. Sedition was built to lead."

Taryn's chin snapped up. "Sedition is dead."

"What?"

"She died at the Black Castle. Please, take her position. She can no longer fill it."

"Sedition's not dead."

"And you are the expert? You never cared about her!"

Petrichor's mouth fell open, her chest heaving, words failing her. Tears hung on her lashes. She lunged forward, shoving Taryn against the wall, her clockwork hand curling around Taryn's throat. Taryn raised her hands in surrender, her frightened green eyes locked with Petrichor's dark ones.

"I would have done *anything* to protect you, *Red*," Petrichor hissed. "Not that you remember any of that." Her eyes flickered to Taryn's forearm, and her demeanor suddenly relaxed. She let Taryn go, stepping back.

"Oh god," she murmured, and the words were the nearest to praying Taryn had ever heard her utter. "You too, huh?"

Taryn swallowed hard, her face betraying some of that feral, terrified wariness she'd brought home from the Black Castle. She did not speak.

Petrichor's voice became much gentler. "How many times did they make you fight?"

Bowing her head, Taryn trembled at her sister's shrewd understanding of what she'd been forced to do at the Black Castle. She shook her head.

"How many times, Taryn?"

It was the first time she'd used her given name, and it stung as if Petrichor had slapped her. "Twice. Then I snapped and they put me on ice. The only reason they did not kill me is because I was worth too much." The words all tumbled out in a heap, piling up on the carpet runner beneath her feet.

"That's two times too many. I am sorry, Red," Petrichor murmured. "I really am. I know how bad the ring can be."

"Do not tell Royal. Please. He thinks me innocent and—and good, and I do not want him to know what a monster I truly am."

"It's your secret to tell. I won't interfere. But..." Petrichor shook her head. "I don't think you can keep it from him forever."

"I will deal with that when I get to it."

"Sure you will." The former assassin reached out, as if to touch Taryn's arm, but when Taryn shied away, she drew her hand back. Her eyes roved the hall, as if unsure where to look.

"So now you understand why I cannot lead. Why Sedition must die like her creator. We—I—betrayed everything Erikkson fought for." Taryn pressed the heels of her palms over her eyes until a headache blossomed at the front of her skull. "I killed for the wrong side. I am a hypocrite and a coward."

The words flowed so easily, as if she and Petrichor had some deep connection, as if Taryn trusted her innately. She could not have had an easier time talking to her biomaton sister if they had grown up together, sleeping in the same room, sharing everything the way only sisters can. Taryn bit down on her tongue, reminding herself that she had never had a sister and could not know what it was like. She'd never even had a childhood.

"You're not the first of us to fight in the ring." Petrichor crossed her arms. "You're not *special* because you killed a few biomatons. I was there for two weeks when I was sixteen. And do you think a face like this gets programmed to be a lady's maid?" She shrugged. "Erikkson's training kept me alive. It kept you alive. We do what we have to in order to survive, because we were built to win the freedom of our kind. I'm not saying it's right that you killed those kids. I'm just saying you did what you had to. They threatened Ace if you didn't fight, didn't they?"

Taryn nodded silently, tears hanging on her lashes. She leaned against the wall for support. She had always been told that talking about a trauma eased the burden of it, but she felt no lighter after admitting her actions to Petrichor. If anything, talking about it only brought the images flooding back to the surface, more painful and vivid than ever. Still, talking to Petrichor eased the weight of Erikkson's specter, and she no longer felt his words of admonishment in her ear. She was grateful for that, at least.

Petrichor leaned against the wall beside Taryn, tucking her long, dark hair behind one ear. "You know, Red, I used to resent Erikkson for building us to fight his war. I thought it was unfair that we had no choice. I ran all the way to New York just to escape it."

"And now?" Taryn murmured.

"Now I realize he never had any stakes in this war. He didn't stand to benefit in any way if our kind were freed. I still don't love the way he did it, but—" Petrichor huffed a little, in awe or frustration or sorrow Taryn could not tell. She had her arms wrapped across her stomach in a kind of protective position, and Taryn thought she was finally seeing through the cocky façade Petrichor wore to the girl underneath. She felt a kind of kinship to the expression in Petrichor's eyes: a mixture of frustration and love, duty and anger. "He built us to fight our own fight. And he'd be rolling in his grave if he knew you wanted to give up."

Taryn held her breath, considering what her sister had said. She had a point. And though Taryn still felt shattered inside—she did not think that could ever truly, completely heal—she found a single spark deep inside her igniting with Petrichor's words. Taryn had believed all the sparks inside her were dead, and now she cupped her hands around this one, breathing on it gently to coax it back to life.

"And what you said earlier, about me not caring about you? You're wrong, Red. I didn't leave because of the Black Castle. I left because I disagreed with what Erikkson did to you, wiping your memory and throwing you out like that. I was the one who'd done something unforgivable. I should have taken the rap."

"I know about Henry," Taryn whispered, turning her head to look at Petrichor.

"You do?"

"I remember," Taryn nodded. "And I remember the way you tried to prevent Master Erikkson from wiping my memory. You may have killed Henry, but I ordered it. I deserved to bear the guilt."

Abruptly, Petrichor grabbed Taryn and pulled her close. Taryn braced herself for a fight, fists clenching— Until she realized that it was an embrace, not a combative maneuver.

Petrichor, the Clockwork Assassin, Taryn's tormentor and nemesis since the moment she had joined their fight, was *hugging her.*

And with a horrible jolt of shock, Taryn realized not only did it feel good, it felt *familiar.*

A gasping sob emerged from Taryn's lips, and she tried to shove Petrichor off, too startled by the emotions and memories that flooded her to bear the tightness of her embrace.

Petrichor, only a few years older than her, showing her how to fight with a dagger for the first time.

Petrichor, sitting beside her on a massive four-poster bed, smiling with her crooked smile as sunlight illuminated her long hair like a halo, and Taryn thinking: *You are the most beautiful girl in the world.*

The two of them racing across the grassy fields of Elmhurst, chasing one another and laughing, faces red with the heat.

Petrichor sick in bed, and Taryn snuggled in beside her feverish body, Erikkson handing them books and cups of broth until Petrichor was well.

Petrichor showing Taryn the places on the body that were most vulnerable to a punch or a weapon. Teaching her to aim for the throat, the eyes, the heart, the groin. Teaching her how to not only harm, but to kill, and kill without mercy.

Another sob burst from Taryn, and she shoved Petrichor hard enough to get her to let go. "You left me alone!" she exclaimed, shock and sorrow and anger and something like *love* tangled around her lungs all at once. "You left me all alone with no memory of who I was or what I had done, and I had to fend for myself on the streets! You knew what his plan was, and you ran away!"

"No, Red, I—" Petrichor shook her head, brown eyes wide and wild at Taryn's reaction. "I would never have been allowed to see you anyway! He hated how volatile I was, hated that I made you more reckless. He would have kept us apart even if I had stayed."

Taryn took a deep breath, trying to calm herself, those flashes of memory returning in fits and starts. She tried and failed to match up that young Petrichor she remembered to the one she saw in front of her.

"I was alone too," Petrichor said in a softer voice. "I was alone two thousand miles away, and the one thing I wished more than anything was that I had tried harder to find you before I stowed away on that ship and left England."

Hot tears tracked down Taryn's cheeks as she stared at this woman—her *sister*—and saw, for the first time, the same scars that her own heart bore. Petrichor had endured the same traumas, the same losses, the same ugly past. And she hadn't had a graft she could hide under a glove. Petrichor's clockwork enhancements were vivid and obvious, and there would have been nowhere in Great Britain she could go without being noticed, captured, and returned to her tormentors. She'd protected herself by running away. Just as Taryn had protected herself by hiding, by ingratiating herself with Royal's family.

"You did what you had to do to survive," Taryn whispered, repeating Petrichor's words back to her.

"Yeah, Red, I did. Doesn't make me any less sorry for it, though."

"We were something like sisters once, were we not?" Taryn asked, untrusting of the flashes of memory after everything she'd been through.

"We were *exactly* like sisters, except for the part where we were being trained to be weapons," Petrichor answered with a grin.

Taryn wiped her cheeks. "I have always wanted a sister."

"Think you can accept one as messed up as me?" Petrichor put her hands on her hips, cocking her head to the side. Some of her old playful cockiness had returned, but it was softer around the edges now. More familiar, now. It felt less like a deliberate attempt to push Taryn away and more like a way to pull her in. To pull her close.

"Aye, I think so," Taryn nodded.

Petrichor smiled crookedly, ruffling Taryn's hair with a playful hand. "I would have done anything for you, Red. Still would, come to think of it."

"I assume you already have some idea of how we can continue this with our depleted numbers?"

"You know I do. Want to join us back in the dining room to hear about it?"

Taryn hesitated before nodding. She suddenly felt closer to Petrichor than ever. She regretted not getting to know her better before. She could tell they'd been good friends once, and she hoped they could be friends again. They both knew how hard it was to live with a monster inside, the struggle every day to choose light over darkness. And they were sisters, after all.

Perhaps it was time Taryn found a strong female friend who would have her back, no matter what.

※

Taryn followed Petrichor back into the dining hall, feeling all five pairs of eyes on her from the table.

"You'll all forgive Sedition's brief absence," Petrichor said as they took their places at the table. Taryn had the feeling she was not only referring to the few moments she'd left the table. "Now, can we get down to business? Our clock is ticking. We have exactly thirteen days to plan the heist of a lifetime. It'll be the first time Queen Victoria takes a ride through London town to take a look at her subjects in almost five years. Everyone will be out for the event. And security will be on high alert."

"Our advantage will be that they believe us all to be dead or defeated," Emmett interjected. "No one will expect the biomatons to attack again, after the defeat we suffered."

"And they are right," Taryn muttered, pressing her fingers to her temples. "We lost so much. Any sane person would give up, cut their losses, and accept their lot."

"Ah, and that is where we have the advantage," Rorin exclaimed, slamming his fist against the table. "Revenge is a powerful motivator, and we have nothing left to lose."

Royal shifted in his seat uncomfortably. "Except your lives," he muttered behind his hand.

"I'd much rather die a martyr than live as a mindless slave," Petrichor snapped. She stood, tapping her jaw piece with one finger, the clink of metal on metal loud over the hushed stares of the other soldiers. "We'll have to find a bottleneck, somewhere the street narrows enough that we can stage an ambush."

"You want to shanghai the Queen's carriage?"

"Cut off the head, and the body will fall."

Taryn could not help but glance at Ace, who had kept

strangely silent. He sat in his seat, jaw clenched tightly, staring straight ahead. She could practically see his patriotism revolting at the plan.

"That is treason," she murmured.

"Treason schmeason, Red. If we're quick, we can install our own ruler, someone sympathetic to our cause." A smile twisted her jaw. "How would you like to be queen, Red?"

Taryn's stomach lurched. She grabbed the edge of the table, and Ace touched her hand with gentle fingers to steady her.

"I—I am not fit to be queen," she choked out.

"Sure you are. I mean, that haircut might cause a stir, but we could get you established in no time."

"I am telling you again, Petrichor, that is not how our government works! The Parliament makes all the decisions. The Queen is a figurehead," Royal exclaimed, his voice hard and exasperated. "You cannot just replace the Queen and expect to rule! We are not living in the feudal ages."

Petrichor shrugged. "Then what do *you* suggest, Your Highness?"

"Stay here. You will have to hide if the soldiers return, but I can get papers forged for you, make sure no one will ever take you from here. Thrawcliffe can be an oasis, as Elmhurst was."

"And forget all our biomaton brothers and sisters suffering at the hands of their slave masters?" Rorin demanded. His voice was thick with sorrow and frustration. "That is as good as giving up. That is as good as saying Ari died for nothing."

"People die every day," Royal answered.

"Not like that," Rorin hissed. "No one ought to die like that."

Taryn traced the whorl of a knot in the wood tabletop in front of her, an idea slowly forming in her mind as she listened to them argue. She'd felt it building inside her since Emmett suggested vengeance earlier, had felt a spark of something that wasn't the killer's instinct beginning to light the darkness inside her. She wanted to win this, yes, but she wanted to win this on her terms. With no more blood on her hands. "Petrichor's plan could work," she began slowly, tasting each word as it left her mouth. "With one alteration."

"And that is?"

"No killing." Taryn raised her eyes and locked them with Petrichor's. "Give me ten minutes to plead our case to Her Majesty. I am certain, with the right words, I can end this peacefully. No one else will have to die."

"But—" Petrichor protested.

"No," Taryn interrupted, surprised to find her chest swelling with some of her old authority. "We have enough blood on our hands. We have lost enough. The only way to win this now is to show we are not something to fear. We do this peaceably, or we do not do this at all."

Every eye in the room stared at her, every mind contemplating her words. She could see on their faces the pain of those they'd lost and, even better, a light of hope at this new plan, dim as the earliest break of dawn but still there, and rising. Taryn's spirits lifted a little.

"This is a suicidal plan!" Royal exclaimed, slamming a fist against the table. Taryn's hope deflated. Her teacup rattled in its saucer. "We will all be hanged for treason, if we make it past the guards at all! I cannot attend a mission like this."

Ace jerked his head around to stare at Royal, his eyes full of fire. "You are not coming on the mission at all. This is not your fight."

"What?"

Taryn turned a gentler expression on Royal. "He is right. This is our fight. We are grateful for all you have done for us, but we must do this alone."

Royal's face drained of color. "Taryn, please—"

"You have the Hall, and responsibilities. That is your place," Taryn snapped, her voice taking on a harder edge than she intended, sharp as the shattered, jagged pieces of herself she was learning to reassemble.

Royal's brown eyes burned with hurt. "I understand," he growled, shoving his chair back and storming from the room. Taryn watched him go, too exhausted to follow. She put her head in her hands, some of that terrified, broken girl inside her returning.

"You were right," Ace murmured, touching her shoulder. "It is not his fight. He will understand, eventually."

"Right," Petrichor interrupted, clapping her hands and turning to survey the dining hall. "Time to get into shape. If we're going to have a chance at this, we all need more training." She looked pointedly at Taryn. "I think this room will do nicely, if we move the table against the wall."

All the biomatons took her cue, rising from their seats and pitching in to move the heavy table. Taryn did her part, too, though she dreaded the training. Ace's face contorted with pain as he helped, but when she questioned him, he responded that he felt fine. Worry blossomed in her chest. She wondered what he was not telling her.

"Great," Petrichor grinned. "Pair off. We start with my personal favorite: hand to hand combat. With knives."

CHAPTER THIRTY-THREE

"Again, Red."

Taryn groaned, struggling to regain her breath, lying flat on her back against the cold stone of the dining hall's floor. Her entire body ached with three days of almost nonstop fitness training, a fresh version of Erikkson's own battle training but increased tenfold in intensity with Petrichor in the lead. Training before had been difficult with a healthy, fit body. This time, she was malnourished and broken, and physical training only wore her down further.

"Not again," Taryn moaned. "Please." Her words were slow, gasped between labored pants as her body tried to regulate. "I need to rest."

"You can rest when this is over! We go *again*," Petrichor insisted, but there was a sparkle behind her crooked grimace that told Taryn she was not pushing to be cruel. Taryn was improving bit by bit thanks to Petrichor's relentless training, her refusal to allow Taryn to focus on anything but the goal ahead. And though she would never admit it, she was grateful to the former assassin for caring enough to help.

Taryn pressed herself up on her elbows, then into a full

sitting position. A tendon popped in her shoulder, a snap of electricity buzzing through her exhausted nerves. "It is not a fair exercise," she grumbled, slowly climbing to her feet. "You weigh twice as much as I with all those prosthetics."

Petrichor put her hands on her hips, her dark locks pulled out of her face in one long braid, ridged over her head like a crown. "Oh, you think you will be evenly matched with the soldiers protecting Her Majesty?"

"No, but I can use my blades against them," Taryn growled, tugging her left sleeve up over her metal elbow. Both women wore training uniforms Gennifer had made by altering some of Royal's old clothes—brown breeches ending just below the knee and white shirts slightly too big. Petrichor appeared comfortable in the clothes, but Taryn had looked positively weightless when she'd first tried them on, her emaciated frame lost in the folds of fabric. Gennifer had taken the clothes in several more inches to prevent them falling off.

"Go on, show me that Sedition fire Master Erikkson bragged about," Petrichor goaded, holding her hands out, a short blade clutched in her clockwork hand.

Taryn rolled her eyes and turned her back on Petrichor, allowing her biomaton sister to approach from behind and catch her wrist, pressing the tip of her blade beneath Taryn's jaw. Taryn stood very still for a moment, sensing Petrichor's form, and then her clockwork hand clamped around Petrichor's blade while her foot came down hard on her instep. She spun, breaking Petrichor's grip on her wrist, trying to wrest the blade from her hand. She brought Petrichor's arm over her shoulder, forcing her elbow to bend the wrong direction, and the blade fell from her fingers into Taryn's waiting hand. She spun, brandishing the weapon.

Petrichor grinned. "Not bad, Red, for your thirtieth time through this exercise."

Taryn scowled, her breath coming in shallow pants again.

"Do not forget I defeated you in your challenge before Elmhurst fell. I could have killed you."

"Yeah, but that was before you got weak." Petrichor jabbed Taryn in the ribs as she padded across the floor to where two glasses of water sat waiting—a courtesy from Ace, who'd completed his own training regimen hours ago and now was off doing god knew what. "You're still not eating enough. I can see right through you."

"I am eating as much as I can."

It was not entirely true. She knew she needed to consume copious amounts of protein-heavy foods to regain her lost weight and muscle, but meat sat in her stomach like lead, so she picked around it during meals. She did her best to force herself to consume enough, but sometimes it seemed too much work. She would never regain that much weight in the ten days left before their London assault anyways, and after that, it did not matter. She did not expect to be coming back.

"You're still limping, Red. How's your foot healing?" Petrichor asked between gulps of water, the clockwork side of her neck shuddering as she swallowed.

Taryn shrugged. The wound she'd so foolishly inflicted upon herself was just another ache to add to her perpetually growing list. "Surprisingly well. Royal offered me stitches, but I would likely tear them out. It ought to be healed enough by the time we run our final mission."

"Don't call it that. If this fails, we will do something else."

Taryn took a long draught of water before speaking, the liquid like a cooling balm on her throat. "If this fails, we are all as good as dead."

"Red..."

She locked eyes with the Clockwork Assassin. "Honestly, I think I liked you better when you just insulted me constantly."

Petrichor shrugged. "What can I say? I get sentimental about my pets."

Taryn felt a smile tugging at the corner of her mouth and wiped it away with the back of her hand. "Sentiment is a defect in the losing side. Master Erikkson took it from us to make us better soldiers."

"Brave words from the girl constantly making eyes at the privateer-turned-rebel."

"We have been through much together!"

"Is that what you call it here?" Petrichor chuckled. "You ready to go again?"

"In a minute. First, tell me about that new pistol you are so proudly toting around." Taryn nodded to Petrichor's belt, carefully folded on the floor by the wall, her dozen throwing knives pristine and gleaming. Taryn referred to the new weapon in her collection, a revolver with a fine, dark wood grip and gleaming silver barrel. "You never carried a pistol before."

"So, you did notice!" Petrichor purred, going to the belt and removing the weapon from its holster, keeping its muzzle pointed down and away from them both. Taryn noticed the pistol's mechanism was different from the flintlocks and revolvers she'd used in the past. "This is the very newest technology," Petrichor explained. "It holds six rounds and can fire them one after another just by pulling the trigger. Easy as pie and faster than anything else on the market."

"You do not need to cock the hammer each time?" Taryn questioned. The deadly potential of the weapon—and Petrichor's apparent glee over it—left a sour taste in her mouth.

"No, it's all automated. Pull the trigger and let the gun do the rest. Pretty sweet, eh?" Petrichor winked, holstering the weapon.

Taryn nodded, though her mind felt numb. "Yes. Sweet." The word felt wrong on her tongue, an American slang term Petrichor had picked up in New York, out of place in Taryn's careful accent.

"You ready to do a little sparring?"

Taryn moved into the center of the room, sighing and shaking the tension out of her shoulders. "As ready as I can be."

The girls squared up, studying one another before beginning the fight. Each was familiar with the other's fighting style—Taryn's a mixture of elaborate, spinning martial arts and scrappy street fighting, a testament to both her time in training with Erikkson and her time on London's streets; Petrichor's equal parts formal street boxing and backhanded gang fighting—a knife hidden between the knuckles, a blow to the eyes, even in what was meant to be a friendly fight—tricks she had picked up on the mean streets of New York. Despite their differences, they were evenly matched; or rather, they would have been, had Taryn not still been recovering.

"Taryn! Petrichor!" Ace raced into the room, stalling their fight. A smile played at the corners of his mouth and his eyes.

"Seraphim is back."

Seraphim looked the worse for wear standing in the front hall of Thrawcliffe, his dark Polynesian skin glistening with the rain beating down outside. His long hair hung bedraggled and tangled, black waves lying limp on his shoulders. His wings were dented and battered, though not crippled, and from their soaked state, Taryn supposed he must have attempted to use them to shield himself from the rain. His right eye—his *real* eye—had burst a blood vessel, and a splotch of crimson darkened part of his cornea.

"S!" Petrichor cried. "You look like death! What happened?"

In answer, Seraphim grinned, little more than a grimace revealing the flash of his silver fangs. "A handful of soldiers caught me when I attempted to return to Elmhurst. I spent the last few days *en route* to a buyer. I broke free three days ago and taught them all a lesson they will not soon forget."

Taryn stared at him numbly, his battered appearance reflecting how she felt within. Part of her had thought him dead, while the rest of her remained quietly hopeful. Seraphim was the anchor that held down the army, the calm to Petrichor and Sedition's firebrands. They needed him. "It is good to have you back with us," Taryn said, but despite her best efforts, her voice fell flat. She could not muster much welcome for him.

"What Sedition means is we could use your strategic thinking skills. We're having some trouble deciding where to intercept the Queen's carriage."

Petrichor led him away from the entry hall as she spoke, toward the back room they had commandeered for scheming. They had a massive map of London laid out on a tabletop, the Queen's most likely route picked out in pins and red thread. Taryn followed them, retreated so far inside herself she felt she was floating two feet above her head.

Was what they were doing the right path? Was there any way to know for certain? She watched her two clockwork siblings walking ahead of her, speaking in low voices. Both appeared confident, determined even, as Petrichor laid out the plan. But some niggling doubt in the back of Taryn's mind would not let go, refusing to allow her peace. If they went through with this, something would go wrong. Something would again get in their way. And this time, there could be no second chances.

"Isn't that right, Red? Red?" Petrichor's questioning contralto jolted Taryn from her thoughts. She blinked, surprised to find they were already in the study.

"I—I am sorry. I was thinking about something else."

"I was just telling Seraphim how you believe you can convince Her Majesty to set us free with a few honeyed words."

"Oh. Yes," Taryn nodded, turning her attention to Seraphim. "There has been too much killing already."

He quirked one eyebrow at her, looking more like an imperious older brother than he ever had before. "And what do you plan to say?"

"I—" Taryn's mouth went dry. Words had come more slowly to her since the Black Castle, at times leaving her entirely speechless but most of the time requiring more thought, more effort than before. "I will tell her how human we are. I will make her see. I—I am still working on it."

"Great. Our futures rest in the hands of an improv artist," Petrichor jabbed. "You better buckle down and start speech writing, or we are all coffin fodder."

"I said I am working on it!" Taryn exploded, her hands balling into fists before she could stop herself. Resurrecting Sedition had meant resurrecting the violence within herself—the violence which had never truly died—and now, her fuse required the merest spark to ignite it. "I understand everything rests on me! That is why I am not rushing into anything!"

Petrichor held up her hands in that placating manner Taryn was slowly learning to hate. "Red, calm down. I didn't mean to insult you."

Taryn dragged her hands over her face, shuddering. "I—I am just tired. I think I shall go rest before supper."

"That's fine. I'll fill Seraphim in."

The way Petrichor's voice tilted reassuringly made Taryn cringe. She turned away, her shoulders hunched, her hands pressed flat to her sides so they could do no damage. What was wrong with her? She was meant to be *better* than this, better than the fear and guilt that still plagued her mind. She was supposed to be getting *better*.

CHAPTER THIRTY-FOUR

SERAPHIM WAITED until Taryn was well beyond earshot before addressing Petrichor, his wings shuffling with the tension that lingered on the air. "The Castle forced her into the ring, did they not?"

Petrichor nodded, crossing her arms over her chest in a way that seemed almost as though she was embracing herself. "Just twice, but couple that with a week on ice and enough survivor's guilt for every one of us, and you start to get the picture. Is it that obvious?"

"I caught a glimpse of her tag," Seraphim murmured, indicating his own forearm. "And she acts similarly to the way you did when you returned from the arena. I am familiar with the signs."

"Oh, like you were so much better after your stint in the ring," Petrichor growled, her hands going to her hips, the position making her appear broader, more dominant.

"I did not say that. If you had been here, you would know Master Erikkson nearly lost me also. I refused to fight for anyone. I even begged him to remove my wings."

Petrichor's brow furrowed, and she deflated a little. "You did?"

Seraphim inclined his head. "I have never had much stomach for killing. And after killing for entertainment, I was not certain I ever could again, no matter the cause."

Petrichor attempted to sneer at him, but the expression seemed empty. "All you perfect Erikksons are pacifists at heart. You ought to take a page from my book. Killing's a lot easier when the only life that matters is your own."

Seraphim smiled enigmatically. "I have proof that is no longer the case for you."

"Oh really?"

"Hmm," he answered, turning his back on her to lean over the map, running one long finger over the red thread. "Explain this suicide mission to me again."

Petrichor pointed to Buckingham Palace. "For the first time in years, the Queen is having a ride around London. Ostensibly, it's a chance for her to look out upon her subjects, but for us, it's a chance to get to her in a way we never could have before."

"So you want to stop the carriage and what... surround her with our humanity?" Seraphim's wings clicked together, emphasizing the sarcasm in his words.

Petrichor shook her head. "*I* want to assassinate the Queen. Plain, simple, no frills. It's Sedition that won't allow it. Says there has been too much killing already, and the only way to achieve our freedom is by talking."

Seraphim cocked an eyebrow. "You disagree?"

Petrichor scoffed, throwing herself into an elaborately carved chair nearby. "Of course I disagree, S! I've lived a long time on the wrong side of the law, and I have never, not once, found that *speaking* is better than a swiftly wielded blade."

Seraphim went quiet for a moment, studying the red threads pinned in several different paths through London, trying to determine the Queen's course. He bit his lip, revealing a flash of one silver fang. "What if we do both?" he asked softly.

"What?" Petrichor sat up straighter, surprised at the suggestion. Seraphim was the peacekeeper, the strong and silent right hand of Sedition. She'd never expected him to suggest going *against* what their leader wanted.

"We give Sedition the opportunity to say her piece. We keep the guards away, we give her the audience she is asking for. But if it does not work..." One wing stretched forward, the razor-sharp tip of one of his flight feathers slicing through the red thread. "You finish the job."

"Sedition will never go for that."

"Then we do not tell her."

"Seraphim." Petrichor had never felt *bad* about secret-keeping before, but this felt wrong. This felt like something Taryn wouldn't forgive her for. And after their fresh reconciliation, after their newly formed friendship, she didn't know if she wanted that. She could hardly admit it, but it felt *good* to be friends with her again. It felt good to have a sister.

He shrugged. "It is a suggestion. It would not even come into play unless Sedition's speech fails." His expression was sharp, hard to read beneath the bruises and the damage to his one good eye, but there was something beneath the flattened surface that was not just sorrow for their fallen comrades. There was a deep, fiery determination. Seraphim didn't want this to fail, and would do anything to enforce its success.

Petrichor's chest clenched tight. "She'll never forgive us."

"If it means freedom, she will."

But Petrichor was not so sure. She'd seen the depths of Sedition's rage. She knew those depths herself. They had already lost so much. Everyone had a breaking point, and Taryn had already been pushed so far past hers. It would only take a little to send her over the edge. Something like this was incredibly risky, especially if they did not warn her of their plan first.

But if they did warn her, Taryn would never allow it. They both knew it.

"Why would you agree to this?" she asked.

"Because a long time ago, Erikkson mentioned this exact plan to me. As a last resort. A toppling of the head of the government could turn the tide, if all else fails. I am following his guide."

"And you do not think Sedition would listen even if we said that?"

"I think she is fragile and wounded right now, and she wants to be noble. She wishes to do this without violence, so we should honor that. But if it fails, we will not."

The words were cold and hard, and Petrichor felt her skin prickle with goosebumps at them. Seraphim *had* changed. He was so much colder than he had been before. Part of her liked this change. And part of her was chilled by it. If even Seraphim had lost his heart, what hope did the rest of them have?

She ducked her head. "Let's just pray that Sedition writes the speech of a lifetime."

"And if not?" Seraphim met her eyes with an intensity that made her stomach churn.

"Then I will do what needs to be done."

Ace caught Taryn as she passed by in the hall, tenderly halting her with his clockwork hand on her shoulder, his piercing gaze full of concern. "How are you?" he murmured, as if he could see right through her.

She shrugged. "I am tired. Still, it is good to see Seraphim. I was afraid—" she broke off, eyes drifting, chewing at her lips, where a bead of blood had already formed, scarlet against the ivory white of her front teeth. "It does not matter," she sighed. "He is here now. We will need him."

"What does he think of our plan?" Ace asked, appearing not to notice her agitation—or perhaps he only pretended not to notice.

"He thinks it is suicide. But it is all we have." Her eyes seemed to see him again, locking with his, suddenly intense and penetrating. "What do you think of it?"

Ace shook his head, offering her his elbow. Taryn took it, and together they made their way through the narrow stone halls. The quiet, companionable stride they fell into had become a habit, Taryn stealing a few minutes away each evening to stroll with Ace in the gardens behind the hall. Despite everything they had endured (or perhaps because of it), it was the one time she felt truly herself, truly whole. In the still of the long spring evenings by Ace's side, the world became just a little brighter.

"I am afraid we will not all return from this mission," he replied slowly as they walked. "I fear it will require more sacrifice than we now comprehend."

She looked up at him, noticing the way the fading light sharpened his features. "Do you think I ought to call it off? Should we wait for some other opportunity?"

Ace shook his head. "We have seen the new laws Parliament has already put into place because of our rebellion. You have rattled them, Tar. They are afraid of you. And now it is up to you to deliver the killing blow before we lose all our autonomy. Before they take even our voices."

She gripped his arm a little tighter, her heart rate rushing at the knowledge that it all relied on her. The biomatons had relied on her before, and she had let them down. How did they know she would not let them down again? How could she succeed this time when she had failed before?

"I saw a little of your training session earlier," Ace encouraged, as if sensing her trepidation. "You are getting stronger."

"Not quickly enough," she muttered.

He stopped, forcing her to halt with him. He gently tucked her hair behind her ear. "You cannot rush healing, Taryn. You are the only one who blames yourself for what happened. Perhaps it is time you forgave yourself."

She shuddered, pulling her hand from his grasp. "If I wanted another lecture on suffering, I would go find Royal."

"I am sorry. I did not mean to bring it up again."

"As long as we are on the topic of painful subjects," she retorted, "how is your cough healing?"

He bobbed his head, though his face had drained of all its color. "It is slowly getting better."

"Do not lie to me."

He sighed, his shoulders slumping. "It is still very painful, but I do not think it is as frequent." He held up a hand. "I swear, that is the truth."

She frowned, but accepted his answer. "Do you think it is related to your graft?"

"Possibly." He glanced around the garden, his eyes glinting in the fading light. He offered her his elbow again. "Come, it is getting toward supper time. They will be missing us soon."

She took his arm, and they continued their turn around the garden, their feet crunching over the wet gravel. Overhead, heavy storm clouds raced by, carried on a chill wind which cut to their cores. Even one another's presence was not sufficient to keep them warm. Taryn shivered.

"Voila, les amoureux."

Both biomatons froze, startled by the sound of their friend's French accent. They turned as one to see Emmett approaching on a secondary, converging path to their own, followed closely by Rorin.

"Emmett!" Ace exclaimed, dropping Taryn's hand. She felt her cheeks grow hot. "What are you doing out here?"

"Not spying, *mon ami*," Emmett replied with a knowing smile. "I assure you. We only came to find you for *dinner*."

"Did not think you the type," Rorin growled, crossing his arms. "And with Lady Sedition, of all people."

"Back to the house, Rorin," Taryn ordered, though her cheeks still burned with embarrassment.

"My lady—"

"You saw nothing untoward, did you? Your accusations are unfounded at best and slanderous at worst. I said, return to the house. That is an order!"

Rorin's expression soured, but he trudged back to the house.

"*Pardonnez-moi*," Emmett interrupted, crossing his arms, "but I will not be silenced and sent away with a word."

"Emmett—" Taryn began, and then trailed off mid-sentence, cheeks still bright with embarrassment. Though it felt like a lifetime ago, Emmett had admitted his love for her, deep in the dungeons of the Black Castle. Taryn had never reciprocated his feelings, nor had she tried to lie to him about it, but even so, she still felt the shame of him discovering them here, arm in arm. Ace had been his best friend before they had become biomatons, and she knew they were still close. She hoped this would not destroy their relationship.

Whatever *this* was.

She and Ace had still not put a name to it, had not done anything further than the occasional brush of hands, stealing minutes away to walk together in the evening light. He had said something about having feelings for her in the Black Castle, but that was long ago, and it hadn't come up again. They were good friends. Maybe more, she thought, in another life. Maybe more, once they were free.

But right now, it was embarrassing to be caught by Emmett,

who loved too big and too deeply, who would see right through her careful, tentative grasp on this new feeling. Would cut right to the heart of it, when she didn't want that to happen. Not yet. Not while it was still in the budding phases of its infancy. Let this grow with time, she told herself. Do not rush it. Let it be whatever it wants to be.

Emmett smiled, though she could read a deep sadness behind the expression. "I may not be able to see as I used to, but I am no longer blind. I have known of your affections for one another for some time."

"You have?"

"*Oui*. The French invented romance. You think I cannot see when two of my dearest friends begin courting?"

"We are not courting," Taryn said too quickly. Ace tensed beside her.

Emmett gave her a knowing smile. "Take your time, *chérie*. Ace is a good man. A terrible roommate, *oui*, but a good man."

Ace chuckled a little, his cheeks warming with a blush that was obvious even in the fading light. "Taryn is telling the truth, Emmett. We are not courting. We are close, that is all."

The Frenchman waved a hand, rolling his eyes. "All you Englishmen with your ridiculous, stuffy decorum! We could die any day, *mon ami*. In France, we seize every day with romance and style!" He swept in and scooped Taryn into his arms, lifting her up by her waist so her head and shoulders were above his head. She yelped, though it quickly became a laugh as he spun her around before setting her down again.

Emmett grasped her hands in his. "To make you laugh like that was all I ever wanted, *belle* Taryn. Your heart belongs to you, as it always has."

She glanced from the Frenchman to the privateer and back again, taking them both in. She thought of how they'd met, the rocky start about the *Dauntless*, and how Emmett had sacrificed everything to try and keep her safe. How Ace had come back for them both, even though it had been too late. How they had worked to help him regain his memories, and how changed he was. Emmett was still the same, mostly. A little angrier, perhaps. A little more vicious. But still Emmett.

But Ace... Becoming a biomaton had blossomed Ace from a cold and cowardly boy into a kind, gentle, caring man. She'd always seen beauty in his high cheekbones, his dark hair, the ice blue of his eyes. But more recently, she'd learned of the beauty in his heart. She wanted time to explore it, to get to know him better.

And maybe that was what love was.

"You are too good to me, Emmett," she murmured softly.

"No, I am too good for *everyone*," he exclaimed, sweeping into a low bow. Emmett's clockwork eyes spun as he came back up, locking on Ace's face. "Take good care of her, *mon ami*. Or I will come after you."

Taryn's ears burned. She turned back toward the house. "We ought to get back. They will be waiting for us."

The others agreed, and the three biomatons headed back toward the house, the dark-haired privateer, the copper-haired revolutionary, and the wiry Frenchman. As they walked, Emmett spoke quietly to Taryn and Ace. "*Monsieur* Erikkson explained your programming to me, the week before he perished. It explained why I fell so hard for you so soon after we met. I do not resent it, but just as your heart is your own, mine is my own as well. Besides, I do not think we would be a good match. After all, you are too English for my tastes." He gave her a wink.

"I am sorry, Emmett," Taryn murmured. In spite of the lightness of his mood, she still felt as if she needed to apologize for manipulating him. "I did not know of that subroutine until just before he died. I never meant to hurt you."

"*Je sais*. I know you did not lead me on purposely. I only have to ask you one thing: Does he make you happy?"

Taryn fell silent, turning to look at Ace, who walked beside her and returned her gaze expectantly. She considered him for a moment, her head tilted to the side. She had not really considered their relationship in a romantic sense. Not yet. Not until this moment, when Emmett appeared to be giving them his blessing. Perhaps she was naive to leave their relationship in the dark in her mind, but she had other, more pressing things to consider. She had to win the war before she could consider courting anyone. And happy? She could remember the last moment she felt truly happy, in the clearing with Ace on her birthday. But happiness now seemed like wishful thinking. She did not think anyone who had endured what they had found happiness easy.

"He makes me feel content and whole, which I believe may be more important than happy."

CHAPTER THIRTY-FIVE

TARYN ROSE the next day and slowly made her way through her morning routine: washing her face, brushing her short, tangled copper locks, dressing in her training uniform. Blearily, she made her way downstairs, readying herself for another difficult day of training. She did not sleep much any longer, plagued by nightmares and a mild phobia of the dark, but she made do with what snatches of sleep she could get, supplementing it with coffee or breakfast tea.

She entered the dining hall, anticipating the babble of voices and sounds of a meal being eaten, seven faces turning to look at her. Instead, she found the floor already cleared, Petrichor and Seraphim standing in the center. The door clicked shut behind her, and she spun to find Ace had closed it, his face a serious mask.

"What is going on?" she demanded, turning back toward Petrichor and Seraphim. "What is this?"

"This is an intervention," Seraphim replied, his soft voice raising the hairs on the back of Taryn's neck. "This is what Master Erikkson did for me when I returned from the Black

Castle, what he would have done for Petrichor had she not left. And now, we do it for you."

"What are you talking about?" Taryn's fingertips buzzed with electricity. Why had they cornered her like this? What did they intend to do?

"You don't wear trauma well, Red," Petrichor answered, and her voice held none of the teasing sarcasm it usually held. She watched Taryn with a deep sadness, her hands held tightly in front of her like a shield. "Everyone heard you scream last night. We know you still blame yourself for what happened."

"It was just a nightmare," Taryn protested too quickly. Her entire body buzzed with the bizarre tension in the room. "I am fine. I can train."

"We did not say you could not train," Seraphim answered. "Consider this another kind of training session."

"I still do not understand what you expect me to do." The words fell flat, strangely calm in the wake of Taryn's fear, her body practically alight with kinetic energy.

"We want to work through what happened in the Black Castle. All of it."

Taryn shook her head, suddenly comprehending. "No. You know well enough what happened there. I have no reason to relive it."

"It may seem unorthodox, but it will help."

Taryn turned back toward Ace, her expression pleading. "Ace, tell them. I do not want to talk about it."

Ace shook his head, eyes sympathetic but unrelenting. "You need to do this, Tar."

She shook her head, backing toward an unoccupied corner of the room. She could not even say *why* she was so terrified, only knew her lungs felt crushed inside her ribcage, like she was drowning on dry land. "I will not do it. I will not."

"You are not leaving this room until we have completed this exercise," Seraphim replied flatly.

It took all her willpower just to remain upright. Taryn swayed, gasping for breath in lungs that refused to inflate. The walls shuddered, suddenly nearer than they once had been. Cold tremors ran down her spine. Worst of all, no one appeared to care. No one came to her aid. They just stood there, staring at her with flat, flat faces while she suffocated.

"The principle of the exercise is simple," Seraphim droned on. "We will ask you questions, and you will answer them. You *must* answer them. But we will also train as we talk. If you need to lash out, we understand. We are here to provide you with something to lash at."

"You will not help me! I will hurt you," she gasped, her breathing shallow, too fast. "I do not know how to maintain control any longer."

"You won't hurt us, Red. It's all right," Petrichor said in that maddeningly gentle voice. Taryn spun on her, her blades snapping open.

"I am tired of you treating me like something that is liable to get broken. I am no longer a child," she hissed.

"Begin with the night Elmhurst fell," Seraphim ordered flatly. He took up a fighting stance, his wings half-raised as counterweight.

"They dropped bombs on the house," Taryn answered bitterly. Every word tasted like poison, and still she could not breathe, but she knew her best way out of this would be to cooperate, to pretend she somehow understood the 'healing' in this whole idiotic process. "Five, I think. By the time I dug my way out of the basement, it was over. No one in the barracks survived."

Seraphim looked at her expectantly, as if waiting for something more. She crossed her arms, locking eyes with him. She had no more to say. No more to give.

"And what about Master Erikkson?" Petrichor demanded.

"Storm was already there. I was too late. So—so I killed

her." Her voice cracked, and she pressed the next words out through gritted teeth, forcing her sorrow to become anger, a far simpler emotion. "I do not regret that."

Out of nowhere, Seraphim attacked her, catching her off guard and pinning her with one sharp feather-blade to her throat. "Was he dead when you found him?"

She froze, nearly demanding that he release her until she realized this, too, was part of the exercise. She dropped her newly sharpened dagger into her waiting palm.

"No." The truth leaped from her lips at the same time she decided to lie. She swung the dagger across Seraphim's chest, barely missing him, forcing him to back off. "He died after I killed Storm. I—I failed him, and he still told me he was *proud*." She leaped forward, attacking again until Seraphim knocked her backward with one wing. Her dagger clattered to the floor. "He was proud of a failure."

Petrichor caught Taryn from behind, her metal arm wrapping around Taryn's throat. "And then you just let them take you?"

Taryn tried to fight Petrichor's grasp, but her entire body shook with the emotion of the night they relentlessly questioned her about, and her fingers could find no purchase. "There was no time to run. I—I wanted to give Ace a chance to escape, but the idiot would not leave!"

His eyes met hers from across the room, blue glaciers melting into tender azure pools. "You know I could not leave you to face them alone."

"Well you should have!" she spat. "They could not use you against me if they did not have you!"

Petrichor's grip tightened around Taryn's throat. "Why did you agree to fight in the arena?"

"I had no choice," Taryn choked. "Release me."

"You always have a choice," the former assassin spat. She shoved Taryn away from her. She stumbled several steps and collapsed to her knees, panting. The air in the room hung heavy with ghosts. Flashes of the past weeks, the nightmarish reality of the Black Castle flickered behind Taryn's eyes. The room spun.

"Why did you agree to fight for them?" Ace asked the question this time, without any condemnation in his voice, but she felt it all the same. She did not look up.

"It does not matter. I fought. I killed. I am a coward. Are we done here?"

"No. We are not done. Why did you fight?" Seraphim repeated the question for a third time, the words ringing through her skull. Taryn shoved herself to her feet, anger lashing through her. She lunged at Seraphim, pelting him with blows from her fists, her heels, her knees, the words pouring from her.

"What is it you want me to say? That they threatened Ace's life if I did not fight? That I knew I could win because I was *trained* for this inevitability?"

She spun, her shoulder blades catching the light. Sparks flew as metal locked with metal, Seraphim blocking her deadly blow with his wings.

"Or do you want to know how it felt to step into the ring for the first time and realize the girl I faced was the same girl who saved my life before my trial in London, the midshipman who prevented Storm from torturing me to death, a person Ace had told me died at Storm's hand?"

She locked in battle again with Seraphim, long enough to turn and stare pointedly at Ace, whose expression had filled with horror.

"Tar, I swear— I did not know—" he muttered, but before he could complete the sentence she swung back into action, fighting with every ounce of strength she had, discovering some fresh reserve deep within herself catalyzing from the pain and the anger and the guilt.

"Do you want to know how I stared into her lifeless eyes before I cut her throat and found no recognition there?" she screamed, throwing Seraphim back with a powerful kick to the ribs. He stumbled, clutching his chest, panting. She stood in the center of the room, her weight low in her hips, body coiled like a cat. "Go on," she hissed. "I am beginning to enjoy this. What else would you like to know?"

"Tell them about how Harper discovered your blades," Ace ordered, his voice both tender and fractured.

Taryn spun on him, ready to direct her deluge of violence his way, but Petrichor stepped between them, her clockwork fist raised. "Tell me, Red."

Taryn stared at her for a single, infinite moment before attacking, metal clanging against metal, the blows almost too fast to see as the sisters parried and ducked, weaving circles around one another, few blows even landing. And all the time, though Taryn's vision had gone red at the edges with bloodlust, though she hardly knew she was speaking, the words continued to pour from her.

"You mean the way the woman tore me apart? She strapped me down and took me apart piece by piece, and I could not even cry out." Something hot and wet ran down her cheek, tears or blood she did not know. She ignored it. "Worse, I kept flashing back, kept remembering Erikkson erasing my memories, and *you* could not protect me! I was awake! I felt every second of it! And I could not even speak! And *you* did not stop him!"

Taryn pinned Petrichor against the wall, her metal fist locked around her throat, both panting for breath. "I tried, Red," Petrichor croaked, and it sounded like a desperate apology. "I tried."

Taryn barely heard her, her mind a blank wash of violence, of fight, of killer's instinct and raw animal emotion. She pressed harder against Petrichor's throat, feeling muscle and bone and clockwork constrict under her grasp.

"Taryn," Ace interrupted, at last stepping into the ring himself, taking up his own fighting position. A hush fell over the room, horrible and heavy. "Tell me about the night you were put in isolation." He paused. "Tell me about the night you abandoned me."

She lunged at him. "I did not abandon you! I would never abandon you!" He kept up with the rapid-fire pounding of her blows, but barely. His breath wheezed in his chest, the gray sheen of his skin gone red with exertion. Taryn did not notice or did not care.

"I killed again in the ring. I did that to protect you. But that was not enough. I was put on display, paraded in front of the rich men who funded the fights. Who fund our subjugation."

Her fist caught him on the jaw, knocking him backward, but he came up swinging, denying her any more than glancing blows.

"I was struggling to control myself as it was. I gave in. I snapped. I killed them, and all I could think was there were two fewer cruel men in the world." Her fists slowed, her green eyes at last appearing to see him. She slumped, her onslaught ceasing. Tears raced down her cheeks.

"When I realized what I had done, and the consequences of my actions, I knew Sedition had to die. I thought they had killed you, Ace." Her breath caught in her throat, transforming from pants to thick, painful sobs. "I thought they had killed you for what I did, and I could not bear it. The cold and the dark and the ghosts I could bear, but not the thought that I had failed the one person I had left."

Her hands fell to her sides, trembling. Her knees shuddered with the weight of her sins. She stood, swaying, and then collapsed to her knees, her body racked with shivers. It felt as though she had been cracked open like a porcelain doll, and all the ugliness, all the evil inside her, was seeping out. It felt as if the blood of all her sins was pouring from every pore, stark and crimson against her skin for all the world to see. The horrible truth had come to light at last, her deeds all laid out for them to see, and she did not know how they could stand to be with her in the same room any longer.

Ace stood, panting, staring at her. His eyes welled over with tears. "I thought the same of you when you did not return. I feared Harper had torn you apart and could not put you back together. And when I discovered you were alive, I begged to see you. They refused. I—I felt like I failed you. I could not protect you. And all along it was you who protected me."

She shoved her tears from her cheeks, looking up at him. "Please do not hate me for what I have done."

He knelt beside her, taking her hands. "I could never hate you, Taryn. Never."

A heat bloomed in her chest at his words, a strange lightness that drove off the darkness. It wasn't being wiped clean, not exactly, but it was a kind of relief, to have all of her worst moments laid out and to be told that it was okay. That they were still with her. That she was not something to be loathed or blamed.

You did what you had to do to survive. Petrichor's voice echoed through her mind.

And Taryn was glad she had survived. It was a surprise to realize it, but she *was* glad. She was ready to carry on with their fight. She wasn't a monster, or evil, or unforgiveable. She was just a girl who had been pushed into impossible situations, who had been abused and abandoned, and told she was a weapon, when all she'd ever wanted was a family.

And maybe that wasn't such a bad thing to be.

Petrichor and Seraphim stood off to the side, observing the scene with a mixture of gratefulness and exhaustion. Taryn held Ace's gaze for a long moment, then turned to her biomaton siblings, her face red with tears.

"I do not know why, but I *do* feel better now, and for that I thank you."

"You suffered much," Seraphim answered, rubbing a long bruise forming on his forearm, "but you must not forget you are not alone. We all have seen and done things we regret. And none of us blame you for what happened, neither at Elmhurst nor at the Black Castle."

The ghost of a smile touched her lips. "Now you know the sum of it, save one final detail you did not question me about."

Petrichor crossed her arms. "Which is?"

"I began hallucinating Master Erikkson's ghost in isolation. He followed me here, to Thrawcliffe. The visions were a way of fending off the darkness and the loneliness, I think." Taryn rubbed her left foot, trying to ease the ache of her healing injury. "The visions stopped the day you returned, Petrichor."

A strange expression came over Petrichor's face, and she crossed the room in three strides, knees hitting the floor in front of Taryn with a clang of metal on stone. Taryn recoiled as Petrichor reached for her, but the Clockwork Assassin just cradled Taryn's face in her hands. Deep sympathy welled in her brown eyes.

"That is because Erikkson has always been *my* ghost," she murmured. "He has haunted me every day since I left."

Taryn grasped Petrichor's wrists tightly. How had they fought so hard to keep themselves apart? Why had they hated each other so much, when they were so alike? "And now? Does he haunt you still?"

Petrichor shook her head slowly, tears coming into her eyes. "No, Red. Not anymore. Not now that I have my family back."

A little laughing sob wrenched itself from Taryn's chest and she pulled her sister close, embracing her tightly. Whatever happened next, whatever was coming for them, be it freedom or death or sorrow, they were together. They were not alone. And that was such a sweet relief. She closed her eyes and she imagined them all, free, living together in Thrawcliffe Manor. Or perhaps traveling the countryside. They could go anywhere they wanted when they were freed. Paris, or Barcelona, or Rome. She wouldn't have to hide. And this little group of survivors, they could do it. They could finally bring about the end of this fight.

She just had to figure out the right words to say.

CHAPTER THIRTY-SIX

THE FEW DAYS they had before what Taryn came to refer to as their "final mission" slipped by silently, lost in the rush of preparations for their attack. Taryn and Petrichor trained together ceaselessly, developing a quick rapport none of the boys could hope to match. Weapons were sharpened and resharpened, their blades and bodies honed to a razor edge. After his initial anger at not being included, Royal quickly became a part of their planning, helping Seraphim to draw up scenarios and instructing Taryn on the best way to get the Queen to listen to her. They would have only minutes. It was best to appeal to her humanity, not her authority. Demonstrate their equality through compassion, empathy, and most of all, logic, not might. Taryn was thankful to have someone who'd been raised in the court to help her construct her arguments, though she could see the sorrow and fear in Royal's face every time they started to plan.

She knew he thought this plan was suicide. But it was their only chance to end this before things got worse. And she knew now that they could get worse. So much worse.

Gennifer assembled armor for them, though nothing so fine

as the original costume she had designed for Taryn, forever lost in the bowels of the Black Castle. She elected to stay behind after all their training and planning, explaining that she would only slow them down. No one refused her the right to stay behind.

No one else chose to stay.

Taryn found her heart and mind strengthening with her body. Which was not to say she never found herself overwhelmed by sorrow for her creator and her friends, nor that she no longer felt guilty about her actions. On the contrary, she fled to the garden on more than one occasion in the following days to weep, and her sleep was still occasionally disturbed by nightmares. Still, she knew she was not alone, and her sins and aches were no longer some great secret she had to bear, and it seemed to make all the difference.

London was two and a half hours hard carriage ride from Thrawcliffe Hall, and only after much debate did the biomatons elect to travel by carriage rather than by airship. They reasoned that the airship would be far more likely to be boarded and inspected before they reached London, whereas another carriage with a biomaton driver would be the most ordinary sight in the world. They readied the carriage and horses as carefully as they readied their weapons.

The night before they were to leave, the night before their raid on the Queen's caravan, Royal caught Taryn's arm and pulled her aside, drawing her into his study and closing the door.

"Do not go."

"I must go, Royal. You know I must." She leaned on his desk, staring at him with eyes almost feverish with anticipation. Her hair swept back from her face in narrow braids, the short copper strands escaping restraint and tumbling around her face in all directions.

"No, I know you say you must. Tiger, allow the others to do

this. Do not go. Stay here, with me. Stay safe." His fingers fluttered over the black cravat at his throat, trembling hands so unlike the steady rock of a boy she knew. Her mission rattled him more than he cared to admit.

"Roy, you have done much for me, and my gratitude and my debt to you is too great to ever repay." She held out her hands to him, one clockwork, one flesh. "You cared about me when no one else could. You bought my freedom. And I am grateful, truly, though it may not seem so. But if I do not do this, I am dishonoring the memory of Master Erikkson, to whom I owe my life. Do not ask me to choose between you."

He took her hands in his, his scarred, slender mechanick's fingers nearly hiding her prosthetic from view. "And if I did ask —who would you choose?"

She shook her head, pulling her hands from his, turning away. Her voice dropped. "You know it is far more complicated than that."

"What is so complicated? You are planning a suicide mission! I am asking you to choose to live!"

"This could still work," she snarled, rounding on him. "This *will* work, or it shall be the last thing I do."

His big brown eyes fell, sadness clouding his irises. "I fear it shall be the latter."

She sighed and touched his shoulder. "You have done so much for me, Royal, but I am afraid I must ask you to do one last thing."

He raised his face to her, eyes hopeful, even pleading.

"I need you to let me go," she murmured.

He shrugged her off, pacing the length of the room. His movements were like a caged animal, hands in fists at his sides, face turning red with frustration. "Gor, Tar, you do not make it easy, do you?" he exclaimed, one hand clenching a handful of his long blond hair.

"I am sorry," she replied, her voice soft, her body perfectly still in the midst of his agitation. "I never meant to lead you on. You have always deserved better than me."

"There is none better than you!" he exclaimed. "You have never been able to see it, but I have only ever had eyes for you! Since the very first time I saw you huddled beneath that bridge, I have loved you! You are my Psyche, my Aphrodite, my unattainable beauty, and you have never known it."

Taryn swallowed hard, finding the room suddenly claustrophobic and suffocating. "I know. I know. And I am sorry. You deserve so much better, Royal. You deserve someone who will see you as I never have."

He stopped his pacing and stared at her, eyes brimming with tears. "I beg of you, do not go."

"I must." She cocked her head, shaking it slowly. "I must. I wish you every happiness. Thank you for all you have done for us. For me. I hope you can forgive me, one day."

"Do not do that."

"Do what?"

"Treat this like goodbye."

She swallowed hard, rubbing the back of her neck with one hand. "It *is* goodbye, Royal. If this fails—well—you know what happens."

"Then do not fail." He crossed the space between them and tenderly kissed her on the cheek. Taryn felt him linger there a moment too long before pulling away, his breath hot against her skin. "Come back to me, Tiger."

She met his gaze and smiled sadly. "Only when the biomatons are free."

He nodded, his lips tightening. "I would expect no less."

The biomatons met outside Thrawcliffe Hall before the sun rose, each arrayed in the armor constructed by

Gennifer—black leather and steel plating, each with weapons and prosthetics honed and polished until they shone. Together, they piled into the carriage, Rorin taking the driver's position and the rest crammed into the dim interior of the carriage, rocking with the swaying movement as they traveled toward London.

Taryn examined her compatriots, these final five who had followed her into the very maw of Hell, who even now willingly accompanied her to see through the single solitary spark of hope that remained. But even a spark may start a wildfire, she knew, and Taryn intended her spark to consume the whole world. No one spoke much. Emmett appeared to be dozing. Seraphim, hunched over so his wings could fold behind him, sat lost in some silent reverie. Petrichor just watched the landscape pass by out the window.

And Ace, seated beside Taryn, held her hand silently, his heartbeat throbbing in his thumb against the back of her hand, like a steady metronome counting down the moments to their final mission.

Finally, Taryn could no longer bear the oppressive silence. "Did Petrichor show you her new weapon, Ace?" she asked.

Ace nodded. "She demonstrated it for me during target practice yesterday. It is an impressive weapon, if somewhat less than accurate. With it firing so quickly, it is difficult to aim properly."

"If you fire enough times, accuracy doesn't matter," Petrichor grumbled from across the aisle.

"Accuracy always matters," Ace replied. "Sometimes all you have time for is a single shot."

A heavy silence fell over them again, and this time, no one tried to break it. Hour after hour, the countryside streamed by, fading in and out of focus. Sometimes, they passed through a town or village, and Taryn watched the people pass by with a feeling of detachment. She wondered how they might react if they knew what the biomatons intended; she wondered if many would care even if they knew.

She considered the long journey to get here, the steps they had taken together and separately as they strove toward freedom. She knew the stories of some of her compatriots; Emmett and Ace's journeys from human to biomaton were intimately familiar to her, while Petrichor and Seraphim were less familiar, though she knew the broad strokes, and moments were still occasionally coming back to her.

She would never regain all her memories, she knew, but the flashes she got were enough. Making so many new memories was enough. She studied each of the faces around her in turn, seeing them range in expression from serious contemplation to pale fear, though there was a stark determination in each as they met her gaze that told her they were ready. They all knew how this ended. In victory or death, either way they would be free.

Either way, they were paving a path ahead for others to follow. If they fell, she had to believe that others would take up their flags in her wake. And maybe that would be enough.

It would have to be enough.

At one point, the road they traveled drew parallel with a vast steam engine puffing across the country, streaming white clouds of vapor and whistling loud enough to rattle Taryn's teeth. As she turned her eyes away from the great machine, she caught sight of Petrichor huddled back from the window, her face pale with terror.

No less than four times during their journey, Rorin tapped thrice at the front of the carriage, their predetermined signal that there was a military airship overhead. The skies over London always teemed with all kinds of airships, but Rorin had an eye for spotting those which appeared naval—and he was usually right. Each time he signaled, the biomatons inside the carriage tensed, muscles knotted and breaths held until, a few minutes later, Rorin gave the signal that all was clear once more.

It was exhausting, readying themselves over and over like that without knowing if the tension would break, and then trying to relax again a few minutes later, but Taryn knew their readiness would make all the difference in the world should any of these ships take an interest in the little carriage.

Their luck held, and no one stopped them. About two hours after dawn, they entered London, Rorin steering them down gray streets with the ease of one of London's own cabbies. The horse's hooves and carriage wheels clattered over the cobbles, and Taryn breathed the familiar stench of London air. No matter how long she spent away, no matter where else she lived, London would always be home.

Rorin steered the carriage into a narrow alley which butted up against the street they had determined best suited to their purposes. Her Majesty would come down the narrow street, and because it was briefly so narrow, there would be few bystanders. Her guard ahead would turn the corner, and then they would strike, driving the Queen's conveyance into the alley where Taryn would make her speech.

If all went well, they would have their freedom in just a few hours. If not, they would be dead, and it would no longer matter. Briefly, Taryn found herself considering the prospect of Heaven. There she might, for the first time in her memory, have two arms. Death did not sound so bad.

Emmett came over and squeezed her elbow affectionately. She gave him a faltering smile that could not hide her trepidation.

"Take heart, *cherie*. We are behind you. This will work."

Taryn sighed, a line from a play she had seen with Royal long ago suddenly coming into her head. "Once more unto the breach, dear friends," she said, loudly enough for everyone to hear, though she kept her eyes on Emmett. "Once more."

"*Henry V,*" Seraphim murmured, flashing his silver fangs. His wings shivered with anticipation. "Very fitting. Master Erikkson would approve."

"To your positions," Taryn ordered, snapping into action herself. "You all know what to do."

As she moved to her own position at the end of the alley, Ace caught her arm. "Taryn—"

She turned and smiled up at him. "In a few hours we shall be free, Ace. One way or another, we shall be free."

He ducked his head, a smile gracing his lips in defiance of the immense sadness in his blue eyes. "Taryn, just in case this goes wrong, I— I want to say—"

"Come on, Blue Eyes!" Petrichor called, lifting her pistol as she readied herself for the attack, impatient for the battle to start. "To your position!"

Ace waved to her, then returned his attention to Taryn. "I—"

"It is all right, Ace. Get to your position. There will be time enough after this is finished."

He hesitated a moment longer, wavering between telling her what he needed to *now,* or trusting she was right, and there would be enough time when this was over. Finally, he ducked his head and moved to his position, trusting Taryn, allowing himself to be a coward one final time.

Time slowed to a horrible crawl, an inescapable agony of tension, every muscle prepared for a battle which refused to come, every second dragging itself into an hour. Taryn gave up on keeping track of time, aware of nothing but the throb of her heartbeat in her clammy palm, the rhythm of her own shallow breathing.

And then came the sound they had waited for: marching feet and clattering hooves, cartwheels and dozens of people. The biomatons instantly snapped to alert, waiting for the procession to round the corner into their line of sight, for the guards to unknowingly march around the corner, leaving the carriage momentarily vulnerable with the rear guard still behind the first corner.

Taryn watched red uniforms proceed past—all identical, perhaps ten men in all, white and red uniforms pristine, rifles over their shoulders. It would take only minutes, perhaps less, for them to realize the Queen had gone missing. That was all the time Taryn had.

The soldiers vanished around the second corner as the Queen's horses drew level with Taryn's hiding place. Right on cue, Seraphim and Rorin jumped in front of the horses, catching the reins and steering them to the alleyway. The carriage driver fell unconscious under an unexpected blow from Petrichor. Taryn stepped aside as the carriage rolled past her, stopping just behind the biomatons' own carriage. Seraphim and Petrichor took up defensive positions at the alley's entryway. Ace and Rorin aimed pistols at the carriage, flanking Taryn. She heaved a deep breath. This was it. Now, or never.

"Your Majesty, step out of the carriage. We have you surrounded," Taryn ordered in a booming voice.

CHAPTER THIRTY-SEVEN

THE DOOR CREAKED OPEN, and a small foot in an elegant black leather pump stepped down. Taryn's breath caught in her throat. Queen Victoria stepped from the carriage, dressed all in mourning black, a veil of sheer black lace covering her face so Taryn could just make out her features. She was small, smaller than Taryn expected, and looked older than her forty-three years. Despite that, she showed no fear or trepidation, even with the biomatons threatening her. She held herself with dignity and poise—and Taryn found herself standing just a bit straighter in her presence.

"Who are you, girl?" The Queen demanded. "What is it you want? If you dare threaten Our life, We shall have you know you have mere seconds before Our army is upon you."

Taryn held up her hands, splaying her fingers both as a symbol of peace and a display of her deformity, her legal identity. "We are not here to threaten you, Your Majesty. We only want your ear. You must forgive us our unconventional methods for getting your attention, but as you can see, we did not exactly have the option of proper channels."

"What do you want, biomaton?" the Queen questioned coldly.

Taryn's words ran fast now, so fast she nearly tripped over them. She had played this so many times in her head, and now it was like opening a dam, with all she wanted to say spilling out.

"My name is Sedition. I have come to petition you for the biomatons' freedom. You may have heard of me and my army—you may even have authorized the bombs meant to destroy me, but I ask you to reconsider your opinion of us. All we ask for is our freedom. Humans have long assumed that biomatons are merely machines, but all of us present here are evidence to the contrary. We possess free will, and can show compassion to other living creatures. We were built from humans, and only the controls *you* have required to be installed in our minds keep us from attaining anything and everything that you can. We are human! We must be allowed to live our lives freely, and without chains! We can contribute so much more to our country than we are currently doing as slaves. You must see that. We are warriors and artists, poets and musicians and inventors. I myself have been trained as a mechanick. If you would only open this door to us, we could contribute to this great empire."

The Queen stared at Taryn, silent, unmoved by her pleas. Taryn could hear Petrichor and Seraphim fighting off the first of the soldiers, and knew she only had seconds to spare. Taryn swallowed hard, drawing her final argument up in her mind, the argument she had not discussed with Royal because she knew he would say it did not conform to logic. But Taryn knew that beneath her stern front, Queen Victoria was a woman who had loved deeply and lost that love. She had a heart. Taryn just had to find the right words to touch that heart.

"There is a young man who I have known for a long time. We are dear friends, and have seen each other through many hardships. He is the newly titled Lord of Oxley, and he has never treated me as anything but an equal. He even purchased me to ensure I did not endure abuse at the hands of another master. But he has never seen me as a slave. He would be here today if I hadn't told him to stay home, to stay safe. He would vouch for us as loudly and firmly as I vouch for myself."

"We can't hold 'em much longer!" Petrichor called over the sounds of gunfire and clashing swords. Emmett was fighting with them, protecting the alley, but the onslaught of guards was becoming too much for even three biomatons in the bottleneck.

Taryn took a deep breath, finally understanding why Erikkson had told her to fall in love. Why he'd said it would make her more sympathetic. What did humans love more than a tragic love story? She closed her eyes and let the full truth of her emotions out.

"Recently, I regained the ability to love. This ability was taken from me by law when I became a biomaton. But I *can* love. I *do* love. I love him." She pointed to Ace where he stood nearby, watching the interaction, one hand on the gun at his hip. "Ace Highmore, privateer for your navy and the man who became a biomaton trying to save me."

Ace's eyes met hers with a light she'd never seen before, bright and full of hope. She quickly turned her face away, afraid that if she looked at him too long she would begin to cry. She held her chin high as she looked back at the Queen. "I beg of you to reconsider. Unless you issue a decree for our freedom, we shall all be hanged. All we ask for is equality. Freedom. A chance to have an equal part in our country as citizens, and not as slaves."

"You have your place, biomaton," the Queen replied coldly.

"Incoming!" Petrichor screamed. "Red, out of the way!"

Time slowed to a crawl.

Taryn turned in time to see Petrichor racing toward them, her automatic pistol pointed straight at Taryn.

No, not at Taryn.

What is she doing? Taryn wondered, even as her body moved on its own, side-stepping just far enough to remove herself from the line of fire. The muzzle of the gun flashed, the thunderclap of gunfire echoing an instant afterward, as if her vision and hearing were out of joint. Three flashes. Three *cracks,* the very air splitting around her head. After the third bullet spun from the pistol's short muzzle, the gun clicked. Out of bullets. The pistol dropped from Petrichor's hand and clattered across the cobbles. All the sounds of fighting had stopped, the world eerily silent. Anger and fear roiled together in Taryn's chest.

Cringing, she turned, anticipating the worst: a crimson blossom of blood on the black mourning gown. Glassy eyes half-hidden by a black lace veil.

The sight that greeted her was so much worse.

Ace stood between Taryn and the Queen, a dumb expression of horror on his face. All three bullets had hit him, penetrating the armor Gennifer had made. One had hit his left shoulder. The second was embedded in his hip. The third found its home in his stomach. Ace touched his stomach, staring numbly at his bloodied fingers. His eyes slid slowly to Taryn's face. His knees buckled and he slipped to the cobblestones, revealing the Queen behind him, shell-shocked and frozen.

"Ace!" Taryn screamed.

"Sedition—" Petrichor gasped at the same moment.

"I will deal with you later," Taryn growled, unable to hold the two things in her head at once. Betrayed by her own sister, and Ace wounded—

She raced to his side, skinning her knees on the stones, breaking the silence with his name. Her legs felt like lead. She could feel her heart pulsing behind her eyes. "No, no, no, no, no," she begged, pressing a hand to his cheek. "Not you, too."

His eyelids fluttered, and a moan escaped his lips. She lifted him into her arms with a love she had not before allowed, blood coating her hands as she did so, though she no longer cared. "Ace, hang on," she begged. His breathing was hot and shallow against her neck.

"Help me!" she screamed. Over the usual smells of him, sea salt and highland breezes, she could not block out the horrible iron smell of blood. "Someone help me! Please!" No one came to her aid. Her companions were overwhelmed as it was, and no one else cared.

Ace was bleeding out in her arms and no one cared.

Ace was bleeding out in her arms and Petrichor had done this to him.

She patted his cheek again, unsure what else to do. "Hold on, Ace. You bloody *hold on*."

His eyes flickered open, locking on her face for the briefest of moments. His left hand caught hold of her sleeve, a fistful of fabric becoming a physical tether between this life and the next. "Tar..."

"Shh. You will be all right," she encouraged. "I swear, you will be all right. I will get you help."

She tried to struggle to her feet, holding him tight against her chest, but he was so heavy. Her legs buckled beneath her, and she swayed back to the cobbles. Blood ran between the stones in rivulets, strangely mesmerizing.

Someone caught his shoulders, lifting him away from her. Taryn blindly scrabbled for purchase, holding his hands, desperate to just keep touching him. Something hot dripped down her cheeks. "No. Ace!"

Strong hands caught her shoulders, her elbows, yanked her to her feet. She lunged for Ace's vanishing form being borne away by two men in white coats toward a waiting cart. Blood dripped from his prone form, leaving a trail of crimson across the stone. Three soldiers held Taryn back, barely keeping her restrained. "Do not take him from me! Please! You must let me stay with him!" she screamed, fighting the hands that held her.

Someone caught a fistful of her hair and held her head still, finally forcing her to stop struggling. The hysterical words and the tears did not stop, though, even as the soldiers clamped manacles around her wrists, tying her bloodied hands behind her back. "Please," she sobbed. "Please. Do not take him from me."

She was forced into the back of a Black Maria cab along with her friends, all of them manacled, bruised, and dejected.

Petrichor raised her head and tried to speak again, but Taryn ignored her. There was no explanation she would accept, nothing that could be said that would possibly make this right. She was so angry, so afraid, that she couldn't even look at Petrichor. She tried to close her eyes, but all she could see were the bright crimson wounds in Ace's chest, the blank look of shock on his face.

Taryn stood and went to the barred door of the cab, kicking at it with what little strength she had left. "Let me go!" she screamed. "I need to be with him!"

If the soldiers heard, they did not care, and a moment later, the cab jolted into motion. Taryn tumbled to the stinking floor of the cab, unable to steady herself with her hands manacled behind her back. "I will get to you," she whispered. "I will save you. This is not the end. This cannot be the end of us. Not now. God, please not now."

The short, rattling, dark ride to the Tower of London took a handful of minutes, all of them oppressed by the silence of her companions. No one sought to console her. No one else spoke on the journey. And that was even worse.

They had failed. Her best laid arguments had failed. They were not human and could never be in the sight of the law. Even when she admitted everything, all her deepest secrets laid bare, it was not enough. And her siblings had known that, had plotted behind her back to enact their original plan if she failed.

They had never believed in her. And there was no way they would be granted their freedom after attempted assassination of the Queen.

The soldiers dragged the biomatons across the inner courtyard of the Tower of London, marching them all to the same cell Taryn had been housed in once before. She turned once over her shoulder and caught a glimpse of Ace on the other side of the courtyard beyond the White Tower, being carried into another building. She broke free and ran toward him, screaming his name.

A soldier tripped her, sending her sprawling across the stones of the courtyard. She did not feel it.

"Ace!" she cried as they jerked her to her feet and forced her upstairs to the cell. Her friends were already inside. "You must let me go to him!"

The cuffs fell away. "You cannot do this!"

The door slammed in her face.

"Ace!"

She shoved her hands through the tiny, barred window of the door, reaching, desperate.

"Please do not keep us apart!"

They turned their backs on her pain.

"Wait!"

Nothing.

"Please!"

The soldiers disappeared from her sight. She grasped the bars, shaking them, but the door held firm. "Ace!" she screamed again and again, until her voice was hoarse and she could taste blood.

"Ace!" as though it would save him.

"Ace..." Like a prayer, like a breath. As though she herself would crumble if she ceased to say his name.

"Ace."

CHAPTER THIRTY-EIGHT

When Taryn's throat could no longer sustain her voice and exhaustion washed over her in waves, she slumped to the floor, her back against the door, swollen eyes examining the cell, with four other defeated biomatons ranged around it in various states of disarray. There were brown stains on the stones near the center of the room, and Taryn slowly realized she had been here before. This was where she was held before her trial. Where Storm had tortured her. And here she was again, awaiting death.

Anger welled up in her chest again, hotter than hellfire. She pushed herself to aching feet and stalked across the room until she stood in front of Petrichor, who stopped pacing to look her in the eye.

"What were you thinking?" Taryn yelled. "I said *no more killing!* You ruined everything, and now Ace is going to die because of you!"

"He will be all right, Sedition," Seraphim murmured from across the cell, his gentle voice only stoking Taryn's fire.

"*He* will be all right?" Petrichor spat, shoving one metal finger hard into Taryn's chest. "*He* will be all right? And what about the rest of us, S? In case you hadn't noticed, we are all headed for the gallows. None of us will be all right, least of all Ace!"

"Sedition's words may yet find their mark."

"Why will you not answer my question?" Taryn grabbed Petrichor by her shoulders. She wanted to shake her. She wanted to stab her. She didn't know what she wanted, just that her hands were itching and her chest was tight. It was too hard to breathe, and she felt like someone had hollowed her out. Anger was all she had right now. "Answer me, Petrichor!"

Petrichor scoffed. "You want me to answer you, Sedition? Why am I the only one who can see that you failed us yet again? It was *your* idiot plan to talk to the Queen rather than assassinating her, and *you* failed. I was doing what we should have done all along. I was making sure this war *ended*. But your stupid privateer had to be the hero, didn't he? He had to jump in at the last moment and take those bullets, and now *everything* is ruined! We are all going to die. Is that what you wanted?"

Petrichor shoved Taryn hard, sending her stumbling back a few feet.

Taryn's fists rose. The anger thrashed like a living thing in her chest. "Ace was following my plan."

"Your *plan* was crap. Even Seraphim thought so. Right, S?"

Shock raced over Taryn as she looked at Seraphim. His eyes held great sorrow, but he nodded slowly.

"Petrichor's plan to assassinate the Queen would at least have been a shock wave that would shake the country. Your speech was an idea that could have worked, Sedition. I wanted to give you that chance. But we wanted a backup in case the Queen refused to listen."

Seraphim's words hit Taryn as hard as physical blows. She'd always trusted Seraphim to follow her lead—to be honest with her, to help her in her role as firebrand, leader of the rebellion. "Petrichor I would expect this from, but you, Seraphim?" Her raw voice cracked, and she hated herself for it. Hated herself for being anything other than the heartless machine the world thought she was, even though that was what this entire battle was about.

If she had just been content with her lot in life, Ace would not be dying somewhere, alone and afraid.

Emmett leaped to his feet. "Enough! We have all made mistakes."

Petrichor swore loudly, repeatedly, until the word lost all form and meaning. "This is not how this was supposed to end!"

"At least we are together," Rorin murmured from the far corner of the cell, where he'd tucked himself.

"Together?" Taryn scoffed. "Together with my siblings who betrayed me? Who did not even trust me enough to tell me that they did not think this mission would succeed?"

"You would not listen," Petrichor grumbled.

"Do you think they will *ever* let us free after you tried to shoot the Queen?" Taryn shouted back. "You have written all our death sentences!"

"As if your speech would have completed anything. It was a mishmash of sentimental bargaining! I thought Royal was supposed to teach you about logic and laws for this?"

Taryn screamed wordlessly and threw herself at Petrichor.

Seraphim stepped between them, spreading his wings wide enough to almost separate the cell into two sections. "Emmett is right," he said in a gentle but commanding voice. The cold breeze through the narrow slits of the windows caught his curls, and in the waning light, he looked almost like the warrior angel he'd been named after. "Fighting amongst ourselves does not change anything. What's done is done. We must wait to see what the verdict is. Perhaps something Taryn said got through, and even if not, the seeds have been planted. Others will take up our banner after we are gone."

The cell fell silent, save for the high, whistling wind still sweeping in through the windows, raising gooseflesh across Taryn's arm and down her spine. She bit down hard enough on the inside of her cheek to draw blood, but crossed the room and sat against the door of their cell again, her hands trembling with unspent anger. She felt betrayed, yes, but she was also terrified. She didn't know if she could survive losing anyone else.

Then again, maybe she wouldn't have to.

"Is it true, Sedition, what you said?" Rorin asked slowly. "Do you love Ace?"

Taryn wanted to protest, but something hot and vile rolled in her gut and she turned her face away, ashamed. "It is too late for that," she whispered.

Every eye looked to Taryn. Petrichor released a dry bark of a laugh that somehow managed to be both ironic and mirthless. "You told Her Majesty you loved the privateer? Had you even gotten up the courage to tell *him* that yet?"

"I should have said it," Taryn croaked, her voice barely more than a whisper after screaming for so long. "I thought we would have the time, after—"

"Don't act so innocent. You knew this was a suicide mission, one way or another."

"I did not know you were going to shoot him!"

"Do not blame me for his attempt to play the hero!"

Taryn lunged to her feet again, but she didn't cross the room, just stood there by the door swaying. "*You* tried to shoot the Queen. You knew my plan and *you* went against it. It is every bit your fault that he is not with us now."

Petrichor's face took on that flat, annoyed look that Taryn was beginning to recognize as the mask she wore when she did not want anyone to see her true emotions. "Seraphim might be right. The romance angle might be a good one, now that Ace took a couple bullets for the Queen. Maybe his heroism will be the thing that *frees us.*" She spat the final words, like they were poison. "Maybe your precious little courting game will have some worth after all."

"Love is not a game," Taryn growled. "It is not a tactic or a *card* to be played." Every word stung, but she forced them out. "What Ace and I had was not something to be used as leverage."

"No, it wasn't. Love is a defect in the losing side." Petrichor marched across the cell and caught Taryn's lapels, pulling her so close their noses almost touched. Taryn could smell the salt on her skin and the metal on her breath. "Do you understand now why Master Erikkson took our love? Do you see yet that it only made us stronger?"

Horror washed over Taryn in waves. All the pain she was feeling suddenly surged back to the surface, threatening to clamp its dark claws around her heart. She pictured Ace in all of his moods: in joy, in sorrow, in fear, in anger. She pictured how brightly he shone, and how pale and weak he had been as he bled onto the cobblestones. How small he had seemed in the arms of those white-coated men as they carried him away.

"If this is love, I do not want it." Tears fell from her eyes again, though she'd thought her tears all spent.

"Let her go, Petrichor," a gentle voice interrupted. Seraphim put a hand on Petrichor's shoulder, and the Clockwork Assassin's lip curled in disgust. She shoved Taryn backward, and Taryn allowed herself to slump to the floor. Her limbs felt heavier than lead.

"Go sit against the wall," Seraphim ordered, pointing across the cell.

"But—"

"You are both too angry. You are not thinking rationally. Remove yourself from this situation before I remove you myself."

Petrichor grumbled her way across the cell, slumping into a corner, her arms crossed. She turned her face toward the wall.

Seraphim knelt near Taryn, his hands on his knees, his wings folded against his back. "Do not listen to her, Sedition. Your love is a gift. Master Erikkson believed it would make you a better warrior, and I believe the same. You have so much compassion. Do not let that die." He ducked his head, his lips twisting into a wry expression. "Ace was alive when we arrived. There is no reason to believe he is not still alive. The doctors here know what they are doing. We may yet see him again."

Taryn shoved her tears away with the back of her hand. "They will not give him medical treatment. He is just a biomaton to them." Her voice caught in her throat, thick with sobs. "What does it matter if one more slave dies?"

"Hush, *cherie*," Emmett murmured. "We must be brave, for Ace. We must believe he will make it through."

Taryn looked up into Seraphim's big green eyes. "Why did you not trust me to finish this?"

"I did trust you," he answered gently. "We made another plan as back up, but I did not think we would need to use it."

"You did," she pressed. "You would not have made it if you had not thought it would not work."

Seraphim closed his eyes and sighed. "Sedition, there are things you still do not know about your past."

Anger flared up in her again, covering the sorrow for the moment. "I do not have my memories. We *all* know that. It has never affected my leadership before."

"It is more than that."

"What? What more is there that I could possibly be missing?"

Seraphim gently took her hands, and it was the first time he'd touched her like that: like a friend, a brother, and not as a mentor. She shuddered, a flash of memory running through her —being no more than eight years old and racing after Seraphim, thrilled to simply be in his shadow.

"Sedition, listen to me very carefully. Your entire journey has been shaped by Master Erikkson."

She tried to pull away. "I *know*—"

He held her hands tightly. "No, you do not know this. When you were found by Ace at Grafton's School of Mechanicks, who was it that tipped Storm and Ace off that you were there?"

She frowned. "I—I do not know. I always assumed it was one of the boys at the school who figured it out. Perhaps I was not careful enough and let my glove slip—"

"No, Sedition. It was Master Erikkson."

"*What?*" she gasped. Her lungs refused to inflate. She had had enough of betrayal today. She could not bear any more. "No, that cannot be— He would not—"

"He did. And he promised me to never, ever tell you. And I have kept it from you until now because I knew it would hurt you. It would hurt our cause."

Tears welled in Taryn's eyes again. "Then it was Master Erikkson's fault I ended up in the Black Castle? *His fault* that Ace and Emmett became biomatons?"

Seraphim nodded slowly, sorrow in his own eyes. "Yes, Taryn, it was."

Her mind spun. Everything she had known, everything she wanted to fight for was manipulated by the man who'd called himself her father. It was a deeper betrayal than any she'd felt before, save perhaps for that vivid memory of his decision to wipe her mind. He had said he loved her. And he had treated her like a pawn in his game, a machine to be moved and deployed at will. She choked on the number of questions she had, angry again. Furious that he had died before he could explain any of this to her. Furious that she could never get a full explanation for why he had been so cruel.

She had been a child. She had only wanted a place to belong.

"And you are telling me this now *why?*"

"Because this decision you made, this act of defiance, it was the first movement that was truly *yours*. Not part of Erikkson's plan. Not part of some greater strategy. Just *you*, Sedition, finding your own voice. I wanted to give you that chance."

He sighed and pressed his forehead against hers. A wave of sorrow prickled over her scalp, and she wondered if he felt the same. "But Petrichor and I are also Erikkson's weapons. And we knew that taking out the Queen was one of his plans. So we set it in motion, in case your words were not enough. I am sorry we did not tell you."

Taryn closed her eyes. There had been too many emotions, too many revelations today. She was tired, the kind of tired that sinks deep into one's bones, that leaves one aching for rest that is deeper than sleep. A kind of numbness washed over her, dulling any feeling to a throbbing ache. "I am sorry my words did not convince her," she whispered.

"We knew the risks," Seraphim murmured. "We chose to come."

"We will be all right," Emmett repeated, but his tone rang hollow and false.

"Don't lie, Frenchie," Petrichor growled from across the room.

※

The sky had grown indigo and stormy when a scholarly man came to the door of their cell with their guard. "Miss Taryn?" he asked in a kind, mousy voice. Taryn rose.

"That is me."

A click, and the door opened. The man peered at her over his spectacles. "Come with me. He may not have much time."

Taryn stepped from the cell, her heart in her throat. She turned and offered the guard her wrists. The scholarly man waved a hand. "Are the handcuffs really necessary, my dear? Would you be dull-witted enough to attempt an escape from the Tower of London?"

Numbly, Taryn shook her head. She knew escape from this place was nigh impossible.

"I thought not. We will skip the handcuffs, then. Let us hurry. We are wasting time."

He marched her swiftly across the square, past the White Tower to a narrow building with barred windows. Warm yellow lamplight shone in puddles across the paving stones, the only brightness in this world painted blue by the indigo clouds overhead. Taryn tried to speak, to ask the man about Ace, but her tongue refused to work. He led her down a long, narrow stone hallway with doors on both sides, all of them closed. Taryn did not need to see into the rooms to understand this was a hospital; she could smell the austere, chemical scent of disinfectant, so strong it burned her lungs, feel the silence of pain and death in her bones.

Finally, they reached a door at the end of the hall and the scholarly man nodded to her. "Take as much time as you like. I shall be just outside if you need me."

She wanted to thank him, wanted to express her gratitude for not being treated like an object, but still her tongue would not work. She could not breathe. So rather than thanking the man, she pressed the door open.

The room inside was small and square, with bare stone walls and floor. A hospital cot sat against the wall to her right. Ace lay on the cot, propped into an almost-sitting position by a cushion. He was naked from the waist up, his torso wrapped in thick white bandages already stained with blood. His warm olive skin had lost all its color, ashen gray like a corpse. Had it not been for his shallow, ragged breathing, she might have believed him already dead.

His eyes blinked open as the door closed behind her, long

black lashes fluttering. The ghost of a smile crossed his lips. "You came," he whispered.

She nodded, walking slowly to his bedside, her feet moving of their own accord. "Of course I came."

He nodded, reaching out to take her hand, flesh holding flesh. His fingers were cold. Her prosthetic hung limply by her side. His lay folded over his stomach. "I knew you would. They could not deny the final request of a dying man."

Her face twisted. "Why did you have to go and pull a stunt like that?"

"Long live the Queen," he replied, an old, wicked grin flashing in his eyes an instant before a cough sent it fleeing; a bubbling, wet cough that told Taryn exactly where one bullet had penetrated—and why even the best doctors in England could do nothing more for him. She suspected even Erikkson, with all his skill, could not have saved Ace now. He wiped at his mouth with his clockwork hand before speaking again. "Old habits die hard," he murmured. "I suppose you never really leave her service, once you are in it."

Taryn squeezed his fingers more tightly. "You fool. You utter fool." She reached out and brushed her clockwork fingers over his cheekbone, suddenly at a loss for words. "You will be all right," she whispered, her face twisting again as she tried to stop the tears pressing at her eyes.

"Tar," he murmured, catching her hand and holding it in his prosthetic palm, though neither could feel the contact. "It is all right. This is the best way."

"No, it is not! The best way is where you live!"

His eyes flickered to the ceiling, and he sighed. The breath rattled in his lungs. "I am—was—am dying. There is something wrong with my graft, and it is killing me. This is better. This way"—another hacking cough—"this way my death shall mean something."

She shook her head, refusing to believe him. If he was truly dying, he would have told her. He would have said something so they could figure it out together. He was lying to make her accept this, and she *would not* fall for it. "No! Whatever is wrong with your graft, we can fix it. You can—you must live—" It took all her strength now to retain the sobs, and she felt as though her heart was being torn from her chest one string at a time. "You cannot leave me here, not after all we have endured. Ace, I love you!" She swore, squeezing her eyes shut. This was not supposed to be how she said those words. "I love you," she repeated, just to taste it again. "I told the Queen I love you and it is the truth. I do not want to live without you."

His face contorted and he let go of her hands, one hand covering his jaw. His breath came in brief, labored gasps. He shook his head violently. "I made my peace with this!" he growled, tears running in sparkling rivers down his cheeks. "I made my peace! Gor, Tar, you had to wait until now to tell me?"

He looked at her again, her face swimming in his watery gaze. "I love you too. I love you so much. I did this for you." He lapsed into a fit of coughing so violent he had to lean forward.

Taryn could hear life itself rattling in his chest, threatening to escape. What had they done? How could *now* be the moment they finally admitted their affection for each other? Tears traced acid-hot trails down her cheeks, and she did not bother to wipe them away.

"This is my fault," she heard herself say.

"No, it is not," he insisted. He patted the edge of the cot, beside his hip. "Sit, Taryn."

"Ace—"

He caught her hands and held her still, locking his gaze with hers. The cot creaked with their combined weight. "This is not your fault."

"I did not know that Petrichor was planning—"

"No. No, you mustn't think like that now. I do not blame

her or you. I would have jumped in front no matter who was firing the bullets." He tucked her hair behind her ear tenderly. His fingers traced her cheek, lingered on the curve of her lips, and then fell away. He knew that face so well.

"Let me come with you, then."

"Taryn—" he warned.

"Let me follow you."

"No. You get to live."

"Not without you!"

He sighed. "Yes. Without me." Another cough racked his shoulders, this time spattering the white sheet with minuscule droplets of crimson blood. "Taryn, I need you to listen to me." He cupped her cheek in his hand, as if just by holding on to her he could remain longer on this earth. "Are you listening?"

"Yes," she whispered.

"You cannot grieve me like you grieved Erikkson, understand? You must move on. You deserve better than this. You deserve happiness." His lips twisted, and he gave a short, ironic laugh. "I cannot believe I am saying this, but give Royal a chance. Just—please, find someone who will make you happy."

Her tears flowed freely down her cheeks. "But that is *you*."

"It cannot be me any longer. Promise me you will try. Promise me."

She closed her eyes, unable to stop the words, though she knew she would regret them. "I promise."

"Good. And Tar—" A shadow passed over his face, fear and pain contorting his expression. "Tar..." he moaned.

She stroked his forehead, his skin cool and clammy under her touch. "Shh, Ace. Lie still. I am here."

"Do not leave me," he whimpered. She had not thought it possible, but his skin had turned even more ashen.

"I will not leave. I am right here." A shaky sob shattered her last word, leaping from her throat. She could not lose him. Not now. Not after they had come so far.

Wordlessly, his arms reached up and encircled her, pulling her to his chest one last time. He smelled like disinfectant and ether, and beneath that, blood. None of his normal Ace scent made it through the hospital smells. He buried his face in her shoulder. His breath burned hot against her neck, and she could feel and hear every burbling, labored breath.

Intense emotion came over her then, and she turned her face, pressing her lips against his. She kissed him as though it could somehow keep him here with her, even as she felt him slipping away. The kiss lasted mere seconds, and he broke off too early to cough, leaving the taste of salt and copper on her lips, but it was a *real* kiss. It was fireworks. It left her wanting more. *All* she wanted was for him to survive. To have the chance to kiss him every day for the rest of her life. But he was in pain, and the thought was a selfish one. She knew that now.

At last, he stopped coughing and leaned his head on her shoulder. She gently stroked his hair. "I am so tired..." he whispered.

"Lie back, Ace. Rest now," she murmured. "You did well."

His breathing slowed, growing more labored with each passing inhale. He lay back, his blue eyes fixed on her face. "Taryn..."

"Shh, Ace. I am here."

His left hand rose, brushing his thumb against her lips. She caught his wrist and held his hand there, weeping silently, feeling the warmth slip away from his fingers. "You..." he whispered, barely audible, "You are so beautiful."

She leaned forward, smiling through her tears. She longed to feel his lips on hers one last time. He stopped her.

"Find love," he whispered.

"Ace..."

"Be happy." A horrible dark shadow crossed his face. Pain came into his eyes. "Taryn—" Her name escaped on a breath. A cloud came over his eyes. All at once, he fell still, and she knew he was gone. She sat staring at him, numbly, almost afraid to acknowledge what had occurred. The room was horribly still without the rattle of his labored breathing.

She leaned forward, shaking his shoulders. "Ace. Ace!" She shook him again, but it felt as though someone was shaking her. She curled on his chest, trembling like a leaf, her tears somehow prematurely spent and now refusing to fall. She could not still her trembling.

"Ace, come back to me," she begged between dry, heaving sobs. "I love you. I love you. I love you."

CHAPTER THIRTY-NINE

ROYAL WORRIED WHEN day drew into evening and still they did not return. He tried to occupy himself with reading, and when even his favorite novel couldn't hold his attention, he tinkered with clockwork, sketching notes in a small leather-bound journal he kept for ideas. He had a few new ideas for fixing Ace's prosthetic, and he sketched details as he waited. Nothing held his attention for long, though, and he constantly rose and peered out the window, hoping for a glimpse of the carriage returning.

Gennifer sat quietly through all of his restless pacing, embroidering. Finally, she sighed, glancing at the darkened windows as he peered out for the thousandth time.

"I do not think they are coming back, Royal," she murmured in her rolling brogue, setting her embroidery on her lap.

"They are. They are. They probably took longer in London than they thought, that is all. Look—someone is coming now. I am sure that is them!"

Royal raced to the front door, his heart lifting in excitement. They had done it! They had won! And now they had come home.

But the clattering hooves up his gravel drive were not accompanied by the crunch of carriage wheels, and as the sounds drew nearer, the shapes in the dusk coagulated into the form of a horse and rider, the man wearing a red uniform. Royal swore beneath his breath, dread suddenly replacing his joy.

The man drew up and dismounted, removing his cap. "Are you Lord Stokker?"

Royal nodded. "What is this about?"

"You have been summoned, my lord. Her Majesty desires to speak with you."

Taryn lay there for hours, unaware of time passing. Her fingers entwined with his, as though if she let go, he would vanish, disappearing from her forever. His body slowly lost its heat, growing cold beside her, and still she did not move, numb with sorrow, paralyzed by grief.

Minutes or hours or days later—she did not know—two guards came into the hospital room. Both were thick and angular. Stupid-looking young men, the type who were cruel just because no one would stop them.

"Get up, girly. Time to go back where you belong," one growled.

Taryn pretended not to hear. Even if she had wanted to leave, her limbs refused to move. She would not abandon Ace to these vultures.

"I said get up. He is dead, can you not see that? Dead."

Trembling, she shook her head. No, he was not d—d—*gone*. She could not even bring herself to think the vile word. He would return to her. She just had to be faithful enough to wait for him.

"Come on. Do not be stupid," the other guard urged. Still, she did not move, tightening her grasp on Ace's cold hands.

One guard grabbed her by the hair, tugging her up from the cot. Taryn cried out, scrabbling for purchase, but the guard's grip on her hair ached, forcing her to let go of Ace.

"No!" she cried, writhing in a poor attempt to escape as they caught her arms and dragged her from the room. "No, Ace! Ace!"

"He cannot save you now, girly," one guard hissed in her ear, eliciting a cruel chuckle from the other.

"But not to worry—you shall be joining him soon enough."

The stone hallway did not seem so long this time. They marched her down the corridor and back into the square. Night had fallen, near inky in its darkness despite the lamps hung about the square. Rain drops spattered across Taryn's cheeks, as if the sky, too, wept for Ace. Taryn's feet dragged along the cobblestones as she half-heartedly fought the guards. Even hours ago, she could have killed them easily, but now, all the fight had gone out of her, as if the violence in her head had abandoned her when she needed it most.

The guards cast her down upon the paving stones with enough force to drive her headlong into the cobbles. Taryn's vision danced with stars, her forehead searing with pain where she'd struck it against the pavers. Her palm burned, skinned where she'd tried to stop her fall. For a moment, she tried to press herself upright again, a little of her old instincts breaking through. And then she let go, collapsing once more. Hot blood ran over her brow, obscuring the vision in her left eye, turning the world crimson.

Let them do what they like to me. It no longer matters.

"Listen to me, freak. You are going to march back to the cell without fighting us, or you are going to spend a very cold night chained to a post in the middle of the square. Do I make myself clear?" the first guard demanded, hauling her up by her collar.

Taryn wanted to refuse, just to see if his threat was genuine. Just to see how far she could push him. She wanted to know if they still beheaded people here, where so many kings and queens had lost their heads. She wanted to know if they would make an exception for her. But then a small voice inside told her this was not what Ace would want, and guiltily, she nodded her head.

Ace would want her to stand strong, and that was what she would do.

She marched the rest of the way across the square and back to her cell obediently, with a guard on either arm, her head bowed, and blood streaming over her eye and down her cheek. Her chest felt hollowed out, but she held on to Ace's last words as tightly as a lifeline. Even with those words, though, hope felt impossibly distant, and every step was a lead weight, dragging her down.

She collapsed on the floor of their small cell, her head hanging, her legs at odd angles. The door locked behind her. She could not even find the strength to cry.

"How is he?" Emmett questioned. "How is Ace?"

Taryn shook her head, her face folding in on itself, though no tears came. Her shoulders shook. She tried to speak, but a tiny, childlike squeak was all she managed.

"*Mon Dieu*," Emmett breathed, his clockwork eyes glittering with tears. "*Ayez pitie de nous.*" He crossed the short distance between them, trying to put an arm around her, a tear slipping down his cheek. Taryn shoved him away, turning and hiding her face against the stone wall. Emmett sighed and sat near her, burying his face in his hands, weeping silently for the man who had been his shipmate and his best friend. Taryn did not even appear to know he was there.

The cell fell eerily still, each biomaton processing Ace's

death in his or her own way. Rorin sat with his head tilted back, staring at the ceiling, his eyes staring and lips moving in a silent prayer. Petrichor stared at nothing, her arms crossed and jaw set, her grief entirely internalized. Seraphim sat cross-legged, his eyes closed in prayer or meditation. Tears slipped down his mahogany brown cheeks.

Taryn rose and crossed the cell, opening the hidden hatch on her forearm and drawing the first of her throwing knives. She stopped in front of Petrichor, dropping the knife at her feet. The other two followed it, clattering against one another and the stone floor. Petrichor sat up, alert, as Taryn knelt in front of her, her arms spread wide.

"What are you doing?" Petrichor questioned, an edge of horror audible in her voice.

"I am allowing you to do what you have wanted since I found you in that pub in Glasgow. I am asking you to kill me," Taryn answered, her voice low and even, unwavering.

Petrichor's mouth fell open, for a moment caught speechless by her sister's request. "I am not going to kill you, Red."

"Do it," Taryn hissed, her fists and jaw clenched, every muscle taut. "I order you to do it."

"No, Red, no!"

Taryn closed her eyes. "Release me," her voice wavered, no longer unflinching. "Let me go to him."

"Are you crazy? I'm not going to assist your suicide! Think about this, Sedition. Is this what Ace would have wanted?"

A sob escaped Taryn's throat, brief and weak and filled with pain. "I do not know how to live without him."

"One day at a time," Petrichor murmured, sweeping the throwing knives behind her silently as she could, removing the weapons from the reach of Taryn's shaking hands. "That's how we all do it, Red. One day at a time."

"Please," Taryn begged again. "Please, do it."

"I can't, Red. Even if I wanted to, I couldn't. Even though I know we'll all be likely dead at the end of this week or the next, I can't."

"You're an assassin!" Taryn's green eyes snapped open to lock with Petrichor's brown eyes, piercing and sharp. "Is that not what you do?"

Petrichor smiled sadly. "Yes, but I don't take contracts for people I know well, and I don't assist suicides. Even mercenaries have a code, Red. I have to draw the line somewhere. *You* were chosen to live. I don't know why, but you were. And I'm not going to be the idiot who gets in the way of that."

Taryn bowed her head, suddenly aware of every eye on the two of them, the boys' concerned faces as they waited to see what the sisters would do. "I want—I need to be with him."

"No, you need to be exactly where you are; here, with us. What would he think, if you left us behind? What would Royal think?"

Taryn stared down at her hands, clenched so long and so tightly in her lap that she could no longer feel her fingers. "Royal is better off without me."

"No, he's not, and you know it. Royal *adores* you, and losing you would crush him." Petrichor clicked her jaw together. "And don't you dare say we are better without you, because that is another lie."

Taryn shook with a sob, knowing Petrichor was right and hating it. She could not see Ace's ghost, not like she had seen Erikkson's, but she could feel him there with her. She could feel him whispering to her to keep going. To *live*. She bowed her head. "You did not trust me to finish this. You were right."

"We knew the risk when we got involved, Red. We chose this, just like you did." She sighed and patted the stone beside her. "Come on, sit by me. You need some rest."

Taryn hesitated, then shook her head, raising herself to her feet. "Not yet." She began to pace the length of the cell, padding silently back and forth, her eyes far away, a slight limp the only indication of her still-healing left foot. Her friends followed her movements for a while, but eventually each fell into a doze, leaving Taryn pacing the cell, silent tears streaming down her cheeks.

CHAPTER FORTY

THE BIOMATONS WERE LEFT to rot in their cell for another day before being summoned to Parliament for sentencing. Taryn alternated between restlessly pacing the cell and sitting in a corner, staring at nothing for hours on end. She replayed every moment of time she'd spent with Ace over and over in her head until every memory was carved into her mind, the few months they'd spent together feeling like a lifetime. Still, she felt robbed. How many more lifetimes she wished they had together. She would gladly trade these few, dull memories for a chance to create new ones with him. She barely slept except for short bursts, and in those dreams, Ace came and sat quietly with her while she read or sat in the sunshine outside Elmhurst Manor. She woke with cheeks sticky with tears, climbing wearily to her feet to resume her pacing. It was easier to move her body than to dwell in her mind.

Only Petrichor seemed able to engage Taryn for a few minutes at a time, and despite their earlier fight, despite the seeming endless well of Taryn's anger, there was something gentle between them. Fragile as a butterfly, a caring side was emerging from Petrichor, and something deep inside Taryn responded to it. She was too tired to be angry anymore, and she knew that Ace did not blame Petrichor for what happened. So she let Petrichor cradle her sometimes, let her quietly make plans they all knew would fail before they started. They were five warriors, but they all had had enough of fighting. Whatever happened next, there would be someone else who took up their mantle. Taryn just hoped they lived to see it.

Finally, on the morning of the second day since their "final mission," a group of soldiers came to take them away. One by one, the biomatons allowed themselves to be handcuffed and led away, down the stairs and into the back of the waiting Black Maria.

As the final swaying journey began, Petrichor nudged Taryn with her foot, urging her to sit up straight. "Chin up, Red. Pull yourself together. Even if we go to our deaths, we go with dignity, right?" Petrichor gave the rest of the biomatons a glare. "We hold our heads high, as Erikkson would have wanted. We don't submit to these people, even in defeat."

The others nodded gravely. Taryn sat up a little straighter, held her head high as she had been trained to do. Everything ached, not least of all her heart, but she would face her end with dignity, as Ace had. Her one consolation was that she would see him again soon.

The wagon pulled up to the Parliament building, and the biomatons stepped out, heads high and jaws set. Big Ben loomed above them, tolling the hour. Ten o'clock. Ten funeral bells. Taryn's heart lodged firmly in her throat. Soldiers took her arms, one on each side, and she and the others were paraded across thick red carpets, through the elaborate halls, and into the main parliamentary chamber.

There must have been a thousand men there—most in white wigs and elaborate robes, all utterly silent, staring at the biomatons as they paraded in. The men sat in tall, tiered seats on either side of a long aisleway, at the end of which stood a box

Taryn could only assume would soon hold the Queen herself. The room smelled of dust, tobacco smoke, and elderly, fading skin. The plush carpet beneath Taryn's feet silenced her steps and she took comfort in it, knowing she would not be executed here, at least, for the risk it posed to the carpets.

The soldiers lined up the biomatons, facing the empty royal box. The men in the stands began to whisper to one another, the sound like thousands of dry leaves rustling against each other. Taryn's stomach tied itself in knots.

And then a second hush fell over the room as Queen Victoria herself appeared, emerging from a door hidden in the elegant wood paneling of the room. She raised a palm in greeting to her subjects, then turned her piercing gaze on the biomatons. Her black crepe mourning dress rustled as she moved.

"You have caused Us much trouble," she began, her voice ringing in the room. "You spat in the face of our laws and traditions. You murdered loyal soldiers, and you threatened Our life. I could hang you all for treason for any one of these charges."

A thrilled murmur rippled around the room.

Taryn's stomach lurched into her throat as the Queen locked eyes with her. She held up a hand for silence. "But you have made Us think."

Taryn bit her tongue to keep herself from screaming at her to just sentence them already. She was so very tired of all this. Her limbs longed for surrender.

"In particular, biomaton, We were interested in the story you told about the young lord who bought your freedom. So interested, in fact, that We summoned him here and spoke with him Ourselves. Incredibly enough, he corroborated your story. He spoke so highly of you We would never have guessed he spoke of a biomaton."

What was the purpose of all this? Did the Queen have some point she would eventually get around to, or was she merely dragging this out to increase the tension in the room? Taryn clamped her tongue between her teeth, breathing hard through her nostrils.

A side door opened, separate from the one the Queen had emerged from, and a young man stepped out. Taryn's breath caught in her throat as big brown eyes met hers.

"Please, let him go," she exclaimed, voice hoarse, tearing her eyes away from Royal's tender expression. "He has nothing to do with this. Our actions were our own."

A ghost of a smile crossed the Queen's lips. "He is not accused of anything, biomaton. He came here at Our invitation. We were curious to know all We could about your little band of misfits. Lord Stokker has been more than helpful."

Royal turned to the Queen, his broad face open and hopeful. It nearly broke Taryn's heart. He had to know he was witnessing their death sentences.

"Permission to approach the accused, Your Majesty?"

She inclined her head. "Granted."

Royal raced to Taryn, catching her in a tight embrace. She buried her face in his shoulder despite her handcuffs, breathing in the scent of him. "I thought I would never see you again," he whispered into her hair.

Taryn could not speak. A whimper rose in her throat. He held her at arm's length, studying her closely. His thumb brushed over the bruise on her forehead. "Have they hurt you?"

Wordlessly, she shook her head. She knew his next question before it left his mouth.

"Where is Ace?"

Taryn shook her head, biting hard on her tongue, her eyes stinging with fresh tears. She turned her face away.

He understood instantly, his hands digging into her arms with shock and sympathy. "Gor, Tar, I am sorry."

"I knew your father, the late Lord Stokker," the Queen said, and Royal turned away from Taryn to face her, his jaw tightening almost imperceptibly. "He was a good man. He would not approve of your friendship. You are aware of this?"

"Yes, Your Majesty. But I am not my father." He glanced at Taryn, a tender expression creasing his brow. "And I have chosen Taryn. My fate has been intertwined with hers for a long time now. Her enhancements change nothing in my eyes. I love her dearly, and she knows this. She is just as human as you or I, and all we have been through has only served to prove that. It is unfair, the way the biomatons are treated. I will put all my resources toward ending this mistreatment of those unfortunate enough to require clockwork enhancements."

A shocked murmur echoed in the stands. Taryn studied Royal in some surprise. She'd feared that after all this, he might try to protect himself from more backlash for his involvement. But Royal's words sounded sincere and earnest, despite everything she had put him through. He could easily have denied her claims and sentenced her to death. No one would believe her word over his.

But he hadn't. He truly cared about her.

"She is also a criminal," the Queen replied.

"Defending herself! How is that any different from what a soldier does in war? It is only that she fought against unjust laws rather than an opposing military."

The Queen frowned, all the lines in her pale face turning downward. Her eyes returned to Taryn. "What was your plan in threatening Our life?"

Taryn forced herself to hold her head high, to answer slowly and clearly, though inside she wanted this all to be over. She wanted to collapse and sleep, all her burdens cast off. "We did not want to threaten you, Your Majesty. We only wanted your ear. I thought perhaps if I appealed to you directly, we could at last find common ground, common understanding."

"You could have killed Us and taken the throne. Why did you not do so?"

A wry smile touched Taryn's eyes. "Long live the Queen." Tears welled in her eyes, and she blinked them back, her cheeks burning with the memories associated with those words.

"And you could have allowed your friend to kill Us," the Queen pressed.

"Ace gave his life because he believed you would make the right decision," Taryn answered, her voice wavering over the words.

She considered this for a moment. "We knew young Mr. Highmore and his parents, long ago. Were he not a biomaton, We would probably award him with a medal for his sacrifice. We are sorry for your loss, biomaton."

Taryn held her head a little higher, her sorrow turning to indignation over the injustice that plagued them even now. "Why does his status as a biomaton matter? He sacrificed his life to save you! And you thank him by denying him even that simple recognition?"

"Taryn—" Royal muttered warningly.

To everyone's surprise, Queen Victoria *smiled*. "No one has dared to speak to me in that tone for a very long time."

Taryn cringed, taking the words as a reprimand, but the Queen waved a hand to the soldiers scattered around the room. "Remove their handcuffs, please. They are no longer in custody."

Shocked, Taryn's mouth fell open. Someone in the stands shouted "Your Majesty!" but the Queen held up her hands for silence once more.

"It has been clear to me for some time that our policies governing biomatons needed reevaluation, but Sedition and her friends have at last made me understand how crucial this is."

Taryn rubbed her wrist as her cuffs fell away.

"Slavery has been illegal for nearly thirty years here on English soil, but we have continued to perpetuate the dehumanization and enslavement of human beings with the creation and trade of biomatons. This cannot continue. Henceforth, I declare all biomatons to be free British citizens, possessing full human rights granted to them with citizenship. *Anyone* who is caught in the trafficking or creation of biomatons for sale will be punished to the full extent of the law. And Sedition and her friends are absolved of all charges."

More than a few of the parliamentary members rose, clamoring for the Queen's attention. Taryn knew most, if not all of these men relied on biomatons to run their households, to provide labor, and even provide their entertainment. They clamored not for justice, but for their own selfish losses. The Queen's dark gaze met Taryn's, a tender smile revealing the crow's feet at the corners of her eyes. "Your fight may be won, my dear, but I am afraid the battle is just beginning. You face a half-century worth of prejudice. Are you prepared for that fight?"

Taryn's chest swelled. Royal reached down to take her hand, and she felt her compatriots—her family—draw a little nearer. She nodded. "Yes, Your Majesty. We are prepared."

And she was, in spite of her exhaustion, in spite of her sorrow, in spite of how long and how hard she had already fought. She knew she was ready for this new battle, as long as her family was there to fight alongside her.

Royal wrapped her into a celebratory embrace. Within moments, the hug had become a dogpile, with Petrichor grumbling as she was trapped beneath Emmett and Rorin, their strong arms squeezing the group tighter. Seraphim draped his metal wings over them all, like a massive clockwork shield. Despite the tender warmth of the embrace, Taryn could not help but feel Ace's absence, there in the center of it all, like a great gaping wound in her chest. All this would never have been possible without him, and she ached to have him here. She closed her eyes and pictured him for a moment, there beside her as the group broke apart again. She blinked, and felt she could see both him and Erikkson out of the corner of her eye, watching her.

"We did it," she whispered to them. "We won."

They smiled twin smiles and nodded.

Now to face your greatest battle, Erikkson said in her head.

Find love, Ace finished. *Find someone to share this brave new world with you.*

She blinked, wanting to argue, to protest. But they both vanished like smoke in the sun. Royal touched her shoulder.

"Tiger, time to go home."

She nodded. It was time.

EPILOGUE

A BRISK AUTUMN breeze swept through the golden evening, carrying orange leaves and the chill of coming winter. The breeze played at the hem of her gray dress and the long strands of her copper hair. She knelt in the grass, bowing her head, breathing slowly.

"Um," she began lamely, her voice barely audible. "Hello. I thought I ought to tell you what is happening, thanks to you."

Hair swept across her face, and she raised one hand—silver clockwork—up to pull it away.

"Most of the Black Castle has been arrested and sentenced. Bellham escaped, but there are people hunting him. Harper was sentenced to hang for her part in the torture and changes to so many people. Their last prisoners have been set free. A lot of them are just children. They are so frightened and broken. Royal and I have been taking them in, helping them as best we can. It is not easy. Seraphim knows exactly how to help them, though. He can convince even the most damaged to trust him."

She smiled wryly.

"It is ironic. He is built for intimidation, and yet children trust him implicitly. The rest of us do our best to follow his example. It is hardest for Rorin. He does his best, but it has not been the same since Ari—since—since Elmhurst fell." She choked back tears. "No change in legislation can make that night disappear for any of us."

"Petrichor and Emmett left three months ago, to hunt down Lord Bellham and any other biomaton merchants who have escaped justice. Once in a while they send us a letter, but mostly I think it is good for them to be away from us. Still, I do not think everyone involved will ever be brought to justice. It is a battle I do not hope to win."

She trailed off, staring into the horizon, the sunset setting the world around her on fire. She sighed.

"I know I have not visited. That is not your fault. It just hurts too much. I miss you. I keep thinking how you ought to be here, enjoying this with us, fighting with us."

She reached out and brushed her fingers over the marble headstone in front of her, lingering over the inscription. *Ace Highmore, 1843-1864. A friend and a hero.*

"I miss you so much. I—uh—it has taken a lot of courage for me to come out here. I am sorry. But—I had to tell you. I could not feel right about it until I told you."

Again, she paused, chewing her lip, tracing his name with her fingers, all the sore places inside her aching even after so much time had passed.

"I am going to marry Royal." She shook her head and laughed dryly. "I know. But—he really loves me. And if I am honest with myself, I love him, just in a different way than I loved you. He has always been here when I need him, and I know he will take care of me."

She bowed her head, twisting the ring on her right hand. A small emerald flashed in the dying light.

"Our wedding is in two months. We have not invited many. Most of the people we would want there are gone now. But Petrichor and Emmett have promised to be there, along with some other old friends. Gennifer is making my wedding dress. White, like Queen Victoria's." She took another steadying breath, the words flowing like a river now that she released them at last.

"Royal tells me this is an important step. This will change the world. In the year and a half since we were freed, people's opinions have been slow to change. Not everyone believes we are equal. Most go out of their way to avoid biomatons, if they can help it. And no human has married one of our kind, especially not a human with a title." She laughed a little. "Can you imagine? Me, Lady of Oxley? I am not lady material. I am a warrior. And now, I have a whole new battle to learn to fight."

Again, she trailed off, rubbing her cheek with her clockwork fingers.

"Please do not hate me for deciding to marry him. It would have been you, Ace. It would have been you. But I—I think—I think perhaps, in some ways, this will better my mission. This will help the cause. And you know better than anyone how important that is. I—I am sorry."

The wind caressed her cheek, blowing her hair back and whispering tenderly in her ear. She closed her eyes, imagining she could hear Ace in the wind, there beside her.

"Tiger?"

Her eyes snapped open, and she rose to see Royal cresting the hill, weaving his way through the gravestones. He waved to her, smiling. She waved in return, then turned and kissed the gravestone in front of her.

"Thank you, Ace," she whispered.

She picked her way toward Royal, and he raced to cross the distance between them. "They told me you had finally come out here!"

She nodded, casting one glance behind her at the bouquet of white roses she'd left at Ace's silent headstone. She knew he was no more there than anywhere, but it had felt good to speak to him regardless. She felt lighter than she had in months.

"I did."

"Are you all right?"

She nodded, managing a small smile. "I shall be."

He took her hand and squeezed it. "Look at the sunset, Tar."

She looked, her heart lifting at the reds, oranges, pinks, and blues painted across the horizon, the sun fighting the oncoming night with such a beautiful array of colors she almost did not want night to come, the sky momentarily burning as the sun fought the inevitable. She smiled, imagining the sunset was Ace giving them his blessing.

Royal tucked her hair behind her ear, touching the place where Ace had shot her so long ago. "You will always carry him with you."

"I know. I carry everyone who died to get us here. And I live to prove they did not die in vain."

He smiled. "That is my Tiger. Ever the soldier. You know they all would be so proud of you, right?"

She nodded, the warmth of the sun's final rays catching her cheeks, painting her in gold. "I know."

"Good. Now then, I am hungry! May I take my fiancée out to supper?"

She smiled and took his proffered elbow, a settled feeling of warm comfort and familiarity washing over her. It would not last, she knew, as nothing did, but for that moment, she held it in her cheek like sweet hard candy. Sure, the restaurant would try to refuse her service, and she would go home tomorrow to try to repair others while her own heart still mourned, but Royal was right. She carried them with her. She was not alone. And she never had to be alone again.

The End

ACKNOWLEDGMENTS

Here we are at the end of Taryn's story, and I am grateful to so many people I don't even know where to start. It's hard to express how long this story has been with me or how many hands have touched it, but I hope to offer just a little insight into what an accomplishment the completion of this story is for me.

Taryn came into being hand in hand with Royal when I was fourteen or fifteen, as just a scene with a pair of young mechanicks in a world where clockwork could be fused with human flesh. This quickly morphed into something resembling the book now known as *Sedition*, but at that age I didn't have the stamina to finish anything more than a few chapters, and the concept sat untouched for a year or so before I finally picked it up again. At sixteen, I was writing at a slumber party and had friends ask what I was working on—eventually compelling me to read a few pages of what I had written. They were hooked, and asked that I continue to write the story so that they could find out what was next. That was my first taste of true authorship, sharing a story with an audience who wanted to hear more, and I found I loved it.

I wrote the whole trilogy in what was likely around a year, though I don't remember the actual timeline. I know I considered self-publishing, even setting a deadline for myself to publish *Sedition* by the time I graduated high school, but then decided that it needed more work. In college, I rewrote the entire series from memory, recreating the scenes I thought worked, and rewriting those that didn't. That was when the structure of the three books really settled into the form you now hold in your hands, though the manuscripts from that time are still truly ugly little monsters that no one should ever see.

I rewrote Sedition *again* in 2018 - 2019, and that was when I began actively pursuing publishing. I tested the new version of the book with beta readers, and found my first fan in a young lady also interested in becoming an author.

In 2020, I signed on with Parliament House Press, and I began the arduous and rewarding process of working with a professional editor. The books changed again, this time becoming the works they are today. Each book has been its own journey, trying to coax the story from the page over and over again as I grow and change as a writer. Now, as I write this in 2025, I can tell you I'm very different from the young woman who started to write about a steampunk world where clockwork cyborgs have to fight for their right to be human. But in many ways, this story feels more relevant than ever. I have always been justice-driven, and I hope that, in spite of the sometimes dark or bleak aspects of my work, the light of truth shines through: that *all people* deserve dignity, safety, and kindness, no matter their race, gender, sexuality, or religion.

But enough about me—this is an acknowledgements section, so let's actually get to what you're here for: the long list of names.

To my parents: Thank you for feeding me books since before I could talk, and encouraging me to pursue storytelling even when it wasn't a "traditional" career. I'm not making any money off of it yet, but hey, that big payout has got to land sometime, right?

To Elizabeth, Leslie, and Kayla: Thank you for being the first audience *Sedition* found, and for pushing me to finish not just one book but *three* with your excitement. I don't know if you'll ever see this, but know that I love you and think of you often, and I wish you well wherever you are now.

To Paden: Thanks for always being here, my love. I couldn't do any of this without you. You know how much you mean to me.

To Nadia: Thank you for being such a good friend, for always encouraging me to keep going, and for writing a banging song for the release of *Sedition! Mrr-mrr-mrr-mrr*.

To Ellie: You were my first real fan, and I cannot express how thankful I am to you. I cannot wait to read what you publish, and be right there cheering you on when you get your big break.

And to the team at Parliament—Mal, Alexandra, Sabrina, and everyone else involved in the incredibly complex process of bringing a book to life: Thank you for seeing the potential in this young author, and for pushing me to develop these characters and this story in ways I would not have been able to achieve on my own. Thank you for the beautiful covers and layouts, and thank you for pushing through in spite of all of the setbacks and changes happening at Parliament during this process!

And to everyone who has read these stories to their conclusion, thank you thank you thank you for coming on this journey with me. I hope to see you in the next one.

E.M. Wright

Oct. 2025

ABOUT THE AUTHOR

E.M. Wright is an author and editor from Salem, Oregon. She's spent her life imagining fantastic worlds full of powerful women, and enjoys reading any kind of speculative fiction. When she's not writing, you can find her reading a book from her ever-growing library, playing a tabletop game, or cuddling her four cats. You can find her on social media as @EMWrightWrites.

x.com/EMWrightWrites
instagram.com/EMWrightWrites

www.ingramcontent.com/pod-product-compliance
Lightning Source LLC
LaVergne TN
LVHW040037080526
838202LV00045B/3375